ALIEN

REVELATION

by

Tony Ruggiero

Dragon
Moon

WWW.DRAGONMOONPRESS.COM

ALIEN REVELATION

ISBN 10 1-896944-57-4 Print Edition
ISBN 13 978-1-896944-57-9

ISBN 10 1-896944-59-0 Electronic Edition
ISBN 13 978-1-896944-59-3
CIP Data on file with the National Library of Canada

Dragon Moon Press is an Imprint of Hades Publications Inc.
P.O. Box 1714, Calgary, Alberta, T2P 2L7, Canada

Dragon Moon Press and Hades Publications, Inc. acknowledges the ongoing support of the Canada Council for the Arts and the Alberta Foundation for the Arts for our publishing programme.

Printed and bound in Canada
www.dragonmoonpress.com
www.tonyruggiero.com
www.artdragon.net

DEDICATION

For Greg and Sarah,
thanks for keeping the dream alive.

Part One

MIND TRAP

"Life is a series of events, or in some cases obstacles, that besiege us in our path. The key is to face them head on and in many cases, the problem diffuses itself…or it explodes in your face. Either way, it's over."

Greg Carlson

Leumas stared at Copolla's emotionless eyes as his enemy continued repeating the words "to become." He thought about the things Copolla had stated in their conversation and how it opened a whole realm of potential dangers. He wondered how much more detail he could get out of Copolla and if he would have the opportunity to use it. Dead men don't talk.

Leumas refused to lose hope about a possibility arising for escape, although the odds of that were virtually nonexistent at this point. He was overdue in reporting back to the council, which probably meant another mission would be launched to find him. But if he had succumbed so easily, what chance did the others have? Worse yet, if Greg came after him he would—

Leumas suddenly realized that was exactly what Copolla probably wanted. *Damn it, I've got to do something!*

"Copolla," he said, hoping to arouse him from his stupor. "I know Greg's father turned against you when he decided to stay on Earth. I won't believe he was still…"

"Before there was one," Copolla slurred the words as if he were drunk.

This reinforced Leumas's growing belief that the procedure Copolla had undergone to develop his influencing ability had caused both mental and physical damage.

"Then there were four," he said with more clarity, as he seemed to slowly rise from the depths he inhabited. "Are you good at riddles, Leumas? I like riddles. You haven't figured this one out yet, have you?"

"No, Copolla. I don't have the knack for figuring riddles, I guess." Leumas realized Copolla was referring to the notes again. He wanted to stay on the previous subject about Greg's "becoming," but Copolla's mind was so erratic, his behavior so unpredictable, that Leumas had no choice but to let him ramble.

"Let me help you then. 'The one' refers to me. 'The four' are my two agents and their earth females. Can you figure it out now?" he asked, with a childish innocence that made Leumas' flesh crawl.

"Why don't you just tell me about what I was asking earlier?" Leumas pressed. "About your agent and—"

"Shut up, you fool!" Copolla screamed at him. "I am trying to answer your question."

Leumas, taken aback by the abrupt change of mood, fell silent.

"Where was I? Yes, the four. The next part is 'now there are three.' Do you know who the three are?"

"No," Leumas answered neutrally, fearing to set off another outburst from this wild creature.

"That's myself, Greg and Sarah—the three," Copolla said proudly. " 'If the reunion is a warm one, then all will be right, but if not, all will end and the one shall be as it was.'"

Leumas still could not comprehend what the madman was talking about.

"I see you still don't grasp it," Copolla sneered. "Still beyond your comprehension, I suppose. Well, let me explain it to you. If Greg and his woman refuse to join me in my little conquest, I shall kill them both and destroy that scum planet he is currently on. I really don't care about the woman. She is insignificant to the whole plan, and I will probably just kill her anyway after a while." The matter-of-fact tone he used sent chills over Leumas' body.

"Greg would never agree to join you in any such insane—"

"Insane? No, not really. I just look at things from a different perspective than everyone else does. I think he might follow me quite willingly."

"I don't think so," Leumas insisted.

"Perhaps if you knew the whole story, you might possess a different opinion," Copolla suggested. "Would you like to hear more, my friend? Hmmm?"

Leumas needed to know more, but he hated having to play this madman's game of "Guess what?" to get it. Copolla obviously had another bombshell to drop on him and wanted Leumas' full attention when he did it.

"Just say please and I will continue. I have time and so do you," Copolla said in a sickening-sweet voice.

Leumas tasted the sour stomach acids that had lurched into his throat. He fought to maintain control.

"Well, Leumas? Do you have anything you want to say?" Copolla taunted.

"Please finish the story," Leumas said between teeth clenched to keep him from saying anything else.

"Very well then." Copolla smiled, obviously satisfied he had gotten this pitiful response from Leumas at a very high cost to his pride..

"Earlier I alluded to the fact Greg's father was still under my control when he supposedly accepted the assignment to Earth with the intention of escaping me. Everyone assumed it was to have him spy on Earth, to see where past plans to undermine the society had gone so wrong and so on and so on. Well, that was only part of it."

He poured himself a glass of whiskey and stared at the bottle for several seconds. He returned his gaze to Leumas as he drank deeply, gulping the entire glass at once, then placed it on the table, wiped his mouth with his fingers and then carefully licked them clean, his eyes never leaving Leumas.

"Would you like something to drink?"

"No, thank you," Leumas said.

"All right, where was I? Oh, yes, the plan. My scientists had been tasked with conducting a very close examination of the Earth subjects after the last fiasco with that Adolf Hitler. They made some interesting findings that garnered my interest. Almost by accident we learned Terran DNA has a very interesting inactive strand in it.

"Further study showed it could possibly be combined with Zirean DNA to produce a hybrid. We felt very certain the result would probably possess certain characteristics extremely beneficial if harnessed and used by the right group...or individual. There is a subconscious trigger required to activate it. I believe the term they used to describe it was 'time-phased' or something like that. Very subtle and hard to detect, but there."

"What kind of characteristics?" Leumas asked cautiously. "You're talking more than just being able to influence, aren't you?"

"Influencing is only the beginning," Copolla crowed. "There is so much more to it: more power and the ability to expand control throughout the galaxy with merely a thought. I wanted that hybrid. I would have it before anyone else realized what was going on. Greg's father carried a little special package inside him compliments of my scientists and, of course, unknown to him."

He bent closer to Leumas as if he were going to let him in on a secret. Leumas instinctively leaned back as far as he could without falling off the bed.

"Part of the influence I interwove into his mind was to ensure he would breed with an Earth woman as soon as possible. The best part..." Copolla chuckled. "The best part is that when he did breed, he would be delivering *my* seed, not his. *Mine!* My offspring would be the hybrid!"

Leumas' cheeks flushed a deep red as his anger at this incredible story rose to a fury. "Greg is your son? It can't be," he shouted. "You're making all this up!"

"Tests can be performed, but I care not about what you believe," Copolla said flatly. "The process was not really that difficult, and Greg's father never knew what had been done to him. As far as he was concerned, Greg was his son and that was exactly the way I wanted it to be, for a while, anyway."

Leumas asked the next logical question. "And what about Sarah? Is she your daughter?" He winced, dreading the response.

"She was the control for the experiment," Copolla said, waving his hand in the air as if dismissing the thought as trivial information. "The other agent was unaffected in that sense. She is a secondary matter that can be dealt with at my leisure. Her only power is the mental capacity to block some forms of influence and to communicate with Greg telepathically; a mere trivial ability compared to what *he* shall become."

"Once this information gets out, everybody will be trying to do the same thing," Leumas argued. "Then what? Even if Greg sided with you, which I am sure he won't, it would be a short-lived advantage. It doesn't make sense to go through all of this."

"That would be the case if the DNA strand still existed in the Terrans. But it doesn't anymore."

"What have you done?" Leumas asked.

"We launched an observation satellite around Earth, or at least that is what the official reports recorded. It emitted a low-frequency radiation pulse that, over the years, destroyed the inactive DNA strand in question in every living creature on the planet. With the exception of a relatively small group, no one else on Earth has it any longer. Except Greg and Sarah."

"You sick bastard," Leumas said. "You crazy, sick—"

Copolla rose from his chair with sudden quickness, grabbing Leumas by the throat with one massive hand. In his other hand, he held a weapon at Leumas' temple. "Another comment from you and I will kill—"

Copolla stopped and tilted his head at various angles, like a dog hearing sounds at a level imperceptible by humans. Achieving verification of what he detected, he laughed as he pressed the point of the weapon harder into Leumas' head.

"Smile for the camera," he whispered, then slowly released his hold. Leumas gasped for air and fell to the floor.

"It won't be much longer now," Copolla said. "Not long at all until our family reunion." Then in his thoughts he sent, ::*Isn't that right…Greg?*::

"Why is it that the things we hold the most precious in life always seem to be the ones that we are in jeopardy to lose?"

Greg Carlson

"I have to go to Acuba to get Leumas," Greg told Vague, who now physically stood in Greg's quarters. "He's in the hands of a madman who will certainly kill him. We were sure he was crazy and dead two years ago. We may have been wrong about him being dead, but we're still sure about him being crazy. I have to get Leumas out of there."

"I would recommend against it. It's too dangerous and you have things you must do yet," Vague countered. "There are many more things at stake you need to be concerned with."

"Things? What things?" Greg asked, frustration evident in his voice. "You talk in circles and mysteries and it's starting to drive me crazy." He turned away for a moment to hide his expression.

"Look, Vague," he began more calmly as he turned back. "I can feel you're here to do me good and to help me, but if you won't tell me anything, how can I believe you or make a decision on what to do to help Leumas? All you tell me is that you are 'going to make me see.' You have to tell me something more in order for me to make the right decision."

Greg watched as Vague lowered his head and turned. He paced a few steps in a very small circle, apparently considering what he had been asked. He made a complete circle and then returned to face Greg.

"Greg, you have only begun to realize your powers. All things happen for a reason, you know that, right?"

"Sure," Greg answered.

"The only thing I can tell you about my people is... Well, think about the organization you represent, the United Council for Developing Worlds. The group I represent is quite similar in purpose, but yet different. It's very difficult to explain."

Greg watched as Vague was silent for several seconds again.

"Let me use a comparison to explain," Vague began.

"Go ahead."

"You have rules about influencing worlds," Vague said. "You keep your presence secret until that world is ready to learn of your existence."

"Yes, to prevent the shock of the existence of another alien race, so to speak."

"Let's think of my organization the same way. I am here to help you develop in a way to help the worlds you represent. In essence, it's the same mission under a similar pretense."

"How old is your race?"

"It's been so long, even they don't remember. Instead of forming physical bodies from elements, we are pure energy. We know no physical bounds. This physical shape before you is for your convienence—to assist in communication. ."

"That's amazing," Greg said. "What about your…"

"No. I can tell you no more. I have gone out on a limb, so to speak, too far already. You will have to trust and believe in me from what I have told you and shown you so far," Vague insisted.

"And what you're trying to teach me—this moving or traveling in my mind—this will help me in leading the council?" Greg asked.

"Yes. But it is more than just traveling through space. It may…" Vague paused, as if rehearsing his next words. "We are not sure how far it can go, maybe even take you through time? You have some limited ability to see into the future, but if you haven't had your doubts yet, you will. The time line you are seeing is based on everything remaining relatively constant. You should know from your own mathematical laws that few things involving a living entity are constant. To believe what you have seen *must happen* is a grave error."

"I think I understand," Greg said. "And, yes, I'll admit I've had my doubts somewhat about the precognition. I can't even control it; it comes and goes as it pleases. In fact, the last time I had a glimpse that made any real sense was over two years ago when I assumed the leadership of the UCDW. Since then, it's been bits and pieces."

Greg paused, as if remembering the day with a certain relish for a few seconds, and it was then realization struck. "So you must be here for a specific reason. You know something is going to happen. What? What is going to happen? You must tell me."

Greg looked into Vague's face, searching for some emotion or expression that might reveal something.

"All I can tell you is that if you are not prepared for what is coming," he stated, looking Greg directly in the eyes, "then Earth will be destroyed. You are the only chance to prevent it—if you are prepared to meet the challenge."

***

Sarah arrived at the UCDW compound and was met at the shuttle bay by Reveb. She couldn't help but be amused as she replayed Greg's press conference in her mind. She had to commend him for his ingenious plan of acting a little crazy; he had done an excellent job of destroying Ray Schume's credibility. The attitude of people around her had changed considerably.

"He's changed, you know," Reveb said. Sarah jumped at the sound of his voice. "I saw it in his face the other day," he added, before she could respond.

"Who?" Sarah asked as she regained her composure.

"The Leader."

"He has a lot of responsibilities now," Sarah pointed out. "It would change anyone to have that much—"

"No, it's more than that. He, himself, is changing. His mind..." Reveb ended the conversation as they reached Greg's quarters. Sarah stared as he hurried down the corridor and out of sight.

Sarah found Greg sitting in his chair, coffee cup in hand as he gazed out the window. It was in these moments she wondered where his mind was. He was spending so much time thinking and planning, he had little time for anything else.

"Ahem," she said to get his attention.

Greg turned his gaze from the window toward her. At first, he seemed distant somehow, his eyes unfocused, but his disposition changed quickly.

"Hi there, lady," he said as he came to greet her. He wrapped his arms around her and kissed her.

"Hmmm, I don't know if I'm safe around a crazy guy like you," she teased.

"I'll be fine as long as you're part of my rehabilitation."

"Cute."

"Thank you. Can I get you something? Coffee?" He indicated his cup. "Fresh and just the way you like it."

"Sure," she said, as her eyes searched his face.

Physically, he looked tired. In his eyes she could see there was great emotional stress, but she would wait until he was ready to tell her. She wrapped her arm around his waist as they walked toward the kitchen.

"What's up with Reveb?" she asked instead. "He's acting very weird and says you're 'changing.' Specifically your mind, he said. Is there something this girl should know before she considers a long-term relationship?"

"Too late for that. We're in for the long haul, sweetheart."

"No, really," Sarah insisted. "It was very strange."

"He's a strange individual." He chuckled. "He came in the other day, and I was really deep into thought and didn't hear him. He came up to me and shook me and I guess I didn't acknowledge him for a while. He got nervous when I finally looked up at him. He gave me one of the strangest looks I have ever seen—or, at least, one of the strangest looks I have ever seen from him, considering his usual bland expression."

"Well, he seemed very disturbed about it."

"Great. It'll only be a matter of time before rumors reach the council chambers that the Leader is behaving very oddly." Greg shook his head. "I'll have to call a meeting of the council as soon as possible to bring them up to speed on what is going on, or at least some of it. I can't go back on the promise we made over two years ago not to hide things from them."

He handed Sarah her cup of coffee and they walked into his living room and sat on the sofa.

"Have you heard from Leumas?" Sarah asked.

"Not exactly," he equivocated. "He's in trouble and it's about as bad as it gets.".

"What's going on, Greg?" Sarah didn't try to hide her alarm as his hesitant silence dragged on. "Stop hiding things from me. I love you. Tell me everything and don't leave anything out. I know you've got big shoulders and all, but you can't carry everything on them yourself. I'm part of the council as well, so let me help you. We'll figure this out together. Isn't that what we are suppose to do, work together?"

She touched his hand. Greg gently grasped and released it. "You're right, as always, Sarah," he admitted and then sighed heavily.

She watched as he rose, went back to the kitchen and refreshed his cup of coffee. Then he reached into an overhead cabinet and produced a bottle which contained a bright yellow fluid which she recognized as Zirean Whiskey, supposedly an alcoholic beverage of considerable potency.

"I don't mean to hide things from you Sarah," he said as he uncapped the bottle. "Yet sometimes the truth hurts and I don't want anyone else to be hurt by it."

Sarah was surprised at the appearance of the bottle of whiskey. "This must be bad," she said. "I can't remember you drinking that unless you are very troubled about something."

Greg looked at her briefly, and then poured a copious amount in his cup. He did not respond to her assertion.

"Keeping it all bottled up inside you isn't good either," Sarah said. As she said this she saw his hand trembling.

Greg walked back into the living room with his coffee in one hand and the bottle in the other.

"Greg, what are..."

"I would suggest you have some of this also. It'll make the story go down easier," he said as he reached for her cup and poured the whiskey into it.

"Greg, what is it? What's wrong?" She felt her heart beating hard in her chest as she waited for him to answer. ::*When will it stop? Why can't things go right for us for a change?*::

::*I don't know...I just don't know anymore.*::

Sarah raised her cup and sipped the doctored coffee. It tasted warm: the flavor reminded her of licorice on her tongue, and it had an immediate effect on her senses.

"It's a Zirean stimulant, non-addictive, of course," Greg explained. "It heightens the awareness and enhances problem-solving."

"It's fine," she assured him. "But, come on, now, let's have it."

He took a deep breath and exhaled as he readied himself to start. "Leumas has been captured and his life is in very grave danger," he began.

Sarah was about to ask something when he placed his hand on her lips and indicated for her to be silent.

"Please, let me finish. He is being held by...Copolla." He blurted the name out in hope saying it quickly would ease the pain hearing it was sure to cause her. By Sarah's initial reaction, he guessed he had been wrong.

The color immediately left her face as it contorted with anger. "How can that be? He was killed!"

"I saw it in my mind," Greg said. "There was no doubt it was him."

"If he's alive..." She struggled with the thought. "...he's probably behind all this strange stuff that's been happening, including the murder of the initial contact agents, the Arcturian ambassadors... All of it."

"I would definitely second that opinion. On the bright side, at least now we know that."

"How are we going to get Leumas back?" She took a large swallow of her coffee.

"I don't know. But I—we'll figure out something," Greg said as he rubbed his forehead.

"I know there's more, Greg, isn't there?"

"Isn't there always?" Greg then told Sarah about the alien who had made contact with him. Sarah paid close attention to the entire story about his mind traveling to the planets in the solar system and what little information Vague had told him about this other race.

"Wow. This Vague sounds interesting. But if his race is pure energy, as he says, wouldn't they be able to do something to stop whatever it is? I mean, they sound like a super being or a god. But it kind of makes sense when you think about it. There's always been a Supreme Being in everyone's ideology. Why couldn't it be an alien? Geez, I'm starting to sound like a tabloid. It's just so damn confusing."

"Still, there are some interesting points. We'll have to press Vague for more information. Maybe I can…"

"Hold it right there, my young man," she began as she slid her arms around his neck and pulled him close. "What I don't like is the 'changes' you're going to go through." She leaned her head on his shoulder. "I'm worried about your health. It was tough enough seeing the changes the first time when this all started. And now more changes. When will it all end?"

"I'll be fine," he tried to reassure her. He ran his fingers through her hair, looping the strands around his fingers and twisting them gently. "And if it's the only possibility of saving Earth, then I have to go through it. You know that, don't you?"

"Yes, I understand it. I don't like it, but I understand. This…Vague… hasn't exactly told you what you will do to save Earth?"

"No, but I'm assuming what he's teaching me now has something to do with it. There seems to be some binding law or procedure that forbids him from explaining too much too soon. It's almost as if he has to wait until other events have happened before he can say or do something."

"Doesn't it scare you? The thought that if you just lose your train of thought your mind could be bounced around like a tennis ball, drifting through some void of nothing but energy? No physical form anymore; loss of all sensory perception?"

"Let's hope that doesn't happen. So far, I've been projecting my mind, but I'm not able to do anything except observe. That doesn't seem like a formidable power unless you want to be a galactic eavesdropper."

Sarah laughed. "Wouldn't that make for a wonderful talk show?"

"But imagine," he continued more seriously. "If the mind could actually affect something. You wouldn't have to move and yet you could travel and do whatever you needed to do from the comfort of your own home."

"I can imagine it and it scares me a little," she said. "What if someone evil like Copolla gets hold of that kind of power? He could spread his sick nonsense all over the galaxy without even leaving the comfort of whatever cold, dark rock he hides under. But as far as you're concerned, it does possess lots of possibilities, until you think about your mind splitting up and heading in several different directions if you make a mistake. It has to scare you, doesn't it?"

After a few seconds when he still hadn't answered, Sarah lifted her head from his shoulder. He appeared to be deep in his own thoughts rather than listening to her concerns.

"Excuse me," she said, trying to get his attention back.

"Oh, sorry. Just thinking about Leumas. Vague doesn't want me to go after him, but I have to. I can't leave him in the hands of that murderer."

"You're assuming he isn't already dead," Sarah pointed out morosely as she looked into his eyes with fear.

"Greg was always a person who cared about the greater good…perhaps too much. I know that sounds selfish and inconsiderate, but it happens when you love someone as much as I loved him and have had to live with the sacrifice."

Sarah McClendon

With Sarah in her place beside him, Greg watched as the council members took their seats for the emergency meeting he had called. She did not spend much time here because of her Washington duties, but Sarah was officially its co-leader, although he normally conducted the meetings even when they were both present.

::*Good luck*::, she whispered in his mind. ::*I hate to be the pessimist, but I think you're going to need it.*::

::*Such confidence,*:: he said back quickly and smiled at her. ::*Maybe I should do my crazed imitation like I did at the press conference. What do you think?*::

::*Funny, but not a good idea.*::

::*All right, I'll be serious. I guess we need to get the show on the road. Let's do it.*:: He grasped her hand and gave it a squeeze. ::*Love you.*::

::*Love you, too.*::

"Members of the council, we're here today with discouraging news to tell you," Greg began, and thought about how he might ease his way into what he had to say. However, he really saw no sense in avoiding the inevitable and decided upon the direct approach. "Our common enemy, Copolla, is back among us," he announced.

Murmurs rose and conversations rampaged through the great hall. He saw the look of horror and disbelief on many faces as the others relived that terrible moment when Copolla had blown up the Council Hall on Zire. Many of those murdered delegates had been family and friends of those who sat in the great hall right now. He waited for a few moments until the noise was reduced to a level he could talk over. Members indicated their desire to speak, but Greg did not acknowledge them. He had more he needed to say first.

"Although I do not have credible proof yet, it appears with certainty that Copolla was behind the murder of the agents on Beta-747, the destruction of the Arcturian ambassadorial craft, and that he now holds our esteemed colleague and friend Leumas as a hostage."

Another uproar as great as the first arose. Members now demanded to be recognized, but again Greg did not acknowledge them.

"There is some good news," he continued, hoping what he was about to add would be interpreted as good news and not make things worse.

"I've been contacted by another race that has offered their assistance to help us in these troubled times."

An abrupt and bemused silence descended.

"This race claims to be the oldest in the universe. They are proud of us and of what this council stands for. They have something like it where they come from and it has prospered through millennium after millennium. I believe we should all have hope in this and not lose our perspective on our own magnificent endeavors within our galaxy." He paused for a few moments. "With that, I'll open the floor for discussion on how we should approach this situation."

The questions came fast and Greg tried to answer as best he could. They debated possibilities of what they should do. Some wanted to attack Acuba; others refused that plan for fear of killing Leumas and the chance of starting an interstellar war with all the non-aligned worlds.

Copolla was a proven criminal and should be brought to trial for his crimes, some members cried, while others sought volunteers to go after him. There was a flat-out refusal of the suggestion that Greg go after Leumas himself. It was too risky if he did, in fact, hold the key to saving Earth from destruction. That had to be his first priority.

Finally, after hours of debate, they reached a plan they could all agree on. A rescue party would be launched to save Leumas. As soon as Leumas was safe, a blockade would be placed around the planet until Copolla surrendered or was turned over by whatever governing force existed. Although the planet was a non-UCDW planet, they were harboring a criminal that posed a significant threat to the UCDW planets. Therefore the right to self protection of the UCDW worlds precluded any thoughts of this action being considered a direct threat of war, but rather self defense. It was also decided that it would be best if Greg remained on Earth and continue to work with the alien race that had approached him.

Greg at first protested, but the Council members would not budge in their decision to not allow him to go along with the rescue mission: in the end, he decided he did have to agree with them. If the choice was between his saving one life and all the lives on an entire planet, there really was no choice.

"This is what the council desires, so shall it be," Greg said when the results of the final vote were announced. "But we must move quickly before Copolla makes another move that may hurt us. The rescue mission departs in twelve hours. The blockade ships will stand by for confirmation of either Leumas' rescue or his…death. This meeting is adjourned."

* * *

"I still think I should lead the rescue mission for Leumas," Greg said quietly but adamantly to Sarah as they left the Hall of the Great Council. "I could get in and out before anyone would even suspect I was there."

"Greg, I know you want to go, but there are other areas you must concentrate on. Remember, you have many obligations now and a lot is at risk at the moment, including Leumas." She touched his arm and slid her hand down to his and grasped it firmly. "The council knows you and Leumas are good friends. It was a hard decision for them, too, but look at what they've done," she said with admiration. "Because of your leadership and the spirit of cooperation you've brought, they were able to work it through and agree on a plan. You should be very proud of them. I doubt they could have done this before."

"I know. And I am proud of them. I just don't think I could forgive myself if anything happened to Leumas. Being in the hands of your worst enemy has to be one of the cruelest scenarios. Everyone remembers that when Copolla took revenge it was extremely painful and very accurate." He sighed heavily. "The odds are against Leumas even being alive."

Releasing her hand, he turned to hide his glassy eyes and possibly even a tear of frustration and fear for his good friend. Sarah gave him a few moments.

"Are you okay?"

"I'm fine. Will you stay tonight?" he asked as he looked back at her.

"Sorry, I have to get back. Edward needs to be briefed and we have some other issues pending that need to be resolved."

"I understand," he said, sounding discouraged. "Maybe you can come back when you're done?"

"As soon as I'm finished, I'll come back and stay until all of this is resolved, I promise. Maybe I can even move my office over to the compound permanently," she said encouragingly. "The project on the new launch vehicle is going smoothly. In fact, with the enthusiasm of the scientists, it's almost on automatic. I can write press releases and do public relations from here as well as I can there. I'll discuss it with Edward when I get back."

"Sounds great."

They held hands as they walked to the shuttle bay, swinging them back and forth like two high school kids out for a leisurely stroll. As they arrived to the end of the corridor, Sarah turned to Greg and hugged him tightly while they still had a private moment together. Greg kissed her and allowed himself to drift within her warmth. No other woman had ever made him feel the way she could. He only hoped...

"Don't worry, we'll get through this," she said as she released him. "When all this is over, and I have your undivided attention once again, we need to talk about something else also."

"What?"

"Later. When the time is right."

"Just what I need—another secret." Greg smiled and continued on into the shuttle area, where Reveb hovered over the main control panel.

"What's going on, Reveb?" Greg asked, surprised to see him here. Reveb was not a technical person by any means or that was what he had been led to believe about the quiet and unemotional alien.

"Just a slight malfunction on the disengaging links on the shuttle," the Monocian explained. "The maintenance personnel have it repaired and are running a test to ensure all is functioning. It should be back in a matter of minutes. I offered my services to ensure it would be ready by the time Ms. McClendon arrived for her trip back."

"I guess we can wait then," Greg told Sarah, smiling at the slight reprieve of extra minutes they had received.

"Leader, I almost forgot," Reveb interjected. "A man named Vague is waiting for you in your quarters. He indicated it was quite urgent." He used a noticeable voice inflexion on the name that indicated dislike.

"Perhaps you should go," Sarah sighed. "I'll be fine. Reveb and I'll wait until the shuttle returns." She looked at the Monocian. "Right, Reveb?"

"Yes, Ms. McClendon. It will be my pleasure."

Greg hesitated for a moment, but saw the look of understanding on Sarah's face that said "go ahead—things to do and people to see, just like always."

"Let me know as soon as you hear something," she added.

"You bet. Talk to you soon." He waved and headed back to his quarters.

He found Vague sitting comfortably in a chair.

"I heard how the council meeting went. It sounds like a good plan," his visitor said. "You have many races and species that work well together. It was a very impressive show of unity and cohesion. You have done well in such a short period of time. I hope it all works out for your friend Leumas."

"So do I," Greg agreed. "So do I. Now on to the urgent business Reveb said you had for me."

Vague looked at Greg with a somewhat blank expression.

"I don't understand," he said. "I did not tell Reveb I needed you back. I knew you were taking Ms. McClendon to the shuttle, so I knew you would be a few moments seeing her off before returning."

"Reveb said you told him that you needed to see me about something very urgent."

"I told him to tell you *not* to hurry because I knew you were seeing Ms. McClendon off," Vague repeated.

"He must've gotten the message mixed up, I guess," Greg said. "Although that's not like Reveb to do that." Greg felt an underlying sense of fear raise its head but quickly dispelled it because he knew that Reveb was trustworthy—he had been cleared by Leumas.

Vague took a step closer to Greg and said, "These are uncertain times. Stress and worry can sometimes cause people to do or say things they would not normally do."

"Or hear incorrectly, too, I suppose," Greg added.

"I imagine so." Vague agreed. "Do you trust Reveb?"

"Yes, but it still seems so out of character for him to get something mixed up. And why weren't the maintenance personnel conducting the check? Let me check with maintenance. It'll just take a second."

"As you wish," Vague acknowledged.

Greg pressed his preset comm link for the maintenance section.

"Yes, Leader of the Council," a voice answered.

"Is the shuttle still under maintenance?"

"Yes, sir, it should be clear in a few moments for Ms. McClendon's departure."

"Why is Reveb assisting?"

"He was at the platform when we did the work and offered to assist to speed up the process. He said it was vital Ms. McClendon get back. Is there anything wrong?"

"No, I guess not. Thanks." Greg felt the questioning fears dissipate like a mist. Everything had been explained and was as it should be. He turned to Vague. "Okay, you have my full attention."

"Good. Now, we have things to do. I want you to close your eyes and blank everything out of your mind."

CHAPTER FOUR

"I will allow nothing to come between me and my destiny, not even myself regardless of whatever forms it comes in."

Copolla

"How is the gathering of the ships progressing?" Copolla asked Kernis, his second-in-command.

Kernis turned to face Copolla, although it wasn't necessary for his species to do so. He knew Copolla was approaching from the small snake-like eye he possessed in the rear of his scaly neck. Kernis was a Mokian, a race where conditions on their desert home-world were so harsh, survival of newborn was less then twenty percent. Those that did survive were highly praised for their survival skills and their viciousness, for they contributed to the low survival rate by devouring their own kind in order to survive.

Their bodies, humanoid in form, were completely covered by a tough snakeskin-like coating that also concealed all their vital organs, ears, eyes and nose when they perceived a threat. All senses were acutely perceptive and their viciousness was reinforced by their razor-sharp claws, poison fangs and their clamp-like jaws which, when latched onto something, never released that something until it was dead.

"They're almost ready. We're waiting for five more to arrive from the Zinta sector. The rest have been outfitted with the weaponry you directed. They should make a most formidable attack fleet, probably the most powerful in the galaxy."

"How many do we have?" Copolla glanced out the window overlooking the landing area where some of the ships were parked. It had taken a long time to acquire the equipment to modify the craft without attracting attention.

"When the remaining five join us, that'll make it twenty-five."

"Good. Very good," Copolla said, smiling.

"Is the primary target still the same?" Kernis asked, although he did not know what the actual target was. Copolla had not told him anything but the basics of the mission and that did not include the name of the target.

"Yes, for the moment. I expect within the next couple of days to confirm either way. How are the crews?"

"Anxious. They've been sitting too long without any real action. I've kept them busy training, but they're eager to acquire the riches you have promised them."

"Well, their wait will soon be over. For now, I want you to heighten security around everything. I expect we'll have company soon." Copolla locked eyes with Kernis to indicate the seriousness of the command he had just given.

"How many?" Kernis asked with interest.

"I don't think it will be more then a handful at best. But if they are spotted, I don't want them taken until I say so and I want them taken alive. Is that understood?"

"Understood," Kernis replied. "Just as we did with the one that came to spy on us, the one called Leumas." He paused and went on. "Forgive me for asking, but why not just kill them?"

"Because one of them, maybe two, will be extremely useful to our cause. So useful it could make our job a whole lot easier and financially greater."

"And if they don't cooperate?"

"Then after I am done with them, you may do as you please."

Kernis smiled. He knew many ways of slow death. The key was to know your subject. He would study his prey before embarking on any trips of pain and torture. He would find all the vital organs and know what it would take to destroy them—or not, if the case warranted an extra-slow demise.

"Have you heard from our contact lately?" Copolla inquired, interrupting Kernis' thoughts of entertainment and delight.

"Not since the last report." Kernis said, forcing his mind back to the moment.

"Perhaps you should check up on him. See if the council has heard anything interesting lately. I want to know what they do when they find out I am back, the whimpering bags of flesh. Not a backbone among the entire lot."

Kernis laughed at Copolla's description of the UCDW. He had, in fact, the same opinion, especially after watching the images of the Arcturian craft carrying their ambassadors being so easily destroyed while one of their ships attacked it at their leisure. Such fools to not to protect themselves. They deserved to die for that reason if no other.

"I'll contact him immediately and get an update," he replied.

"Let him know if our present bait is not strong enough to lure our friends here, we will move on to the next plan. Ensure he understands it must be performed exactly as I have laid it out. I want no mistakes, Kernis. Is that clearly understood?"

"Yes, I understand perfectly."

"Very good," Copolla said. "And then I have another task for you. I want you to pick up our helpful reporter friend from Earth and bring him here."

Kernis looked at Copolla oddly, wondering why he would take such a large risk over the useless human he had used to toy with the leaders of the council and the Earth government.

"Him? What purpose will he…"

"Don't question my orders!" Copolla screamed.

Kernis reeled back several paces. His head throbbed with the pain that had accompanied both the vocalized and mental invasion of Copolla's warning.

"Don't *ever* question my orders if you wish to live," Copolla added as his face contorted into an evil, sardonic expression.

"Yes, Copolla," Kernis whimpered, his head pounding from the pain.

Copolla smiled at the Mokian's obvious discomfort as he waved a hand in dismissal. He kicked back in his chair, lacing his fingers behind his large neck. His thoughts danced in his head.

Soon, my friends. Not much longer now and there will be a new order of things. Come on, Greg, my dear, sweet boy. Come on. I'm waiting for you…

"There are days when I really hate this damn job…you can fall from the top so quickly it makes your head spin."

Reporter Ray Schume

Ray Schume was mumbling as he placed what few mementos he had left in his office into the brown cardboard box. "Idiots, that's all they are. Damn stupid idiots. They think I can't get another job? Hah! There'll be other papers that'll love to have me. I'll show them all!"

His editor had suggested he move on after the embarrassing press conference that he, in essence, had prompted. Ray didn't really care much about the story anymore—he had lost interest after the press conference—but that didn't change the fact his boss had fired him for it.

"How quickly these assholes forget about all the other breaking stories I've done. One little aw-shit comes along and years of good work are conveniently forgotten. Screw them, then, and the shit-for-brains source!"

His source had set him up. Some other reporter, person or organization he had pissed off in the past wanted to get even with him or something and had arranged the whole thing. Lord knows there were surely enough of them out there. What better than to have the mud-slinging reporter end up with mud on his own face?

But there was still something that bothered him about the whole damn affair. After the strong first positive lead he had received proved out, what was the point if not to expose? He stopped as his head suddenly pounded. He grabbed the tin of aspirin from his pocket and quickly downed a handful as he winced at the acrid taste in his mouth.

"I'm done with the whole thing. To hell with it," he said as he threw the last item in the box and headed out the door.

There weren't any fond farewells as he walked across the press floor and pressed the elevator key. Heroes left with fanfare and loads of new friends; failures left without notice for fear of being associated with a loser. The elevator arrived. Inside stood a man in dark khaki clothing; above his right pocket his name—Fred. Immediately below that was Trace's Cleaning Service. As Ray stepped into the elevator he couldn't help but notice the broad smile on the man's face. Probably heard the news and had a good laugh, Ray thought as he fell back into his musing on his future.

"Tough break, Mr. Schume," the young man said.

"Yeah, you could say that," he said, wondering if there was one person around who hadn't heard of his demise as a reporter. He looked at the man, realizing this was not the usual person who performed the cleaning. He couldn't recall the name of the usual janitor, but this man was not he.

"You're new here, aren't you?" Ray asked, watching the lights on the panel glow as they moved.

"Yes, first day, as a matter of fact."

Ray settled back into the silence as he wondered who the hell would hire him after this mess.

"So, you think you were set up," the man said, which caused Ray's attention to be momentarily drawn back.

"Yes, I do. How do you know that?"

"How would you like to have the story of a lifetime—with indisputable proof?" the man asked, ignoring the question.

"Give me a hint." Ray shifted the box in his arms as he imagined hearing the same story he had heard hundreds of times before; especially the one where some family relative or pet possessed supernatural powers. Or will it be the typical alien abduction and birth story or something?

"You will be given the proof of all that you have been told and a chance to interview all of the people involved. Interested?"

"Who the hell are you?" Thoughts of the alien conspiracy rose in his mind, causing him to wince from the head pain again noticeably. "Damn headache, that's all this story has given me. Every time I think about it!" He reached into his pocket for more aspirin.

The young man grasped Ray's arm and shook his head. Instead, the janitor removed a small pill from his pocket. "Take this. It will ease the pain. You have had mental influence applied to keep you away from the truth."

"Mental influence…who are you?" Ray asked. "And what the hell are you talking about?" Ray found the ridiculous situation amusing. After the rotten day he had, why not indulge this lunatic for a while—he could use the amusement. His reporter instincts also agreed that sometimes you just have to go with the flow regardless how crazy it sounded. There might be that one time where there actually is a pile of gold at the end of the rainbow rather than the usual pile of shit he was accustomed to.

"I am a friend of a friend. Now, take the pill. It will work immediately."

Ray did as instructed and was quite surprised that his newfound friend was correct; the headache vanquished almost immediately. Mind over matter, he thought, either that or some good drugs.

"Do you still want to know the truth?"

"Why not?" Ray said with a shrug of his shoulders. "When do we get started?"

"We leave immediately." He pressed the elevator button for the rooftop.

"We're going to the roof?"

"Yes, that is where my vehicle is."

"On the roof? Your vehicle?" Ray chuckled. "Okay, buddy, why not? It can't possibly get any worse."

They arrived on the roof level and the door opened. Ray followed the man down the short corridor leading to the exposed roof area. He saw nothing there except the vacant helicopter pad.

"Okay, my friend, where is your 'vehicle' at?"

"It is right there, cloaked so it will not be detected."

"Why don't they just beam you up, Scotty?"

The man looked at Ray with puzzlement, obviously not understanding the humor.

"Forget it. Look, my friend, I'm going to go back down in the elevator, find the nearest bar and get drunk. Adios, my alien friend, and thanks for the headache stuff, whatever it was." He turned and headed back to the elevator. He did not see the man pull out the little handheld weapon.

"Mr. Schume, I would suggest you…"

"Bug off, you asshole," Ray said without turning around. "I've had enough of alien conspiracies to last me a lifetime!"

The man fired and Ray crumbled to the ground. The attacker removed another device from his pocket, clicked it and a small spacecraft appeared on the helicopter pad. He carried the body on board and dumped it on the floor.

Once inside, he quickly set about removing the fake facial features he wore to give him a human appearance. He was desperate for relief from the itching. Finally free, he exhaled strongly. "Stuff makes you sweat too much." Kernis looked into a mirror and, satisfied with his cleanup, prepared to resume work on the task at hand.

He keyed in the coordinates, and the computer announced the destination of Acuba confirmed. With time to spare during the flight, he removed his laser tool from the console and began to burn little holes in Ray's clothing.

"Oops," he said, as he underestimated the distance and strength of the laser and singed the flesh. Kernis smiled. He didn't really mind the smell of burning flesh. Actually, it enticed him to keep going.

"We are basically creatures of habit…I should have remembered that and perhaps I could have avoided what was to come."

Sarah McClendon

As Sarah waited for the shuttle she tried to occupy her time thinking of what she needed to do on her return to Washington, but she couldn't help notice Reveb's uncharacteristic nervousness, a distinct difference from his usual behavior. He stood at the control station, his hands quickly moving across the keyboard as his eyes watched the small monitor built into the console. His stern glare was appeared to reflect impatience as if things moved too slowly for him. He would tap the keyboard furiously, then watch the screen as if interpreting the outcome of what he had just done. This action repeated itself over and over.

Was that perspiration she saw glimmer on his forehead? Had she ever seen him like that before? Perhaps the task he had been given by the maintenance personnel exceeded his capacity, she thought. But she knew that Reveb was proud, and he would never have turned down an assignment just for fear of not—

"Don't worry," he said, catching her off-guard, as if he had read her thoughts. "It's almost ready. The system checks are almost completed. I just want to be sure the maintenance personnel completed the diagnostics portion of the checks so we can get you where you need to go. I know how valuable your time is."

"Thank you, Reveb. Can I help you with something?"

"No. Thank you," he said as he wiped the perspiration from his brow with a piece of cloth.

Sarah watched as his expression changed to something between embarrassment and anger. She wasn't sure which.

"Please excuse my harried appearance. I'm a little rusty with these procedures. Rest assured, I have everything under control." He returned his full attention to the control panel and fell silent.

Embarrassed, she thought, nothing more. *Just my nerves making me jumpy.* She began to stroll around the platform. *Just so much happening… I still can't believe that Copolla is alive. And Leumas—Copolla has him. Good Lord knows there was no love lost between those two. How much better it would be to—*

"The shuttle will be here in about one minute," Reveb said, breaking into her thoughts.

"Thank you, Reveb." He was looking at her strangely now. His eyes were wide and wary, as if he were anticipating an attack.

What is it with him today?

"Reveb, are you sure you're okay? You seem very much on edge. Is there anything I can do?"

"Yes, er… I mean no. I am quite well, thank you," he said. "I am sorry if this delay has caused any problem in your schedule. We will be on track in a few moments."

"That's alright. The delay is not a concern. But you're acting…"

"Did you see the change in him, Ms. McClendon?" he asked, surprising her with this change of topic. "The emptiness in his eyes, as if his mind is elsewhere? His body is here, but his mind is off somewhere. It's not natural."

"No, I saw no change," she told him. "I think you're misinterpreting whatever it was you saw, Reveb. You caught him when he was deep in thought. It happens to all of us at times." She chose not to add that he was, in truth, partly correct about Greg's behavior. It would only add to his obvious fear and confusion.

"I know what I saw," he said, his voice rising. "His mind was elsewhere. And now with this new alien race that has contacted him, many wonder why he is becoming secretive and distant. Some even say he will cause the downfall of the great council because of this affiliation he has developed."

"Nonsense," Sarah said, keeping her voice low and even. This line of conversation was becoming extremely discomfiting. "The meeting with the council went extremely well. No one in there suggested any of that." She paused. "Perhaps that is purely your own opinion?" She began to feel uncomfortable about his conduct and with the fact the shuttle still had not arrived.

"And why does he not go to Acuba to save Leumas? Leumas would go for him," Reveb continued.

"Reveb, I don't know what's gotten into you, but you need to stop and look at these things rationally." Her eyes locked onto his and she thought she saw something strange in them, as if he were having an attack of conscience.

An instant later, the sound of the shuttle caused her to look in that direction and she felt glad she would be departing Reveb's company. She also made a mental note to tell Greg what happened as soon as possible. Perhaps Reveb was having a mental breakdown of some sort.

The shuttle coasted into the stop area and opened up for boarding. She quickly turned to enter, and as she took a last look at Reveb, her stomach bottomed out. He was standing right next to her with a stun weapon in his hand.

"Reveb? What are you…"

"I am looking at it very rationally, Ms. McClendon, for my family and myself," he said as he fired.

Sarah collapsed onto the pavement. Reveb picked her up and placed her into the shuttle, then sat in the other seat. He keyed in the destination. It was not to the compound where Sarah was supposed to go, but to the launch area.

As the shuttle departed, he quickly removed a portable computer link and began to type the UCDW override codes that superceded any previous one a vessel in the launch area might have had put in place by its operator. He went from screen to screen, accessing onboard computers for each ship in the staging area, which included all ambassadorial ships and the council security force vessels. He instructed each vessel except his own to shut down their engines and go into a mandatory preventive maintenance and diagnostic mode because of suspected risk to all passengers.

That would result in a shutdown of twenty-four to thirty-six hours for each vessel, depending on the size of its engine. Any attempt to start the engines could result in irreparable damage and possible implosion.

As he keyed the last code into the computer and received confirmation the final ship had entered the maintenance cycle, he shut down all internal communications to the council area except his. He sat back and sent a coded message.

"Have package; will be arriving soon. All vessels inoperable; have agreed compensation upon arrival."

The message flashed to Acuba.

"Was I suspicious about the alien called Vague? Of course I was, but there was no alternative left for me to pursue if I was to become what I must."

Greg Carlson

::*Do we travel today?*:: Greg asked.

::*Yes, but I want you to try something different when we arrive at our destination,*:: Vague told him.

::*What's that?*:: Greg was curious.

::*Let's get to where we're going first. For now, focus your thoughts on this sector.*::

A star chart appeared to Greg. He stared at it with no recognition of the area of space it depicted.

::*Why this area?*:: he wanted to know.

::*Why not?*:: Vague countered with a slight hint of impatience. ::*Concentrate, please.*::

::*Okay, okay,*:: Greg said and did as instructed. He concentrated on the image of the star chart. Slowly, his mind opened up to it and he was floating in space. It was wonderful, he thought. He felt the consciousness of Vague there with him.

::*It's beautiful,*:: he said.

::*Yes, it is,*:: Vague agreed. ::*Do you see the comet to your right?*::

Greg willed himself to turn in that direction. ::*Yes, I see it.*::

::*I now want you to reach with your mind and seek to join with the comet, to merge with it. But remember, you must also maintain your own consciousness. This is very important. Do you understand?*::

::*But how?*::

::*You must never commit yourself totally to an object. Always keep a portion behind. Your thoughts are comprised of energy. This energy is a stream incorporating what you are, what makes you be who you are as long as it is attached in a physical sense.*

::*In simpler terms, imagine a rope or lifeline, this stream of energy, which links back to anchor you to your physical body. The anchor is that part of your mind that must never leave its position in your physical body in order for you to find your way back. Do you understand?*::

::*Yes,*:: Greg said, feeling a little unsure. ::*I think so.*::

::*Try doing it in increments. Very slowly.*::

Greg centered his concentration on the comet. Slowly, he felt a shifting of his consciousness. Shadow images of the stars appeared as his earlier image of the comet weakened in intensity. These shadow images were the images he saw from the comet; the part of him within the comet. After a few more seconds, he felt his consciousness spread over the entire shape of the comet. The immensity of its size was overwhelming as it hurtled at terrific speed through the universe. Although fascinated by this shift, he carefully maintained the link back to his own consciousness, the image of the comet still occupying a portion of his thoughts.

::How do you feel?:: Vague asked.

::Strange, but wonderful. It's...hard to explain. I can feel or sense some things about the comet. I'm not sure how I know things about it, but I do. Its birth was very long ago. When the galaxy was formed.::

::Yes, the comet is old, formed at the beginning of the universe. By becoming part of it, you experience its age. If you committed more of yourself, you possibly might see its birth.::

::Travel back in time?::

::Yes. That is a very important lesson you must remember. Time is of the utmost importance.::

::If you can control time, you can influence the course of events?::

::Yes. Very good. You have done well.::

Greg didn't know how to exactly put this all into perspective. Even now, a part of him was the comet while another part knew it was Greg. A question stirred in his mind.

::Can you do this to a living being? Have two consciences exist within the same confines?::

::That is a very dangerous thing you speak of. There are those who tried it and never came back, absorbed by the existing mind. Others went insane.:: Vague's tone was sad, as if someone close to him had been one of those to attempt such a thing. ::When you are in this state, you must be very careful. Remember we once talked about the danger of trying to be in two places at the same time. A non-living organism, such as the comet is one thing, but a living organism is totally different. If you are not sufficiently cautious, your mind can actually lose its hold on the physical body, the anchor we spoke of earlier, split in two different directions, and never combine again.::

::But how does this all tie together with seeing?:: Greg asked.

::To see is to understand everything around you, to understand it by being it. And by being a thing through time, you experience the true essence of life. When you reach this pinnacle of comprehension, then you shall truly see.::

::I'm not sure I understand. Is it–:: Greg stopped as he suddenly felt himself being pulled in another direction. ::Vague! What's happening?::

He felt as if his mind were being torn into fragments. Suddenly, blackness swept into his mind. In the darkness, he faintly heard Sarah calling to him, distant and hard to make out.

::*Greg, concentrate on home. Focus your thoughts! Focus on the image of your quarters; follow your lifeline back to the anchor.*::

He did as instructed. Concentrating, he used the images of the lifeline; the line appeared and he followed it back. Gradually the darkness began to lighten as he felt more and more of him rejoining within himself.

Greg opened his eyes. His vision was blurred, but quickly sharpened to reveal that the shadowy form standing in front of him was Vague. They were back in his quarters at the UCDW.

"What happened?" Greg asked, his heartbeat racing as he tried to catch his breath. "I thought I heard Sarah calling me, but it was very distant and faint."

"Sarah was attempting to reach you, and you weren't prepared for it. Your mind was beginning to split."

Greg, although badly shaken by what had almost happened, quickly shifted his mind to Sarah and searched.

::*Sarah! Sarah, can you hear me?*::

::*I'm here, Greg. Copolla has taken me hostage. I've been instructed to tell you that he'll kill Leumas and me unless you come here to Acuba. But you have—*::

Her thoughts were suddenly cut off by the sound of brief laughter. Greg knew to whom that laughter belonged. It was Copolla.

* * *

"I don't have any choice now, Vague," Greg said. "If I don't go, he'll kill them both, and I can't live with that." The image of Sarah calling to him in his mind as Copolla threatened her life was too much for him to bear.

"I understand," Vague told him, "but I must remind you that a whole planet's survival may rest in the balance of your decision." He gave the warning softly to emphasize his understanding of Greg's thoughts and concerns.

"I know. But I must go." He turned and looked out the window.

Vague took a deep breath and exhaled slowly as he appeared to go into a state of deep concentration. A few seconds passed before he spoke again.

"There may be another way," Vague began as Greg turned to face him. "If you can travel in your mind to Acuba, and get close enough by attaching your thoughts on nonliving elements, you might be able to apply influence through that connection."

"What? Would it really work? I don't want to take any risks with their lives."

"We won"t really know until you try," Vague admitted. "But I want you to realize what you risk. You are the only chance of saving Earth, and you must not jeopardize yourself in any way. The greater good is to save a world, even if it means the loss of two people you care about."

"I understand. Can you go with me?"

"No, I can't," Vague answered. "But remember what I have taught you so far. Control is the key. Concentrate and maintain control over your thoughts."

"Against your rules? Is that why you can't come along?" Greg asked.

"Yes, I'm afraid so." Vague accompanied his answer with a shrug. Greg knew it meant he couldn't answer with any more detail. Then Vague indicated Greg should lie on his bed. "You must be totally clear on what you are going to do, and you must free your mind of everything...*everything*. One mistake and you could leave your mind trapped in some other object rather than returning to your own body. You will have to jump from object to object to get close enough to do anything. And you must be part of something of substance in order to use your influence."

"I understand," Greg said and closed his eyes.

He tried to focus but his mind was a jumble of images: Leumas, Sarah, the council, Copolla, Earth. One by one, he willed them away and concentrated on the image of Acuba. The image in his mind quickly altered as the actual planet became visible to his thoughts. He found himself looking down on the surface. The moons of his dreams were there and added a strange sense of familiarity to the setting.

Okay, what next? he asked himself.

Suddenly, as if an answer was given to him, he saw a craft entering orbit. With a flick of his mind, he willed himself to be part of the vessel. In his thoughts, he also maintained his crucial lifeline and anchor back to his physical body. The transition was very different from the moment with the comet. The ship felt empty, without any kind of life force. He knew he shouldn't feel the coldness of its hull of steel or any other physical sensation for that matter, but he could have sworn he did.

He immersed himself into the coldness and became the vessel, able to glimpse into its working machinery or right down to the cloth on the command seat. He could flow through the cables and piping by just thinking of it, but the further he went into the matrix of the ship, the more the process required a stringent and tiring focus on what he wanted to do. He learned this the hard way as he was pulled in several different directions until he learned to control the focus of his thoughts.

::*Give it more, but not too much.*::

He moved into the ship's computer and verified the ship would be landing at the major spaceport on Acuba. Further investigation surprised him as he learned the last stop of this vessel had been Earth and that there were two passengers on board, one of them human. He flowed through the craft to get a look at the two who occupied it.

The non-human one he did not recognize, neither species nor by appearance. The other brought a strange relief and surprise. It was his favorite reporter, Mr. Ray Schume.

So, that's how the information was leaked to the papers. Copolla was giving the information to Schume and he took it from there.

Greg's attention was suddenly drawn to the fact the reporter was not awake. He appeared to be unconscious, and there were strange burn marks on him. *Perhaps Mr. Schume was not a willing partner. Either way, I think if I tag along with these two, I'll find what I'm looking for.*

Greg knew he would soon have to leave the confines of the ship and latch onto something else in order to move with his only connection to where, possibly, Sarah and Leumas might be. He sent his mind gently in the direction of Schume, focusing on the man's jacket. He merged into the threads of the material and their interwoven texture. He had to be careful to not go too low on the molecular level for fear of being lost in the molecular matrix. He had learned from his experience with the ship it was a delicate balance that had to be meticulously maintained.

As he became part of the clothing, he detected it, and probably the body within it, had been exposed to some type of burning. As he explored the fiber content, the texture of the material, and the precision and neatness of the damage, it became apparent Mr. Schume's captor had a thing for poking holes in unconscious life forms with a laser. He suspected this perverse behavior was a trait Copolla encouraged in his personnel—a ruthlessness and lack of respect for life in general. His suspicion was confirmed when, after the ship was docked, the alien lifted Schume off the deck and slung him over his shoulder in a careless and obviously painful manner.

The alien, whom Greg had learned from the ship's computer was named Kernis, was met by a vehicle at the docking ramp. He quickly stowed Schume in the trunk. The darkness severely disoriented Greg. That alarmed him because apparently, darkness was very disturbing, for some reason. However, he fought to maintain his composure, concentrating on where he was to overcome the sense his mind had been thrown into some unfathomable darkness from which there would be no escape. After a few moments, he had his fear and the disorientation under control.

A short drive and the vehicle stopped. The trunk was opened, flooding the interior with bright light. Once again Schume was slung over Kernis' shoulder and this time was carried inside some type of building.

Greg contemplated what his next move would be. His main goal was to rescue Leumas and Sarah, but if an opportunity to thwart Copolla presented itself he would take it. He would, however, do nothing that would jeopardize his return to whatever role he was still to play in the saving of Earth. He decided that, for now, he would have to wait and see what happened and take it from there.

"Well, what do we have here, Kernis?" The voice was instantly recognizable.

Moving through the garment to get a better look, Greg sensed the large ominous figure of Copolla. He had been face-to-face with Copolla only once when Sarah, Leumas and he were brought before the council the first time to refuse membership. The former leader had looked overbearing then, but was even more so now. Something had changed in him, something that made him look as if he would kill anyone for any reason at any time. His features were hardened and fraught with evil, and his eyes glistened with a darkness that appeared to defy the light.

"Your favorite Earth reporter," Kernis responded as Copolla looked closely at the figure slumped over the alien's shoulder.

Greg imagined he could smell his enemy's foul breath even though he knew that was impossible.

"You've been playing with your laser again, I see, Kernis," Copolla said like a stern father to a child.

"I didn't damage him...much." Kernis smirked.

"How much longer do you think he'll be out?" Copolla asked.

"Probably about another two hours or so. These Earthlings are so fragile."

"Yes, they are," Copolla agreed. "Put him with the other two, and I will deal with them all later. I have something I need to attend to, some little additional alteration that will provide added insurance when we attack Earth."

"Then we will attack?" Kernis asked.

"There was never a doubt. I plan to be rid of that scum council and organization once and for all. It's payback time."

"I look forward to it," Kernis said.

"Now, do what I said. We have things to attend to."

Kernis headed toward the room that held the other two captives. Greg felt anger welling up. Copolla intended to attack Earth no matter what happened. He must find a way to stop him and it had to be soon. If he stayed on the reporter he, too, would become a captive, but the question of how to get them out haunted him as precious seconds ticked away.

Kernis slid his card in the magnetic lock and prepared to hurl the reporter into the room. Copolla must have warned him to protect himself against Leumas' influencing ability by staying out of Leumas' line of sight. Kernis quickly rid himself of the body as soon as he opened the door, then slammed it shut behind him.

Greg jumped at just the last second before the door closed.

"I questioned everything when I realized that Copolla was still alive. Life, death, hate, and love…and I have come believe that to be evil is to have nine lives."

Leumas

"Sarah? Sarah? Can you hear me?" Leumas pleaded as he gently shook her. She slowly opened her eyes and stared into his face with glassy and unfocused eyes.

She had been brought in rather unceremoniously and dumped on the floor unconscious before Leumas could even see who had brought her in. Seeing a familiar face raised his spirits immensely, even though he was disappointed Sarah had been thrust into harm's way.

"Yes," she said slowly. "I can hear you."

Leumas sighed with relief now that she was conscious. Her eyes cleared as she looked around the room and tried to sit up. Her clothes were ripped and disheveled, and he knew her body ached immensely from the stunner.

"Where am I?" she asked.

"In a hotel on Acuba. But you might as well call it a jail cell, thanks to Copolla."

Slowly she rose from the bed, testing her balance. "I'd like to get my hands on that Reveb," she said with a notable amount of disdain as she rubbed her neck with her hands.

"Reveb? Why him?"

"Because that emotionless freak is responsible for me being here. Pulled a stunner on me and used it! The little alien trash tricked me while I was waiting for the shuttle."

"I can't believe it," Leumas said and immediately received a stern look from Sarah. "Okay. Don't shoot! I believe it."

Sarah's stern look vanished as she gave a little smile at his usual humor.

"I'm just very surprised," he continued. "Reveb was checked out very thoroughly before he got the assignment as Greg's secretary. This is very confusing."

"How're you doing?" Sarah asked.

"There've been moments," he said reflectively. "Close moments, when I thought he would kill me. I know he wants to—payback and all for the way I humiliated him out of his position, but I think he wants to make sure he gets Greg here first. Which, I assume, is why you are here?"

"Yup. I'm also the insurance to make sure he comes. I vaguely remember Copolla forcing me to contact Greg so there wouldn't be any doubt where I was. I was still groggy from the stunner, but…" Sarah's face took on a look of fear and confusion. "Where did Copolla get the mental power to block with? He cut me off precisely when I was going to warn Greg."

"He says it was done surgically, but I don't know if you can believe anything he says," Leumas answered. "He's become quite dangerous and with this plan of Greg's joining him because he is his son…" Leumas stopped in mid-sentence when he saw Sarah's face. "I'm sorry, Sarah, I forgot you didn't know."

"It can't be true," she said.

"Copolla says it will bear up to any scrutiny. I've seen that look on him before, when he knows he has you. He may be crazy, but he's not stupid." Leumas then recited the complete story Copolla had told him. She listened in utter disbelief, turning pale on several occasions.

"My God," she said. "What a maniacal bastard! This will break Greg's heart."

"That'll be minor compared to what Copolla will do if Greg doesn't join him," Leumas pointed out. "He's assembled some kind of attack fleet here, and they're going to pay a little call on Earth if things don't go the way he wants them to."

Sarah thought about this for a few moments, mulling the possibilities over in her mind. "Have you tried to influence anyone to try and escape?"

"I made the mistake of trying it on Copolla, and he nearly blew my mind out of my head with his power. No one else has been allowed near me. What about the council? Are they planning anything?"

"Well, they were going to send in a rescue team. Not Greg, though, because he's made contact with an unusual visitor, an alien he calls Vague who's taken the physical form of someone named Robise."

"Robise? He was the librarian at the archives on Zire. He was the one who saved the computer core from destruction and help bring Copolla down. He was also…my friend."

"Apparently, this race does not possess a physical body anymore, and the one who is meeting with Greg used Robise's appearance to be able to communicate in a way that's more familiar for our sake." Sarah explained that the alien brought a warning of some great impending danger and had told Greg he alone had the power to prevent it. Before he could do that, however, Greg had to learn some new and expanded abilities only the alien could teach him.

"I don't know about all this," Leumas said. "Where have they been all this time? We have no way to prove their story."

"Greg says he trusts him, even though he's secretive. I know if Greg trusts him, he's okay."

"I leave Earth for a little while and look what happens," he said, shaking his head.

Sarah smiled again. "So, what's next?" she asked.

"If Greg comes, Copolla will kill us. If he doesn't come, Copolla will kill us. Looks to me like our fate is sealed no matter what."

"Then we have to find a way out." Sarah began to walk around the room, carefully inspecting doors and windows.

"We are on the thirteenth floor, there is only one door and it is magnetically sealed. Unless we can get someone to come in, we're not going anywhere," Leumas told her.

As he finished his statement, the door opened and a body was thrown into the room. Leumas ran to the door hoping to reach it before it closed but was too late; the magnetic lock latched down tight. Sarah went to the body lying on the floor and indicated for Leumas to give her some help with it. The man lay unconscious, face down on the floor. Sarah and Leumas knelt and slowly rolled him over. A smell of burnt fabric and flesh reached their nostrils.

"Well, misery certainly does love company," Sarah said. "Welcome to our happy little family, Mr. Ray Schume."

* * *

There was a solid and resounding thump as the reporter hit the carpeted floor. Greg, from his new location on Kernis' shirt, saw Leumas immediately get to his feet and spring toward him. His friend was charging at full speed but he wasn't going to be quick enough. Kernis teased him by indicating with his thumb and index finger how the space of the door was quickly closing with Leumas still at a safe distance away.

"Not today, Council boy,' Kernis taunted. Greg had a quick view of Sarah with a shocked expression on her face as she stared at the body so unceremoniously thrown on the floor. He was overwhelmed with relief they both were alive and looked in shape to try and escape. That is, if he could figure out a way to do it.

He was appalled at this alien's lack of compassion and wished Leumas had been in time reaching the door. Between his taunting Leumas and the vicious torture of the unconscious and defenseless reporter, Kernis obviously needed a good lesson at the hands of someone.

Kernis laughed as he turned away from the door. He could hear Leumas on the other side yelling for him to face him instead of hiding.

"You'll get your chance soon enough, Council boy," Kernis said. "Then you'll regret you even thought of the idea."

If there were going to be any chance of escape, Greg knew he would have to move now. He formed the thoughts and gently pushed them to Kernis. ::Stop! You will unlock the door and escort the prisoners to your craft. You will protect them, and if anyone asks, you are doing as Copolla has directed you to do!::

He felt immediate resistance to the suggestion. Copolla may have equipped Kernis with some type of mild resistance to being influenced. Greg pushed again, this time with much stronger emphasis. ::STOP!! You will unlock the door RIGHT NOW! YOU will escort the prisoners to your craft. You will PROTECT them, and if anyone asks, you are doing as Copolla has directed you to do!::

This time Greg felt the strain. He fought to maintain his position as brief seconds of darkness flashed over him along with a sense of detachment that scared him. One second he was aware of being submerged in the weave of the clothing, the next he was in Kernis' mind. He realized he somehow had to maintain his focus within the confines of the fabric and send the thoughts to Kernis from there. He also still needed to keep a portion of his mind attached to the crucial lifeline and anchor to his physical body. He gathered his concentration until he was once again securely enmeshed in the fabric, then, keeping his sense of place intact, launched the influencing thoughts outward without attempting to establish the usual intimate connection.

This time Kernis felt the full affect of Greg's influence. His eyes glazed over, as if he had taken a drug that had finally reached his nervous system. He stopped and slowly turned back toward the door. His hand moved slowly and hesitantly toward the card he had placed back into his pocket. He began to move it toward the slot, then reversed the motion as his will fought against Greg's. Greg reinforced his thoughts one last time, and removed the last bit of resistance.

Suddenly, Greg felt a severe pull toward the darkness again and gripped onto his mind with every fiber of will he could muster. His vision of his lifeline showed it stretched very taut and he fought to ease the strain upon it. Then Kernis slid his card through the magnetic lock, and Greg relaxed his control of the alien and focused on stabilizing his self.

The door clicked open.

"No matter how much good one has done in their life, dealing with evil places you on the path that can only end in death. I do not argue with that assumption."

Reveb

Reveb stood as Copolla entered the room where he had been waiting since his arrival from Earth with the stunned Sarah McClendon. The gesture was not out of respect for Copolla, but of fear at Copolla's domineering physical appearance.

The look on Reveb's face as he looked at Copolla was mixed: full of shame of what he had done and revulsion toward the alien who had made him do it. He tried to hide it but it was easily readable.

"You have done well," Copolla said.

"Thank you," he answered automatically and then with some fortitude added, "But I am sure you realize that what I have done, I have done for my family and not any allegiance towards you."

Copolla smiled. "Please, you will hurt my feelings," he said, coloring the statement with sarcasm. "But I have learned to ignore such insults. After all, I am not an easy person to understand. And it is for that reason I must resort to certain tactics required to get the job done. Such as in your case, my friend Reveb."

"You held my family hostage unless I spied on the Leader of the…"

"Do not call him that!" Copolla exploded, his face reddening with anger. "I am the Leader of the Council and soon will be much more then that. You may refer to *him* as 'the young master,' if you wish. After all, he is my son."

"I have done as you have asked of me," Reveb responded, his voice calm and even. "I have spied on him and kidnapped the Earth woman. I have fulfilled my commitment to you. Now, I want…I request that my family be given back to me as was our deal." In the end, despite his efforts, his voice quavered.

"Now?" Copolla said slowly. "That is a word that you really shouldn't use with me, Reveb. You know how it upsets me." He fought to control his temper. "Am I not a man of my word? You have done as I requested, and now I will give you what I promised you." He reached into one of the drawers on the desk and produced a disc. "Here, place this in the viewer."

"But what has this to do—?"

"PLAY IT!"

Reveb cautiously took the disc and did as he was ordered, his hand visibly shaking. The screen flickered for a moment and then stabilized. He immediately recognized the images of his wife and two children. Reveb's face became outraged and stricken with grief as the images showed his family working in some mountainous area, chained together and laboriously carving at the face of the mountain with hand tools obviously substandard to the task. They were gaunt and malnourished, clearly on the verge of collapse, as if they had been at this toil without relief for a long and sustained period of time.

"What have you done?" Reveb gasped. "What have you done to my family?"

Copolla didn't say a word as he stared at Reveb's face. Reveb returned his gaze to the screen as the images played on. An alien wearing a hooded cloak that obscured his face entered into view. The expressions on the faces of the members of his family reflected fear, horror and outrage as the alien approached them. The newcomer removed a golden hand-laser weapon from his holster beneath his cloak and fired it three times, killing them all.

"My God!" Reveb fell to his knees and wept, but between the sobs he spoke. "Why? Why? Why did you do this?"

"I don't trust traitors like you, Reveb," Copolla said without a hint of emotion. "And when they have outlived their usefulness, they shall be discarded along with their families because they, too, have been tainted with treachery."

Copolla removed the same golden hand-laser Reveb had seen only seconds ago from underneath his jacket. He paused and then handed it to Reveb. "In fact, death is too easy for you."

Reveb stared at Copolla, his face filling with rage as emotion began to overwhelm him. Just as Reveb was about to use the weapon, Copolla placed the thoughts he had developed in his victim's mind. Reveb's face turned horrific as he twisted horribly and fell to the floor. Copolla laughed as he watched in amusement at the display of self-inflicted agony.

* * *

Reveb's view of Copolla and the room vanished. He was walking toward his family as they toiled unmercifully as he had seen only seconds ago. His feet crunched along the rough rocky surface and he could smell the foulness of the air around him.

"Claish, Sourchs, Tuolon," he called. He watched them look up at his approach. He expected to see happy expressions at his sudden arrival, but instead their drawn faces showed fear.

"It's me. Don't you recognize me?" He moved his arms and realized that he was no longer in the clothing he had been wearing. Instead he was wearing the hooded cloak he had seen on the person who had killed his family earlier.

What? No...can't be.

His hand moved under the cloak and found the golden hand-laser in its holster.

NO! He removed it from the holster. *NO! What am I doing?* His arm and hand refused to obey his own thoughts. He pointed the weapon at his wife.

NO-NO! Please don't let me do this!

He squeezed the trigger and felt the weapon discharge. He watched as the blast leapt from the weapon with agonizing slowness and into his wife, tearing her body apart. His arm moved automatically toward his children and squeezed off two more shots, and his children joined his wife. He stood and stared at the three bodies lying on the ground. Their burnt flesh and clothing was all he could smell.

The scene began again. As he walked to where his family was, he knew it would happen again and again. He would not be able to alter the nightmare Copolla had placed him in. As he watched his family die again, he knew what he must do. He would be surrendering to Copolla's desire, but it would also end this nightmare. He raised the weapon to his head.

"The true Leader of the Council, Greg Carlson, will destroy you!" He screamed and squeezed the trigger.

* * *

Reveb's body lay on the floor in Copolla's chamber. The laser blast to his head had cooked a portion of his brain. Copolla inhaled deeply.

Ahhh, death by thought, what a novel idea. I never realized it could be so much fun. I really must explore this further.

Satisfied that this loose end was now tied up, he prepared to tend to the other pressing matters he had to deal with. As he walked by the body, he bent over and picked up his weapon and placed it in its holster under his robe. Then he kicked Reveb's body aside with an air of disdain.

*"Sometimes it seems as though everything is connected in some way…
although most times it ends up in a perverse way."*
Sarah McClendon

Sarah and Leumas stared up from where they were kneeling over Ray Schume's body, their gaze focused toward the door that had closed a few moments earlier and was now open again. The alien Kernis was standing at the open door and just looking at them with a strange blank expression on his face. Leumas stood and charged the door as he had done before. This time, however, he used influence as he moved toward Kernis instead of focusing all his efforts on speed. He formed the thoughts in his mind and let them go, instructing the Monocian to hold the door open.

Suddenly, as Leumas approached within a few feet of the door, his own thoughts returned to him as if they had ricocheted off the alien brain. The only way that could happen was if Kernis were already under the very powerful influence of someone else. He would have to proceed very carefully at this point. Once someone was under heavy influence, they could be driven mad if given contrary instructions.

"What are your instructions?" Leumas inquired as he stopped a few feet away from the alien.

At the sound of his voice, Sarah raised her head from examining the reporter. "What's going on?" she asked.

"He's already been influenced by someone," Leumas whispered. "From the indication, it's someone powerful. I want to see if he will tell me what his instructions are."

As if on cue, Kernis responded in a robotic-sounding tone. "I am to take all of you to my ship at the spaceport. I am to protect you from any harm. If anyone asks, I am to tell them I am doing as Copolla directed me."

"Sounds like a plan to me," Sarah said. "But can we trust him?"

"As long as it gets us outside this door, I'm game," Leumas replied. As they approached the door, however, Kernis blocked the exit and did not allow them to leave. Leumas feared he had been the brunt of some terrible joke.

"All of you," the alien said, as he pointed toward where Ray Schume lay on the floor. Leumas looked at the unconscious reporter, then at Sarah.

"This guy has been nothing but trouble," he said. "I have no strong desire to take him with us."

"No argument here," Sarah concurred.

"My directions are for all of you,' the alien intoned again.

Leumas knew he could not override the influence, and that if they didn't take the body with them, the whole plan would collapse as they stood here and tried to reason with the alien.

"I'll carry him," he sighed. He picked Schume up and slung him over his shoulder. With that, Kernis led them out of the hotel and acquired transportation to take them to his craft at the space port.

* * *

Greg had been watching the chain of events all along from Kernis' jacket and was becoming extremely tired, finding it a real struggle to concentrate. The effort of remaining merged with the fabric, keeping his influence over Kernis and maintaining his lifeline was resulting in extreme mental fatigue. He couldn't even foster enough strength to communicate to Sarah through their normal telepathic link. Once back on the ship and out into space, he would make the mind-jump back to his body on Earth.

When they were aboard the craft, Kernis became immobile and submitted to being restrained by Leumas and placed out of the way. Sarah strapped the unconscious reporter into one of the extra seats and met Leumas back in the cockpit.

"Ready?" he asked.

"I've been ready to leave since I arrived," Sarah responded and with that, Leumas sped the craft off into space and set destination to Earth.

Greg was about to make the leap back to his physical body before he ran out of strength altogether, but a piece of conversation between Leumas and Sarah caught his attention.

"How are you going to tell Greg?" Leumas asked.

"I'll just tell him, I guess. He has to know about Copolla," she said with a strong sigh. Greg heard the frustration and disappointment in her voice and knew she was pained deeply by something that concerned him.

"What are you going to say?" Leumas pressed her. "I mean, how do you tell the guy that his father is the object of all his hatred? A man who does not possess one ounce of compassion for anything and totally contradicts everything that we stand for."

My father? No, it can't be. My father was a good man! Copolla is a sick animal! No! No! No!

He lost his concentration in a tremendous wave of confusion and anger. He was blown out of the shell of the ship he had been occupying and was hurtling through space at an enormous speed, totally out of control. His mind lost coherence and his awareness of his physical shell. Its neural energy was like a hundred candles being extinguished one by one, causing the darkness to overcome the light. He saw his lifeline untwining strand by strand as he fought to refocus.

::*Greg! Greg!*:: a voice called. ::*You've got to concentrate! Focus your thoughts! Think about my voice. Follow my voice. Forget what you have heard. You must follow my voice if you wish to live!*::

Some part of Greg knew that voice. He used whatever small force of will he had left and focused on it, but the strain was enormous. Slowly he regained control, each neuron regrouping to form his consciousness. It was like holding his breath. Any second he would burst and exhale all the air he had in his lungs and his life would be over.

::*You've got to concentrate! Focus your thoughts! Think about my voice. Follow my voice. Forget what you have heard. You must follow my voice if you wish to live!*::

The words became clearer and stronger as a shadowy image of Earth appeared in his mind. *I'm going to make it,* he thought as the pressure continued to build. Just a few more seconds would be all he needed.

::*Yes, my son...soon we will be together,*:: Copolla's voice called to him.

Suddenly, the view of earth weakened and wavered before him. His lifeline snapped and everything around him was replaced by total darkness.

* * *

Leumas and Sarah arrived at Greg's quarters after depositing the still-influenced and quite humble Kernis with UCDW security. Ray Schume was taken to their medical facility with orders to keep him sedated until they figured out what to do with him after consulting with Greg.

As they entered, they were met by the alien appearing as Robise. Leumas stared intently at him. The image of the old custodian brought back memories from a difficult period. Robise's actions had saved millions of lives, but also brought about his own death at the hands of Copolla's henchmen. Now they were faced with that same madman once again; it was an odd symmetry Leumas found quite disturbing.

"Was there a reason for selecting this form?" he asked as he eyed the other man cautiously.

"It was deemed appropriate for the work at hand," Vague answered with a tone indicating he did not choose to debate the issue. "We have things at the moment that warrant your concern; this shape should not be one of them."

"What's happened?" Sarah asked as she realized Greg was not present. "Where's Greg?"

Vague indicated Leumas and Sarah should follow him into the bedroom. They found Greg lying on his bed apparently asleep; his respiration very slow. Sarah immediately rushed to grasp his hand.

"His pulse is very faint," she said. "He needs medical attention."

"He is in no immediate danger, at least physically. He is in a deep coma from a shock to his mind," Vague explained.

"From what?" Sarah asked without taking her eyes off of Greg.

"He saved you both."

"How could he? He was here the whole time, right?" Leumas asked.

"His body, yes. But his mind traveled to Acuba and influenced Kernis to help you in escaping."

"That was the influencing I felt when I tried using my own," Leumas realized.

"Did something go wrong? You've been his teacher the whole time. You should be able to tell us what has happened," Sarah said, anger and frustration in her voice. "Something must've happened to cause this state."

"He lost control of his orientation."

"What does that mean?" Leumas demanded.

"He lost his focus on what he was doing. The key principle to all of this is to keep the mind focused on what it is doing. If you lose that, there's no telling what could happen."

"Where was he? We didn't sense him or anything," Sarah said.

"During the escape he blended his mind into the craft," Vague told her.

Sarah and Leumas looked confused, so Vague took a moment and gave a quick accounting of the ability of the mind to travel using objects that were available and how doing so conserved precious mental energy.

"Okay, so what happened?" Sarah repeated.

"What caused him to lose his orientation?" Leumas asked at the same time.

"On the trip back, he was very fatigued from maintaining the link to his body after what he had been doing on Acuba. He was distracted by a severe emotional shock. It was when you two were discussing how you were going to tell him Copolla is actually his father."

Sarah and Leumas stared at each other in shock.

"We caused this?" she asked incredulously.

"Not intentionally, by any means. You had no way of knowing he was there and could hear you," Vague assured her.

Leumas' look had grown wary as he listened to Vague's explanations.

"How come you know all of this? We haven't told you anything about the trip." He challenged the stranger suspiciously.

"I observed the events as part of the training process," Vague replied.

"All of it?" Sarah asked.

"Yes."

"If you observed the entire thing, then you probably have the power to assist him," she pressed.

"I tried to assist him when he was in trouble, but he was too tired."

"By then he was already in trouble, wasn't he?" Leumas asked.

"Yes."

"Why didn't you help him earlier?" Sarah wanted to know.

"He needed to finish the training in order to learn how to use his power..." Vague began.

"You risked his life for a training evolution?" Leumas interrupted incredulously.

"The training is crucial," Vague shot back. "You don't understand what is about to happen."

"You're damned right about that," Sarah lashed out. "You aren't telling us very much either."

"I can't," Vague said. "And I can't really explain why other than that it is a rule of my...organization." He paused before going on. "I can tell you the training Greg is undergoing has been arranged very carefully. The whole event of your capture, both of you, was arranged or orchestrated in order for Greg to learn how to open his mind."

He paused again to let his statement sink in. After a few moments of silence without any response from either of them he said, "You don't see it, do you? Reveb was not working for Copolla. Oh, he may have thought he was, but in actuality he was really working for me."

Leumas and Sarah just stared at him, speechless.

"What do you mean, Reveb was working for you?" Leumas asked Vague, appalled at the statement and its implications. Sarah found herself unable to speak.

"Not directly working for me," Vague clarified. "You see, what I required was a series of events that would force Greg to harness powers he has within himself. If he had not gone to Acuba to rescue you and Sarah, he would not have learned how to utilize them."

"I'm confused," Sarah said. "I thought you were against him going there?"

"I was. I did not want him to go there in person, but in his mind," Vague answered. "When the council decided to send the rescue team, I thought the only way to get Greg to go was if you were kidnapped."

"But if Reveb was working for Copolla, how did you get him to carry out what you wanted?" Sarah asked.

"It's hard to explain," Vague began. "There are certain restrictions on what my...organization...can alter, I mean, do and what it can't. It's very complicated, but we can discuss that later. Right now we need to get through to Greg and bring him back to consciousness. I can't do it, but maybe Sarah can."

"Wait a minute. I'm getting mixed signals here," Leumas declared as he recognized Vague's attempt to dodge Sarah's question. "With all of this that is going on, I still see no credible evidence you're helping us. All I know is Greg said he trusted you. On what basis he came to that, I'm not sure." He looked at Sarah, who shrugged her shoulders in agreement.

Vague stood still and silent, his face expressionless as Leumas continued.

"You can't or won't tell us any more about this group of yours, and you have had a role in doing things which, in my mind, are highly questionable. Sarah could've been hurt, but you risked her life so Greg would do something that would risk his. Now he's lying here in some kind of coma. I'm sorry, but can you honestly believe we should be helping you or listening to you?" Leumas finished with an almost pleading look on his face as he looked for more information.

Just then one of the security chiefs entered the room. The look on his face betrayed he was not bringing good news.

"Excuse me," he announced. "We've discovered another problem."

"Now what?" Sarah asked, reacting to the tone of trouble in the security chief's voice; a tone she had heard all too often the past couple of days. Leumas rubbed his forehead from frustration as he prepared to hear the report.

"Let's have it," he said, spreading his arms as if baring his chest to a person with a weapon.

"The fleet that was to blockade Acuba is unable to depart."

"Why?" Leumas demanded.

"The ships have been sabotaged. All the reactors have been tampered with and the anti-matter drives are drained."

"Great," Leumas muttered. Then, aloud, "Do we know who did this?"

"Investigation reveals Reveb was responsible," the security chief said. "As the Leader's personal aide, he has all the required clearances to access the main computer and drives of the ships."

Leumas just looked at Sarah as they both realized the significance of this news at the same time.

"Time to reenergize the reactors?" Leumas asked.

"Thirty-six hours," the security chief said.

Leumas thanked him and told him to return to his post and await further orders.

"So, for the next thirty-six hours we're defenseless," Sarah commented needlessly.

"Perfect time to attack," Leumas agreed. "It couldn't get any more perfect for Copolla."

"Well, we've got some work to do then," Sarah began, trying to sound energized. "Let's start working on recharging as many ships as we can and meet with the council members to get additional ships here as soon as possible."

Leumas nodded and turned to leave, but stopped. "What're you going to do?" he asked as his eyes drifted from Sarah to Greg.

"I'll stay here for now and see what I can do to try and bring him out of it," she said.

During the entire conversation, Vague had not said a word. Leumas glanced in his direction and received a slight shrug of his shoulders. *He's not going to do anything,* Leumas thought. *All part of the grand plan he won't tell us.*

"Sarah, I would let President Samuel know what's going on," Leumas suggested.

She thought about the statement, then nodded her head as he turned and departed the room.

Sarah was about to leave but stopped and turned toward Vague who was looking at Greg. She studied the old man's face. It looked different—changed, somehow, from the look of confidence it usually possessed to one afraid and confused about what to do next.

"The last thing in the world I wanted was for Greg to be harmed," he said. He turned his gaze from Greg back to Sarah. "If only you knew how important this is. Millions upon millions of lives depend on what happens very soon. I can't do it without you…"

"What do you want me to do?"

"Bring him back, Sarah. Bring his mind back or it will all be over before it even begins."

"I'm not sure what you want me to do," Sarah said. "I want to help Greg, but how? Tell me what I need to do. I'll do anything to get him back."

"I want you to focus your mind and think about Greg and nothing else," Vague instructed as he placed his hand on her shoulder and pressed gently. "Think about what he means to you," and then he repeated with emphasis, "what he *really* means to you." Sarah saw in his eyes the significance of what he was telling her. "Project more than your thoughts. Project your feelings and emotions."

"I'll give it a shot," she said.

She pulled a chair alongside the bed and looked at Greg for a few moments. She let her mind drift with images of how their lives had changed so much since their first meeting. She smiled and felt the warmth of their relationship and their rough beginning during their indoctrination to the United Council for Developing Worlds. How clumsy he had been then compared to how mature he had become in taking on almost the entire leadership of the council.

She grasped his hand gently, feeling the warmth in it, and raised it to the side of her face and caressed it across her cheek. They never seriously spoke about their future together, even though it was clearly understood by both that they would be bonded together forever, not only by their mental connection but also by their emotional one. Greg had spoken of how he had seen the future with *their* children. The thought of having children made her blush, and she basked in the warmth that accompanied it.

As she closed her eyes, she found herself beginning to float on the seas of her consciousness. She flowed with the waves of thought, riding and moving in the direction they chose. She had never experienced this kind of sensation before; it was a detached feeling, yet she felt reassured she was still tethered to her physical self. She opened her mind and called to Greg.

CHAPTER ELEVEN

"Regrets? The only thing I regret was not killing Leumas more than once."

Copolla

Copolla walked into the surgical laboratory he had installed in his compound on Acuba. He inspected the computer-operated surgical equipment as it performed its magic on one of his personnel. The precision required could only be achieved by use of the automated surgeon, and precision was a must if the operation was to be successful.

The machine first applied a local anesthetic, then drilled a small hole through the skull. Next it inserted a long needle into the hole that would inject a deadening agent to make the area of the brain less sensitive to being influenced for approximately one week.

Influencing was accomplished by the application of directed biochemical neural energy. Those areas of the brain connected to survival were more susceptible to being influenced over greater distances because, when stimulated, they used the subject's instinct for self-preservation.

Copolla's plan to attack Earth would not require an actual landing on the planet, so any attempt to influence his crews would not come from close range. That UCDW ships would not even get off the planet to offer any resistance would simplify matters immensely. There was, unfortunately, no way to completely block a close-range influence without destroying parts of the brain itself. Copolla had considered this possibility for some of his men, but after seeing the results, had decided against it.

He looked for Kernis but did not see him anywhere in the facility. Normally, Kernis, an extreme pessimist, liked to keep his fingers in everything to ensure all was going as planned. He had no tolerance for failure or ineptitude and was quick to inflict his corrective methods on anyone guilty of either. Copolla rubbed his chin as he wondered what he should make of Kernis' absence. Could there be a problem?

Copolla turned and saw Zeur, one of Kernis' assistants, watching the surgical procedure while checking off names on a palm-sized device in his hand.

"Zeur," Copolla said. "Where is Kernis?"

"I have not seen him since his craft arrived at the spaceport from his mission to Earth," Zeur replied warily as he kept his eyes lowered in obvious submissiveness.

Copolla considered that perhaps his aide was still with the captives, maybe taking a little early pleasure with them. If so, Copolla would have to punish him severely for taking advantage of the situation before his employer. He keyed his communication link for Kernis. There was no response.

"Zeur, do you have a surveillance monitor in the room where the prisoners are?"

"Yes, but it is not active." He quickly added, "Kernis didn't think it was necessary with the magnetic locks."

"Activate it now," Copolla ordered. Zeur quickly moved to a monitor and keyed in the appropriate code.

The room was completely empty and the door ajar.

"Check the spaceport to see if Kernis' craft is still here," Copolla commanded. Zeur checked and came back with an answer.

"Gone. It left about two hours ago," Zeur said, his voice and expression revealing his concern over what Copolla's temper might bring.

However, Copolla calmly sat down at a table and indicated Zeur should join him. He slowly took the indicated seat, mistrustful of the spontaneous mood swings he had heard Copolla was capable of.

"What do you think about what you have seen?" Copolla asked.

"Kernis and the prisoners are gone. The security of the room would not have allowed the escape unless they were helped. Either Kernis helped them or someone else disabled him and used his key card."

"And his ship?"

"They took it and went back to Earth."

"And if Kernis or his body is not found?"

"Then the plan to attack may be revealed," Zeur said in a displeased tone.

"What would you recommend?" Copolla asked.

"Search for evidence of Kernis' body. If there is none, then attack as soon as possible before any preparations can be made in defense," Zeur said, his confidence growing.

"Exactly my idea," Copolla concurred and smiled. "How much longer will it be before all the surgical preparations are complete?"

"Approximately twenty-four hours."

"That's it then. That works out quite nicely. Just enough time…"

"May I be of further assistance?"

"No. I have some loose ends to tie up—some family matters. Kind of personal."

***

Greg floated in darkness with no indication of where he was going or where he was. The last thing he remembered was an image of Earth that quickly faded away. There was nothing to gauge distance or reality by; no way to tell if he was alive or dead. *My mind is okay,* he thought. At least, he assumed as much, being able to think again, but he was unable to perform his return to Earth. He could see it in his mind but could not reestablish the link that tied him to it. He knew that Vague had tried to help him and it had almost worked, but he had lost the connection and had gone…to this—wherever "this" was.

Greg had no desire to stay here in this nothingness. He knew what had caused his abrupt arrival in this place—his loss of concentration because Sarah had said Copolla was his father. Just the thought of the words almost drove him mad again with anger and disgust.

He knew Sarah wouldn't have said it unless she thought it was true. As much as he wanted not to think about the possibility, he couldn't stop himself from doing so. All he could do now was put it to the back of his mind and concentrate on trying to get back to the living. If he failed, there would be lots of time to think about those facts and what they meant, because there would be nothing else he could possibly do.

Greg assumed this void was a place between where things existed physically and another area of time and space, maybe a parallel universe. It was critical he develop a reference point from which to start his search, but if there were none in this place of darkness he was trapped.

Greg realized he could be occupying the same space the planet Earth did, just not in the same dimension.

But how do you cross over? What divides the two?

Vague had said maintaining the connection to the physical body was the most important thing, but what actually was that connection? What was the most strongest basis of human beings?

What makes us what we are? Could it be the soul?

Greg wondered at the aspects of a theoretical debate. The soul was comprised of emotional feelings and the associated acts of love, hate, and all the other emotions known to every living thing. *The most important aspects of how we define ourselves,* he thought. If the lifeline back to his physical body was comprised of fibers of these emotions and feelings, could he use these emotions as a way back?

With this realization, Greg began to see colors before him that gradually formed into squares. He reached out with his thoughts and found he could touch them and feel their content; they were alive with the electricity of a million souls wrapped up into them. He began to fold each square over and over. The images changed and he somehow knew what he was folding. These were dimensions, and he was folding them into themselves and then into time. It became so simple as he went on. He wondered why he had not discovered it before.

Because you didn't know how to see it. Yes! That's it!

It all made sense. He saw what Vague had been trying to explain.

A tunnel formed in front of him, then flattened out into a horrific maze with thousands of possibilities and directions that offered journeys along different paths in time. As with all mazes, there were many possibilities but only one path that was the correct one—the one that would take him back home. As he thought it, he found he could orient the maze, or himself, in such a way now as *to see* the one true path that would lead to the center. To go down any of the other ones would lead to recklessness and a waste of not only time, but things associated with it: life, death, war, peace, love, hate, and everything else.

And time is the key, the key to everything that will fit the lock to reveal the correct path.

The maze vanished as quickly as it had appeared.

He saw his way home now, but knew he could not go it alone, not without help to guide him back. He thought about Sarah and their love for each other as he projected his mind outward. He had no point of reference. If he failed, his mind would disperse all over this void and that would be the end.

"But that is not going to happen because this is a leap of faith and in the end, that's all that really matters. One life willing to put everything at risk for another life, all based on their faith and caring for one another."

He reached out, calling with his mind, oblivious to everything else around him.

* * *

::*Sarah? Sarah, can you hear me?*::

::*Here!*:: She cried back. ::*I'm here, Greg. Can you hear me?*::

::*Yes!*:: His relief flowed through the simple word.

::*Where are you?*::

::*That's an interesting question,*:: he said, sounding amused. ::*But what I need is to get back to you. I've been places and seen so much. I understand it now, Sarah. All of it. It's all about time, place, and circumstance.::* He paused. *::But we can talk about that later. I need to get back.::*

::Can you follow my voice?::

::I don't know, but I'll try. Just keep talking.::

::Greg, I know you found out about Copolla being your father.::

::It's okay, Sarah. I've come to terms with that in my own mind. It doesn't matter what Copolla says or has done. My father was on Earth with my mother, and I remember him clearly and nothing will replace that or change it in any way. Copolla is nothing to me except a... Well, let's not go there right now.::

Sarah felt comforting warmth settling over her. It was as if a warm blanket had been placed around her, coddling and caressing every inch of her.

::You're getting closer,:: she said. *::I can feel you.::*

::Same here,:: he said, then, hesitantly, *::Sarah, how would you feel about getting married?::*

The question caught her off-guard with surprise and happiness and she found that she could not respond for a few seconds.

::Is this a proposal, young man?:: she said, regaining her wits.

::I believe so.::

She imagined him blushing with his usual shyness in these matters. *::Well, you're going to have to deliver your request in person if you want an answer,::* she teased.

Then, suddenly, she was engulfed by an aura that totally enveloped her. She basked in warmth and feelings of intense love and caring. It was overpowering and filled her with immense pleasure all at the same time. She had never felt anything so strongly or completely before in her life. Her only thought was to not let it ever end.

Sarah opened her eyes and found herself back in the familiar surroundings of Greg's bedroom. Greg was looking up at her from his bed. She smiled warmly at him as her eyes glistened with moisture.

"I'll take that to be a 'yes,' then?" he asked as he sat up. He reached his arms out to her and she folded herself into them.

As they kissed, Sarah felt herself being drawn back within the warmth of the aura that had encompassed her earlier. Bathing in his love for her, she projected her own feelings to him. The intensity of their emotions mingling together was indescribable as they drifted together both in their minds and their physical passions of their love for one another.

::Well.:: Greg thought. *::I didn't actually hear you say yes.::*

::Yes, yes, yes! Of course, I'll marry you.::

::I thought so.::

::Very funny.::

::I gotta be me.::

::Yes, you do. Otherwise I wouldn't love you, now, would I?::

::I suppose not.::

::You know you had everyone really worried. We thought you wouldn't be coming back.::

::I know. So did I. It was very close there for a while. I imagine they're waiting in the next room to see what happens. I guess we should rejoin the world of the living.::

::Do we have to? I know, I know. Dumb question.::

Greg and Sarah stepped from his bedroom into the living room of his quarters. Both Vague and Leumas were there. Their eyes opened wide with shock and happiness as they saw Greg.

"Hey, it's good to have you back, Greg," Leumas said.

"It's good to be back," Greg said and stretched his hand. Leumas took it and shook it warmly. Vague placed his hand on Greg's shoulder.

"I hope you understand why I couldn't help you," Vague said quietly.

"I understand," Greg confirmed. "I understand everything now."

Another person quietly entered the room as if not to disturb what was happening among the occupants. President Edward Samuel slowly stepped forward, his eyes darting to and from a piece of paper in his hand.

"Edward," Sarah said, her face still beaming with a smile and wetness around her eyes. "You told me earlier you wanted the first invitation to the wedding. Well, I am giving it to you now."

Edward hesitantly smiled at her words but didn't respond to her good news; his face reflected deep concern.

"What's wrong?" she asked.

"I'm sorry to be the bearer of bad news, but the communications officer handed this to me on the way in. We need Greg to accept a communication immediately." He raised the piece of paper in his hand.

"From who?" Greg asked.

"Copolla. He wants to talk with you."

"I have never and will never accept Copolla as my father, not even biologically."

Greg Carlson

Before Greg went to accept the communication from Copolla, he received a quick briefing from Leumas about their current status, including the degraded fleet of ships sabotaged by Reveb. Sarah, Edward and Vague listened to the situation report with grim expressions. There was not much good news to hear.

While listening to Leumas, Greg struggled with the sour feeling of knowing they were discussing how to defeat his biological father. It made him feel dirty and part of the deranged plans of this madman. *He used my father and mother and now he is trying to use me. This all must end now, once and for all, no matter what the cost, even if it takes my life.*

He suddenly realized there was an uncomfortable silence in the room. Leumas had completed his briefing and everyone was waiting for him to respond.

"We will be virtually wide open for attack," he said, after apologizing for letting his mind stray.

"The best thing you can do right now is to stall for time," Leumas suggested with resignation.

"I don't think Copolla will be willing to cooperate," Edward stated. "I've never had the pleasure of meeting him, but I've heard enough to form the opinion he's some kind of monster, and insane at that."

"And knowing him and this attempt at communication, he's probably on the way already," Sarah added.

"You can bet he knows we've called for reinforcements from the UCDW worlds, and he knows how long it'll take for them to get here," Leumas said.

"That doesn't leave many options, does it?" Greg sighed. "Unless we try and trick him into thinking we'll surrender and go along with his plan."

There was no comment from the rest of them; only silence as they chewed and digested what Greg had said.

"There's always Earth defenses," Edward pointed out.

"That would be asking for total destruction of the planet," Greg disagreed. "Right now I'm assuming we're the focus and target of his attack, not the entire planet. Besides, you know Earth's weaponry is no match for their ships."

Again silence covered the small group. Greg felt all of this was upon his shoulders. He looked at Vague and received no encouragement on what decision to make.

"Okay," he began. "Leumas, you check on the progress of getting some of our ships off the ground. Sarah, you and Edward check where the reinforcement ships are and how much longer before their arrival and brief the other council members. I'll talk with Copolla and see what I can do."

Everyone left the room with the exception of Sarah. She placed her arms around Greg and held him tightly.

"Don't forget, we have a date at the altar, my friend," she reminded him sternly.

"You can bet I'll be there. As soon as we finish all this craziness." Greg kissed her gently. "Now, go ahead and see what you and Edward can find out. I need to do this on my own." Sarah left him alone at the communications console. He pressed the button to open communications to the preset channel Copolla would be waiting on.

The former council leader's image appeared immediately; large, dark and haunting, with a casual look of madness in his eyes that scared Greg.

"You wanted to talk," Greg said coldly.

"Yes, my son," Copolla responded, placing particular emphasis on the word "son."

"Don't call me that," Greg barked. "You may have claim to the biological creation of me, but not the parenting one. My father was a better person than you could ever hope to be." Greg tried to get hold of himself, to calm down. Making their enemy angry was not going to help them in trying to stall for time. "I am nothing but an experiment to you, your idea of creating a being who would possess powers you could harness for your dark visions of the future." Greg slowed his mind and let his anger dissipate. "But this is not what you want to talk about, is it?"

"The council is mine and always has been, just as is the rest of the galaxy. I will capture it all, and with it, my destiny. I will be the supreme ruler I have always been meant to be." Copolla paused for a few seconds then went on.

"I am giving you the chance to rule by my side and be a part of this. You can still control the council as long as you do my bidding. Together, as father and son, our powers combined, we would be unstoppable." Copolla paused to study Greg's face. Then he said in a disdainful voice, "You can even keep the Earth woman you are so fond of."

"That 'Earth woman,'" as you refer to her, is going to be my wife," Greg snarled through clenched teeth. As angry as he was at this creature, he would not allow him to taint Sarah in any way, now or ever.

"How disappointing," Copolla said, shaking his head. "You could have…"

"I'll never join you or commit the other members of the council to follow you under any circumstance," Greg interrupted. "They can make their own choice on that matter. You have this god-like vision of yourself, but I can tell you there are other races more powerful than you at work here."

"That nonsense Reveb told me is just that, pure nonsense. If there were a race with the power you say, they would have made their presence known a long time ago. Are you so blind you have not recognized this?" Copolla gave him a look of rueful distaste that reflected his disgust Greg could have believed such a story.

"Believe what you must," Greg told him. "Now, what are the options?"

"They are simple. You and the council join me and live or you die. That's it."

"And if we refuse?"

"After I destroy Earth, I will move on to each world one by one and destroy them until those left surrender to me."

"That's sick. Why destroy the entire planet? The planet and its people have done nothing against you. Earth is not even aware that the council exists."

"A trivial matter," Copolla said as he looked at a fingernail. "You have three hours to decide because that is how much longer it will take for me to arrive in orbit. And don't bother thinking your reinforcements will arrive in time. The closest is twelve hours away; and by the time they reach here, if you and the council haven't joined me, all they will find is the rubble of a planet that once was."

The conversation was over, or so Greg thought as he reached to cut off the transmission, never taking his eyes from the evil image before him. Instead, Copolla spoke again.

"Think it over carefully…my son."

* * *

Greg stared out the window at his beloved mountains as he thought about Copolla and his threats to destroy everything they had built. He wished the thoughts away and thought about Sarah as he awaited Vague's return. It was inevitable he would come now. Time was short and the critical moment the strange alien had warned him about was fast approaching. He wrestled with how he would tell Sarah what lay ahead for them and decided he would have to stretch the truth somewhat in order to do what he had to do. She would come to understand in time, he hoped.

There was a knock at the door and Vague entered. For the first time, Greg really felt he understood what this alien represented and why he had come to begin with. Everything and everyone has their plans, he thought. If one thing is consistent in all of that which is creation, this is a certainty that transcends everything else.

"So how did it go with Copolla?" Vague asked in his usual calm voice.

"I think you already know that answer, don't you, Vague?" Greg replied with certainty in his voice.

Vague did not answer, but let his gaze drift to the view of the mountains outside the window.

"They really are magnificent, aren't they?" Greg asked. "The mountains are so strong and enduring. They change very little over the span of our lifetimes, but over great periods they do, in fact, change. They are molded by the climatic and geological changes of the planet. They become what they must in order to survive."

"Yes, I suppose they do," Vague responded. "Time holds many surprises for us, but yet it is one of the most constant factors that we have." He paused to look at Greg before he spoke again. "You know that now, don't you?"

"Yes. I know that, along with many other things. Time is a constant for those who can't manipulate it. So how is it you can manipulate it?"

"Manipulate is too harsh a term," Vague said without any surprise at the question. "I prefer the term 'shaping' as a better analogy."

"Call it what you will," Greg observed, "but tampering with some things may cause multiple and unpredictable outcomes, don't you think?"

"That is a possibility, but when the most likely outcome is certainly a bad one, might not other possibilities be a chance at a better ending?"

"You're gambling on me here and now to produce a better timeline than the one that actually happens. I may fail."

"You may, but it is a known certainty Copolla will destroy the planet and the council worlds unless he is stopped. Is it not better to go down an alternate path and take our chances a greater good will result and civilization will rise up instead of being utterly destroyed and falling into years of tyranny, death and destruction?"

"That would be the logical approach," Greg conceded. "But logic is a cold, hard method that doesn't take into consideration the factor of emotions."

"I know this is something very difficult for you to decide upon. It means giving up a lot," Vague said compassionately.

"Yes, it does. A great deal," Greg answered vehemently, "but I'm sure you realize I always have the greater goal in mind."

"I know that. We have always known that about you. The one thing that has been a constant in all of this is your willingness to sacrifice for the greater good." He paused for a few moments. "Time is getting short and there are things you must do."

"Yes," Greg agreed. "I have things to do. What about you?"

"I must take my leave of this place and time. I also must make arrangements in the event things should not turn out well. I wish you luck." Vague held out his hand. Greg took it and shook it. He felt the warmth and physical shape of it dissipate in his grip as Vague slowly faded out of existence.

::We're counting on you, Greg. Even if it means the end of our existence, we gladly accept that in light of the potential for the creation of a better place for everyone.::

"I hope so, Vague. I hope so."

* * *

Greg entered the Council chambers as Sarah and Leumas finished their briefing on the current situation. He walked in slow measured steps, his eyes searching the magnificent chambers and the members who occupied it.

At one time or another he had spoken with each and every member and had developed a rapport with them through the past couple of years. They were all dedicated to the safety and peace of the galaxy.

The room fell silent as he took his position next to Sarah. He smiled quickly at her and grasped her hand, giving it a little squeeze for reassurance. He turned toward the members of the council, took a deep breath and exhaled to calm himself before he spoke.

"Members of the Great Council, I am sure you're all aware of the situation and the gravity it presents. I have just finished talking to Copolla, and I've agreed to meet with him and discuss terms of our surrender."

Voices blurred as the races interjected with their opposition to such a plan. Leumas, Sarah and Edward stared at him in amazement.

"I have told him this," Greg continued, having to raise his voice over the uproar to be heard, "as a way to stall for more time until our reinforcement ships can arrive." He let these words settle on the members and saw their acknowledgement now instead of their disagreement in their movements. He wanted his next couple of sentences to be perfect, the inflection and tone had to be correct.

"We have come too far to let an evil creature like Copolla ruin what we have done," he said in a tone reflecting his anger and frustration. "We shall not lose what this Council stands for to the likes of him or any other creature that challenges our premise. The council will go on!"

Members rose up on whatever appendages they possessed. By various methods, what would be construed as unanimous approval was demonstrated. Some slapped their hands on the tables and pounded their support. Others emitted whooping sounds and calls of praise. Greg was proud to see the unity in the group; he only hoped it would be there later.

As the sounds of approval receded and the members returned to their seats, he said, "One last point I'll broach before taking my leave of the Great Council. Purely as a matter of protocol while I'm gone, Leumas will fill in my role with Sarah McClendon in joint leadership of the council."

There were a few mystified stares at this, especially from Leumas and Sarah, but before any discussion could be born, Greg asked for the appointments to be acknowledged and they quickly were. With that, the meeting was over.

Greg hastily departed the hall. He knew some of the members would wish to discuss some aspects of the plan. He didn't want to get caught up in any lengthy sidebar discussions right now. He had other things that required his immediate attention. A barrage of questioning delegates moved in on Sarah, Edward and Leumas. Sarah, seeing what was coming, managed to duck most of them as she hurried to catch up with Greg.

"Greg," Sarah said as she grasped him by the arm. "What was all that?"

"Not here. Let's get to my quarters."

A few moments later they reached his quarters. Leumas and Edward arrived shortly after that.

"What is that all about?" Sarah exclaimed. "Meeting with Copolla? Leumas to fill in for you? I don't like the sound of this, Greg!"

"Calm down, Sarah," he urged her. "We're running out of time and that's the best I can come up with. Copolla is less then three hours away from Earth orbit. I'll go and talk with him. It's the only way to stall him."

"I don't like it either," Leumas argued. "I'll go instead…"

"He doesn't want you, Leumas, he wants me!" Greg snapped. "He wants his prodigal son to stand by his side and look up to his father as the omnipotent one. If it buys us some time, then so be it. There's no other choice."

"And if you can't convince him to change his mind?" Edward asked.

"I'll try and use influence on him in some way."

"Greg, I'm telling you he has more power than I've ever felt," Leumas said. "He overloaded me with no problem whatsoever. It was if I were a little child compared to a mental giant."

"But you weren't expecting that either. I'll be expecting it and I think I can counter him." Greg told him. "And I have had additional training now. I think I'm ready to take him on."

"I still don't like it," Sarah insisted. "You can't trust him. Even if you are his son, do you think that will give you any extra protection? What if he…"

"No more what if," he said, touching Sarah gently. "I know you all mean well and I'm extremely grateful. I'm open to another plan if anyone has one."

There was no response.

"Then it's settled." He turned to Leumas. "Leumas, I want a ship ready within the hour to take me to Copolla's fleet. I will pilot it."

Leumas nodded his head in reluctant agreement.

"In the meantime," Greg continued. "I want to keep working on getting our ships off the ground and preparing to mount some kind of defense in case I fail. Also call those reinforcements and tell them to push those ships to the limit to get here!"

"Do you still want to keep the Earth forces out of this, Greg?" Edward asked.

"Yes, keep them out. I don't want to give him any excuses to launch his attack. Oh, and one more thing, Edward."

"What's that?"

"I don't know if its legal or not, but can the President of the United States marry people?"

Edward looked confused at first, and then recognized what Greg wanted to do.

"I don't know," he said, "but if not, I'll change the law or something when I get back to Washington."

Greg took Sarah's hand in both of his. "You think you can get ready in about ten minutes? Or do you need more time?"

Sarah slowly smiled, struggling to force away the fear and trepidation she was feeling. This last-minute decision delighted her beyond her dreams—and terrified her with the realization even Greg believed he might not return. Tears formed in her eyes as she tried her best to put forth her genuine feelings for Greg while ignoring the impending others.

"Don't you know a girl never has enough time to get ready?"

Neither do the rest of us, Greg thought.

"The one truly happy day in my life was when I married Sarah, even though I kept the truth from her about what was going to happen."
Greg Carlson

The formation of formidable attack ships cruised through space on their way to Earth. Each and every ship's crew was aching to go to battle after the long wait Copolla had made them endure on Acuba. They would be merciless and ruthless, just the way he wanted them. Killing required a certain mood if it was to be enjoyed, and that was what he had tried to obtain for his minions. He even added an incentive. He offered an extra bounty to those causing the most destruction on the planet.

Copolla was composing one of his poems in his mind to occupy the time. He played with the verses as he arranged them to his liking.

The choices were given along with the ultimatums. It was their last chance to make the final decision that would either start or finish them. But the fools were so predictable, as was most things with them. Many races would die and to that I would say—to hell with them and kill them all.

Copolla laughed as he mouthed the last words. With the exception of the last two lines, the rest was mediocre. But it was satisfactory enough for the moment. Later, when he had someone record the events for posterity, he would change it as he saw fit. History would show how today was the first day of the great reformation, the crusade he had been chosen to undertake. It would be a glorious start, a new beginning.

"How much longer until we arrive?" he asked Zeur as he impatiently paced the command deck, now tired of his poem and other musings.

"One hour at the most," Zeur responded, as his hands moved across the navigation and helm panels.

Copolla was anxious to begin the assault on the planet. Zeur saw this as an opportune time for conversation. He wanted Copolla to remember how valuable he was to him this day. Soon Copolla would need to pick those to be governors of the worlds they conquered and he wanted to be one of them.

"Is there any change to the approach we shall take?"

"No. Unless my son comes away from the planet, we shall begin the attack upon arrival. If he does come, the attack will commence after I leave the vicinity. Is that clearly understood?"

"Yes," Zeur answered. He understood perfectly that Copolla would not want to appear as the murderer of the entire planet. He would say some renegade commander took it upon himself to destroy the planet. "I understand." Zeur hesitated for a few moments then went on. "Is there anything special you want done in the attack?"

"Special? Such as?"

"Leumas is there. I thought you might want him captured for further interrogation and possibly some personal enjoyment. I could handle it myself." Zeur smiled.

"You're really trying to get on my good side, aren't you, Zeur?" Copolla sneered. "What is it you seek? Money? Power? What?"

"I see the chances of your son coming along as being virtually none. I also see you will need a trustworthy assistant now that Kernis is gone. I want to prove my worth to you…Lord Copolla," Zeur said, with emphasis on the new title he had just made up and uttered with the utmost reverence.

Copolla was impressed with the title. No, not impressed, but he loved the sound of it, even though he knew Zeur was merely flattering him.

"I'm impressed with your thinking, Zeur, and I like that in an assistant. Let the others know that is to be my title from here on."

"As you wish, my Lord Copolla," Zeur said as he applauded himself for maneuvering into a position of importance.

"And, yes, I also like your idea about Leumas. It's a splendid idea."

"It will be done then," Zeur said.

Copolla looked reflectively out into the darkness of space, his eyes vacant as if he had lost or forgotten something. Suddenly, he turned to Zeur with those eyes burning with intensity. Zeur felt a coldness from his head to his bowels overtake his earlier gratification.

"It's probably time to stir up things a little bit," Copolla said excitedly. "Activate the device in our reporter friend that Kernis installed. He may be able to add to our amusement and to their fear."

Zeur moved his hand across the control panel and flipped a switch. "Yes, my Lord Copolla."

* * *

Greg and Sarah decided to hold their impromptu wedding in the hall of the council; it seemed the appropriate place because the council had been the catalyst to their original meeting. The members had gathered and saw this event as inspiring hope in their upcoming hour of uncertainty. To Greg's surprise, Ray Schume was present, looking both shocked and exuberant all at the same time.

Edward, noticing the look on Greg's face, walked over to explain. "I know you have to be wondering what he's doing here," he said, clasping

Greg on the shoulder. "But I figured whatever happens, there'd have to be a legal witness of some sort, and," he paused as he swept his arm around them, "with the exception of me, he's the only other human here."

Greg smiled, then laughed outright at the president's appraisal of the legality of the situation.

"Does he have any clue what's happening?"

"I gave him a quick synopsis. I figured, what the heck, no one is going to believe him anyway. He probably thinks this is some kind of dream or something. He's still a little groggy from whatever it is they did to him."

Greg watched the reporter staring with amazement at the different aliens of the council. It reminded him of his own first sight of the members two years earlier. *It seems a long time ago now,* Greg thought as he fought back pangs of guilt about his decision to get married. Maybe it wasn't fair to Sarah, the way things were going to get quite strange around here soon.

Sarah walked in, dressed in a plain white dress. The wall of aliens parted, forming a path for her to walk down. Leumas entered and Greg motioned for him to come and stand beside him. As Leumas arrived next to him, Greg bent over and whispered into his ear.

"I know I didn't have a chance to ask you formally, but would you mind being my best man?"

Leumas looked into Greg's eyes and with heartfelt emotion said, "I'd be honored. What do I do?"

"Just stand here next to me for now," Greg said, and received a look of acknowledgement from Leumas.

Sarah looks wonderful, he thought as he admired her beauty in the simple dress she had chosen. As he watched her, he was suddenly distracted by a sudden pang of uneasiness. Unsure of what might be causing it, he looked nervously around the room. Something was not right.

"Nervous?" Leumas asked.

"Uh, no," Greg said. "Just had a strange feeling. It's nothing. Probably just nerves."

"Is there something I'm suppose to do during the ceremony?" Leumas asked. "I've not been this 'best man' before."

"You just stand by me and hand me the rings when…" Greg suddenly realized they had no rings for the ceremony. Noticing Leumas had several on his fingers, he asked, "Can I borrow two of your rings?" Leumas raised his hands and held them out to him. Greg plucked two rings from his fingers and then lowered Leumas' hands. "Thanks," he said.

Sarah, watching the entire exchange between Greg and Leumas, laughed and shook her head in amusement as she joined Greg in front of Edward.

"I am not an historian by any means," Edward began, "but this may be the first time in my nation's history that a President of the United States is performing the marriage ceremony. I consider this honor commensurate with my responsibility to these two people, and to the organization that we stand in company with."

Leumas listened intently to the service as it proceeded, but suddenly found himself thinking about what Greg had said about feeling something was just not right. Leumas had learned to respect Greg's hunches because usually they were correct. It might have been some side effect of their influencing abilities that allowed them to detect stray emotional thoughts, but now he was getting that same feeling, too. He moved his head inconspicuously to look around, trying not to draw any attention to himself. He closed his eyes and tried to follow his feeling.

"We have grave challenges ahead of all of us," Edward continued. "But the time we take in these few minutes to perform this ceremony is indicative of our emotional bond to each other and fellow members of the council."

Edward paused, looking at Greg and Sarah. "Are you ready?" he asked softly. They both nodded and Edward spoke softly again. "I'll abbreviate the vows to conserve time, not to mention I don't remember the whole thing anyway. Okay?"

Again they nodded.

Leumas' thoughts centered on the reporter. It didn't make any sense that this person could pose any threat; after all, he had been thrown in with Sarah and him back on Acuba. The burns in his flesh were evidence that...

"Greg, do you take Sarah to be your wife?" Edward said.

"I do," Greg responded.

"Sarah, do you take Greg to be your husband?" Edward said.

"I do," Sarah responded.

"Exchange rings," Edward whispered. Greg handed Sarah a ring and she placed it on his finger. Greg placed his ring on Sarah's finger.

"Under my authority as the President of the United States, I now pronounce you man and wife. You may kiss the bride."

Ray Schume stepped forward at this exact moment; Leumas saw him out of the corner of his eye. In those seconds, Leumas saw into the mind of Ray Schume, but it was no longer his own mind. He was under the control of someone else, and in those precious seconds, Leumas saw it all. In his thoughts, he saw Kernis leaning over the reporter while he was unconscious on the ship, not burning him for sport, but for the implantation of a monitoring device, the internal loyalty device—Copolla's trademark. Except this one was designed to be hidden in some way not detectable by the council medical scans.

CHAPTER FOURTEEN

"I still curse the moment I befriended the reporter Ray Schume. If only I had known…"

President Edward Samuel

At the exact moment that Greg and Sarah kissed, Ray Schume moved toward them and Leumas lunged for him, hitting him squarely in the chest and knocking him several feet backward away from the crowd. Leumas' momentum was so great he was carried toward where the reporter had been thrown. Seconds later, a blinding white light encompassed the area where the reporter had been, causing all of them to be momentarily blinded.

"Leumas," Greg cried. "Where are you?"

There was no answer.

As the smoke cleared and their vision returned to normal, they saw Leumas lying on the ground near the burnt remains of what had been Ray Schume. Greg and Sarah ran to where he lay, hoping he was still alive. From the look of his clothes it was apparent he had been badly burned by the combustion forces of the device planted in the reporter.

Greg placed his hand along Leumas' throat, searching for the carotid pulse. He tensed as he slid his hand from one spot to another, searching.

"I can feel it," he said with relief. "It's weak, but regular. Someone get a stretcher in here and take him to medical." His voice rang with authority. Security personnel began clearing the area to make room for the medics who had arrived already.

Greg thanked God that Leumas was still alive. He wished he could stay and accompany him to medical, but knew it was time to go. This madness had to be ended once and for all.

"I didn't know…" Edward began from behind Greg and Sarah. "It was my idea to have him here in the first place. He didn't really have to be here, I thought that…Well, just to make it official, you know."

"It's okay, Edward," Sarah reassured him. "There was no way you could've known. The device was obviously hidden from scanners or they would've been detected when he was examined."

"Still, I should have done something or…" Edward struggled with the words.

"There's nothing you could've done," Greg said, placing his hand on Edward's shoulder. "But there is something you can do now. Would you mind going with Leumas to medical? I've got some things to attend to before I go."

"Sure. But you're still going to go? You know who is behind this, and it just confirms again that he cannot be trusted."

"I know, but there's no other choice. Don't worry. I can handle myself," Greg said confidently and he extended his hand to Edward.

Edward grasped it and shook it warmly.

"Good luck, Greg. We'll be waiting," Edward then turned to follow the stretcher that carried Leumas.

Greg grasped Sarah's hand and led her to a quiet spot in the hall away from the commotion.

"Sarah, keep an eye on Leumas," he begged with obvious stress and concern in his voice.

"You know I will," she said. "Is it time for you to go?"

"Yes. We're running out of time. And I don't want to lose the anger building up inside of me. I promise you, Copolla will pay dearly for this." But as he looked at Sarah, he diverted his rage toward Copolla and focused on her face—the beautiful face of his wife.

"Some wedding, huh?" he said.

"It'll do for now, Mr. Carlson. But when this is all over, we'll have a nicer one. Okay?" Her hand caressed the side of his face, her eyes filling with tears.

"Okay, Mrs. Carlson," he said and kissed her.

They stood there, holding one another for several minutes, neither one saying anything for fear of speaking what they really thought—or feared.

::You've got to keep it together here, Sarah,:: Greg said to her in his mind. ::This little tactic of Copolla's may have destroyed what courage was left among the council. He's so damn good at doing that.::

::I'll try,:: she said. ::But only if you promise to come back to me. I have something… So many things I want to tell you.::

::You know I will,:: he answered. ::It'll take something much worse than old Copolla to keep me away from you. When this is all over, we shall make our own time…together.::

Greg started to feel uncomfortable about not telling her the whole story and what really lay ahead. But, for now, he had no choice.

::Keep pressing to get our ships up and the reinforcements here.::

::I will,:: she said. ::Greg, I love you.::

::And I love you. Remember, whatever happens, I'll be with you always. Do you understand that? Always.::

::Yes, I understand…:: Her voice faded with the intensity of her emotion.

Without another word, Greg turned and walked away. Sarah stood motionless as she watched him. In her mind, his voice resonated with the one word...*always.*

* * *

Greg quickly programmed the ship, pressed the auto sequencer for takeoff and sat down. As the ship left the council compound and Earth's atmosphere, he took a long look at the blue-white globe that fell behind him, wondering if it would be the last time he saw his home.

No time for this now, he scolded himself and set to work clearing his mind of everything so he would be ready to begin the process of projection as soon as he needed it. Methodically, he cleared each thought—Copolla, the council, Leumas, and finally, he came to his lovely Sarah. Perhaps he dwelt somewhat longer on this last image, but he figured he was entitled and he wanted it burned into every square inch of his mind. After a few moments, he broke the concentration, bidding Sarah a fond farewell, and felt prepared for this final encounter with Copolla. One way or the other, it would end in the next few minutes.

One way or the other...

"Time to approaching ships?" Greg asked the computer.

"Two minutes to nominal range."

"Computer, prepare to receive instructions," he ordered. "Program automatic setting for return to takeoff point upon incapacity of pilot, then open communications channel."

"Program complete. Channel open."

"Copolla, can you hear me?" Greg asked coldly.

"I can hear you," Copolla's ominous voice boomed back, as if he had been waiting for the communication.

"That was a sick stunt you pulled with the reporter. But, then, that's what you are, isn't it?" Greg let his voice fill with intimidating anger and sarcasm. He had to enrage Copolla to the point of carelessness; any mistake he could capitalize on would be an advantage.

"It served its purpose," Copolla replied airily. "The council is quaking on its foundation, just perfect for my arrival. They will roll over and submit to my every whim...or die. And now they know beyond any doubt that I am the Supreme Being."

"Copolla, nobody wants all this bloodshed. It serves no purpose. I offer myself as token for their lives. Do with me as you wish, but leave them be."

"That's not what I asked for, is it?" Copolla told him and then snickered. "But then, I knew you never would agree to any of this willingly. You will be taken prisoner. I have plans for you anyway."

"You're not stupid enough to think I would cooperate with any of your…"

"What I have planned does not require your cooperation. Your DNA will suffice to start the breeding program of my super army of mind-altering beings under my control. But that is another story. Right now, you can watch the destruction of your precious planet."

"Do you think I came here not knowing that?" Greg sneered, again focused on enraging this creature. "You are so predictable, just like the little child you are. A very spoiled child!"

"How dare you talk to me like that!" Copolla snarled. "I am Lord Copolla! Ruler of all that is and will ever be!"

"Oh, shut up, you idiot! Come and get me! Better yet, why don't you use your petty mind powers against me?"

This is it, Greg thought. He could clearly see all the ships in formation. He had to move now and quickly if he were going to be successful. He drew his mind inward.

Concentrate and project. Concentrate and project.

He felt his consciousness leaving his ship and taking position directly in line with the attack craft. There were at least twenty-five of them, and he would have to take them on almost simultaneously, dividing his mind amongst all of them. He heard Vague warning him not to project to more then one location in the back of his mind. *No choice,* he thought.

Slowly, he inserted himself into each of the craft; the difference in sensation from a single projection to multiple was dramatically different. Each position was a blur, and the neural feedback was excruciating as it was multiplied by a factor of twenty-five. He felt his link to his body quickly slipping away from him like ropes snapping from his consciousness, each snap bringing him closer to oblivion and the darkness. And the feel of the snaps was amplified, leaving no doubt of what was happening. Greg wondered how many snaps he would have before the last one left him…wherever.

Concentrate and project. Concentrate and project.

As he approached the consciousness of each pilot, Greg felt the block placed in their minds to prevent what he had come to do. But Copolla had erred—and badly. He had blocked the region against influence from a distance, not from up close.

Snap!

More precious ties and fibers of his mind were gone. For a moment, he saw the black void, each snap making the darkness stay longer and longer. He tried to not think about the void; he pushed it out of his thoughts and began the influence.

::*There are new orders from Copolla! An imposter has taken my place on the space cruiser. You are ordered to destroy the craft by any means possible. ALL of you! Do it now and don't stop until I tell you to!*:: Greg repeated it continuously.

Snap! How many more could be left, he wondered.

::*There are new orders from Copolla! An imposter has taken my place on the space cruiser. You are ordered to destroy the craft by any means possible. ALL of you! Do it now and don't stop until I tell you to!*::

The void appeared again, and Greg thought it was permanent this time. His mind-vision now flickered and flip-flopped between the two areas—here and there. The first ship began its run on Copolla's vessel, then the second, and the third. Copolla reacted to the first ship in time and destroyed it, but the second struck his vessel slightly before blowing up. The third caused slightly more damage, but not enough to cripple it. It was apparent Copolla was fighting Greg for the control of the minds of the pilots. More ships joined in the barrage.

::*You whelp! You think you can challenge me! I will squash you like a bug!*:: Copolla's voice boomed into his mind.

Greg shut it out as much as he could, but he was already overburdened beyond any point of safe return.

Snap! The images flickered faster now as he felt the last threads of his hold on his mind sever in order for him to maintain his focus on the pilots and against Copolla. Greg saw no sense in dwelling on it at this point; his destiny had been sealed before he even left his body. He understood that, as had Vague.

He pushed hard at Copolla, as hard as he could ever remember pushing in his life. He saw more of the ships had gotten through, and Copolla's vessel was heavily damaged. *Just a couple more hits should do it*, he told himself. More than half of them had been destroyed in their runs against Copolla, but the darkness was becoming more stationary in Greg's mind view. Time was getting very short.

::*Give it up, Greg,*:: Copolla called to him, but Greg detected weakness from the previous connection and this spurred him on.

::*Never!*:: he said.

::*You would see your own father die?*::

::*My father...no. You? Gladly!*:: Greg used the anger and rage that suffused him at the thought of Copolla as his father and how it degraded the memory of his real father. He pushed with all the strength he had remaining one last time.

Snap! His last view was of the remaining vessels under his mind control exploding as they impacted Copolla's ship, totally obliterating anything in that area. His mind dissolved into space, and as the final darkness settled on him, he used his last shred of energy to call out.

::Sarah…::

C H A P T E R
F I F T E E N

"I wished I had told Greg everything before he left to go and meet Copolla.
Maybe if he had known the truth it would have saved him."
Sarah McClendon

Sarah sat in the control center, monitoring the video link with Greg's craft. She promised herself she would not try to contact him. He didn't need her to deal with right now and he must concentrate on what he had to do. She nervously twisted the ring he had placed on her finger not so long ago, then suddenly jumped at the sound of his voice as he began taunting Copolla. It definitely did not seem like a cordial conversation.

Edward entered the room, pushing Leumas in a wheelchair. Sarah was glad to see him conscious, but concerned about such a quick return.

"You should be in bed," she suggested.

"Would you be?" he retorted.

"No, I guess not."

"What's happening?" Edward asked.

"Greg has been…talking with Copolla, but it's no good."

Suddenly, the view from Greg's ship erupted as ships from Copolla's fleet began attacking their flagship.

"What the devil is going on?" Leumas wondered.

"I think Greg is influencing Copolla's people," Edward said and then added, "but how can he do that from where he is?"

"He's projecting his mind," Sarah said, then realized what was happening. "No, Greg," she cried as she remembered what Vague had told him. "He's not suppose to be in more than one place at one time. He might…"

Suddenly, the alarm in Greg's craft sounded, and the computer voice spoke.

"Bodily functions erratic."

"What's happening?" Edward demanded as his eyes darted between the visual of the battle in space and the monitors on Greg's ship.

"It's Greg," Sarah cried. "His mind and body are under great stress because of his consciousness being in so many different places. If he does too much, he will not be able to return to his body."

"He'll die?"

"The body will live on, but without his mind." Sarah fought back her tears. "His mind will be somewhere else."

"Make him stop," Leumas shouted, gripping Sarah's arm.

"I can't," Sarah answered. "You know that as well as I do. And Greg knew that before he went up there."

"Maybe he can make it back into his body in time," Edward said hopefully.

"Look at the attack," Leumas told them. "Copolla is fighting back. But I think Greg is slowly gaining on him. Copolla can't last much longer."

The visual display became a blur of ships colliding and explosions in the center as the space battle approached some kind of climax. Suddenly, there was a violent surge and Copolla's vessel disintegrated along with the last two fighters in his fleet. Then there was nothing but the blackness of space remaining.

::Sarah.:: She heard Greg call in her mind, his voice sounding distant and far away as it faded. Dark gloom settled over her heart. The computer voice sounded from Greg's ship, breaking the silence.

"Pilot incapacitated. Returning to base."

Sarah's shaking fingers moved swiftly across the console. "Computer, link me to the medical and diagnostic module. Display all functions of the human in vessel."

Her screen lit up with numerous views of information as Edward and Leumas came alongside her. They all knew which indicator was the most important right now as they looked at the brain activity scan. It was a flat line, no activity. Silence descended as the realization that Greg was brain-dead settled over them.

Sarah fell back into her chair. She tried to hold back the pain but couldn't any longer. She quietly wept. Edward lifted her from the chair, encompassing her in his arms as she began to sob without restraint.

"I'm so sorry," he told her. "I know nothing I can say can change what has happened or how terrible it feels. It was a great sacrifice by a great man."

Sarah said nothing. Leumas staggered from his chair and laid his hand on Sarah's shoulder. "I would've gladly given my life for him if I could," he said. "But he was the only one who could've done what he did to save all of us."

"I know, I know," she said between sobs. "That doesn't make it any easier, though, does it?"

"No, I guess not." Leumas sighed. "I'll go and tell the council what's happened."

"No, we'll tell them together," Sarah stated. "That's what Greg would've wanted."

"All right," Leumas agreed as he grasped her hand. "Do you want to do it now?"

"Yes. It's best they know as soon as possible so…" She was interrupted by the computer.

"Time encrypted delay message for Sarah McClendon, Leumas and President Edward Samuel from the Leader of the Council."

* * *

After they had given the appropriate responses in order to view the encrypted message, Greg's image appeared on the screen. The time track indicator displayed the time of recording as one day earlier. Sarah fought to stifle more sobs at the sight of her husband.

"If you're seeing this," the stoic image began, "then things have fortunately worked out the way they were supposed to. The threat by Copolla is gone, but I am…no longer with you."

Leumas and Edward looked at each other with the same realization. Greg had known all along what the outcome was going to be.

"I wanted to share with you why I did what I did. There were some things I couldn't tell you and there were some things I didn"t want to tell you because I feared you might've persuaded me to change my mind as to my course of action."

Sarah, Leumas and Edward momentarily looked at each other in awe at this revelation of the depth of Greg's devotion to their cause.

"The organization Vague told us about is not another alien race. They are our race, the United Council for Developing Worlds. He came from the future back to this time and place to train me for what I had to do. The purpose of his visit was, in fact, to train me how to see the correct path to take and what I had to do to achieve it. Never at any point did they force me to do anything. It was always my own decision and it was not an easy one.

"Their future was a terrible one filled with war and pain. Copolla won this battle in their timeline. Vague's future and the continued reign of Copolla included decades of terror and suffering. Eventually, they regained control, but by that time, more than half of the civilized worlds in the galaxy had been destroyed at a cost of billions of lives. They decided to come back in time, knowing if they were successful they themselves might not even exist anymore. It was a gamble, but if they could save some of those worlds, it would've been worth it to them.

"As for me, I am existing—or, at least, my mind is—in some other realm not too distant from where you are; a different dimension not easy to get back from. But all is not lost. Before Vague departed back to his time he shared with me a theory of how I might get back, but it takes much mind conditioning to perform it. Much more conditioning than I currently have.

"Still, in a while I should be able to do it. Don't ask me what 'a while' is. I don't know if it means years or centuries. Time, where I am, does not exist in the same context as it does for you. Here, time is nothing.

"As far as my physical body is concerned, I would ask you place it in long-term stasis. Hopefully, I'll have need of it again sometime. Council leadership, as we laid out at the last meeting, will fall to Sarah and Leumas. Don't worry about having to explain all this to the council members; I have sent them a message that explains all of this in great detail, along with my request they pledge their allegiance to all of you." He stopped, his voice at the end sounding somewhat relieved at completing business.

"Now for the tough part," he continued. "I've never been good at saying good-bye, so please bear with me. Leumas and Edward, thank you both for being my friends and for all your help in creating an organization that will live on for a very long, long time. I love you both like brothers and will miss you very much. I hope to see you in the future, so for now, I'll say 'until next time' and ask you for one final favor—a few moments alone with my wife."

Edward placed his hand on Sarah's shoulder. "We'll be right outside if you need us," he assured her, then helped Leumas back to his wheelchair and left the room.

"Sarah, my wonderful wife, forgive me for being selfish and asking you to marry me. I just wanted to know that, for a brief period of time, we'd be husband and wife. I will love you always and I will always be with you in your thoughts.

"I can't ask you to wait for me until I return because I may never do so, and I want you to go on with your life. Lead the council with Leumas. Lead from your heart and it will be fine. Please, don't grieve for me. It would take away from the true meaning of what we've accomplished. Instead, remember me as the young man who befriended you so long ago in a strange bar in our dreams where we met, and all the wonderful and exciting adventures that followed.

"I look forward to seeing you in my dreams for they're the precious things no one or nothing can ever take from any of us. It is there that we met the first time and it is where we'll meet again. I love you…my beloved."

The screen went blank. Sarah stared into the darkness and cried.

"I still can't help feeling responsible for his loss since it had been my idea that led to his leadership of the council in the first place."

Leumas

The council took the sacrifice of their Leader as a symbol of dedication and nobility to their cause, vowing devoutly that their service would be in tribute to the man who'd laid down his life to defeat the greatest tyrant of them all. They resumed their duties with renewed zeal, promising Sarah and Leumas their utmost support in the time to come, and held the hope Greg would return to them.

There was no religious fanaticism about his promise to return, but they held his truths steadfast in their minds, for he had promised never to lie to them or hurt the foundation of their cause by hiding the truth from them. He had been special in many ways, and the thought he would find his way back was a promise they felt he was sure to keep, even though it might not happen in their lifetimes or even in their children's lifetimes.

There were no more visits from Vague. Speculation contended that the timeline had changed, and the time from which he had come no longer existed. Others suggested things had been changed according to what was supposed to happen, and that Vague had been sent to just ensure time went on the way it was supposed to. Regardless of which philosophy was subscribed to, the lack of any confirmation led the discourse to a quick demise, and it passed quietly and quickly from conversation.

As promised, Sarah spent more time at the council complex familiarizing herself with the day-to-day business of running the organization. She still continued her efforts with the space flight program, attending monthly meetings to monitor their progress. The momentum of the program had been escalating. The fervor to explore was becoming more popular by the month as public awareness grew, oddly enough, from the accusations of the existence of other alien races that Ray Schume had begun. With presidential and congressional support, the program would soon be leaps and bounds ahead of their own expectations.

Leumas redoubled his efforts in the initial-contact agent program, searching for new recruits to help rebuild it. As news circulated through the member worlds of the events of Greg's death, Leumas soon had more requests to test for the program than he could handle. They all knew very few of them would actually meet the requirements, but it was the inherent call of responsibility and reverence for the death of Greg that inspired the masses to try. Out of respect for Greg's memory, Leumas found supporting roles within the organization for those who could not qualify to become a contact agent .

Greg's body was placed in long-term stasis in the UCDW complex as he requested. Sarah insisted it be where those who wished to visit would be allowed to view it from an observation area. Leumas didn't agree at first, but after Sarah insisted it be done so all life forms would never forget what Greg had done, he agreed.

* * *

Six months later Sarah sat down next to the chamber where Greg lay enclosed in the stabilization chamber that would keep his bodily functions working indefinitely. His appearance was as peaceful as it would have been during sleep and at times she would close her eyes and allow this fantasy to play itself out expecting Greg to wake up at any moment. She knew it was a fantasy, but it was all she had to cling onto...

::Greg? Greg? Are you there?:: she called to his mind.

She did this every time she visited him. Perhaps she even let herself believe that, possibly, because of the mental link they had possessed, he might still be able to hear the thoughts she sent to him and follow them back as he had done before.

::I'm having the dream almost every day now. I don't understand how to interpret it. It's so vivid I feel I'm actually in it. But I'm so confused about what it means and why I'm seeing it.::

The dream was the vision Greg had told her about the day they accepted control of the council two years ago. They were in the council hall, passing control of the council to their successors, a young man and woman. Greg had not told her who the man and woman were. But now, as she gazed on their faces, seeing the striking resemblence in their features to Greg and her, she knew that the man and woman were their own son and daughter.

::Is this vision the ways things would've been before you altered the timeline? Or is it what the new timeline will be? I can't figure it out, and with you not here, how can it happen? My beloved, we never had that chance to talk. I know you promised later when everything was over and we had a moment. But it never came.

::*I wanted to tell you I'm pregnant. It's a boy, a son, Greg.*:: The dream flashed in her mind again, the two children. ::*But what of the daughter?*::

She struggled to not become fixated on these ideas of what might or might not be. She had to plan for the future, the future of their son.

::*I've got to go now. Council business never waits. I'm sure you, of all people, can understand that. I'll be back tomorrow. Sleep well, my husband.*::

Sarah rested her hand on the chamber directly above Greg's face for a few seconds, then departed. Her dream would stay her own private concern, as would the expectation of the day Greg, her husband, would return to her.

She cleared her mind to return to the present-day business with the council.

***

::*Where am I?*:: Greg asked. The scene was familiar—the large moon, the trees, and the shoreline. ::*It looks like Acuba, but everything is different. Not like before. There isn't any color to things, just black and white. Is that because my mind was torn apart?*::

::*You're safe in a place where you may rest,*:: a calm and reassuring voice answered simply. ::*Your mind has been damaged and needs time to heal.*::

::*So, I'm not dead?*::

::*Death deals in physical terms. That state does not exist here.*::

::*Am I in some kind of galactic void like I was before?* ::

::*No, you have gone beyond any criteria that you have known.*::

::*Who are you?*::

::*I am the caretaker of this place.*::

::*Is there a way to get back?*::

::*For every action there is an equal and opposite action. Such laws do not change. Even here, they still apply.*::

There was a pause.

::*You will go back when the time is right.*::

Part Two

INNOCENCE

OF THE MIND

CHAPTER ONE

Entry from the personal diary of Greg Carlson:
the Leader of the United Council of Developing Worlds.
(Last entry--Archive Record released one year
after the historic battle in which Copolla was defeated.)

The future. Everyone always asks me about the future and what I see. I tell them I see the same things they do: Life and Death. These are the only constants that exist. That does not satisfy them, and they ask me to tell them more.

I tell them about the first vision that came to me on the day I stood before the council as their leader. It showed me the future contains many dangers that will threaten the United Council of Developing Worlds. Why is that, some ask? Have we not conquered all that is evil? I tell them as long as life forms walk the surfaces of planets, both good and evil will always continue to exist. What will save us is how we proceed against them, and our faith and conviction to overcome.

This vision enlightened me to two important things. First, I have seen the council on Earth many years in the future, and it is still here. I have seen those who shall take Sarah's and my position: our children, a boy and a girl. I will rest easy knowing that the future is in their hands; what better testament can one ask for in regards to the sanctity of such an important organization? As long as it exists, there will always be hope that peace will be maintained.

End record.

Archive Scholar Note: A portion of the text was erased from the original entry, reason unknown. It has been recovered and placed in as an addendum.

However, my second point, I must reluctantly admit my own fear and concern. Contradictory to what I have already mentioned, the events that have led up to the battle to save Earth involved influence from the future. Vague, the life form that assisted me, came from the future and gave us the opportunity to prevent a great catastrophe. But by doing so, and if we are successful in changing the outcome, does that not alter the timeline and the future? What effect does that have on my own vision? Upon my own children and their destiny for the council? I don't know and it is this that I have come to fear.

End Entry.

***

Earth Year 2008

Personal Diary Entry - Sarah McClendon Carlson: I wanted to keep that part of me that was human—as human as I could. That is what led to my decision to use a doctor outside the confines of the UCDW compound to deliver my baby. I wanted the birth of our child to be done the human way because it might potentially be the last human experience that the child would have and I wanted it to have it. I think Greg would have agreed with me on this. Leumas and the rest of the council were against it, but I wouldn't give in on the issue. No bodyguards, nothing like that. Just myself and my son.

County Hospital, West Virginia

"I'm going to have to sedate you now, Sarah," Doctor Robert Caruso said as he dabbed at the perspiration on her face. He hoped that Sarah wouldn't be able to tell he was lying to her by the look on his face or in his eyes. He had grown quite fond of her over the past seven months and didn't want to see her hurt. The only redeeming thought he had at the moment was that all the lying was almost over.

"It's almost time?" Sarah croaked in between the contractions. Her eyes were fuzzy and unfocused from the pain. Her breathing was heavy as she exhaled deeply in spurts.

"Yes, soon. But we're not going to be able to do the local as we thought," he said, trying to sound convincing.

"Why not?" she asked. "I thought we agreed?"

"We did. But, remember what I said about the baby having to turn and face the right way?"

Sarah nodded as she expelled a large burst of breath.

"Well, this young man has not turned in the correct direction. We're going to have to do a cesarean in order to ensure the safety of the child."

"Will he be all right?"

"Of course he will. It's just required that you be under during the procedure. Can you handle that?"

"Sure," she answered, her voice quavering. "How long will I be out?"

"Just a couple of hours. As soon as you wake, they'll bring the baby to you, I promise. Are you ready to begin?"

"Yes, but..."

"What is it, Sarah?"

"Are you sure about--I mean--well you know, is there any chance about there being a second child? Maybe you couldn't tell before?"

"Sarah, we've been through this," he said as he gently gripped her hand while trying to keep his eyes and voice from betraying his true thoughts. "There are not two children. Only one." He felt remorse at forging the test results in order to satisfy her, but she had been adamant about her having twins. She was correct, of course, but he couldn't allow her to know that—not if he wanted to keep his family safe..

"Yes...of course," she muttered. "I'm ready."

Caruso motioned for the anesthesiologist to begin. "They are going to put a mask over your mouth and nose now. You'll be asleep very soon."

"All right," she answered.

As Sarah was put under the anesthesia, the doctor and his team of two assistants stood off to one side so they would not be overheard.

"Assistants" was a term Caruso applied to the man and woman who had accompanied him into the delivery room. In actuality, neither one were from the hospital staff, no matter what the forged identification badges (which indicated that the man was a doctor and the woman was a nurse on the staff of the hospital) said. Caruso didn't know much about them except that they had leveraged him into this situation, making him regret the day they had walked into his office announcing they had taken his wife and daughter.

"Is everything prepared?" he asked them, his voice not much above a whisper.

"Yes," the man he knew as Sosam answered.

Caruso watched him carefully, the dark eyes with their barely distinguishable pupils, the nose partially covered by the mask he wore but still showing the hawk-like nose, the jet black hair, greasy and unkempt that stuck to the side of his head. Caruso guessed his age at about thirty years.

"We shall not be disturbed during the procedure," Sosam continued. "We have someone outside the doors just in case."

"Good. Well then, let's get this over with before I change my mind."

"That would not be a good idea, Doctor Caruso, if you wish your family to live," Sosam said, his voice stern and unwavering.

Caruso could tell by the way his cheeks raised and moved under the surgical mask that Sosam was smiling. He surmised that nothing would give Sosam more pleasure than to kill him at this very moment if he could. Caruso smiled back, thinking how much he wanted to grab the scalpel off the table and plunge it into the bastard's heart. His thought was distracted as he heard a low but audible chuckle of amusement from the woman, whose name was Deloh.

"It's an expression, you idiot," Caruso said sarcastically as he looked at the woman. She was so nondescript in her features he could only describe her face as clay-like in appearance, with all her features blending together smoothly. The only features that stood out were her vivid green pupils. He guessed her age at somewhere between twenty and thirty.

Caruso exhaled strongly to calm himself. The frustration and fear of not having seen his wife and daughter for nearly seven months seemed to be pushing him over the last edge that had kept him going up to this very moment. These "people" had kidnapped his wife and daughter, only allowing an occasional phone call to prove that they were still alive. He was ensured his family would stay that way as long as he did what they said.

"Doctor, I would suggest you do what needs to be done instead of wasting time. Time is precious to us all, especially your family," said Sosam.

Caruso returned to the table without saying another word. He knew there wasn't any point. This whole affair hadn't any point. They never explained why they kept the truth from Sarah about the second child or why they were doing any of this.

He turned his attention to the anesthesiologist, who stared at the equipment that monitored Sarah's vital signs. He wasn't sure what they had done to him, but the man had not said a word since he came into the room. He just set up the equipment and did his job appearing oblivious to everything else.

"Ready?" he asked.

The anesthesiologist nodded without comment.

Caruso removed the sterile implements from the table and began.

Thirty minutes later, he handed the second child to Deloh. She had proven to him, by his interrogation of medical questions, that she was qualified to assist in the procedure and to properly handle the care of the newborn. But he doubted that it would have mattered if he objected, they still would have taken the child away whether he agreed to her qualifications or not.

The first child, the boy, had been placed into the standard hospital transporter to go to the nursery. The delivery room nurse arrived and took the child, a boy, from the delivery room to the nursery. As soon as she left, Caruso delivered the second child, a girl. Now, he watched as Deloh placed the second child into a specially designed carrier for transport. This transport had been disguised as a piece of medical equipment that was on a cart with wheels so it could be easily moved. The child would be stored in a compartment underneath, which consisted of an environmentally controlled area to keep her safe as they moved it out of the hospital. When she had finished the preparations required for the child, she then changed her identification badge and clothing to a hospital equipment specialist, who normally took equipment in and out of the hospital on a regular basis. At a busy hospital such as this, technicians constantly moved equipment and would raise no suspicion. She had a few muffled words with Sosam, then took the carrier and headed out of the delivery room.

A few minutes later the delivery nurse returned from the nursery. "That's it," Caruso said as he finished. "Can you Ms. Carlson into recovery?"

"Yes, doctor," the nurse replied and pushed the table out of the delivery room. As if on cue, the silent anesthesiologist left immediately after her.

"You are finished," Sosam said, his voice not questioning Caruso, but affirming the fact.

"Yes. Now when will my wife and daughter be returned?"

"Very soon. I will make the phone call and they will be brought to your home immediately."

"They better be," Caruso said. "Or I'll…"

"Please, no threats, doctor. We will live up to our end of the bargain as you have lived up to yours." He removed his surgical mask, revealing the rest of his face. His skin was mottled in the cheeks as if he had suffered a prolonged and devastating acne problem. But there was something else that had bothered Caruso the whole time he had been in the presence of Sosam. It was something about him that just wasn't right, something in his mannerisms or lack thereof.

"As a gesture of our good faith, you can talk directly to the man who will release them, that way you can be sure it is done as you wish. One moment." Sosam removed a tiny cell phone from his pocket, pressed a button on it and placed it to his ear.

Caruso removed his mask and gloves as he waited.

"It's completed as planned. No problems," Sosam spoke into the phone. "Yes. Yes. The doctor wants to speak to you."

Sosam smiled and handed the phone to Caruso. "Here you are."

The doctor quickly snatched up the phone and placed it up to his ear. "Hello?" he said. "Who am…"

As soon as the first syllable had crossed his lips, Caruso's face contorted and twisted into a painful expression. The phone dropped from his hand and it crashed to the floor, smashing into pieces.

Sosam took a few steps back, still smiling, and reached into another pocket and removed his sunglasses. He flicked them open and placed them on his face.

Caruso's face turned a dark red as his hair began to smoke. Then, there was a sudden burst of white light.

When the flash of light had extinguished, Sosam removed his glasses. He walked to where Caruso had been standing and stopped, looking toward the floor. Only a pile of ashes remained where Doctor Caruso had been standing. Sosam removed another small phone from his pocket and pressed a button.

After a few seconds, he spoke. "It's done. Yes, he's gone. Everything is going according to your plan. The child is being transported to the address you gave me. What?"

A high pitched sound emitted from the phone Sosam held in his hand. His face grimaced from pain and the betrayal that he had fallen prey to. There was a flash of light and the delivery room was empty, with the exception of the two piles of ash, which lay scattered upon the floor.

"Imagine what existence would be like if you removed the factor of time."

The Caretaker

Where am I? Greg thought, as the feeling of suddenly being awakened from a long sleep encompassed his mind.

As if responding to his command, the darkness transformed itself into an image of a landscape that filled his vision. The scene was familiar to him--the large moon encircled by several smaller ones, the trees standing in the marsh in the near distance, and the shoreline only a few feet away.

It looks like the planet Acuba, but something is different. It's not like before when I was here. Wait...there isn't any color to things; it's all just black and white. But how did I get here?

Suddenly, images flashed in his mind. He saw Earth below him.

The ships...their weapons firing upon the other ships. No. Not other ships, but on their own. Copolla's ships! The battle. It was over--Copolla was dead!

And then he remembered the ships around him exploding and his mind slipping away from his physical body that was in the small spacecraft he had taken from Earth. *His body.* He no longer possessed a physical form. Only...only the energy of his consciousness remained.

Is that because my mind was torn apart? Is that why it all looks...so strange, so unreal?

::Yes,:: a soothing voice said. ::Don't be afraid.::

Greg oriented his thoughts in the direction from which the voice had come. He didn't see or sense anything.

::*Where are you?*::

::*I am all around you. You're safe in a place where you may rest. Your mind has been damaged and needs time to heal. The images you see of the planet are being provided to comfort your senses. Physically, there is nothing around you but the fabric of space and the energy that surrounds it.*::

::*So, I'm not dead?*:: Greg asked, his voice sounding hopeful.

::*Death deals in physical terms. That state does not exist here.*::

::*Am I in some kind of galactic void like I was before when I lost contact with my physical body?*::

::*No, you have gone beyond any criteria that you have previously known. A void is without attachment. Here there is an attachment or association to your energy that keeps your mind focused, otherwise you would drift through space.*::

::Who are you?::
::I am the caretaker of this place.::
::And this place?::
::Think of it as a hotel, a place of temporary lodging.::
::You brought me here?::
::I have no control over whose energy arrives here. It just happens for reasons that are determined by a greater source. The consciousness of the neural energy is scooped up and deposited here.::
::Is there a way to get back?::
::For every action there is an equal and opposite action; such laws still apply even here.:: The voice paused, then continued. ::You will go back when the time is right.::
::How will you know when that time is here?::
::Excuse my use of the word "time." I am trying to simplify terms for your understanding. Time is a matter of no consequence here. Perhaps "need" is a better expression.::
::I don't understand.::
::How long do you think you have been here?::
::I just arrived, a moment ago.::
::Compared to the time you are familiar with, six Earth standard years have elapsed.::
::Six years? How can that--::
::That is not relevant at the moment!:: The voice sounded harsh, almost condemning.

Greg was shocked at the abrupt change.

::What is relevant is the balance.::
::Balance? I don't understand what you mean.::
::This place exists on the fundamental principle of balance. Only so much energy can exist here. Equilibrium must be maintained. Think of this place as a glass of water. If you keep adding, eventually some will spill out. Your arrival has had that affect.::
::My arrival? I thought you said it was planned or expected?::
::I do not know the particulars. But even planned things are susceptible to errors. Nothing is perfect; it will do you well to remember that.::
::Of course,:: Greg agreed, not really understanding the point the caretaker was trying to make. ::What happens to the energy that spills out?::
::It returns on the path to the area where the new arrival came from.::
::So someone…or something else has returned to where I was? To Earth? Six years later?::
::Yes.::
::What…who was it?::

There was a pause of a few seconds before the caretaker's voice entered into Greg's mind.

::*Something evil. Something so evil it shook the fabric of the universe.*::

Greg's mind knew he didn't have a physical body -- but he could have sworn he felt a chill run up his spine.

"Many times we look elsewhere to place blame for our failures. However, sometimes we need only look toward a mirror."

Sarah McClendon

Earth Year 2008

Personal Diary Entry - Sarah McClendon Carlson: For being half-alien/half-human, and possessing abilities above many of the species of the council, I wish I had received more talents that I could use to control my own thoughts. Although I have the talent to block my thoughts from others, I cannot block them from myself, for it is my thoughts that have become my worst enemy. They are relentless and uncaring as to what they show me from the past...and what the future may bring.

* * *

Headquarters of the United Council of Developing Worlds
West Virginia

The automated lights slowly illuminated the chamber as Sarah entered the room where her husband's body lay at rest. She stopped a few steps through the doorway and waited as the lights came on slowly, allowing her eyes time to adjust. She thought she could have walked here blindfolded. She knew the way well, having traced these steps for six years now.

She also knew there wouldn't be anyone here at this hour of the morning, 4:00 A.M. She chose this time of the day for two reasons: so she would not be disturbed, and it was the only time not commandeered by the demands in her life.

Time. Time had become so precious to her. At the age of twenty-nine, she had more responsibilities than anyone else on the planet. Being the co-leader of the alien organization, the United Council of Developing Worlds (UCDW), with her alien partner Leumas, and helping United States President Edward Samuel with the public relations of the space program kept her too busy to offer her any moments of idleness. But busy was a good thing, she thought. Busy meant not dwelling on Greg.

Greg lay in the stasis chamber. He'd been there for six years now since defeating his *father*. No, not father -- Copolla was anything but a father to Greg. He was an evil creature that sought out his own goals over the good of the rest, whatever the cost. Copolla's armada would have destroyed the Earth, but Greg used his mind to trick and defeat him. He saved the Earth and the United Council of Developing Worlds.

The room was now fully lit. Sarah took a moment to comb her long dark hair with her fingers, leaving it to drape over the left side of her face and shoulder. That was the way Greg had liked her to keep it. It was also the way she did her hair the day they were married.

They had been husband and wife for only a few brief hours. She tried to force the images of that day from her mind, but they always appeared to her when she came here. She took a deep breath and took the remaining steps that would place her beside the chamber.

She looked through the glass compartment that ran along the top of the chamber. Greg's face looked so peaceful. Her eyes were drawn to his dark, combed-back hair and the way it accented his olive-colored skin. She imagined running her hand across his cheek and him blushing. She felt a smile briefly appear on her lips but quickly fade. Greg's body was alive but it was an empty shell without his mind. His mind...was somewhere else. The neural energy of the mind control required to avert the disaster and defeat the armada had severed his mind from his physical body.

Although she knew he had done the right thing, at times she still wondered at the fairness of him losing his mind and virtually his life. He had been the most important person on Earth -- in the galaxy for that matter -- as leader of the UCDW. Greg, with Leumas' help, had reformed and strengthened the council and placed Earth on the path of space exploration so Earth could join the other sentient races. But closest to Sarah's heart was her own personal grief, the loss of her husband and the father to their child. A child Greg had never seen, or even known of. She hadn't had a chance to tell him before he left. A boy, their son Soren, had been born seven months after Greg sacrificed his mind in order to defeat Copolla.

Sarah sank into the soft and comfortable chair. She didn't know who had placed it beside the stasis chamber for her, but she guessed it had been Leumas. He was not only the co-leader of the UCDW, but her friend. Greg thought of him as his brother, and so did she.

She closed her eyes and focused her thoughts. Whenever she came here, she never talked to Greg in a verbal voice, but instead continued with the mental telepathy that they shared, their private hotline to each other, she remembered Greg had called it.

::Greg, are you there?:: She always tried to call to him when she came here. Once, before the tragic battle, she had been able to reach him when he had separated from his body caused by the shock of learning that Copolla was his father, which resulted in a loss of his concentration at a critical moment. He had been able to follow her voice and find his way back. But that had been a long time ago.

::Well hon, I've got a busy couple of days coming up. We're going to test the prototype design of the interstellar spacecraft. Of course we know it's going to work. After all, the best council scientists developed it. You remember that, don't you? The agreement for the council to secretly and slowly release technology to the Earth scientists, making them think it's their own breakthroughs? Of course you do...I'm sorry. I don't mean to ramble about all of this. It's just been so long since you've been gone and...I can't...::

She felt her emotions preparing to rise over the walls she had built to hide them. She never cried when she came into this room. It was her unwritten rule. She wiped at her eyes and fought back the tears.

::Greg, it's Soren. It's beginning. He's been perfectly normal up to this point. There weren't any unusual readings or anything perceivable through the examinations. Everyone was wondering what type of mental powers he would possess considering you and I are both human/alien hybrids and have the ability to influence and block others from affecting our thoughts. When nothing turned up for the past few years, the doctors and scientists figured there must have been some kind of cancellation or alteration to his DNA. For all practical purposes, he's human.

::Then the other day, he touched my mind. It was barely there but I could feel it. It was as if he were exploring or unsure of what to do with his discovery. I can't comprehend... He's only six years old, Greg! We never realized our own powers until a few years ago and we barely handled it. How is he going to deal with it?

::I haven't told anyone about it...yet...but my God, if he does possess the mind powers at this young age, and if they grow and develop within him over the years, how strong will his abilities be and what will he become? What kind of life will he--?::

The monitoring device at her waist buzzed, driving Sarah from her thoughts. She abruptly unclipped it from her belt and pressed the receive button. "Yes!" she shouted, half perturbed at being disturbed and the other half surprised at receiving a call at this hour.

The computer voice sounded from her device: "Bodily functions monitor indicate Soren Carlson is in a disturbed state. Do you wish to..."

Sarah shut off the device as she started to run, her heart pounding in her chest at what she would find when she arrived at his bedside. What had the computer said? Disturbed state? What the hell did that mean, she thought as she ran through the empty corridors that led to her quarters? He'd been asleep when she'd left. Thank God the corridors were empty instead of in their usual crowded state, bustling with members of the council.

She turned the corner, grasping the wall for support as she slid to a stop at her quarters, and placed her hand on the ID plate. Before the door had completely slid back, she lunged through the opening and banged her shoulder on the metal door. The computer voice sounded: "Warning. Entering before the door has fully reached its open position is dangerous."

"Shut up!"

She entered Soren's bedroom. The six-year-old boy was sitting upright in the bed. His long, dark hair was tousled and strands stuck to the side of his face where it was wet from perspiration. His pajamas, the ones Leumas had given him recently, were twisted around his body. He appeared to be re-arranging them so he could look at the pictures of the planets and galaxies on them. He stopped when his eyes met hers as she moved towards the bed.

"Hi, Mom." His voice portrayed no hint of discomfort. She felt the wave of fear begin to dissipate.

"Are you okay, Soren?" she said, forcing calmness into her voice as she sat on the side of the bed and caressed his face. She could feel the moisture on his skin. He was warm. A fever?

"Ah-huh. I'm okay. I was just having a dream."

"What kind of dream? Was it scary?"

"A little," he said without looking up. He continued straightening his pajamas, staring at some of the pictures with fascination.

"Were there scary people or monsters in it?"

"There was both good people and bad people in it." He looked up at her, his dark eyes sparkling in the light of the small table lamp, and continued. "But it ended before anything bad could happen."

"That's good. Did you know any of the people in the dream or were they all new?"

"I knew some of them but nooot aaaalllll," he said as he yawned and tried to keep talking. "I'm going to go back to sleep now, Mommy, okay?"

"Sure, honey," Sarah said, although she was curious about the dream. She would have to wait until later to see if she could learn any more about it. Perhaps she might be able to understand what was happening to Soren if he would talk about it. When he'd touched her mind the other day, she thought he would have asked about his newly discovered ability with his thoughts, but he hadn't -- not yet.

He lay back down in the bed and Sarah pulled the covers up to his chin and tucked them in. "Comfy?" she asked.

"Hm-hmm." He snuggled under the covers, turned his head, and closed his eyes. Sarah bent over him and gave him a kiss and then tickled him along the side of his face. He smiled with only the innocence that a child could do and giggled.

"Good night," she said. She stood and began to walk out of the room.

"Mom?"

"Yes?" Sarah stopped at the doorway. Soren had sat back up in the bed and was staring at her intensely. She looked at him, waiting for him to speak.

::Daddy was in the dream. I think he's coming home soon.::

The words came not from his mouth, but entered into her mind with such intensity and emotion that Sarah was involuntarily slammed against the bedroom wall with tremendous force.

CHAPTER FOUR

"Peace is a fragile commodity that always seems to be broken."
President Edward Samuel

President Edward Samuel stepped out of the limousine at Ramstein Air Force Base in Germany and marveled at the sight of Air Force One, where it sat in the bright illumination of the runway. "One hell of an airplane."

"Sir?" one of the Secrets Service Agents asked. "Is something wrong?"

"No, of course not, Frank. I was just admiring the plane," Edward said as he felt a wave of nostalgia flush through him. He knew there wouldn't be many more trips on the magnificent airplane in the eighth year of his presidency.

"A Boeing 747-200B. All the fancy electronic gadgetry aside, did you know that the galleys on board can prepare up to a hundred meals at one sitting?"

"No, sir, I didn't realize that."

"Sometimes it's the simple things we always miss," Edward said, still standing in one place and looking at the plane

"Sir, we should move onto the plane."

"Of course, Frank. Let's go."

The President and his entourage moved toward the boarding ramp and began the climb up the steps to enter the plane.

"Welcome back, Mr. President," Colonel Robert Barker, the flight commander from the 89th Airlift Wing out of Andrews Air Force Base said as he saluted.

"Thanks, Bob," Edward said warmly as he returned the salute. "Did you have a chance to get out and see any of the sites?"

"Yes, sir. Thanks for asking."

"You didn't forget to get the wife something, did you?" Edward asked with a hint of humor in his voice.

"No sir! I learned my lesson a long time ago. Don't go home without anything for the Missus."

"Good man." Edward patted his shoulder. "The key to a happy marriage is always ensuring you bring something home for the little lady. I always used to do that for my Julia. Always kept me in the black, if you know what I mean."

"Yes, sir!" The colonel smiled. "Roger that."

"We ready to head home?"

"Ready, Mr. President; should be a nice smooth flight all the way back to Andrews Air Force Base. I'm going to have Colonel Mitchell fly you home; I'll be second seat."

"Great. Let's get the show on the road," Edward said as he made his way into the plane and down the corridor.

As he walked, he nodded greetings to his staff and the usual conglomerate of the press corps that traveled with him. Seeing the press always reminded him of Ray Schume, leaving him with an uneasy feeling since that last affair a few years ago with the tabloid reporter. With help from Copolla, Schume had learned the truth about Edward's, Greg's and Sarah's connection to the alien organization, the United Council of Developing Worlds, and had threatened to tell the world about it. Schume had come too close for comfort on almost completing his wish.

By the time Edward finished greeting and exchanging a few words with some of the entourage, the announcement from the flight crew of their impending departure was made. Edward just made it to his executive suite as the plane began to taxi toward the runway. Within minutes, Air Force One was airborne and began its climb to its cruising height of 50,000 feet.

"Yes, John, I think it went very well," Edward said, relaxing into the reclining office chair in the bedroom. As he spoke to Vice President John Bishop on the secure communication phone, he used his other hand to push off his remaining shoe.

"All indications that the global market will continue to expand as a result of the united effort in the space program was agreed upon by the economists present at the summit. Employment forecasts are up, as are the anticipated demands for materials and additional investment opportunities."

"So everyone went home happy," John said.

"Yes, I think so," agreed Edward. "With the test of the new interstellar spacecraft in a few days, that should make them even happier."

"Happier than a pig in the mud," John offered.

"Now that would look good in the papers, wouldn't it? United States says foreign countries are as happy as pigs in the mud...oh boy."

They both laughed.

"You know, Edward," John began, his voice sounding serious, "if something should go wrong with the test..."

"Nothing will go wrong, John. Everything has been triple checked. Security is the tightest it's ever been. Speaking of which, is there any new intelligence on the terrorist cells?"

"Nothing credible. Just the usual rumors about the destruction of the world because we plan to go where we don't belong. You know, the standard rhetoric about the religious consequences and all."

"The usual," Edward agreed.

"Pretty much...but..."

"Yes. Come on, John. Spill it."

"I'm just concerned. Some of the countries that have been going along with the plan to move out into space are under a lot of pressure from their people -- an almost religious fanaticism. If something should go wrong, you know they will have a field day at our expense."

"Well, I guess we'll have to make sure nothing goes wrong then, won't we? Relax. I feel confident that we have this one in the bag."

"But aaaalllll..." John yawned.

"You sound tired, John. Get some rest. Sorry you can't come with me to the launch, but the security precautions of us both being in the same place...well, you know the drill."

"I understand. I'll watch from the White House."

"You get some rest. I'll talk to you in a while. Good night."

"Good night, Edward."

Edward hung up the phone. He, too, was tired. It had been a long week and an even longer year drumming up support for the interstellar spacecraft program. But he wanted to make sure things would remain on track after he left office at the end of this year.

Still, he couldn't help but smile at John's concern. At times he wished he could tell him about his affiliation with the UCDW, but it was too risky. And he wasn't worried about the test launch because technologically speaking, nothing could go wrong. The technology came from the UCDW and was not a new design, but already proven.

Thinking about the agreement reminded Edward of Greg's mind death six years ago. He had truly liked Greg, and thought of Sarah as a daughter. Nothing had made him happier than the day he had married the two -- right before Greg's death.

He knew that Sarah frequently remembered the past. At times he'd seen her eyes grow glazed and dreamy and he knew she was thinking about Greg.

Edward shook his head. "It's been six years and she still can't let him go."

He rose from the chair and stretched his body out on the bed. The aches from continually sitting and standing inflamed his lower back. Maybe he should take some Tylenol before he grabbed a few hours of sleep.

He rose from the bed and entered the bathroom. The Tylenol sat on a shelf in the medicine cabinet. Edward removed the Secret Service security tabs, poured out two capsules, and popped them into his mouth.

He'd just taken a gulp of water to wash the medicine down when the airplane suddenly shook and bounced, first sharply in a down direction and then back up again. The movement caused Edward to fall backward onto the floor, expelling the mouthful of water and pills.

"What the heck was…" He stopped as his body received a painful jolt. The sensation was something along the lines of an electrical shock. His entire body stretched flat on the floor and began to shake; his limbs convulsed as the pain wracked his body. He heard a screeching sound, like a freight train right on top of him, and felt a tremendous pressure in his head.

Then it was over.

The plane straightened out and returned to the smooth path it had previously been on. After several minutes passed, Edward slowly rose from the floor, his head aching. As he walked into the main room, he heard the sound of running footsteps in the corridor.

There was a knock on the door followed by, "Mr. President, are you all right?"

Edward recognized the voice of the flight captain, Colonel Robert Barker.

"Come in," he croaked.

The colonel came in followed by several Secret Service agents. "Sir, are you okay?" Eyes wide, they nervously studied the President.

"Yes, just shaken a little. I'm fine." Seeing the reluctance in the Secret Service agents, he said, "You can go back to your stations. Everything is okay here."

The agents left Colonel Barker and Edward alone.

"Now, what happened?" Edward asked.

"Some kind of bizarre turbulence, I think," the colonel said. As Edward listened, he felt as if a curtain were being lowered on his thoughts, like they were being pushed aside for the next act of some show. Anger began to well inside of him.

"Never seen anything like it before," the colonel continued. "It just hit out of nowhere without any warning. I don't know…"

Edward turned his full attention to Colonel Barker. "That's not the right answer, Colonel," he barked, his face suddenly contorting into a sneer as his insides burned with anger. Edward grabbed the colonel by the flaps of his pockets on his flight suit and drove him against the wall. "Maybe it was incompetence on your part! Or did that thought not cross your mind?"

"Sir?" the surprised colonel said.

"Incompetence! Don't you know what the word means?"

"Yes, sir. I know…"

"Well then, we're making some progress, aren't we?" Edward released his hold on the flaps of the colonel's pockets and used his hands to smooth the grip marks his hands had left in them. A slow grin appeared on his face. "Now, Colonel…you get your ass back into the cockpit where it belongs. If this plane so much as moves a hair for the rest of the flight, I'll see you'll be flying the shittiest run I can find for you! Is that CLEAR?"

"Yes, sir!"

"That's good, Bob. Good. Now get the hell out of my face."

The colonel turned and exited the cabin quickly.

President Edward Samuel began to laugh as he listened to the footsteps of Colonel Barker hurriedly returning to the cockpit. "Stupid SOB," he muttered.

He dropped into his desk's chair, exhaling strongly and closed his eyes as he massaged his temples. In a few minutes he opened them. He had the immediate but vague feeling that something odd had happened, but he couldn't remember what it was. He went to the bathroom and got a glass of water. It was then that he remembered he had been looking for some Tylenol. He opened the medicine cabinet, retrieved the bottle, and shook two capsules out of it…but then remembered doing the same thing earlier, and also remembered the sudden turbulence.

He returned to the sitting room and pressed the intercom to the cockpit.

"Yes, sir," Colonel Barker's voice answered.

"Bob, is everything alright?"

"Sir?" the colonel's voice answered questioningly.

"The flight. Did we hit some turbulence?"

"Yes, sir. I've checked the rest of the way and it should be a smooth ride."

"Okay. Thanks, Bob. Have a good night."

"Yes, sir."

Edward returned to his chair wondering how that moment appeared to have been…misplaced. As he sat down, he felt a dampness on his shirt and pants.

"I must have fallen and spilled my water on myself. I probably hit my head and blacked out for a few seconds."

He rose, removed the damp clothing, and tossed them on the chair. Feeling thoroughly exhausted, he lay down on the bed. As he closed his eyes and tried to sleep, he felt the oddest sensation. He had the strongest urge to laugh, but he didn't know why.

"Memories either haunt or nourish the consciousness of a life form. I only wish someone would invent an on/off switch by which they could be controlled."

Leumas

Personal diary entry -- Leumas: Although it has been six standard Earth years, I have decided to allow a select group of trusted agents to continue monitoring for any residual Copolla supporters that may have escaped in the aftermath of his attempt to destroy the council and Earth. The depth of his infiltration into the council, or his associated contacts, has never been discovered. Although my agents have not found anything to contradict that there is a presence, I still cannot help but feel the need to be vigilant. I remember the words from the Great Catastrophe: The most feared enemy is not in the direct assault, but those that adapt their ways to camouflage their actions and under the cover of darkness, quietly slit the throats of their opponents.

* * *

Planet Zire

Leumas' footsteps echoed on the hard floor as he walked. He was in the halls of the shrine that had been erected on the planet Zire in commemoration of the council members who had been killed when Copolla destroyed the complex in an act of rage. It had also been the place where he'd had his first meeting with Robise, the custodian of the library. He couldn't help but smile at the remembrance of the old man. *Cocky as hell.* Yet Leumas remembered the emotional commitment the old man had toward his work in the archives and how he'd saved the computer core that led to Copolla's downfall. *There should be a plaque or something with his name on it,* he thought. *I'll have to see that it...*

"What are your feelings on it?" the Zirean ambassador said, interrupting Leumas' thoughts.

Leumas, irritated by the interruption, turned toward the ambassador. The humanoid, at approximately seven feet tall and extremely skinny with a pale, waxen skin color, appeared nervous; his hands were in constant motion. Noticing Leumas' gaze, the ambassador quickly placed his hands behind his back.

"I'm sorry, Ambassador Corin, my thoughts were in the past about this place. I have many memories here. Please forgive my wandering. Now what were you saying?"

"I was asking what your position was about moving the council back to Zire? Many members have been giving it thought and debates have begun on planets throughout the galaxy."

Leumas' stomach flipped. *Not this again.* He'd heard of the movement, and felt it was a bold presumption on the ambassador's part to openly ask him this question. Perhaps that accounted for the Zirean's nervousness. Leumas made a mental note that maybe it was time to take a closer look at the issue.

"Ambassador, I don't believe such action would be in the best interest of the council at this time."

"But here is where the council was born. Earth was a valid but temporary measure given the crisis of the time. It has served its purpose, and all that facilitated the move there has been resolved. This is…"

"Ambassador," Leumas stopped him in mid-sentence. "I understand your concern in this matter. However, I must disagree with your assessment that all of the council concerns have been resolved. I believe there is still an element of Copolla's followers lurking about who seek to interfere with council actions toward Earth and the rest of the planets we are influencing."

"Have you evidence to support this claim?"

"Nothing solid; just call it a feeling."

"Perhaps you fear something that does not exist." The ambassador placed his hand on Leumas' shoulder. "Leumas, it's simply that many feel we are doing too much for the humans on Earth. More than what we're doing for other races. We cannot help but wonder if this is because the Leader was human…"

"Half human," Leumas reminded him, as he abruptly removed the ambassador's hand from his shoulder.

"Yes, that is correct, half human. Please forgive my error. I understand you had a personal bond with him."

The ambassador's voice had a tone to it that Leumas didn't like. What did this life form know of his and Greg's relationship? *He was like a brother to me,* Leumas thought.

"Leumas, you are the co-leader of the United Council of Developing Worlds and as such you must realize that there is validity in the movement for members wishing to return to their roots on Zire. If enough members bring it to the council, a vote will have to be taken on the issue. It would be prudent for you to address the issue before it comes to that moment, don't you think?"

"Ambassador Corin, I assure you that when it becomes an issue it will be addressed. I will bring your concerns to co-leader Carlson. But until that time, I see no need for any action."

"Many do not wish to wait. There are…"

"Thank you for the tour," Leumas interrupted him. He didn't wish to hear any more on this issue. "But I must really get back to Earth."

"Of course," he agreed. "I will escort you back to the space port."

"Thanks, but I think I'll head back alone. I wish to contemplate on some things."

"As you wish."

* * *

Ambassador Corin stepped into his office and turned on his privacy shield so no one would hear his words. "That arrogant freak!" he screamed, as he slapped a porcelain sculpture off his desk. He watched it sail through the air and shatter into pieces on the floor. "He wants to head back alone. How dare he embarrass me like that!"

He went to his liquor cabinet and removed a bottle of Scorintian Whiskey. He grabbed a tumbler, filled it halfway, and gulped down the liquor. As it warmed him, he felt his temper begin to simmer, a sure sign his tirade was now complete.

Returning to his desk, he contemplated in a somewhat more rational train of thought what had just occurred in his discussion with Leumas. After a few moments, he removed his secure communication device from his desk and keyed in the coded channel.

A voice answered. "Yes."

"I just finished talking with Leumas."

"And?"

"He doesn't appear favorable to our suggestion of relocating the council on Zire."

"Are you surprised?" the voice asked smugly. "Leumas and many other members are tied to the memories of the former leader, Greg Carlson. Even though dead…well, virtually dead," the voice corrected itself, "for six years now, they still maintain hope of his return. They are to be commended for their loyalty and perseverance."

"You sound like you are having a change of mind," Ambassador Corin stated. "Has Leumas convinced you to…"

"No, he has not," the voice replied sharply. "He must have stepped on your toes while he was there, didn't he?"

Ambassador Corin felt his flesh become heated again with embarrassment, but quickly willed it away. "No," he replied trying to keep his voice even.

"I think perhaps he did. Anyway, that is of no matter at the moment. What I am implying is that I understand their position. Many of us were not part of the council during that upheaval period. Those who served during that time are to be commended for their roles in the saving of the council. If the great leader were still alive, it would be different. But the divided leadership of Ms. Carlson and Leumas is not effective. I applaud the woman for her abilities and efforts, but she is also living in her memories, and more concerned with Earth than the other planets. Nor are her powers as strong as the great leader."

"And Leumas?"

"He is also to be commended for his role during the upheaval. But he does not possess the charisma of a leader. He would not have been chosen if not for the great leader's insistence upon his death."

"So what is our next move?"

"First, we shall further predispose the council to the idea of returning to Zire. But it must be done carefully. The religious fanaticism over the death of the leader is a sensitive issue and that cannot be touched in any way. The reason for the move must be on another account."

"Such as?"

"We are exploring some possibilities. One option does appear to hold a greater chance of success than the others. If we convince the council members, both Leumas and Ms. Carlson will have to go along."

"And that option is?"

"That the planet Earth and its internal conflicts make it too volatile for the council to remain and that its presence is in jeopardy of being exposed to the humans."

"You would expose the secret?"

"Not directly, but in an indirect manner. We don't want any harm to come to this world, but just enough concern to sway the council's decision."

"You speak of a very fine line. It may be dangerous."

"Things that are worthy of accomplishment are at times dangerous, but necessary for the greater good."

"Even one's own mind can be a lonely place."
Greg Carlson

As Greg wondered about the chill he felt, the air in front of him shimmered. A humanoid form began to materialize.

::*What's this?*::

::*Perhaps it will be easier to converse with you if I take a form you are more accustomed to,*:: the voice in his mind said. ::*You also will assume a physical shape of familiarity.*::

Greg immediately felt some kind of change come upon him. Instinctively, he raised his hand and saw he actually possessed one now. He looked down and saw his chest, legs and feet. He felt where his head should be and found it solid also. He was back in his physical shell...

::*Not exactly. Your mind has only been convinced that you are back in your physical shell. In truth, there is nothing physical about you or anything that you see.*::

Greg watched as the image of the entity sharpened and became more defined. He mentally clicked off the characteristics: male, about a hundred and sixty pounds, dark hair, five foot eight or nine. Olive skin complexion, about roughly twenty-nine years old, hawk-like nose and... wait a minute. Greg couldn't help but laugh when he saw the shape the entity had chosen: it was his own. He was looking at himself.

"Couldn't get any more original, could you?" Greg asked. He felt his voice speak, heard the words and thought it was good to sense that feeling again.

"This seemed the easiest way," the entity responded. "Please, let's sit." He indicated a direction to Greg.

Greg turned and saw that a simple table and two chairs had materialized. He turned back toward the image of himself. "After you, Greg -- wait a minute, this is going to be too awkward if I call you Greg. It's odd enough that I am literally going to be talking to myself. How about I call you something else?"

"Do you have a preference?" the entity asked.

"No."

"Then call me...Caretaker. You seemed to adjust to that term when you used it earlier. Will that suffice?"

"Sure," Greg answered. *Why not,* he thought as he followed himself to the table...no, not himself, he corrected, but the look-a-like. They sat and Greg couldn't help but feel awkward as he studied himself across the table. But as he remembered their earlier conversation, questions began to rise in his mind.

"Caretaker, you must be aware that I am concerned about going back to Earth. You said when I arrived that I would return when the time is right. I was doing something very important and if anything should jeopardize…"

"Your career has been followed and scrutinized closely. You should be honored. Not many are followed that closely. What you did was very heroic."

"I did what I knew had to be done. The entity that came from the future, Vague, he helped me to learn…"

"I know. We sent him," the caretaker said, a grin edging onto his face.

"You sent him? But I thought he was from the future?"

"He was. As I said earlier, time has no meaning here. To you, he has not been born yet, but the others, well…they see him in various stages of living and dying. To them, time is circular."

"These…others? Who are they?" Greg asked.

"They are…everything. They are what compose the fabric of the universe."

"If that's the case, why do they have to maneuver everything to keep it going?"

"The correct laws of physics override everything. Since the beginning of time, many have thought that for every reaction there is an opposite equal reaction. However, this is not exactly the case. Reactions are tempered by many other things that make them unequal or out of balance. What they strive to do is keep a balance."

"What do you mean, tempered by other things?"

"This is very complicated. The simplistic way of stating it is that too much of anything is not good. Too many people and not enough food cause war and death. Not enough people cause a decrease in diversity of species. Too much evil causes hate and pain. Too much good causes stagnation and decay. So on and so forth, so you see, what they do is seek a balance. By doing so, they ensure that everything around us goes on."

"And you?"

"The only thing I know is balance of this place. Balance is the key to everything."

"You mentioned that earlier. This balance. You said I upset it when I came here."

"Here," the caretaker began by opening his arms wide to indicate everything around them, "is like everywhere else. An intricate balance of energy must exist. I don't pick who or what comes here, the others do. But I must maintain a balance; not too much of one or another, otherwise the others get upset, because if too much of one is here, then not enough is out there where it needs to be to keep the balance. Balance is the key…"

"Okay, I get the drift on the balance thing already. Forgive me and my impatience, but how does all of this apply to me?"

"Impatience is a trait I do not understand," the caretaker said, with a questioning look on his face. "Is it because you want to get back to your planet to resume your work, to see your people, your wife and child?"

"Of cour-- Child? Did you say child?"

"Yes. When you sacrificed yourself for the better good, you saved millions of lives and left behind a wife and unborn child."

"A child…"

"Yes, an offspring, a genetic makeup similar to your own, a…"

"I get it! I get it! Was it a boy or a girl?"

"It was of the male species."

"A boy. I'm a father. How old is he?"

"Six Earth standard years."

"Can I see him? Is his name Soren? That is what Sarah and I were going to name a male child if we ever had one."

The caretaker waved a hand and an area of the landscape of the planet Acuba wavered and then reformed into an image of a chamber where a little boy sat. Greg immediately recognized the features of the child that made him his and Sarah's. The boy had the dark hair of both his parents, Greg's olive skin tone, and Sarah's soft facial characteristics.

"He's beautiful," Greg said.

As Greg's eyes looked at the other contents of the room, he saw the stasis chamber where his real physical body lay. The boy had come to visit his father's body. Greg automatically focused his thoughts and sent them. ::Hello, Soren.::

The image blurred and vanished.

"Thank you, Caretaker," Greg said with a rush of pride and love for his son. A son. He thought back and remembered that Sarah had wanted to talk with him before he left, but there hadn't been enough time.

"We should finish our discussion," the caretaker said, interrupting Greg's thoughts and without acknowledging his thanks. "We were speaking of balance."

"Yes." Greg agreed. "You mentioned about the *evil* being released upon my arrival." The word *evil* associated his thoughts with only one thing. He didn't want to ask the question…it seemed too horrific of a possibility to even consider. The joy of seeing his son was quickly swept away by the thought.

"In simplistic terms," the caretaker began, "energy can also be defined as good and evil, just like physical beings. When you arrived, some of the energy had to be discharged. Your energy is positive, so negative energy had to leave."

"Yes. Yes," Greg said impatiently. "Balance. I know. You said it was negative or evil energy and that it went on the path back to where I came from. You described it as something so evil it shook the fabric of the universe."

"Yes it was. An evil so malignant it defies explanation or logic."

"Tell me it wasn't Copolla's energy." Greg watched the image of himself, which sat across from him, looking and hoping for some sign that would reassure him that the worse could not possibly have happened. "It wasn't him?"

The caretaker sat and remained silent, simply looking at Greg.

* * *

Sarah fought to maintain her composure as she stood against the wall next to the doorway of Soren's bedroom. His words continued to reverberate in her mind, ::*Daddy was in the dream. I think he's coming home soon. Daddy was in the dream. I think he's coming home soon. Daddy was in the dream. I think he's coming home soon.*::

The pain from the overwhelming energy of his mind tore into hers with such raw force, she thought her head was going to explode. She felt weak, her knees threatening to buckle, as she tried to think of what to say or do. Finally the words formed in her mind and she sent them to her son. :: *Stop, Soren! Stop your thoughts. They are too strong and are hurting Mommy.*::

A moment later his thoughts slowly faded from her mind and eventually ceased. Sarah felt her tensed body relax and her breathing begin to return to normal.

Soren's face twisted into a painful mask as his eyes filled with tears. "I'm sorry, Mommy, I didn't mean to be bad..."

"It's okay, honey," Sarah said as she made herself move toward his bed. The effort required much of her strength. Her entire body felt as if it had been overexerted by some kind of electrical shock. The muscles and tendons were stiff and unyielding. She eased her way down, sat on the bed, and hugged Soren as he cried against her chest. "It's all over now. Mommy's okay."

"What is it?" he asked, his voice muffled against her chest. "What is it with my...thoughts? What's happening?"

"It's a gift," Sarah said. "It's something very special." She stroked his hair as she struggled with her own emotions. She knew he had been experimenting with the power, the way he had touched her mind the other day, and could understand the frustration and fear he felt about using it. She so much wanted to ask him why he had said what he had, about Greg being in his dream and that he might be coming home, but she thought that could wait.

"It's scary sometimes," Soren said softly.

"It can be until you learn about it and how to control it, but then it becomes a good thing. It's like being able to talk to people without having to say anything. When you did it, it was like...turning your stereo up all the way. You have to keep the volume down."

"Will you show me how?"

"Yes."

"When?"

"Tomorrow. But you have to promise not to tell anyone. Okay?"

"Okay, I promise. So it's like secret talking?"

Sarah saw the change of his emotion from fear to excitement. *The luxury of being a six-year-old*, she thought.

"Yes. But you have to remember; not everyone likes secret talking. It scares them, too."

"What about Uncle Leumas? Will he like secret talking? How about Uncle Edward?"

"I think they will. But let me talk to them first, okay?"

"Okay. When?"

"When what?"

"When will you talk to them?"

"Soon. I'll talk to them as soon as they get back."

"Okay. Can I go to sleep now?"

"In a minute, hon." Sarah thought it was safe to approach the subject she needed to talk about. "Soren, can you tell me what you meant about Daddy being in your dream and he might be coming home?"

"I was dreaming that I was in sitting in his room."

"His room? You mean where I take you sometimes, where Daddy is asleep in the stasis chamber?"

"Yes. I was sitting there and the long case opened up. I was scared at first, but I couldn't run away. Daddy called to me and said to not be scared. He said everything was going to be all right now that he was home. And then I woke up."

It took Sarah a few seconds to find her voice. She imagined the image in her mind of Soren sitting next to the stasis chamber and--
 :: *No, Mommy, not like that. Like this.*:: he said in her mind at a perfect volume for her comprehension.
How quickly he learns, she thought. What happened next caught her off guard. She received the images of his dream in her mind with such clarity it was as if it were her own dream and she was actively seeing it in her own thoughts. But even that hadn't prepared her for the sound of the voice that came from the stasis chamber. It was Greg's voice, she was certain, although he spoke only two words. *"Hello Soren..."*
The images vanished. She focused her gaze back on Soren and discovered he'd fallen asleep.
Sarah quietly rose and walked from his room. Tears streamed down her face as she struggled with what she had just seen. Was it true? Would it happen? Would Greg come back? Or was it just a dream of a young boy who wanted his father?
She sat on the sofa, her legs folded under her, her chin resting on her hands. She wiped the tears from her face with a tissue as she forced the images of Soren's dreams from her thoughts. She was somewhat relieved that the ability to communicate telepathically was now in the open where they could talk about it and she could teach him how to control and use the power. *That way I can...* She stopped midway in her thought when she suddenly realized what he had also done. He had sent her "his dream." But not as thoughts. *He placed me inside of his dream.*
Not even Greg had the power to do that...and Soren was only six years old.

"For better or worse, emotions make us what we are. Yet when we are driven to love, anger, or sorrow because of these emotions, we seek an explanation."

Leumas

"Dora, how much longer before we arrive?" Leumas asked as he walked onto the bridge of his ship. Dora was the name he had bestowed upon the computer along with the feminine voice, a remembrance of an old acquaintance that held fond memories for him.

"Six hours and ah...thirteen minutes, *L-e-u-m-a-s*," the computer voice answered, adding a little touch of promiscuity to its already overly sultry tone.

"Thanks, Dora."

"Would you like a mirror to check your appearance?" she asked.

"Not right now, Dora. Maybe later."

"That's okay, you look *f-i-n-e* anyway. Are you sure you're not getting younger? My records tell me you are thirty Earth years of age, but your physique and metabolism..."

"Thank you, Dora. That's all for now."

Leumas plopped into the control chair of his ship, the *Blessed*, as it made its way back to Earth from the planet Zire. As co-leader of the council, he was entitled to the use of the diplomatic craft reserved for such purpose, but he preferred his own ship. He had completed many of his initial contact missions with this ship, and he knew its capabilities. As he became older, he felt a fondness for things he knew he could trust.

He ran his fingers through his long blond hair. It was one of the many human characteristics and gestures he had picked up over the years. He already looked completely human with one exception, the webbing between his fingers that usually made the results of running his hands through his hair an exercise in futility. He sighed as the hair slipped over his hands and fell to the sides.

He pondered why he was feeling so blah. Usually Dora's playfulness kept him upbeat. After all, that was the way he'd had her designed, to detect his emotional state and apply whatever stimulus was required to keep him from being upset or distressed. *I shouldn't have gone to Zire*, he thought. Too many memories there: Greg, Robise, and many of the council members he'd been friends with and whom Copolla had killed. And then, Ambassador Corin had to bring up the movement to return the council to Zire. Didn't anyone follow proper channels anymore?

But he knew it was more than that that had upset him. The issue of moving the council was a personal affront toward Greg and that really pissed him off. Greg had become like a brother to him. When Greg got married, it was he, Leumas, who had been the best man. And hadn't Greg sacrificed everything to ensure the stable relocation of the council to Earth, and saved the council's lives by forfeiting his own? *Doesn't anyone remember that? Was it that long ago?*

::*Do you want to talk about it?*:: Dora asked in his thoughts. Her abilities had been enhanced to communicate telepathically with Leumas. ::*It sounds like your emotions are getting in the way and biasing your decisions.*::

::*I don't know, Dora. Maybe they are. It just seems like everyone wants to move on and I don't.*::

::*You have a strong emotional attachment that makes it harder to see perspective in this matter. I hate to sound like a psycho-therapeutic computer, but you should look at the facts of this issue*::

::*Maybe you're right, Dora. I want you to analyze any data you can find regarding the movement to return the council back to the planet Zire. What I want to know is how deep this fervor is running and who is leading it. And are there any ulterior motives that need to be considered.*::

::*I will get back to you when I have the information.*::

::*Thanks.*::

::*There's something else bothering you, Leumas. Can I assist you?*::

::*You already are, Dora. The monitoring of any signs that indicate any presence of Copolla's old regime.*::

::*There has been no evidence for the past six years that indicates such a thing.*::

::*I know.*::

::*So why do you pursue it? Perhaps none exists within the parameters in which you seek.*::

::*We know we didn't catch everyone involved with Copolla simply because we didn't know who everyone was. Call it a feeling. An instinct that I'm missing something.*::

::*You should have more confidence in--*::

"Wait a minute, Dora," Leumas said interrupting the computer's thoughts as he changed back to vocal communication. "What did you say? About parameters?"

"I said that perhaps none exists within the parameters in which you seek."

"The parameters. What are the current search parameters?"

"Current parameters include the monitoring of all unusual communications, ship movements, monetary transactions, general planetary disturbances and similar protocols between the planet Zire and other planets in that quadrant. I am searching for any abnormalities that might possibly indicate a resurgence or movement that fits any previous pattern used by Copolla."

"So what does that leave? What are we not watching?"

"Any planets outside of the quadrant, of course," Dora answered confidently.

Leumas slapped his forehead with his hand. "Wait a minute. How foolish could I have been?"

"You are never foolish, Leumas," Dora asserted adamantly. "You are the co-leader of the United Council of Developing Worlds."

"Well, in this case, I have been foolish and overlooked something that should have been obvious. How could I not have realized?" He paused for a few seconds and then spoke. "Earth is outside the quadrant."

"Yes, it is, Leumas. You have made a...slight misjudgment."

"Yes, I have. I only hope that I haven't made any other misjudgments. Dora, change the parameters to include the monitoring of Earth. Reexamine records to see if we have missed anything. Start from present time and work back. Let me know as soon..."

"We have one event which meets criteria. It occurred less than one day ago."

***

President Edward Samuel sat restlessly in his chair in his private office at Camp David, which was about seventy miles from Washington, D.C. At Camp David, the term "private office" was an understatement. The site, first established as a retreat by Franklin D. Roosevelt in 1942, was in the isolated and heavily wooded section of the Catoctin Mountains in Maryland. Operated by the United States Navy, along with armed Marine guards and other agencies which provided security, the compound was sealed from any form of possible threat, whether physical or other, from the outside world.

Although he hadn't been scheduled to come to Camp David, Edward hadn't been feeling or sleeping well since his return from the overseas meeting in Germany two days ago. Also, it was brought to his attention by Vice President John Bishop that he was becoming extremely short-tempered with many of the White House staff. The White House doctor gave the usual recommendation: rest and a change of scenery for a few days. Part of Edward wanted to resist, but another applauded the suggestion and he went along with it.

Feeling the need to do something that would relax him, Edward removed from his desk drawer what a steel case. It was about ten inches wide by thirteen inches long; however, it weighed barely a pound. There were no visible seams on the container. He set it on his desk and firmly placed his hand, palm down, in the center of it. The box folded itself flat and retracted into a paper-thin sheet. In the center lay a book. The book was his private journal -- his memoirs -- and never left this room. The container had been a gift from Leumas and was totally tamper-proof. It was keyed to the bio-rhythms of Edward's body, which could not be duplicated. Any other attempt to get at its contents would take an explosive device so large it would devastate a small island.

The book itself was also a unique gift from Leumas. Whatever was written was automatically encoded into harmless but coherent prose of a predisposed story line that had nothing to do with the actual contents.

When Edward felt restless, he would come here and write down the events that had occurred since his last entry. He thought of it as a memory dump and as a form of therapy. Most folks just talked it out with their spouse or children, but having lost his wife many years ago to cancer, and with his two children grown and attending college, that didn't leave many options.

Being the President of the United States for a second term had offered more than enough challenges for one man to be tasked with, but his affiliation with the UCDW added upon it tremendously. There was nobody in his administration who knew of the alliance, except for Sarah, but she was also kept busy by the demands of her double affiliation. So he wrote, knowing that the day that such writings could be publicly viewed would probably not come in his lifetime.

He picked up the writing device, which appeared as a normal pen and began to write: "All goes as planned for the test of the new launch vehicle. There is skepticism from some staff, but that is to be expected. Leumas and Sarah have been assured by the UCDW scientists all will go as planned. I have been-- *I want to know what you know…I want to know what you know…I want to know what you know…tell me!*"

Edward dropped the pen on the desk blotter and looked at the words. The last few sentences were…very strange.

"That's not what I was thinking," he said to the empty room. As his words resonated from the walls, he had the strangest sensation briefly cross his mind that his hand was communicating someone else's thoughts, not his own. He quickly dismissed it as absurd. "What the hell is going on here? Someone playing some kind of joke?"

He examined the pen closely. Leumas was a prankster at heart and it wouldn't be difficult for him to get in here.

He forced the thoughts from his head. *No—it's just stress, that's all. Everything is fine. I just need to rest. I'll write for a while and then get some sleep. It was just a freak thing...a brain fart. The mind is playing games.*

He slowly picked up the pen and tried to return to what he had been writing: "Our allies are supportive of...*YOU TELL ME WHAT I WANT TO KNOW OR IT WILL BE EXTREMELY PAINFUL. SHOW ME EVERYTHING!*"

"No! What's happening? It's not me writing this!"

Something was very wrong here. Either he was losing his mind, or he was somehow being controlled by an outside source. Some kind of psychological attack? Either way, he needed help right now. His hand moved to the intercom on his desk.

His forward movement stopped abruptly. He dropped the pen again as his body violently jerked in the chair. Pain ripped through him, sharp and hot, and then centered in his head. He gripped his head with his hands. "NO! Help me...stop..."

::*Didn't I tell you it would painful?*:: A voice manifested itself in Edward's thoughts. ::*Now you be a good human and tell me what I want to know and I won't tear your brain apart in agonizingly painstaking detail, cell by cell.*::

"What...what do you want? Who are you?" Edward gasped.

::*Questions? Did I say you could ask questions? I don't think so.*::

Edward's upper body suddenly surged forward and slammed into the desk. Pain surged through him.

::*I hope I have your full attention. Listen carefully. There are two rules. Rule number one: I ask the questions. Rule Number Two: defer to rule number one. Is that understood?*::

"Yes," Edward said. "I understand..." One hand gripped his side. He didn't think anything was broken, but it hurt like hell. Through the pain, he felt confident that he had not gone over the edge, so whatever was happening was coming from someone or something else...and it wasn't human.

::*Good. See, that wasn't too difficult. Now...where were we? Oh yes... I believe I asked you to tell me what you know.*::

"One day I woke up and everything just looked different."
Soren Carlson

Soren slowly opened his eyes and sat up as he looked at the clock with the big numbers that glowed a bright red in the nighttime. They said it was 7:30, and the little day number in the corner said it was day number 6, which meant it was Saturday. That meant there wouldn't be any school today. He lay back down on his back and stared at the ceiling.

It's not that he didn't like school; it was fun. But he missed not going to school with other children like he saw on television. Mom said it was too far away and not as good as individual attention like what he got from Mr. Scofield, his private teacher.

Soren turned over on his side. He knew his mother hadn't exactly told him the truth. He could sense those things -- when someone wasn't telling the truth. But he also sensed that she thought it was safer here at home, and that was more important to her.

He knew about "here," although everyone tried to hide it from him. He was restricted from going outside of the "designated" area, as they called it. But he could sense the thoughts of the "space people," as he called them. There were many of them and they weren't human like him. Although he never saw them, he heard their strange thoughts in his mind, and based on those thoughts, he sometimes drew pictures of what they might look like.

He hid the drawings and didn't tell anyone about these things. It was his secret and he liked secrets. Although the doctors didn't come as often anymore as they had when he was younger, they always asked him questions about what he thought and if he could hear things others couldn't. And special talking, without words but just thinking about it like he did the other night with his mother, they always asked about that also.

Talking with his mind was something new he'd just discovered. The doctors would find out about it if his mom told them. But for some reason, he didn't think she would tell. It was one thing for Uncle Leumas and Uncle Edward to know -- they were good friends. But besides them, he felt sure she wasn't going to say anything because she was scared how others might think or react.

Soren knew he was different. He saw other children sometimes when his mother took him to the movies, but he knew he didn't think or act like them. When he asked his mother about it, she said he was "very mature" for his age. That made him feel proud, but he still missed some of the aspects of playing with kids his own age. They weren't allowed to come back to his home because it was the secret place of the space people.

Uncle Leumas was really nice. He always brought something for him when he returned from a trip...and he went on a lot of trips. When Soren asked him why he was gone so much, Leumas had told him it was his job, plus he'd promised Soren's father he'd do the work he'd started and to help his mom also. It was very important work that they were doing and his father was the one who had started it.

Uncle Leumas would tell him stories about his dad and his mom. He said he knew them before they knew each other and he helped bring them together.

Soren recalled a conversation. "Like the little angel, Cupid, who shoots the arrows into people and makes them fall in love?" he'd said.

"Well...I guess so," Leumas had responded. "I can't say I understand how shooting a pointed object into someone could make one person fall in love with another. But the one thing I am sure of is that your mom and dad were very much in love and that your dad would be very proud of you if he were here right now."

Sometimes Soren went with his mom to see his dad in the special room where he was sleeping. Both Leumas and his mom said that Dad was going to come back some day. That's why they kept his body alive and in the special place instead of burying it in the ground like most people did. So that when he returned, he would slip back into it. *Like he had said in the dream*, Soren thought.

The dream. Yes. At first there had been nothing but darkness, then he'd reached out, imagined his father, and there he was! He sensed his father was lost and needed to find his way back home. But Soren also sensed he needed something to guide him, a sense of urgency for something he had to do. That feeling of need lingered in Soren's thoughts, and he felt he must somehow be a part of what his father sought.

The dream excited Soren, but he was also a little scared, because what he hadn't shown his mom was the shadow in the corner. Someone else had been in the dream, too. Someone who wanted to hurt his dad and a lot of others. He flipped the covers off and got out of bed. He didn't want to think about the dream anymore. What he wanted was breakfast.

He skipped from his bedroom and headed toward the kitchen. His mom lay asleep on the sofa. He picked up the throw blanket that had fallen off her and tucked it in around her shoulders. "Snug as a bug," he said as his gaze settled upon a strand of hair that dangled over his mother's face and fluttered as she exhaled.

Soren brushed it behind her ear. As he did so, he momentarily touched the side of her face and...he felt a strange sensation. Something had traveled up and through his arm but quickly dissipated. *Like an ant...no, like a lot of ants crawling along the skin.*

Inquisitive as to what had just happened, he let his fingers gently trace their way along the side of her head seeking the source. There was something there--he could feel it--but it wasn't very strong. He moved his hand slightly trying to determine in which direction to go. He stopped alongside her temple. It was stronger here.

As his hand remained in place, he felt the skin-crawling sensation travel through his arm as it had earlier. But it was changing. This time it felt stronger. It was being replaced with a snap-like feel of a static charge, the kind you got when you walked on a carpet and then touched something. But it wasn't scary or painful. It was kind of neat.

As Soren thought about this, the charge-like feeling moved into his shoulder. His shoulder twitched as the muscles reacted to the small electrical shock. He giggled at the feeling. A few seconds later, it went into his neck and then suddenly entered into his mind.

Everything went dark for Soren. For a brief instance, he became scared at his lack of sight. But then he was quickly overcome with a tremendous wave of emotion...sadness.

Shocked at the overwhelming sense of despair, he removed his hand from his mother's head. As he did so, the emotional wave he felt vanished and his sight returned.

What was that?

"No...no," Sarah moaned in her sleep, causing Soren to step back. He immediately sensed that what he had just felt was also making his mother feel sad, very sad. He watched as she grew restless, her body squirming on the sofa, her face contorting into a frightened countenance.

She's having a bad dream. That was what I felt? Mommy's dream! Maybe I can chase away the bad dreams like Baku did in the book Mommy used to read to me? But I would have to go inside of her head. Can I do that? I know I can talk that way, but...I don't know if I can be in two places.

He hesitated for a moment, wondering if he could really help her. He thought of Uncle Leumas and how he always said that if you didn't try something, you would never know if you could do it or not. He stepped forward and gently placed his hand back on the spot where it had been before. As soon as he made contact, the feelings of sadness took him over as everything went dark.

CHAPTER NINE

"The way home had always been before me…I just couldn't see it."
Greg Carlson

Greg held his breath as he waited for the response to his question from the look-a-like being known as the caretaker. None came. Instead he just sat with an unemotional expression on his face.

Greg felt his patience slipping as he repeated the question. "I said, tell me it wasn't Copolla's energy."

"I cannot," the caretaker finally responded. "For that would not be the truth of the matter."

Greg's mind filled with rage. "What the hell is going on? Every time we defeat him, every time we think it's safe, that son-of-a-bitch comes back!" Greg stood and walked up to within inches of the caretaker's face. "Where is the justice in that? Do you understand what he tried to do? He would have destroyed Earth if I hadn't stopped him. He's sick! He's demented and insane! What idiot decided that his energy should leave?"

"Balance is necessary…"

"I don't want to hear about balance anymore!" Greg shouted.

"That is all I know," the caretaker answered calmly. "Things are the way they are for reasons beyond my understanding. I explained that to you earlier. I can understand this frustrates you, but you think of only one planet. There are many more in the galaxy and beyond."

Greg stared at the caretaker for a few seconds in silence. He couldn't believe it was happening to him again; the greater good of something larger than his own life, planet or his own race was being thrust in his face. *Why couldn't I have had a normal life? For once, I want to be like everyone else.*

"I understand what you're saying," Greg said as he turned away from the caretaker. "I know there is always a greater good. But that doesn't make it any easier to swallow. I just can't understand what possible good can come from saving the energy of a madman? Can I talk to the others? Those who make the decisions? Perhaps I can make them understand what he has done and what he is capable of doing."

"That is not possible."

"Why?"

"They understand everything. I am sure they have taken all of this into consideration. You must also understand that they do as they wish, not as others wish."

"No time for us inferior species? Too busy playing with the destiny of the galaxies?"

Greg walked in a small circle for a few seconds trying to figure a way to get through to the caretaker. He was obviously just the servant for these others. He needed to know more about them. He turned back to the caretaker. "If they understand everything, surely they must know that Copolla is evil and that nothing good will come of his energy. But if..." Greg paused. "Wait a minute. I have a body to go back to, Copolla does not."

"His energy will reside in another life form, suppressing it if it is weaker than his own."

"Whose body?"

"That is not important at the moment."

"That's why I'm going back, isn't it? You need someone to physically go to Earth and capture him."

"Yes. You must bring his energy back."

"Bring it back? You mean destroy it, don't you?"

"No!" The caretaker said with an unusual display of emotion that surprised Greg as he saw the seriousness of his own face and the undertones in his voice. "Under no circumstances are you to destroy it. You must bring it back to be placed here where it belongs. That must be clearly understood or you will not go back."

"Okay, I get your point, but why is that so important?"

"Balance," the caretaker replied, offering no further explanation.

"I should have guessed," Greg snickered ironically. "And after his energy is brought back, what happens to me?"

"Balance must be maintained."

"Aw, come on! Look, I'm getting tired of this balance thing you keep laying on me as the answer to everything," Greg said, his anger rising again. "How about a straight answer for a change?"

"Your energy will return and remain here."

"But I have a perfectly good body waiting for me on Earth. Why can't I just slip back into it and stay there?"

"Bal..." the caretaker began, then stopped. "Because you must return. That is all I know."

"No other options?" Greg thought about Sarah and his son Soren. "What about my son? My wife?"

"There are no other choices. As far as your son is concerned, he has his own destiny to fulfill."

"Destiny?" Greg asked, his body becoming tense. "My son, who I haven't even met yet, has a destiny? Why do I feel there is more to this than you are telling me? What are you talking about?"

"Balance," the caretaker said and turned away.

* * *

Leumas' thoughts hung on the words Dora had spoken as he waited for the computer to expound on what it had said. As seconds ticked by, he remembered that Dora, being a computer, would not elaborate unless prompted. "Explain, Dora."

"We have one event which meets criteria that occurred less than one day ago," Dora repeated. "At approximately 1830 hours, Earth EDT, there was a severe atmospheric disturbance."

"Define the nature of the disturbance," Leumas said.

"A burst of electromagnetic energy appeared over the European continent. Its duration was approximately four seconds."

"Cause?"

"Unknown."

"Is there any information on this type of disturbance? Is it a natural atmospheric disturbance or are they caused by something?"

"There is no record of a naturally occurring phenomena that matches this type of disturbance."

"Could it have been fabricated or caused by another life form?"

"Possibly. There are elements within the electromagnetic range that are not naturally occurring."

"Source?"

"It appeared in Quadrant three of Earth space."

"Appeared? You mean it originated in Quadrant three?"

"No. It just appeared there. There is no detectable trajectory of it traveling from another point."

"That doesn't make any sense, Dora. How could something just appear?"

"Unknown."

"Theorize then," Leumas said, raising his voice.

"One moment please..."

Leumas sighed. Sometimes it frustrated him the ways things had to be spelled out to a computer. *Quadrant three? What was it about--*

"Given the data available, the most probable explanation for the appearance of the energy was due to a shift in spatial dimension."

"A shift in spatial dimension? What do you mean?"

"The energy came from another dimension in time or space."

"Explain."

"According to theory, other dimensions of space exist. If there were to be an opening in that fabric of space, it would theoretically be possible to cross over from one dimension to another. This would explain the lack of trajectory."

"But for what purpose?" Leumas asked.

"If we stay with the same assumption," Dora said. "The most common assertion would be either to bring something in or out. Given the available data of the electromagnetic burst, it appears to be coming in."

"If we continue with this assumption, that something arrived through or across another dimension, where did it go?"

"Unknown. The burst completely dissolved in the atmosphere. There are no further traces of it after that point."

"Well, in that case it sounds relatively harmless," Leumas offered. "Maybe a hazard to navigation for craft...Dora, check to see if there were any aircraft in the area when it occurred."

"Within a three hundred mile range, there were seventy-five aircraft."

"Who was closest to it?"

"There were several aircraft in a less than a five-mile radius."

"Check and see who they were."

"This will take several minutes as I tie into Earth databases."

"That's fine," Leumas said. "While you're doing that I have another query for you. Quadrant three sounds familiar to me for some reason but I can't remember. Is there information about that area that I am missing?"

"Quadrant three was the area where the final battle took place between Council Leader Greg Carlson and Copolla."

Leumas felt his heartbeat quicken and his stomach take an uneasy turn. "Yes. Yes it was. I don't know how I could have forgotten that. Thank you, Dora. Let me know when you have the other information. Until then, I'd like some private time."

"Yes, Leumas. All sensors going off-line."

Leumas walked over to the observation window and peered out into space. He felt anger, shame, and sadness because he had not remembered what quadrant three represented.

Why won't it stop? As soon as I think I'm over it, putting it behind me, something pops up and reminds me about that day. Maybe I wasn't meant to forget it. After all, I was the one who insisted on Greg taking the reins of the council. Hell, I virtually crammed it down his throat. What would have happened if I had just left things alone? Copolla was defeated, we could have relocated the council anywhere and allowed Earth to go on its own path -- found other life forms to lead it. Then Greg would have been safe and not lost somewhere in space with no physical body. Was I trying to save my own precious reputation or was it the best choice to make? I don't know anymore. All I do know is that I'm so sorry, my dear friend…so sorry.

CHAPTER TEN

"Evil wears a well tailored suit made of deception."
President Edward Samuel

Soren felt as if his body were floating in an ocean, but there wasn't any water and he could breath. His head began to throb as the sadness he was linked to assaulted every nuance of his mind. He knew he would have to push the feelings aside to be able to figure out how he could stop them. *I'm too close here. I need to...back up...*

As the thought blinked through his mind, the darkness began to give way and images of people appeared before him. The forms took shape and he recognized the three people: his mom, Uncle Leumas and Uncle Edward. They were standing around a screen watching something on the monitor. They all looked unhappy and worried.

This is Mommy's dream. I'm watching it like a TV show or a movie.

Soren watched as Uncle Edward walked over to his mom, who was crying, and put his arms around her. "I'm so sorry," he said. "I know nothing I say can change what's happened or how terrible it feels. It was a great sacrifice by a great man."

Soren felt the intensity of her sadness increase as it washed through him. He knew this was what was causing her to have the bad dream. Now he had to figure out how to stop it. *But how?* And then he remembered what he'd done earlier. *Back up more?*

The images shimmered and when they reformed, Soren found himself in a dark corridor. Water dripped from the ceiling and a black substance oozed from between the large stone that comprised the walls and ceilings. Torches provided the only means of light, and the smell of dampness was overpowering. Doors of different shapes and sizes filled the corridor. The door in front of him was open. When he peered through it, he could see the images he had been previously watching. He sensed the sadness oozing its way through the opening. Instinctively, he shut the door, hoping that closing it would stop the feelings from getting out. As he did so, the resounding thud of it closing echoed in the cavernous corridor. All sensations of sadness stopped. Now there was nothing but silence.

Each door must be a dream. If there are bad dreams here, there must be good ones, too. Mommy needs a good dream. But how can I tell which door leads to a good dream?

Soren remembered that when he had been faced with the earlier problems, all he had to do was think about an action. In those two cases, he backed away from what the problem had been. Now he wanted to find the right door to open, one that had a happy moment. *But how?* He had found his way here by following the sad emotions that emanated from the room, so if he thought of good things, happy things, it should take him to where he needed to go. *Right?*

He thought of his mom hugging him and tucking him in at night. Uncle Leumas playing a game of cards with him. Uncle Edward bringing him his favorite ice cream. The images of his dad when he had still been alive...

The dark corridor changed, replaced with another corridor of the same size and layout, but of a completely opposite nature. Although it was also constructed of the same stone materials as the previous one, it was lit from an outside light source that shone brightly through the square holes the size of small windows cut in the stone. There was no moisture here and the air smelled clean and fresh. Everything looked warm and inviting. Doors lined the long corridor, glimmering in the bright sunlight that flooded the area. This was a much better place.

Now to find something good, something Mom would like to make her feel happy. He looked at the numerous doors, trying to decide how to pick one. The corridor appeared to go on forever as he looked down it for some kind of sign of how he should proceed. Finally he decided he would pick one at random...well not exactly at random. He would move down the hall until something gave him a feeling of what he looked for. He believed that something would tell him which door to open.

As he drifted along, he closed his eyes and let his senses search for what he wanted. He knew his mom was most happy when she talked of his dad. So something with them both in it should work nicely. After a few seconds, he felt a...pull, like that of a current in the water, toward one of the doors. It looked like all the other doors, but he was definitely being drawn to it, although he had no idea how. He stopped within a few inches of the door and with his thoughts, he sent one word: *open.*

The door opened soundlessly and an aura of golden yellow light emerged. When it touched his skin, his own thoughts were overwhelmed and replaced with his mother's thoughts. There were no images for him to see. Only emotion. He felt what she felt as warmth settled over her, as if a warm blanket had been placed around her, coddling and caressing every inch of her.

::*You're getting closer,*:: he heard his mother say in her thoughts. :: *I can feel you.*::

::*Same here,*:: another voice answered that Soren recognized as his father's. He had heard several recordings of his father speaking and easily recognized his voice now. They were talking to each other via their thoughts. His father continued. ::*Sarah, how would you feel about getting married?*::

The question caught her off-guard, and her heart filled with surprise and happiness, so much so that she couldn't respond for a few seconds.

::*Is this a proposal, young man?*:: she asked.

::*I believe so,*:: his father responded quickly.

Although these words and emotions were only thought without images, Soren felt his mother imagine how his father was probably blushing with his usual shyness in these matters. ::*Well, you're going to have to deliver your request in person if you want an answer,*:: she teased.

Suddenly a golden aura appeared and it expanded all around him. Soren thought it was like the grand finale of fireworks on the fourth of July. He felt his mother's emotions, the warmth of intense love and caring. It was overpowering and filled her with immense pleasure all at the same time. She had never felt anything so strongly or completely before in her life. Her only thought was to not let it ever end.

As Soren watched, the golden aura dissipated and images appeared. He was watching his mom and dad in a room. His father lay on a bed and his mother sat in a chair next to him, holding his hand. His mom opened her eyes and looked at his dad who now had his eyes open and was looking up at her. She smiled, but Soren saw that her eyes glistened with moisture. *I guess she's happy. There are happy tears like when you laugh too hard at something.*

::*I'll take that to be a 'yes,' then?*:: his dad's thoughts said as he sat up and reached his arms out to her. Smiling, she folded herself into them.

They kissed.

Aw…man, Soren thought. *Yuk!*

::*Well.*:: Soren's father said to his mother. ::*I didn't actually hear you say yes.*::

::*Yes, yes, yes! Of course, I'll marry you!*:: They hugged and--

Suddenly Soren felt a tremendous tugging sensation as he was torn from the room and hurtled through the corridor he had earlier traversed. Faster and faster he went, the images all vanishing, leaving nothing but darkness. He felt he was falling…falling…

* * *

President Edward Samuel, a man of impeccable appearance and physically in good condition for his fifty-two years, cowered in the corner of his secure room at Camp David. Sweat covered his face; his shirt was drenched with it as he tried to resist the infiltration of his mind. He knew he was losing the battle. His mind was slowing giving everything away, all his thoughts peeling away like the layers of an onion. Still he tried to hide that fact from his tormentor because Edward suspected that if he gave in, he would lose any hope of keeping his own consciousness intact.

Edward knew he wasn't crazy. Whatever had gotten into him, into his mind, was not human. It had to be an attack from an alien entity. They were the only ones who had the capability to enter into another person's mind. But he'd never heard Leumas speak of any this powerful. This was not just the influencing of his thoughts. This alien controlled his physical body and was quickly gaining control of his mental capabilities as well. He needed more time to figure out how he could get help. Someone was bound to check on him pretty soon and...

::How noble you are,:: the annoying voice in his mind spoke. ::I remember when I used to think like you. That was a very long time ago when I was young and foolish enough to think things could be different.::

"Who are you? What are you? And why have you come...to me?" The action of speaking to the empty room no longer seemed strange to Edward.

::Who am I, you ask? You already know who I am but you refuse to accept it.::

"What? What do you mean?"

::Never mind for now. You have a very well-organized mind; much information that will be useful to me. There is no point in you trying to stop me from learning certain things, it will all come to me, one way or another.::

"You can't kill me or damage my mind," Edward said defiantly. He felt fairly sure about his statement. It just seemed to make sense that if the entity possessed no physical form itself, it was planning on occupying his.

::Very smart for a human. That is true. But I could make you wish you were dead and that can sometimes be worse than living.::

"I won't let..."

::Don't even attempt to tell me what you won't do! It is irrelevant and you know it. Let me give you an example. Those precious thoughts you have been trying to hide from me about the council and your affiliation with it. That's old news, my friend. I can even replay the memory of your meeting in that coffee shop with Leumas and the other two humans.::

"Common information," Edward said, his voice wavering slightly in his own ears. "That meeting was over seven years ago and was known to many." He tried to hide the fact that he was lying; no one knew about that meeting aside from himself, Greg, Sarah and Leumas.

::*Stubborn, aren't you. You don't want to see the obvious because it frightens you so much, you insignificant piece of life form trash. Okay then, how about this, I can tell you whose DNA exists in young Soren, son of the late Greg Carlson.*::

"I don't get what you're implying," Edward asked. "The answer is obvious. Greg's and..."

::*Wrong answer! Mine!*::

"Yours? I don't think so." Edward found his muscles in his body tightening as he sat upright in the corner.

::*It's not exactly common knowledge that Greg is my son. Is it? Only you, my good friend Leumas, who I can't wait to see again, Greg, and the woman knew. Isn't that correct?*::

"No! That would mean..." Edward's head begin to spin. How could that be? He was dead. He died when the ship exploded.

::*That's right. Congratulations. You are in the presence of the only true leader of the galaxy. Don't you feel special?*::

"Copolla? No... No... No..." Edward's mind nearly went blank with shock. Could it be possible the alien entity that had invaded his body was the feared and sadistic alien Copolla? "You're dead..." The ramifications of Copolla still being alive caused Edward to relinquish the guard he held on the remaining areas of his mind. Before he realized what had happened, Copolla shot in and claimed final victory.

::*Ah...thank you. See how easy that was. Now you take a nice nap, a very long nap. I don't want to hear you again,*:: Copolla said in a voice that was frothing with victory. ::*Oh now, isn't this interesting...you really were keeping secrets from me.*::

Edward stared blankly in front of him as a lone tear shimmered and slid down his cheek. Slowly he closed his eyes, as what remained of his mind was vanquished from his consciousness.

"How appropriate I was given the human president's body to inhabit. It made everything so easy to accomplish...and I didn't have to kill anybody, well, at least in the beginning."

Copolla

The ringing of the telephone woke him. Edward, now totally in Copolla's control, opened his eyes and slowly stood. His legs wobbled unsteadily. His entire body ached as he moved. As soon as he could, he reached for the desk to support himself as he continued on toward the chair. When he was close enough, he let his body drop into the chair as he exhaled strongly from the exertion. With a shaky hand, he reached for the receiver. "Yes?"

"Mr. President, you have a call from the Secretary of State. Shall I patch it through?"

"When's dinner? I need to eat something," the President replied, ignoring the question posed to him.

"Er...dinner is ready now if you would like, Mr. President."

"Fine, then I want it now."

"Mr. President, what shall I tell the Secretary?"

"Tell him I'm eating."

"Yes, sir."

Copolla hung up the phone. As he stood, he tested his legs before moving. They felt slightly stronger but not much. He needed food and water to replace what that fool had wasted. He paused at a mirror and stared at himself. Shaking his head, he cursed his luck. His shape was puny compared to his old form of over seven feet in height and several hundred pounds.

"Oh well, beggars can't be choosy, now can they?" he said to his reflection in the mirror. "That doesn't mean I can't have any fun. And I *am* going to have some fun. There is some unfinished business I need to attend to. My son may be dead, but I have a grandson I need to visit."

* * *

Leumas turned away from the observation window from which he had been watching the stars and thinking about Greg's death. He knew he had to get on with things and just accept what had happened, no matter how difficult and painful those memories may be. There could be no changing of the promise he had made to Greg to keep his ideals alive and moving forward. Plus there were young Soren and Sarah to think of.

"Dora?"

"Yes, Leumas, shall I turn sensors back to active mode?"

"Yes...and thank you. I needed a few moments to gather my thoughts. Let's get back to what you discovered. Earlier you said there were traces of unnatural elements in the burst in quadrant three. What did you mean?"

"There are elements that would not be considered a natural part of the electrical makeup of such a disturbance."

"Explain?"

"Please look at the monitor above the main control console," she said.

Leumas turned in that direction. A spectrographic image appeared on the display.

Dora continued. "The normal characteristics of energy found in a natural occurring electromagnetic burst are defined by the color red."

Leumas watched as the majority of the image shifted to red in color leaving a smaller portion of golden color spikes. "What are those?"

"Unknown without further examination."

"Run a comparison with all known electrical occurrences."

"Yes, Leumas. It should only take a few minutes."

"Good. What have you found about the air space activity in that area? Did anyone report anything about the disturbance?"

"The nearest aircraft was a government jet and fighter escort belonging to the United States. The flight designation is Air Force One."

"That the President's plane...Edward. Was he on that flight?"

"Yes. The plane was returning from a Global Conference in Germany."

"Did the pilots log any reports about the incident?"

"The plane and its escort experienced turbulence for a few seconds. There is no other mention of any abnormalities."

"Well, that doesn't sound like it was anything too bad. I'll give Edward a call and see if he can add anything to it. Dora, I'm beginning to think we might be chasing something that doesn't need to be. What about..."

"Excuse me, Leumas," Dora interrupted. "I have the results of the comparison of the electrical characteristics."

"Go ahead."

"I believe that the data obtained by the analysis of the disturbance may be flawed."

"Why do think that?"

"Because the highest probability of a match is unexplainable."

"What do you mean?"

"The type of energy has been identified as neural energy or brainwaves; that which is responsible for the conduction of energy into and from the brain. Its presence in a disturbance such as this is highly questionable."

"Is there nothing else that matches this type of energy?"

"No."

"So you think the data is flawed?"

"Most probably."

"You say probably. So you're not saying that it's positively not this neural energy?"

"I must re-examine the data."

"Dora...just for the heck of it, let's say it was neural energy. What would that mean?"

"That would be speculating on a broad basis, Leumas. I could not verify any of the information derived from that hypothesis."

"Understood. Just humor me."

"As you wish. If we return to our earlier supposition that this was a doorway opening between two areas of space."

"Yes," Leumas said, drawing it out to get Dora to move faster.

"Adding another supposition that a mode of travel existed that could transport the energy that comprises an entity life thought process through this doorway…"

"Would equal the arrival of something or someone," Leumas added before Dora could speak again.

* * *

"Balance," the caretaker said in response to the question Greg had posed about Soren. The caretaker turned away as if searching for something in the image of the landscape of the Planet Acuba.

Greg was about to say something again about the caretaker's standard answer to everything, this balance, but didn't see the point in it. He was beginning to believe the caretaker didn't know anything else on the issue, or he was very good at hiding it if he did. But there was another issue, something else here. Something to do with Soren...

"Caretaker?" Greg called to him. The caretaker turned. Greg recognized uneasiness in the image of his own face. "There is something about Soren you're not telling me, isn't there?"

"I tell you what I can," he said. His eyes moved side to side nervously. "But there are things that you must concede will happen."

"What do you mean?"

"You know what you are, a mixture of both alien and human, a hybrid from which certain powers have arisen."

"Yes. Through Copolla's scheming, I am what I am. I cannot change that. Nor can Sarah. She is what she is. I also understand that no other human on Earth can ever be altered to be like us since Copolla eradicated the gene in humans that allowed the recombination. But it also is because of those powers that I was able to defeat Copolla."

"That is somewhat correct."

"Somewhat? What do you mean?"

"You said that no one else on Earth could ever be altered."

"That's correct. Copolla can be very thorough in the most devious ways. He sent a council probe to Earth that eradicated the inactive gene in humans so the results could never be reproduced. He wanted a monopoly in me. He thought he could convince me to join him in his campaign to take over the galaxy."

"But you're forgetting your son."

"My son..." Greg realized what direction the conversation was moving. Soren was the unknown. What powers would he possess? What characteristics would he have?

"Your son could upset the balance if he possesses powers greater than the sum," the caretaker said.

"Greater than the sum? What do you mean?"

"If he exceeds the powers of both you and Sarah, how will it be controlled? Will it be for the good? If he does possess some of Copolla's genetic traits, how will..."

"As I do," Greg interrupted. "I must possess some of his qualities also and I have not used them in an evil way as he has."

"Yes, however you did not realize your power until a much later age. Your mind had a chance to develop and you were predisposed to the world. You knew and understood of right and wrong and good and evil."

"All of that can be taught."

"To a mind that is not already conscious of the power it possesses, I would agree. But that is not the case here."

"You're making some pretty large assumptions. How do you know they will be correct?"

"Correct or incorrect, my position is not the judgmental one. But you must understand and be prepared: Soren is the next generation. He is not only *your son;* he can be a vital link in the future of the galaxy, whether for good or evil. There are no assurances as to what he shall become in this new being. Until his powers have been realized, he will have to be watched."

"Watched?"

"Yes. To see how much and what kind of powers manifest themselves within him. To see what traits he possesses and how he uses them."

"And if you are not happy with what you see? Then what?" Greg asked.

"Balance is to be maintained. No matter what," the caretaker said in a most assured voice as he locked his gaze upon Greg.

Greg stared at his own face, searching for some sign of optimism, or that the decision would be a carefully chosen one. He saw nothing that reflected either, as the words reverberated in his thoughts. *Balance is to be maintained. No matter what.*

CHAPTER TWELVE

"I was never so scared for Soren as I was the first time he entered my thoughts; however, the sharing of thought with your child is one of the most intimate things one can do."

Sarah McClendon

::*Yes, yes, yes! Of course, I'll marry you!*:: Sarah said as she hugged Greg. She felt his arms wrap around her and squeeze her body next to his. She could remember the smell of his cologne and she felt herself smile, then...it was gone.

The dream of her and Greg began to fade. As she passed from her dream state to the one just before waking, Sarah immediately felt a deep presence in her thoughts and mind. The intrusion scared her. She jerked awake and sat up

Soren sat on the floor next to her, his arms and hands outstretched as if they had been touching something and it had been removed from his grasp, leaving his arms fixed in that position. She saw something glisten on the edge of his fingertips. She ran her finger along his palms and fingers and found they were moist with perspiration. She felt something on her skin at her temples and automatically reached up to find droplets of moisture running down the sides of her face. Looking back at his hands and the moisture they contained, she assumed that had been where Soren's outstretched hands had been in place.

His eyes were closed but she could see rapid movement underneath his eyelids. He was dreaming, she thought at first, but his awkward position indicated it was something more than that. *He's been touching me*, she thought and then remembered that she had been dreaming of Greg. But it was not the horrible dream that she relived often, the one where he defeated Copolla and lost his mind link to his body. Instead, it was the dream where Greg had proposed...one of the happiest moments of her life. A dream she had not had for a very long time. *Could it have been Soren?*

"Soren?" she called. He gave no response. "Soren! Soren, can you hear me?" Sarah said as she grasped him by his shoulders and shook him gently. "Soren? Can you hear me?" Where she grasped him by the shoulders, her hands felt his sweat-soaked pajamas. He also felt warm, as if he had a high fever. "Soren, can you hear me? Wake up!"

His arms fell from the stationary position they had been in and made a slapping sound as they hit against the sides of his small chest. His eyes fluttered open and shut. "Mommy? Is that you?" He slowly opened his eyes. "Hi, Mom," he said. "I'm really thirsty -- cold, too."

"Come and sit up here," she said as she lifted him. "I'll get you some water." She situated him on the sofa and wrapped him in the blanket. She quickly went to the kitchen, filled a large glass full of water, brought it back into the living room, and sat next to him. "Here," she said, handing him the glass of water while still holding onto it. "Drink."

Soren grasped the glass with both hands, his palms pressed atop Sarah's hand. His skin still felt warm, but it seemed to have faded some. He drank the entire contents of the glass.

"Let's get you into some dry clothes." She refilled the glass and gave it back to him. "You stay here and don't move, okay?"

"Okay."

Sarah went to his bedroom. As she opened drawers to get things for him to put on, the seriousness of what he had done settled over her. *How could he do that? It's one thing to place thoughts into another mind, but he had been able to retrieve a dream and play it as if it were a movie in a theater.* She felt tears of fear threaten to invade her, but she forced them back...for the moment.

She returned with the clothes and helped him dress.

Should I call the doctor? His temperature seems to be returning to normal. No. They would ask questions and Soren might say something about his newfound ability and that might arouse suspicion. As long as he's alright...

When he was dressed and had had enough water to drink, she placed him back under the blanket and sat next to him. She traced his forehead with her fingers, combing his black hair back. Finally she spoke. "Soren, what did you do? I know you were in my thoughts. I sensed you there."

"You were sleeping and having a bad dream. I fixed it."

"How?"

"I made the bad time go away. I found something you liked, something to make you happy. It did, didn't it?"

"Yes, it did. But how did you find it?"

"I followed it."

"Followed it? How did you do that?"

"I just closed my eyes and followed the...the feeling I guess."

Followed a feeling. He must possess a heightened sensitivity along with his mental capabilities. "Well, I don't want you doing that. You see how thirsty and wet it made you. It isn't healthy for you right now. Maybe later when you learn how to do it so that it doesn't make you so tired."

"Okay," he agreed. "No more bad dreams for you."

"No more bad dreams," she said and sincerely hoped it was true.

* * *

"Leumas, I would remind you that nothing is substantiated by any proof in these suppositions," Dora said.

"I understand that, Dora. But it does sound rather intriguing, doesn't it? Traveling across dimensions?"

"All of this is purely hypothetical," she answered.

"I know it is and I can see you're not going to go out on any limbs, are you?"

"If you mean agree to this theory, no," she said flatly.

"Well, I want you to keep examining the possibilities. Link back to the archives on Zire and see if there's anything there on it. I also want you to continue monitoring for any reoccurrences."

"Understood. I also have the data you requested earlier about the group that is initiating the council move back to Zire."

Leumas frowned at the mention of that issue. He felt his anger notch up a few degrees. The diversion of the electromagnetic disturbance had flushed the thoughts from his mind and the disrespect he felt the subject brought to Greg's memory. He tried to couch his demeanor so that he could objectively evaluate the information that Dora would give him. "Go ahead," he said.

"The group formally consists of six members. The delegates from Omega 214, Sarusa 121, Alpha Quintilian 187, Cosmora 7, Norina 34 and Zire. Corin is the chair of the group and the central contact for issues. There is an unknown amount of followers, but statistically speaking, I believe the number is less than fifty. Their symbolic argument for the movement is that the council should be relocated back to Zire due to the historic significance of the planet, the birthplace of the council. They agree that at the time of the council relocation to Earth, the reasons justified the actions. But now, with Greg Carlson, the former leader of the council gone, and with the elimination of any potential threat to the organization, they see no reason to remain on Earth."

Leumas shifted uncomfortably in his chair as he digested the information. The reasons stated were somewhat true. Yes, Zire was truly the home of the council. And yes, the main reason for relocation was to re-establish the council on a neutral world to ensure there would be no favoritism. As far as the potential threat, he wouldn't agree. Sure things were going okay, but he still had a feeling that something was... what? He didn't know. It was just a feeling.

"On the spiritual side of the debate," Dora continued, "there is also the position that the former leader's vision of the future was incorrect. He stated that his successors would be a boy and girl. Only the male child exists and there is no chance…"

"I don't want to hear this!" Leumas shouted. He rose from his chair and paced. His cheeks flushed red with anger.

"Leumas, I understand your emotional conflict with this issue. But this is an important part of understanding the reasoning behind their motives. It cannot be ignored if you are going to try and sway opinion of those members who believe in this."

"I understand that, Dora," Leumas sighed. "But if these religious fanatics believe that, why can't they believe in the return of Greg? If he came back, then another child is a possibility. Then the vision he told us of is also true, the council would remain as he saw it, on Earth and safe from harm."

"I don't have a precise answer for you, Leumas. If I were to speculate, I would suggest that in the case of life forms, perhaps some things are easier to believe than others. If the two children were here, perhaps the concern over this issue would not be happening."

Leumas looked warily at the main sensor for Dora's input. "Why would you say that?" he asked.

"Then part of the vision would have been fulfilled and lead to credibility of the remaining part."

"Yes, I suppose so." Leumas looked away from the data input sensor as he felt the guilt from earlier resurface.

"Leumas, are you all right?" Dora asked.

"Yes, why?"

"My sensors recorded a spike in your heart beat and respiration levels."

"I'm fine, Dora. It's just this issue. It doesn't sit well with me," Leumas said as he focused on slowing his heartbeat and respiration.

"I understand."

"Thank you, Dora," he said, then changed the subject. "I need to speak with President Edward Samuel. Can you give me a secure channel please?"

"It will be my pleasure."

"Humans are frail and weak, they don't deserve too live unless it is under my rule and of course...only if I am in a good mood that day."
Copolla

Such an insignificant planet, Copolla thought inside President Edward Samuel's body as he chewed the meat of the second large T-bone steak he'd had the cooks prepare. Now that he was in control of the body, he tried to rationalize what had happened that led to his mind being here, in this poor excuse of a physical specimen.

I remember the battle, explosions all around. My wonderful son turned my own fleet against me; pretty sneaky of the little bastard...something I would have done. He smiled wryly as he chewed a piece of fat. *Too bad he's dead; such a waste of talent. We could have ruled the galaxy together.*

After the last explosion, everything went dark and now...I'm here. According to my friend's thoughts, six Earth standard years have passed. I don't understand it, but it's better than being dead. Yes, there will be difficulties with this body, but given the alternatives, it will do. Terror can emanate in many different ways, and it will do just as well from this form as it did from my other.

Copolla possessed the full cognizance of Edward's mind. His thoughts, his memories, were all there for Copolla to examine at his leisure. People, his staff members, what current affairs he had been working on. While he ate, he perused them to learn what he needed to in order to behave and act in a manner that would avoid any outward displays of aberrant behavior that might attract attention. He needed time to formulate what he was going to do.

"Mr. President?" a voice called, retrieving Copolla from his thoughts.

Copolla turned toward the sound and saw a man dressed in a uniform. His mind told him this was Major John Berman of the United States Air Force.

"Yes, Major," he answered, fighting back his initial reaction to being disturbed while he ate. "What is it?"

"Mr. President. Your private COMSAT station has an incoming call," he answered, still standing at attention.

::COMSAT, what's that? Edward...is there something you're trying to hide from me? You know you can't do that. Give it to me! What's COMSAT?:: he demanded with his mind. In a fraction of a second, he found the information. *::COMSAT is the secure communications channel*

for the United Council of Developing Worlds. Only two people had access to it. Sarah and Leumas.::

"Thank you, Major. I'll take the call in my office."

"Yes, sir," the major barked and hastily departed.

Copolla returned to his private office. He placed his hand on the scanning device outside the door. The white light moved slowly up, then down. *Antique devices!* The door locking mechanism clicked open and Copolla entered.

His attention was immediately drawn to the phone on his desk with the flashing light. He debated not answering it, but that would attract unnecessary attention because he knew Edward always answered it without delay. *I must proceed carefully,* he thought as he picked it up and placed the receiver to his ear.

"Yes," he answered.

"Edward, this is Leumas. How are you?"

Copolla felt his stomach tighten and his anger flare at the sound of the voice. He violently opened and closed the fist of his free hand. *LEUMAS. You piece of alien trash! I should have killed you when I had the chance!*

"Leumas. I'm fine, my good friend. It's so nice to hear from you," he said as he fought to control his words. His free hand reached for the pencils that sat within a coffee cup that stated: "Fishermen have the best rods." He picked up the first pencil and snapped it in the palm of his hand. He picked up another.

"Same here, Edward. I know you're probably busy so I won't keep you long."

"I always have time for you, Leumas."

SNAP, another pencil shattered. *Calm down...you need to milk this proverbial cow. Find out what he knows that you can use.*

"Tell me about your flight from Germany."

"What do you mean?"

"My observations show that you encountered some form of electromagnetic disturbance shortly after take-off. Do you remember that?"

"Oh, yes," Copolla answered. *Yes...my arrival.* "It was nothing, just some turbulence. It gave us a good shake and bounce there for a few seconds."

"Nothing unusual?"

"Didn't I just..." he began and caught himself before he went too far. *Leumas, you're such an idiot! Why do I have to repeat myself!*

"Edward?" Leumas asked.

"Oh, sorry," Copolla quickly said. "One of my assistants brought me the wrong thing. It's hard to find good help these days." He made an effort to add humor into his voice. "But no, there was nothing unusual. Like I said, just a little bumpy."

"Well, that's good then. I just wanted to check to see if everything was okay."

"Fine...Fine. How about you? Anything interesting happening?"

Interesting. Isn't that one of those oxymoron statements when talking to an idiot? Well, it certainly fits the situation, doesn't it? How the hell did you ever manage to defeat me?

"Interesting?" Leumas said. "I don't know if I would call it that. Apparently there is a movement to relocate the council back to Zire. I had heard of it earlier but didn't give it much thought. Now, though, it seems to be gathering some speed and I'm concerned that a radical element may develop. I'm keeping an eye on it."

"Who's the leader. Is it anyone I -- you know?"

"It's the delegate from Zire, his name is Corin."

Copolla smiled at the mention of the name. He knew Corin. Yes, he knew him quite well. If he was acting up, Copolla knew someone else was pulling his strings. Corin didn't have the balls for it and he felt quite sure he knew who was leading Corin. And now that he knew about this COMSAT, which was obviously of council technology, he could make some calls of his own and find out more. "Let me know if I can do anything to help."

"Sure will. I'm heading back to Earth now. Will you be at the council headquarters?"

"In the next day or so," Copolla answered. "I've got a few things of my own I need to set into motion."

* * *

Greg saw nothing in his own face of the caretaker that reflected either any sign of optimism, or that the decision about Soren would be a carefully chosen one. The words reverberated in Greg's thoughts: *Balance is to be maintained--no matter what.*

For Christ sakes! All they care about is their precious balance, Greg thought as he stood. Was the caretaker being pig-headed or was it that his matching physical appearance to his own, the act of arguing with himself, was becoming more and more frustrating?

I don't understand their concerns about Soren. He's only a child...how can they be certain that...

"Nothing is for certain," the caretaker said, startling him.

Greg looked at him, studying his own face. "You're monitoring my thoughts?"

"All thoughts here are...available to be heard," he replied.

"I see," Greg said. "I forgot that's all we are. This appearance of a physical body was deceiving. Perhaps it was meant to be." The caretaker did not answer. Greg moved on. "You said nothing is for certain. What about your precious balance?"

"Balance is the realignment of the results caused by an event or particular situation. Events are things that happen. You yourself once said that there were only two things that a person could be sure of, life and death."

"Yes, I did," Greg acknowledged. He remembered the time he had said it; it was when he was being questioned about his visions of the future.

"Do you still agree with that?"

"Yes," Greg said assuredly.

"And the vision you spoke of? The legacy of your children taking over the United Council for Developing Worlds, do you still believe that?"

Greg thought for a moment. He remembered the alien known to him as Vague, who had come back through time to teach him how to project his mind to defeat Copolla. His own actions had obviously altered the outcome. The Earth had been saved instead of destroyed. But Greg couldn't help wondering of the vision he had seen of Earth and even his own life. Would all those be altered now as well? He wasn't sure.

"Yes, I do," Greg answered, his voice sounding more hopeful rather than confident. "So...your intervention must have been included somehow in my vision, or else how could it come true? If I was killed in space, then it wouldn't be going to happen. Correct?"

"You understand you must return Copolla's energy?" The caretaker asked, ignoring Greg's question.

"Yes, but how..."

"It will all become clear to you."

"When am I going back?" Greg asked.

"Soon. There shall be no further communication on the subject."

"What is..."

::Remember. Nothing is for certain -- except what you truly believe. The key to all things is balance...::

Suddenly everything around Greg became unsubstantial as it faded into nothingness.

"There can be no greater fear then the thought of one's child being harmed."

Sarah McClendon

Sarah was just about ready to doze off when her personal communicator sounded.

"Yes," she said.

"The medical monitoring system has determined that Soren Carlson is experiencing physical distress. Bodily functions are outside of normal parameters. Should medical personnel be notified?"

"Yes!" she screamed as she rose from her bed and dashed toward Soren's room. *What the hell is going on now?*

When she entered Soren's room, she found him lying in bed, drenched in sweat. It reminded her of his earlier physical appearance when she had awakened and found him next to her. She placed her hand on his forehead and felt the extreme warmth. High fever.

"Soren? Wake up, Soren."

Sarah watched nervously as Soren opened his eyes and stared at her as if he were looking through her, as if she wasn't even there, as if he were somewhere else.

"Nothing is for certain -- except what you truly believe," he said softly and then closed his eyes.

"Soren? What did you say? What do you mean?"

The announcing of someone at the door interrupted Sarah.

"Who..." she began, then remembered she had instructed the computer to send medical personnel. "Enter," she cried, knowing that the voice command would open the door. She waited for a few seconds and then called, "In here!"

She heard footsteps slap against the carpeting and turned to see the medical team enter. One was tall, a Corsican, a member of an aquatic race with a humanoid body but a fish-like head. The other was a Serian, a reptilian-like race, who possessed a stocky build and scaly skin with a head that reminded Sarah of a dragon. Seeing the two of them, Sarah selfishly wished she had a human doctor within the council area.

"What has happened?" the Corsican asked.

"I don't know. The computer monitoring system alerted me and I came in and found him like this."

The Serian scanned Soren's body with a wand-like device and then handed it to the Corsican, who studied the results.

"It appears the young child has had some form of physical exertion. His body requires electrolyte stimulus."

"What?" Sarah asked.

"His body fluids are unbalanced. He has loss much of his fluids and needs to replenish them."

"Oh," Sarah said, remembering his earlier thirst. "It's not serious..."

"No. Is this the first time this has happened?"

Sarah hesitated before answering. If she said no, that might indicate that something was wrong with Soren or that something else was happening to him. She didn't want rumors to begin, not now when he was just beginning to realize he had some type of power.

"Yes. It's the first time," she said.

"I will give him an injection to help restore his electrolyte balance. Keep him in bed and give him plenty of fluids. The fever will dissipate over the next thirty minutes. If anything else happens, please notify me."

"Yes," Sarah agreed, as she watched the Corsican give Soren the injection. "Yes, I'll call you if anything happens. Thank you."

The two aliens left Soren's bedroom and Sarah listened until she heard the sound of the door to her quarters shut. She returned her attention to Soren.

"Soren? Soren, can you hear me?"

"Mom?" he asked softly as his eyes fluttered open.

"How do you feel?"

"Tired."

"You need to rest. The doctor gave you something to help. Do you remember what happened?"

"When?"

"What caused you to become so drained? You said something about nothing being for certain, except what you truly believe?"

"I don't remember," he said and drifted off to sleep.

Sarah remained sitting on his bed and watching him as he slept. She wished she could have gotten him to tell her something that might give a clue to this second occurrence of exhaustion, but she would have to wait.

But that wasn't all she wanted an answer to. There was something that bothered her about what he had said. *Nothing is for certain, except what you truly believe.* She could have sworn she had heard that statement before. *Nothing is for certain, except what you truly believe.*

***

Ambassador Alpha looked over the reports of the unofficial analysis of the council members in regards to the issue of moving the council back to the planet Zire. He was not satisfied. Less than one third agreed with the effort.

He lifted himself out of the chair, his back protesting, reminding him that he wasn't getting any younger. *If only things had worked out...it wouldn't be like this now. I wouldn't have to be groveling to get things done. I would be a life form of status under the old regime.*

His short, pudgy body looked like a mound of flesh rather than having a definitive shape. He was hairless and possessed four tentacle-covered arms. His head contained four eyes and a large mouth, which almost covered the entire circumference of his head. What he lacked in physical body, he made up for in brain. He was very intelligent. He could develop plans and devise methods to get things accomplished. However, what he lacked was the strength or will to carry them out -- it just wasn't in his nature to do so.

This fault led council members to ignore him in an unofficial and even an official capacity at times, even though he was one of the original council members going back under the rule of Copolla. But that had worked to his advantage at the time. It had enabled him to devise Copolla's plans of personal conquest without attracting attention from any of the other council members. Even Leumas' private detail that still searched for signs of Copolla's influence didn't pay him a second look, even though they had located some of the life forms that he had used to carry out his plans.

Copolla had been the only life form that treated him as if he were important. But Alpha wasn't stupid or blind to Copolla's intent; he knew he was being used to mastermind the plans that Copolla wanted. But that didn't matter. With Copolla's backing, things got accomplished and when it was all done, he was to have had a position that would have commanded respect from everyone. Copolla had purposely left him out of any interaction on his last attempt to take over the council and destroy Earth. He said he wanted him safe for the next phase that would be crucial. Alpha's mound of flesh swelled with pride as he remembered those words from Copolla. But his plans of grandeur had been ruined when Copolla perished in the battle. The only consolation was that the leader, Greg Carlson, had not returned whole. He was only an empty shell of what had once been the leader.

Call it misguided respect for Copolla, or just picking up where he'd left off, Alpha had taken on the role of coming up with methods to upset the balance of the current council lead by Leumas and the trivial

Earth woman. He saw this movement to go back to Zire as a chisel that he could use to cause division amongst the members and destroy the vision that Greg Carlson had promised to everyone. Once the chaos and confusion settled, Alpha would approach whomever stepped in to take over and then he would use them to get what he wanted: wealth and respect. By using Ambassador Corin, he had already accomplished the first part, which he had to admit was ingenious even for him. There was no movement to return to Zire -- he had created it to be a thorn in the side of Leumas and the Earth woman.

This second part of the plan was posing more difficulty because of the sensitivity of the issue and it required...

His personal communicator on his desk beeped.

"Yes."

"You have an incoming message on private channel Z4," the voice of a computer told him.

Alpha felt an uncontrollable shiver coarse through his body. Channel Z4 was the channel reserved only for one person to contact him. It hadn't been used in over six years because that person was dead.

CHAPTER FIFTEEN

"Salvation only comes from one place — one's own mind."
Greg Carlson

Greg plummeted through darkness feeling isolated and alone. There was no cognitive perception in his thoughts of any type—only the fear that he might be dying.

How will I get back?

::*Follow the path.*:: a voice called to his thoughts.

:: *What path?*:: Greg thought back.

::*The path you created in life.*::

::*The path I created in life? I don't know what you mean!*::

::*Remember and believe the things you care for the most.*::

::*Memories. Do you mean memories?*::

::*In simplistic terms that you can understand…yes. If you follow them, they will lead you to the path which shall return you.*::

::*And if I don't?"* Greg asked.

::*You must.*::

"Trust only those that are close to you — the closer, the better."

Leumas

Leumas stepped out of the shuttle as he arrived at the main UCDW compound. He spotted a familiar shape: Clorice, one of Sarah's personal assistants, and also his handpicked bodyguard for her. She was a petite female, humanoid in appearance, with short black hair and light blue skin. To the casual observer, she might seem young, perhaps twenty Earth years of age, possibly fulfilling a position of personal assistant. However, the inhabitants of Beta-7, Clorice's home world, possessed unique features. Their body mass was inversely related to their strength and stamina; the smaller and lighter, the greater the physical strength they possessed. The relationship applied to their mental capabilities as well; the younger they were, the higher their reasoning capabilities. These two attributes -- strength and a high analytical ability -- made them the perfect bodyguards.

"Clorice, how are you?" Leumas asked, wondering why she was here. "Is there something wrong?"

"I am well, Co-leader Leumas," she responded. "Co-leader Sarah Carlson asked me to meet you and wishes that you stop by their living quarters as soon as possible."

"What's going on?"

"I am not aware of anything, but she has canceled all of her appointments today. I suspect perhaps there is a problem with Soren."

"Soren? What's happened?" Leumas' mind began racing with possibilities of what may have happened.

"The medical team was summoned last night to her quarters. According to the log, they were for Soren, not her. Given that information, it appears logical that she wishes to speak to you about the incident."

"Thanks, Clorice. Well done," he said as he hurried off, worrying what could have happened with Soren to cause Sarah to cancel her appointments. In all the time he'd known her, she'd never cancelled anything dealing with the workings of the council, not even after Greg's death. As Greg had been like a brother to him, Sarah was a sister. He loved them both dearly, along with Soren.

When he arrived at her door he pressed the announcement button. The door slid opened. Leumas immediately noticed Sarah's haggard appearance. She had dark circles under her eyes and her eyes looked red, as if she hadn't been sleeping.

"Sarah, what's wrong?"

"Come in, we don't want to discuss this out here," she said and turned away before he could ask anything else.

Leumas stepped inside. The door slid closed.

"It's Soren," she said.

"What's happened?" he asked. "Is he all right?"

"He's resting right now. It just seems like it happened all at once..."

"What's happened, Sarah? He's alright, isn't he?"

"Yes, I think so..."

"Then what?"

Sarah paused for a few seconds, appearing to be trying to decide where to start.

"Why don't we sit down?" Leumas offered as he gently grasped her elbow and led her to the sofa. "Do you want something to drink?"

She shook her head slowly. "I'm okay."

"Take your time, start from the beginning, and tell me everything." He gently lifted her hand and placed it into his, then placed his other hand on top of it.

"Soren has the mind abilities," she blurted. "He can do everything we can."

"What? I haven't sensed anything from him. When did this happen?"

"The other day. I thought I felt something, another presence trying to assert itself."

"He was exploring?"

"That's exactly what I thought," she agreed. "Then, last night he was having a dream or something so I came in to see him. He communicated to me telepathically and almost knocked me off of my feet."

"What?" Leumas asked, surprised. He knew that both Sarah and Greg had received strong telepathic powers from their genetic mix, but he couldn't fathom that a six-year-old could already possess a greater force.

"He's extremely powerful. And then early this morning, he...he came into my mind and was able to alter my dreams."

"Alter your dreams?"

"He's able to perceive what I'm feeling or what I'm thinking about and then enter into my thoughts and alter or change them."

"What was happening when he did this?"

Sarah explained about the dream she was having and the way Soren had entered her mind and replaced that dream with another. When she finished, Leumas sat silently, rubbing his face with his hands. When he looked up at her, he noticed that she looked a little better after talking about it.

"Well, we're going to have to run him through some tests and see if we can identify how strong he actually is."

"He must be very strong, because I have a natural block that prevents anyone from trying to enter my mind," she said pointedly. "Remember?"

Leumas smiled briefly at the memory. "I remember. You kicked me out without any trouble." He also remembered the mind strength that Greg possessed: the strongest telepath he had ever known and he also possessed the ability to allow his mind to travel through space. If Soren possessed even more power...it was hard to even comprehend.

"Leumas, I don't want anyone to know about this yet," she said, as she reached out and touched his arm.

"I understand. The ramifications of this kind of power could be frightening, especially if there is a problem of controlling it. If he can alter a person's thoughts, he can change their entire perception of reality. Influencing allows us to place individual thoughts in another person's mind, but his power goes way beyond that."

Leumas thought about the mind powers Copolla had used against him when he was captured on Acuba. Would some council members make the same association to Soren? Would they consider him a threat because of that power?

"Did you see or experience anything else?"

"He was extremely tired and dehydrated after he manipulated my thoughts. Then last night, he appeared even more affected. I don't know if it was a delayed effect of what he did or what? Somehow the power appears to be affecting his body chemistry in some way and depletes it."

"We'll have to get a doctor to keep an eye on him. We'll let him rest the rest of today and start tomorrow on testing."

"A trusted doctor," she added. "I had one here this morning. I didn't tell him anything about what was happening. He gave Soren a shot. The fever dropped and now Soren's resting comfortably. I didn't want any stories or rumors to get started."

"Good idea. Was there anything else?"

Sarah rose from the sofa and slowly paced around it. Her head remained bent over as her eyes remained fixed on the carpet.

"Sarah?"

"There was something else. He said something that was...very odd and it scared me."

"What was it?" He saw Sarah's eyes shimmer as moisture crowded their way into them. "What was it?" he asked again.

"He said...Greg was in the dream and that he thinks he's...he's coming home soon."

"Sarah, you..."

"I want to believe that, Leumas!" she shouted. Tears streamed down her face as she continued to shout. "I need to believe that! He has to come back...do you hear me? He has to come back!"

"I know, Sarah. I know." Leumas placed his hands on her shoulders and gently pulled her toward him. She began to cry uncontrollably. "Shhh. Sarah, I would like to believe that as well. But we don't know if Soren's dreams mean that or not."

"They have to...they have to...." she cried.

Leumas hugged and gently rocked her from side to side. He wondered if there could be any truth about the young boy's dream. Deep down inside, he could only hope.

***

Alpha's tentacle hung poised over the button to receive the call on the Z4 frequency reserved for Copolla. As was his nature, he was unsure of what to do. He knew Copolla was dead. There was no doubt he and his attack fleet had been destroyed six years ago. But...the Z4 frequency had many safeguards assigned to it. Passwords and coded entries were required to access it in order to even place a call. Passwords could be found eventually -- any worthwhile computer, if given the time, would be able to achieve the correct combination -- but Copolla had even thought of that. He had designed an evolving password that changed with each use. So, if the secret had died with Copolla, and there was no way another life form could use it, then who could be calling?

"Incoming call on frequency..."

"I know that!" Alpha yelled at the computer. "What am I going to do? Maybe it's a trap? Perhaps Leumas and his agents are probing the frequencies looking for hidden and coded channels? What am I going to do?" His heartbeat quickened as he felt a panic attack looming over him. "Can't think..."

"Frequency verification protocol available," the computer offered in response to his question.

"What?" Alpha asked as he tried to remember what the term meant.

"Frequency verification protocol available," the computer repeated.

"Specify?"

"The channel is secure. There are no indications that routing protocol has been tampered with. Receiving source is hidden from caller. Verification options include coded queries."

"Queries?"

"You may ask questions in order to achieve verification of the caller."

"Yes...yes. I forgot," he stammered. He had let his emotions get away from him to the point of not remembering the security precautions he had designed and put into place. He could ask a question or a series of questions to the caller while remaining hidden from any detection sources.

"Query to sender," Alpha said as he tried to think of what he would ask, something that only he and Copolla would know.

Alpha slipped back into a calm analytical mode. He closed his eyes and thought back through the years, searching for something very particular he could use.

"Standing by," the computer reminded him.

"Query to sender. Describe our business arrangement in exactly the same way you expressed it when it was formed."

A smile appeared on Alpha's face as he completed the query. He remembered exactly the words used that day. But more explicitly, he remembered the affect those words had had over him. Several seconds passed as he waited impatiently for a response.

"Incoming response," the computer said.

"Display on my screen," Alpha commanded.

He turned toward the small screen implanted inside his desk and watched as the words appeared. He read:

A merger of the best mind and the strength to see it through. A partnership to be the beginning of what surely is to come. In secrecy we shall conjure and move the elements that would resist. To those who fail or disobey, death shall greet them like a long lost friend.

The chilling affect of the words, exactly as he had remembered them, stunned Alpha. They had been spoken to him directly by Copolla in a rare moment the two of them had been together. When he and Copolla had worked together in the past, Alpha had only met privately with Copolla twice, the necessity of secrecy and non-association a prime concern. There was no way those words could have been overheard or recorded.

The thrill of this verification coursed through Alpha's body. He had never thought that a chance for a renewed opportunity to continue what he started years ago would ever present itself. All his hopes of prestige and importance that he'd lost, now returned in a rush.

"Computer, open verbal line to sender and verify location of transmitter. Send location information to my screen, non-verbal."

"Understood. Line open."

'This is Alpha."

"Alpha, my good friend," an unfamiliar voice said. "I'm glad to see you are still taking the usual and thorough precautions."

"You have me at a disadvantage. According to all data available, there is no possibility you survived."

"Yes. I understand. It's not particularly clear to me either. I have returned in an energy-state and taken the physical form of a human. You will no doubt find my story worthy of examination and further study."

"A human?"

"Yes, it is rather revolting. But what is it the humans say? Sometimes you can't be choosy?" Copolla laughed.

Alpha saw the words appear on his screen. "Location of transmission. Earth --Washington, DC, secure line of President Edward Samuel." Alpha studied the words for several seconds.

"But you have chosen an excellent choice of position," Alpha offered in lieu of his new information.

"Your skills are still as I remembered," Copolla said appreciatively. "I would have assumed this call was untraceable."

"It is to anyone but me," Alpha said. "How will you continue this ruse with the humans?"

"I have all the information that the human President possessed. But most importantly, there is a second in command, a vice president. I'll shove most of the things off on him while I figure out my next move."

"A smart and methodical action," Alpha agreed. "The dealings of the humans are inconsequential to someone of your stature."

Copolla laughed. "It's good to hear a familiar voice among the strangers I have found myself surrounded with. My last memory is of the battle and the deceitful attack of my son. The fool! We could have done many great things together."

"It was a most regrettable loss." Alpha spoke in a conciliatory manner. He had helped with much of the planning that had almost brought them victory. If there hadn't been the interaction of the time traveler from the future, they would have been victorious.

"But I understand there is another chance. A child exists...my grandson?"

"Yes and..."

"Alpha, tell me what's been going on," Copolla began. "This human has some knowledge but I think your version will be more interesting. I want to know what's really happening and how we can exploit it to our benefit. I'm ready to pick up where we left off. Aren't you? You still want to be in a position where they will grovel to you, don't you?"

"Yes. Oh yes...very much so, honorable Copolla."

"Well then, let's get going," Copolla said. "Important life-forms such as us have things to do. Tell me everything."

CHAPTER
SEVENTEEN

"There were things I just knew...I didn't know how I knew them, I just did."

Soren

Soren drifted up from the depths of his sleep to the sound of voices. He slipped from under the covers of his bed and crept toward the door. He peered out and saw his mother and Leumas in the living room. At first he was glad to see Uncle Leumas, but then saw that his mother was crying.

"They have to...they have to...." he heard her cry as he watched Uncle Leumas hug and gently rock her from side to side.

Soren slowly walked toward the embracing couple in the living room. Tears glistened in his eyes as he approached them.

"Mom, what's wrong?" he asked.

Both Leumas and Sarah turned toward him.

"Nothing," Sarah said.

Soren saw the surprise in her eyes as she and Leumas parted. He also saw the tears she wiped from her eyes.

"You're not having any more bad dreams, are you?" Soren asked.

"Hey, young man, no greeting for me?" Leumas said as he distracted Soren from seeing Sarah's distress. Sarah took advantage of the moment and moved off into the kitchen.

"Hi, Uncle Leumas," Soren said with only a half-hearted smile, his eyes still fixed on his mother.

"What kind of greeting is that? Come and give me a hug."

Hearing the usual challenge in Leumas' voice, Soren brightened and ran over to him. Uncle Leumas swooped him up in his arms.

"That's more like it," Leumas said as he tickled the boy viciously.

"Stop...stop," Soren cried amidst uncontrollable laughter.

"Say the magic words. Come on, I want to hear them!"

"Uncle--Uncle," Soren cried.

"Okay, I'll let you off easy this time." He lowered Soren gently toward the floor.

"Are you hungry, Soren?" Sarah called from the kitchen.

"No," he called back, then turned toward Leumas and whispered, "Mom had a bad dream and I helped it go away."

"So I heard." Leumas sat in a chair and motioned for Soren to come and sit on his lap. "You've been very busy the past day or so. Can you tell me about the dream you had?"

"Maybe later," Soren answered. He didn't want to talk about his dreams because he knew they were part of the reason his mother was so upset.

"Well, how about the neat trick you did on your mom?" Leumas asked.

"Trick?"

"Yeah. The way you switched her dreams around. That was some accomplishment. I'm very proud of you."

Soren smiled at the bestowed praise. "Well, I..." his voice drifted off as he heard the sound of movement from the kitchen. He didn't want to do or say anything that might upset her again.

"It's okay, Soren," Leumas said. "Your mom and I want you to talk about this."

"Mom won't get upset again?"

"I don't think so. This...ability is very important. But you must be very careful with it. It's not something you want to tell anyone. Only us. Do you understand?"

"What about Uncle Edward?"

"Sure. Uncle Edward is okay. But not when anyone else is around, just us three. It'll be our secret."

"Okay," Soren said as he held out his hand to shake. Leumas shook it and smiled.

"Now tell me how you did it."

Soren took in a deep breath. "I followed the bad feelings until I found them. They were in a room. I closed the door to keep them in there. Then I looked for the good feelings and I opened that door and everything was okay. It was easy."

"You weren't scared?"

::No way!:: Soren shouted in his thoughts.

Leumas cringed. "Easy there, Soren. Not so loud."

"Sorry."

"That's something else we need to talk about: control. You just can't go around shouting your thoughts without making sure you won't hurt people."

"Sorry," he repeated.

Sarah came in from the kitchen and sat on the sofa. She had stopped crying but the red splotches on her cheeks were noticeable.

"Hi, Mom. Are you feeling better?" Soren asked.

"Yes. I'm okay now," she said and produced a small smile.

Leumas continued. "And no more snooping into your mom's or anyone else's dream until we do some tests."

"Tests? Yuk!" Soren curled his lips and twisted his face.

"I know. I know. But we have to, Soren. Sometimes these things you can do might cause your body harm. It's not good for you. You were very tired and thirsty when you moved the dreams around, weren't you?"

"Yeah," he agreed. He remembered he couldn't keep his eyes open and all he wanted to do was sleep after he drank glasses of water.

"That's why we have to do some tests. They won't hurt, I promise."

"When?"

"Soon. We'll start later if it's okay with your mom."

Soren looked toward his mom and concentrated on gently sending his thoughts. ::*Mom, is it okay?*::

***

Sarah, surprised at the intrusion into her mind, involuntarily shuddered at first in hearing his thoughts. But it was not as much as from the act as much as it was from the sharpness and clarity of the intensity of his thoughts. It was perfect. Soren had already begun to master the thought sending process.

::*Do you feel strong enough? Or do you need to rest some more?*:: she asked.

::*I'm okay, Mom.*::

Soren turned back to Leumas. "It's okay, I just asked," he responded matter-of-factly.

Sarah nodded in agreement to Leumas. Still, she couldn't help feeling that things were happening too fast for Soren and worrying about the possible implications of what his increasing mental capabilities meant.

CHAPTER
EIGHTEEN

"Always be more conniving than the other, if you can't — then kill them."

Copolla

Copolla listened as Alpha began summarizing events since his disappearance six years ago. Things were bleak as far as his organization was concerned. Only a handful of loyal followers existed. Leumas had done an amazingly thorough job in eliminating or chasing anyone out of the system if they were implicated in any way as having ties to him. The base Copolla had launched his attack from on Acuba had been leveled shortly after the fleet had been destroyed. Destroyed by his son's doing, he thought, feeling the reminiscent burn of disgust within him. *What a waste of good breeding. But what's done is done.* The loss of a life was insignificant in the grand scheme of everything he wanted. He quickly moved on to other concerns.

The thought of starting from scratch, rebuilding his organization, creating a network of agents to spy in the council, made his goal of galactic domination seem almost impossible for even a creature with his long life span, but that option no longer existed. The fallacies of the body he occupied, a human body, now redefined his plans. He wondered if there would be any way to rid himself of the puny physical form for something of more substance.

When Alpha spoke of the movement he had initiated -- the return of the council to Zire — Copolla's interest perked up. There were possibilities there he liked. Use one goal to attain another, he thought. Use the dissatisfaction of council members as a launch pad for other issues...his issues. Or better yet, use it as cover while he moved in another direction, a distraction for Leumas and his other council cronies to chase while he quietly maneuvered in the background. Yes, there were possibilities there.

Then there was the issue of Alpha. Alpha was just a worthless piece of alien brain he had used to devise some of his plans. And they had been good plans, he had to admit. If he had not been foiled by his son Greg, he would have been well into his control of the galaxy, and Alpha would have been killed by now. At times Alpha could be too smart for his own good, he just didn't have the guts to know it. He was nothing but a living machine that did what it was told. He would develop plans based on logical assumptions of data, but he lacked the element of emotion and that was what Copolla added. He doubted Alpha could ever mount a threat to him by what he knew, but his simple rule of eliminating any chance of that possibility remained a priority. Alpha would live for now, at least until Copolla got re-established. Allies were far and few at the moment.

Copolla knew Alpha still craved prestige. That was the lever he had used to control the tentacled ambassador before, and it would work just as well now. It just needed a little lubrication to get it pointed in the right direction.

"There is a second child," Alpha said.

"What?" Copolla asked, driven from his thoughts. "What did you say?"

Alpha smiled, seeming to take pleasure in his announcement. "There were two children born to Sarah McClendon."

"Two?"

"Yes. Don't you remember the vision your son had? He said there would be *two* children to take over the council."

"Yes, I remember the stupid vision!" Copolla tried to keep his voice normal, but the reference to his son's vision riled him. Such nonsense! His son wasted time on visions and promises of galactic friendship and unity. His utopia. There would never be such a thing as long as life-forms inhabited the galaxy. There would be only one way to rule: by submission of all races to one supreme being. And that one being would be him.

Another child. He was quite surprised to learn this information and it immediately raised his suspicion about Alpha's abilities. "How did you manage to keep it a secret? Surely she would have known?"

"Co-leader Sarah Carlson, excuse my use of the term *leader*, but it is appropriate I describe her…"

"Out with it!" Copolla yelled. He wanted information, not useless terminology. *Calm down*, he scolded himself. Getting angry wouldn't solve anything. He calmed his tone and continued. "Excuse me, Alpha, you must understand that this is quite a surprise and my impatience sometimes gets the better of me. Please continue."

"It is understandable," Alpha said.

Copolla heard a slight quavering in the alien's voice. He found it appropriate, and more to his liking than Alpha's earlier confidence.

"Go on, please," he said tersely.

"Although Leumas disagreed with her, she insisted that a human doctor handle the requirements of her child's birth. The human complications of her position in Washington, working on the President's staff and being unwed by all practical Earth standards, required additional secrecy on her part. It was said she was on assignment to…"

"Alpha, please skip over these inconceivably tiny details. Go on."

"Yes, of course. I was able to develop a method of control over the doctor. These humans are a relatively simple species. I arranged for the doctor's family to be removed and held to ensure that the doctor did what I wanted him to do. All information, including reports and examinations, regarding the second child was hidden from Sarah Carlson. When it came time for the birth, the doctor placed her under an anesthetic during the procedure. Through his maneuvering of hospital staff and the few remaining loyal subjects to our cause, the records were altered and the second child was removed. The child..."

"What was the gender?" Copolla asked, interrupting Alpha.

"The child is female."

"So...there are one of each," Copolla mulled aloud. He tried to place it into the context of the other information Alpha had told him. "If the birth of the two children was openly known, the council would use that to believe in the so-called vision my son insisted upon, and resist the return to Zire."

"Yes, Copolla. Exactly," Alpha agreed. "This way the council members believe his vision to be incorrect. Even his fanatical believers are losing some of their faith that he'll return. Doubt equals chaos."

"Excellent, Alpha. You have planned well." But as Copolla said the words, his thoughts cautioned him to keep a closer eye on Alpha. What he had done actually showed the existence of some backbone, which could be dangerous.

"Thank you, honorable Copolla."

"Where is the female child?"

"She is hidden in the care of a human family under my--our-- control."

"Perfect. This is so perfect! Perfect--perfect--perfect." As the last syllables of the word "perfect" faded, Copolla began to laugh.

When at last he got hold of himself again, he said: "Show me the girl."

***

"What do you have in mind?" Sarah asked as she and Leumas spoke quietly. Soren was in his room getting dressed.

"I want to see how strong his power is."

"Don't we already know that? He was able to get into my mind without difficulty."

"You weren't prepared. This time we both will be."

"Both?"

"Yes. If he can get into one, then we'll push him to see if he can get into the other mind. That way we can gauge his abilities."

"I don't know, Leumas. Shouldn't we proceed in a better test environment?"

"I don't think we want any of this getting out. Not yet anyway."

"Why are you so worried about that? He's only a child, for God sakes."

"But he may be a child with enormous power. A child could be easily persuaded to do things for others. There might be some out there who would want to harness that power for their own benefit."

"I swear you're still paranoid about secret plots," Sarah scoffed.

"Maybe I am, but I figure for Soren's sake, better safe then sorry," Leumas replied. He knew his answer was rather blunt, but he also knew Sarah was not thinking clearly since Soren had told her of his dream about Greg.

Leumas felt her staring at him for a few moments before speaking. He watched as conflicting emotions raged across her face; first anger at what he had said, followed by a look of assurance.

"You're right," Sarah agreed. "I just want to be careful. He's just a child."

"I know he is," Leumas said as he reached for her hand. "But you know we have to find out so we can plan what to do next."

"I know." She squeezed his hand. "Let's do it, but I want to keep an eye on him. We don't want to go too far."

"I understand. We'll…"

"I'm ready!" Soren called as he returned to the living room.

"Hey, big guy," Sarah said. "Come here and give me a hug."

Soren smiled and ran to her, jumping the remaining last steps to where Sarah had to catch him.

"Arg…you're getting too heavy. I'm going to have to stop feeding you."

"No more cereal?" he cried, his voice sounding serious.

"Well, maybe cereal's okay."

"Yay!"

"Soren, do you feel okay to try some of what you did earlier with my dreams?"

"I think so," he answered.

Leumas thought he heard some hesitation in the child's voice.

"What I want you to do is promise that if you feel unsure about something Leumas or I ask you to do, or if you feel tired again, you raise your hand and say so. Okay?"

"Just like in school?"

"That's right, honey, just like in school."

"Okay."

"Let's sit on the sofa," she said as she led Soren by the hand. As they sat, Sarah looked toward Leumas and nodded.

"Here's what I want you to do, Soren," Leumas said as he sat across from the boy. "I'm going to imagine something in my thoughts and I want you to try and find out what it is. Okay?"

"Fun!"

"But," Leumas added, "I'm going to try to hide it from you. Do you understand?"

"Sure!" Soren was obviously delighted at the opportunity to play a game.

Leumas conjured up the image of a horse in his mind. "Okay, Soren, I'm ready," he said and then focused his mind to block any attempts to infiltrate it.

"It's a horse, you silly," Soren said immediately and then giggled.

"Ah...good," Leumas said, although he was surprised Soren had had no difficulty whatsoever in entering his thoughts. "Now your mom is going to try and I think she'll be a little tougher then I was."

"Okay, Mom," Soren said anxiously. "Your turn."

"Hmmm...let me see," Sarah said. "I'm ready."

"It's a dog!" Soren exclaimed.

"Sarah?" Leumas asked.

"I blocked as best I could," she answered.

"Well, I think that concludes the first part," Leumas said. There was obviously no doubt that Soren could bypass any attempts to hide thoughts.

"Soren, are you okay?" Sarah asked.

"Fine, let's play some more!"

"All right, young man," Leumas said. "This time, I want you to try to send something to us."

"That's too easy!" Soren exclaimed. "Something harder!"

"Don't be in such a rush," Sarah told him.

"Okay...okay," he agreed. "Are you ready?"

Leumas looked at Sarah. "Okay," he said. "Send it on."

As the last syllable rolled off of his tongue, Leumas collapsed into his chair as images lunged into his consciousness. He felt nauseous as the onslaught of information continued, throwing off his equilibrium. Finally they slowed and he was standing in the great hall of the council next to Greg. Leumas immediately recognized the images as the memory of the day that Greg and Sarah got married.

"Is there something I'm supposed to do during the ceremony?" Leumas asked. *"I've never been a 'best man' before."*

"You just stand by me and hand me the rings when..."

Leumas remembered that Greg hadn't any rings for the ceremony.

"Can I borrow two of your rings?" Greg asked as his eyes remained fixed on Leumas' hands. Leumas raised his hand and Greg plucked two rings from his fingers. *"Thanks."*

Leumas remembered what was to come—the explosion. Copolla had implanted the reporter, Ray Schume, with an explosive device. He remembered seeing the reporter begin to come forward after Greg and Sarah had been pronounced man and wife. Leumas had lunged toward him.

Suddenly the images went dark and he heard a voice calling to him.

"Leumas, help me!"

He slowly opened his eyes and the familiar scene of Sarah's quarters greeted him with a reassurance of the here and now.

"Leumas, help me!" the voice came again. He turned toward the sound of the voice he recognized as Sarah's. She was still sitting on the sofa where she had been earlier, except she now cradled Soren in her arms. The boy appeared to be unconscious and his clothing was soaked.

"He collapsed!" she cried.

CHAPTER
NINETEEN

"It was a ruse, I knew it from the start but I had no choice but to play along."

Cindy Carlson

The six-year-old girl with black shoulder-length hair sat on the floor in the corner of her room, playing with a doll. Using a small hairbrush, she slowly combed its long dark hair that matched her own. When satisfied, she placed it in the little chair that sat next to the small table in the dollhouse kitchen. She then began to set out teacups upon the table: one for her doll and another at a vacant spot at the table as if she were expecting the arrival of another.

Then without any warning, her body jerked and she sat upright. Her facial features were calm. Her dark eyes set into her round face did not blink as she remained motionless. Her heartbeat and respiration slowed, and her small chest rose and fell with barely a noticeable movement.

An alarm sounded in another room of the house and footsteps could be heard approaching the child's room. As they neared, the slapping of shoes against the hardwood floors echoed ominously.

"Cindy?" a woman's voice called as the door opened. "Cindy, are you okay?"

Christine Williams stepped into the room, her eyes searching. "Cindy?" Looking toward the dollhouse in the corner, she saw Cindy with her back facing her. She moved toward the child, fearing the girl might be having another seizure. *I can't take this shit,* she thought.

She grasped the child by her shoulders and immediately felt for a pulse on the side of her neck. It was there, but faint. She let out the breath she'd been holding until she confirmed that Cindy was alive. After the episode the other day, she feared any further seizures might kill the child...and that would ruin the convenient arrangement she had.

"Cindy!" she shouted as she laid the unresponsive child flat on her back on the carpet. What had the doctor told her? She needed to shock her body to kick start it again or something like that. Christine raised her right hand and began to lightly slap Cindy's face, hoping to bring her out of whatever state she had sunk into. The child's eyes now presented an all-white appearance, lacking any pupils. This scared and disturbed Christine, which caused her to continue to slap her, this time with more force.

"Come on, Cindy, snap out of it!" Christine cried.

A low moan escaped the girl.

Christine, hearing this validation of possible returning consciousness, lifted the child's back off the carpet a few inches and then let it go. The girl fell backwards and hit the floor. She opened her eyes and this time Christine saw that her dark pupils were there and that her eyes were fluttering as if struggling to return to a normal state.

"Cindy!" Christine said, her tone becoming more angry than scared now that the apparent danger seemed to have passed. "Wake up!"

Cindy's eyes slowed in their fluttering and eventually stabilized as they focused on Christine's face. The child let out a large exhale of air and began to breathe normally.

"Hi, Aunt Christine," she said nonchalantly.

"Don't give me that 'Hi, Aunt Christine' crap like nothing has happened."

"Did I do something wrong?" Cindy asked.

"You most certainly did! You went off into one of those trances again like you did the other day."

"I did? I don't know..."

"Yes, you did," Christine snapped. "Remember what I told you. If you keep that up, I'm going to have to take you to the hospital and they will give you all kind of needles and things that will hurt. You don't want that, do you?"

"No!" Cindy's voice trembled. "I don't know anything about why this is happening. It just does! Please don't take me to the hospital. I'm scared of doctors and needles and things."

"I bet you are," Christine agreed cynically.

During the six years the child had been in her custody, there had been regular visits every other month by a doctor sent by her mysterious benefactor, Mr. Alpha. She had watched what they did only once. The strange man constantly tested her and took bodily fluid samples from her, but not in a caring way. He was quite crude and harsh in his manners. It took at least two days after each visit to get the child to calm down and stop crying, which gave Christine problems in managing her. When she complained to Mr. Alpha, the answer had been short and curt: "If you don't like it, I can find someone else."

Christine didn't want that. Mr. Alpha paid her extremely well for taking care of the child and pretending to be her aunt...as long as she didn't ask questions. If she did, Mr. Alpha, whom she had never met in person, threatened to inform the authorities of her location. Christine had an outstanding warrant for her arrest: on the charge of drug distribution to minors.

She had been approached by a Federal officer, CIA, or Secret Service or some organization that showed her the warrant and gave her the choice of servitude to her government, or a speedy trial and conviction, which meant a sentence of at least ten years. At twenty-eight years of age, and without much consideration, she agreed, and was placed in the house she now occupied to await further instructions.

Shortly afterwards, she met Mr. Alpha, via the telephone. He explained all the details of the arrangement. A baby would be delivered to the home and she was to care for it in every way, assuming the role as the child's aunt. She would provide proper nutrition, care, education and amusement for a period of undetermined time. Christine almost balked at the term of "undetermined time," but Mr. Alpha reminded her that she would receive at least ten years in the federal penitentiary for her crimes.

For her services, a generous monthly stipend would be provided with a bonus at the end of each year. The bonus alone was such a substantial amount that in five years or so, she wouldn't have to work ever again. As long as she didn't ask questions. Christine had agreed. Less than a week later, the child arrived, a baby girl, and so began the relationship that had continued for six years.

Christine did not have any maternal instincts. Her philosophy was simple: she tolerated the child for the money. She did what she was directed to do by Mr. Alpha and was allowed certain freedoms: two days a week she was allowed to obtain a sitter so that she could go out. It wasn't necessary that she spend a lot of time with the child either. The home was equipped with state-of-the-art monitoring systems that conveyed vital signs and alarms if anything was wrong. She was aware that the home was also under continuous monitoring by Mr. Alpha and associates because she had been reprimanded if she did anything that was not to their liking. The reprimands resulted in a loss of "out" time and/or financial consequences.

"I don't want to go to the hospital!" Cindy repeated, bringing Christine's thoughts back to the present.

"No, I guess you don't," Christine agreed. "But you have to stop these...seizures or whatever they are. You know *they* are watching and they will send the doctors."

"I don't know why they are happening...they just do. Someone else is causing them."

"You and I are the only ones in this house. Are you saying that I'm doing something to you?" Christine asked. If anyone was watching, and there probably was or would be later when the video would be reviewed, because of the abnormality of the child's physical readings, she wanted the absurdity of the question out in the open.

"No. Of course it's not you, Aunt Christine," Cindy answered. "Someone else."

"Who then? You remember what the doctor said...he said that these episodes may be self-induced."

"I don't know."

"Well, you think about it for a while. You're not going to come out of your room until you come up with the truth."

"But..." Cindy began to protest.

"No buts. Stay in your room." Christine took one more look at the child to see if she was going to change her mind. She saw no sign in the girl's face that conveyed such a notion, so she turned and left the room, locking the door behind her.

"I would never allow any harm to come to Soren, I owed it to Greg."
Leumas

Sarah laid Soren's limp body on the sofa. The feel of his skin, clammy and soaked with sweat, scared her.

"I'll call the physician," Leumas said as he moved toward the communication center in the kitchen.

"Hurry," Sarah cried. She wiped the moisture from his face with a cloth she had retrieved from the bathroom.

She listened as Leumas spoke with the physician, telling him to come immediately. When he completed the call, he returned and stood next to Soren.

"His breathing is shallow," Sarah said. "It's as if he's been through a strenuous physical workout that's burned him out."

"It's like what happened before?" Leumas asked.

"Similar, but worse."

"Obviously it was too much of a strain for him when he manipulated my thoughts," Leumas said.

Sarah looked at him puzzled. "Your thoughts? I thought he did my thoughts."

Leumas now looked perplexed. "He delved into my mind and picked something I felt strongly about."

"Was it...was it the wedding day?" she asked hesitantly.

"Yes. You saw it too?"

Sarah silently nodded, then returned her gaze to the unconscious child.

The door entry buzzed and Leumas escorted the doctor in.

Sarah looked up and hoped it wouldn't be the same doctor that had been on call the other night. The questions posed could be a problem and she wasn't in the mindset to be explaining. As the doctor came into view, she saw it was not the same one. This doctor was an Alpha Centaur humanoid, remarkably similar to Earth humans except with a bluish skin color.

"Good evening, Co-leader Carlson. I am Doctor SP911. Please explain what has happened," he said as he immediately sat next to Soren and began taking vital signs with his medical recorder.

"Soren collapsed. We were sitting here on the sofa and he just... passed out."

"What was the child doing before that?" the doctor asked as he studied the readouts on his display. "His electrolyte count appears to be severely depleted to a dangerously low level."

"Nothing, we were…"

"He was getting a pretty good workout, well…me, too," Leumas interjected and then looked toward Sarah. "I'm sorry, Sarah, we were horsing around before you came in. Maybe we overdid it a little."

"Well, Leumas, I told you," Sarah began, unsure of what to say as she focused on the words the doctor had spoken…*dangerously low level.*

"Has he not been feeling well? Any other symptoms?" the doctor asked, without waiting for Sarah to finish.

"He's been thirsty a lot," Sarah offered, remembering the effects from the earlier episode.

"The amount of electrolytes he appears to have lost would indicate an excessively high metabolism rate. Has he complained about his heart beating extremely fast or shortness of breath?"

"No," Sarah said.

"Well, we will need to run some tests to determine why he is so out of balance. But first we need to get him on a saline solution for a couple of hours to get his electrolytes and fluids back in check. I'll send in a nurse with an IV and set him up. Why don't you put him back in his bedroom. He needs to rest and he'll probably sleep for several hours. The nurse will be here in a few minutes."

"Are there long-term effects for this fluid imbalance?" Sarah asked, worried about any continued use of his abilities.

"If it continues and is not treated, or if the episodes of imbalance increase, the body will basically burn itself out. There have been reported instances of delusions and loss of memory. Definitely not something to be taken lightly; however, we don't know if that is the case here or not. He may have only over-exerted himself, as Co-leader Leumas has suggested. Let's wait until we do some tests."

"When?" Sarah asked.

"I've got some preliminary readings I can look at already," he said, indicating the medical recorder. "When he's feeling better we can run the tests. I can have some of my colleagues look over the results also."

Sarah shot a wary eye toward Leumas, who turned toward the doctor.

"Thank you doctor, I appreciate your efforts this evening. I would ask that your visit be kept under the strictest confidence."

"Of course," the doctor agreed.

"Thank you. I'll escort you out," Leumas offered.

As Leumas let the doctor out, Sarah carefully picked Soren up from the sofa and carried him into the bedroom. Laying him upon the bed, she removed his wet clothes, and placed dry pajamas on him. When finished, she tucked him under the covers, not liking the feel of his dead weight, kissed his forehead and then sat in the chair next to the bed. She brushed the damp hair from his forehead with her fingers as the tears inside her begged to be released. A soft knock on the door drew her attention away from Soren.

"Excuse me," a voice called from the doorway.

Sarah looked up and saw the nurse the doctor had sent. She was also an Alpha Centaur.

"This should only take a few minutes to set up," she said.

Sarah noted the small metal tripod with a bag of clear liquid at the top.

"Sure, come on in." Sarah stood and moved out of the way. The nurse set up the stand and inserted the needle into the vein in Soren's arm. Sarah couldn't help wincing at the sight of the needle going into the small child. Then the nurse placed tiny sensors onto his skin and attached them to a small monitoring device.

The nurse finished setting up and turned toward Sarah. "That bag should last for a few hours. I'll check back later. In the interim, we'll monitor his vital signs through the computer link," she said, pointing to the small device she had placed on the nightstand next to the bed.

"Thank you," Sarah said appreciatively.

"You should get some rest yourself," the nurse added. "He'll sleep for several hours."

"Thanks, I just might do that," Sarah agreed.

When the nurse left, Sarah sat back in the chair next to his bed. In a matter of minutes, her exhaustion caught up with her and she had just closed her eyes when suddenly she felt a hand on her shoulder. She lurched up, thinking that Soren had awakened.

"Easy, Sarah," Leumas said calmly. "It's only me."

"Oh...must have dozed off," she said as she tried to drive away the numbness that had wanted to encompass her into sleep.

"You need to get some rest," he said. "I'll..."

"Leumas, he can't use this power. It will kill him."

"Let the doctor do a through examination and see what he finds. We'll decide from there what to do next."

"Next? What do you mean, next?" she said, turning toward him.

"Sarah, Soren obviously has an uncanny ability. He was able to maneuver both of our thoughts at once. The ramifications of such power are..."

"No," Sarah said, cutting him off. "I don't want to hear this now." She turned back toward Soren's prone body. "Look at what we're doing! We're gambling with his life. I won't do that. I can't do that."

"Sarah, listen…"

"No. I don't want to talk about this anymore."

"Well," Leumas began, exhaling a long sigh of a breath. "Go and get some rest. The test of the new interstellar spacecraft is less than thirty-six hours away. You have to get down to the Kennedy Space Center tomorrow."

"I can't leave him, not like this," she protested.

"I'll stay with him. I promise I won't leave the quarters."

Sarah saw the concern in Leumas' eyes. He was a good friend and she knew he would be true to his word. Still, the thought of leaving Soren seemed callous and self-serving.

"The launch will be a monumental accomplishment," Leumas said. "It's what you have been working for the past four years. You can't miss it. It would look very strange if the President's top advisor was not present, wouldn't it?"

His reasoning was right on the mark, as usual. She had to go. "Right, you're right," she agreed.

"Now I want you to get some rest. I'll sit with him for a while. You go to bed." He grasped her elbow and helped her rise from the chair.

Her legs felt like rubber and resisted her attempts to move freely. Finally, she stood straight and began to walk toward the door of her son's bedroom. Thoughts jumbled through her mind and they made her wince at the shocking realization of what they were asserting. She stopped at the door and turned back toward Leumas.

"With this…power he has," she began, her voice trembling. "Do you think he has the ability to see into the future like Greg did? His dreams?"

"I don't know, Sarah. I don't know…"

She thought his voice sounded nervous, as if he knew what she was thinking about, what she was always thinking about. "I know…I know," she said. "I'm a hypocrite. One minute I curse his powers and forbid his use, and the next I look for a way to use them to see if Greg is alive or ever coming back. My husband, and now my son. I feel so…so damned selfish at times," she said and then added, "Or maybe just damned."

She turned and left the room before Leumas could respond.

***

Copolla watched the images on his view screen from Alpha, showing him the little girl with the black hair.

"Seems rather trite," he commented. "Does she possess any abilities?"

"None. In fact, she has a limited capacity for comprehension. She has been under constant surveillance by either myself, or one other. She receives regular examinations to check for any signs of any unusual neural activity. Nothing has been discovered or noted. She appears to be a plain human."

"A dud," Copolla blurted. The word came to him from the thoughts that existed within the vocabulary of the body he possessed.

"A what?" Alpha asked.

"Never mind. And nothing on the boy either?"

"Not that we can detect. They keep him secreted away most of the time. He is rarely seen outside of his quarters."

"I have memories of the boy," Copolla said. "The memories from the human President. There aren't any indications that he has seen anything either, but given the intelligence of this species, he would only recognize something if it hit him in the face."

Copolla heard Alpha emit a sound that sounded like laughter, and he couldn't remember if he had heard Alpha demonstrate that characteristic before. He ignored it for the moment and moved on.

"I also have access to the boy. I'm...Uncle Edward. Good...Good. I can use that to take a closer look at him. I will want to take a look at the girl also at some point. Sometimes these powers have a strange way of manifesting themselves or just lie dormant. Look at my son and the female. Their powers lay dormant until they began to undergo indoctrination procedures. Something stimulated those areas of the brains and poof...they had powers they could have used to control the galaxy. Instead they wanted to use them for the betterment of all races. How pathetic. I think its time I paid a visit to the United Council of Developing Worlds and checked on my grandson."

Copolla drifted off into silence as he remembered his ruined plans; the way Leumas and his son tricked him and then destroyed his fleet.

"There is one issue we discussed earlier that I need to bring to your attention," Alpha said.

Copolla returned his mind to the conversation. "And that is?"

"Earlier we discussed our plans to interfere with the test of the human's interstellar spacecraft. I have several council members who could be persuaded to volunteer their services. Do you wish us to proceed?"

"Oh yes, most definitely. I've been thinking about that since you mentioned it. We want to begin my welcome home party and this event will light it off perfectly. Here is what I want you to do..."

***

Alpha waited for Ambassador Corin to receive his call. Corin was no doubt verifying the source to ensure he was not being spied upon or being set up to be incriminated.

Earlier, Alpha had encrypted a synopsis of the plan he'd developed based upon Copolla's wishes, and sent it on for the Ambassador to review before he called. He had to admit it was perfect, the way he'd incorporated Copolla's plan into what he had already set into motion. Things were going to change, he thought. He would have his position of authority under Copolla as he had planned years ago, his position of respect and power. He would no longer have to submit to other race's insults and insinuations. Those days would be long gone and he had kept a little list, a list of all those who had crossed his path. Yes...the day of reckoning would finally come to him. Just a few alterations to the scheme of events and it would be done.

Not much longer...not much longer.

"Yes," Ambassador Corin finally answered, driving Alpha from his thoughts.

"Have you managed to convince some of our followers that the time to act is upon us?" Alpha asked.

"Yes. I think I have enough who agree with our concerns. But..." his voice drifted off.

"But what?"

"The plan you sent earlier, it's rather...severe. The others may not agree with it. They might perceive it as a direct attack against the humans."

"Nonsense. There will be no loss of life involved; this is purely an attack on the technology...our own technology, I might add," Alpha offered, having anticipated the type of response. "A clear signal must be sent if there is to be any hope of returning the council to Zire where it belongs."

"I understand. But how can you be sure that..."

"I know this will work," Alpha stated calmly. He knew Corin well enough to know how to work issues until he accepted them. Just a few assurances and he would fall in line. "Have I not been right so far? Have I not anticipated the outcomes of the council actions?"

"Yes, you have. But there are still many who could prevent our desires."

"I know. I assure you that after this event, you will see many more council members lose their religious fervor and side with the movement. We don't belong here on this planet anymore; it has served its purpose."

"But those that still believe in the possibility of the return of the leader, they may be more difficult to sway."

"You must remember not to take any actions or say anything against the former leader, Greg Carlson. He must remain clear of the issue entirely. As for the more staunch believers, I have another idea that may help sway the remaining holdouts."

"I understand, but what is this other idea?"

"Not now. It's time to move forward with our plan," Alpha said calmly.

There were a few moments of silence as Alpha waited for the response he was sure would come.

"I will make the preparations in accordance with the plan you submitted," Corin said.

"Good." Alpha smiled. "I'll be in touch," he said, as he terminated the communication.

"Well done," Copolla's voice sounded from a small speaker. "I love the way you maneuvered the idiot to your way of thinking. Are you sure he can be trusted?"

"Yes. He was harshly rebuffed by Leumas on the issue. If he was unsure of himself, he would have stopped after that. In fact, I think it solidified his position more than anything else."

"Leumas does have that affect on many," Copolla said as he snickered. "He has constantly been in my way on numerous occasions. Even when I think I've gotten rid of him, he somehow manages to come back. We have to be sure he is out of the picture at some point. I want you to think of a way to do that."

"Of course. I already have a plan in mind," Alpha answered confidently.

"You will go far in the new organization, Alpha, very far," Copolla said.

"I hope so," Alpha agreed.

"I knew something was out there...I just didn't know what."
Cindy Carlson

Cindy looked at the door as she heard the lock being turned. She wasn't really concerned with the action of her aunt; it had happened many times before. She smiled and held back a laugh from the view of the camera that monitored her room. Aunt Christine's tactics and tirades could be quite amusing at times.

She had realized a long time ago that she was different from other children. Different in many ways that she couldn't completely comprehend, but enough to realize she knew more things than most kids did. She didn't know how she knew them, she just did.

Because her time outside was limited to very short periods, she read lots of books. Her requests received raised eyebrows from her aunt, but she quelled those questions by saying that she wanted the books for the pictures in them and encyclopedias had many pictures. She could somehow see through the grownups, understand that they were doing things for reasons that were not supposed to be known by someone like her. But she did know. Sometimes it felt as if she could feel their thoughts.

She understood that living with her aunt was not typical. Most children had a mother and father who loved them and took joy in seeing them grow and doing things with them that were fun. Where her mother and father were she didn't know, but Aunt Christine was certainly nothing like a parent. Cindy thought their arrangement was more like an animal in the zoo that people came to watch and study. In her case, they were watching her, waiting to see something happen, but she didn't know what. Her supposed aunt was just a zookeeper, someone whose job it was to keep the animal healthy.

Cindy found the doctor visits scary. He was an ugly man. His head didn't have any hair on it and his skin looked different, almost scaly. His dark eyes never showed any kind of emotion, especially not sympathy or any form of caring. He never asked her anything except the standard questions every visit.

"Have you heard anything in your thoughts?"

"Does anyone talk to you in your mind?"

"Do you have strange dreams?"

"Can you move objects by thinking about doing it?"

Each time the same questions, nothing new or any personal questions about how she felt. Then came the needles and the samples he took from her. She hated that part, for he was cruel and didn't care that he caused her pain. Cindy supposed he was just doing his job like Aunt Christine, but Aunt Christine usually didn't cause her pain...until recently.

And why was that? she asked herself. Today had been the second time that she had experienced...something. Something that took her away to somewhere she didn't understand. And she was supposed to do something; she sensed that in some way she couldn't explain.

She shrugged and returned to her doll house. She began putting away the tiny cups and saucers she had placed on the table earlier. It suddenly occurred to her that she'd put an extra cup on the table without thinking, like she'd been expecting someone. *Who? Was someone supposed to visit? If so, how would I know that?*

She'd experienced premonitions before--twice? Or maybe more. She wasn't sure. There was a feeling just prior to the occurrences when she couldn't remember what had happened. That was when the seizures Aunt Christine talked about came on. She felt as if she were going to be with someone, but then at the last moment, it was all gone. Both times she'd awakened to see Aunt Christine bending over at her and yelling for her to wake up.

Whatever the meaning behind these occurrences, it was obvious that something strange was happening--something the doctor would want to know about. *Something that she was not to tell him*, the voice inside of her said.

She agreed with the voice. The mentioning of anything outside of the ordinary might prompt more painful testing, and she didn't want that. It was definitely best to keep this to herself.

***

President Edward Samuel stepped out of the unmarked helicopter as it landed at the high level retreat in the secluded area of West Virginia. The site had the same facilities as Camp David, but was cloaked with even more security--was generally used for high-level meetings where a need for secrecy was required. The President did not depart or arrive as he normally did on the Presidential helicopter when he came here; instead he was ushered out of the White House and secreted to a commercial heliport on a helicopter owned and operated by the CIA.

At the beginning of Samuel's presidency, the main thrust of the revitalization of the old US Navy satellite communications site was mainly for its access to the council chambers. They were under the Blue Ridge mountains approximately seventy-five miles away and connected by a high speed shuttle system only known to Greg, Sarah, Edward and Leumas. Among the intimate presidential staff and high ranking military personnel required to have knowledge of the site, it had been designated for meetings and as an additional retreat for senior members to work on highly-classified matters.

As they entered the tunnel to the underground facility, Copolla, already possessing the images and memories of the facility, was reminded that *he* was actually seeing it for the first time. He admired the cunningness of the arrangement and the manner in which the levels of redundancy had been built into it and did not allow room for error of discovery. It was obviously planned and constructed by council members. He was sure any concept such as this was far beyond the limited mental capabilities of the humans.

He greeted members of the permanent military security detail, smiling the ridiculous grin that Samuel used and saying a few words in greeting as they made their way to the elevator. The humans repulsed him as they smiled and waved, a few of them were even allowed closer by the Secret Service agents to shake his hand. If he had been in his old body, he would have crushed a few of their hands, taking great satisfaction out of hearing their tiny bones cracking within his grip. But he maintained the illusion that was required, and smiled and waved at the insignificant and idiot humans.

They rode down the elevator to the third underground level that contained the living and meeting quarters. Copolla remembered the criteria that had been established for this area. People were not to be disturbed for any reason without being contacted either by secure phone or by the internal electronic system. Each room was equipped with state of the art communications equipment designed to keep in touch with anyone in the world.

As they exited the elevator, they walked along the brightly lit corridor and polished cement floor. Reaching the junction that led to the President's quarters, the Secret Service agents stopped at a desk and chair where they would maintain a post. An overly redundant security layer, Copolla thought. He smiled at the agents, threw in a wave for good measure, and opened the door to his quarters. When he stepped into them and closed the door, he exhaled. "Finally. I'm surprised they didn't want to come in here also."

Remembering there was a well-stocked bar in the living room, he headed in that direction. Looking over the bottles, he knew what the human would drink, but Copolla wanted to drink what *he* wanted.

Unfortunately, he also knew there would be no Arcturian whiskey and he would have to settle for what was here. He scanned the bottles and settled upon whatever contained the highest proof of alcohol. He examined the bottle closely, and saw a label that said "Scotch" in prominent letters.

He poured himself a large water tumbler full, and gulped it down. This was quickly followed by another and then repeated until the bottle was emptied. When the last drop dribbled out of the glass into his mouth, he realized what he had done. *Fool! You're not in your body! This human's body cannot take the same levels as you're used to.* No sooner had he thought it, he felt the human alcohol coursing its way back up his throat. He ran to the bathroom and vomited copious amount of Scotch his body refused to accept.

"Damn alien trash...humans," he said as he grasped a towel off the rack and wiped his face. His stomach angrily churned as if to remind him there was still more to come. He dropped the lid on the toilet seat, sat down, and waited to see what this body would do next.

A beep from his personal communicator sounded. The code indicated it was Alpha calling. "Yes!" he snarled, followed by a large belch that tasted of bile. He grimaced at the taste and went to the sink for a glass of water to wash it down.

"All is ready for tomorrow," Alpha's voice said.

"Good," Copolla acknowledged weakly, his voice sounding scratchy and uneven. He felt the urge to vomit, but couldn't if he had to talk with Alpha, furthering his frustration.

"Are you all right?" Alpha asked.

"Do I sound all right?" Copolla said sarcastically. "No, I don't! Come now, you're supposed to be intelligent. Does that sound like an intelligent question to ask? Does it?"

"My apologies," Alpha said softly.

"I don't want your apologies! You just stay on top of the plan, Alpha. Can you do that without any assistance or do I need to hold your hand? Hmmm?"

"I will handle the details."

"Good! Now leave me alone! I'll contact you later."

Copolla hastily returned the communicator to his pocket and then leaned over the toilet and vomited. As his stomach contracted violently against the urges to rid itself of the alcohol, Copolla heard the sound inside his thoughts...the sound of someone laughing.

CHAPTER TWENTY TWO

"To deceive is sometimes necessary."
Soren Carlson

::Nothing is for certain--except what you truly believe. The key to everything is balance.::

The thought sounded in his mind like the sound of an alarm clock going off in the morning. Soren's eyes fluttered open as he struggled toward consciousness, lingering in that area of oblivion between sleep and awake. His mind was a clutter of the last images he remembered, the images he had sent to his mother and to Uncle Leumas. He wanted to show both of them something that they both felt good about, something happy. He searched through both of their minds and found the same memory that they each valued and then gave it to them. He thought Uncle Leumas was probably going to be angry with him because he had not done what he had been told to do...but this had been more fun. Well, more fun until the darkness had come.

Soren knew that whatever this darkness was, it was something that he couldn't control when it came. He didn't know what caused its arrival, only that it was certain to come the longer he stayed in someone else's mind. It was as if his batteries wore down quickly and as soon as they were depleted, that was when it came. He didn't like it because it ended his fun of helping his mom and Uncle Leumas, and made him tired and weak.

But soon all that will end... The thought crossed through his mind like a car driving by so quickly you only catch a glimpse of it. He wondered where it had come from, but at the same time, felt that he knew there was something about it that made sense. There was a sense of balance to it.

Full wakefulness upon him, Soren sat up and immediately felt the tug of something on his arm. As he looked in that direction, he saw a needle poking into his arm that led to a tube that snaked its way up toward a bag of liquid held upon a pole. He wondered what it was and why it was here. He didn't like needles so he looked away from it. The sound of someone breathing drove his attention to the other side of the room. He saw Uncle Leumas sitting in a chair next to his bed, asleep.

Uncle Leumas was pretty neat, considering he was an alien from another planet. No one had ever told Soren that fact, he just knew it the same way he knew about the council and the other alien life forms. He never mentioned it because he knew he was not really supposed to know these things. But he also thought the time was here when that would no longer be the case.

"Uncle Leumas," he called.

Leumas immediately jerked awake in his chair and stared at him, his eyes blinking rapidly.

"Hey, my little friend, how are you feeling?"

"Okay. A little tired. Where's Mom?"

"She's resting. You gave us a bit of a scare, young man," he said, as he rose from the chair and walked to the bed and sat down.

"I know. But I wanted to do something...different."

"More like you wanted to show off," Leumas suggested.

Soren smiled. "Yeah...I guess so. Are you angry with me?"

"Not angry," Leumas said as he ruffled Soren's hair with his hand. "But you can't do that anymore. There is something about it that hurts you inside. That's why you have this attached to you." Leumas pointed at the IV. "I think it's okay to talk to us in that special way without saying it with your mouth, but the other part, going into memories, is dangerous."

"I know," Soren agreed. "The darkness comes."

"Darkness?"

"Yes. Everything just...goes away. It's a strange feeling. I can't explain it well, but sort of like something is missing, something that can keep it away, but it's not here to do it."

"Interesting. We'll talk more about that later. But right now, before your mom awakes and talks to you, you need to make me a promise that you won't do it anymore unless your mom or I ask you to. Okay?"

"Okay."

"Your mom has to go away for a day or so, to work with Uncle Edward. You don't want her going away worried and sad, so you have to make her happy by telling her you won't do that kind of stuff. You have to really mean it, Soren, okay?"

"The new spaceship?"

"That's right. She has to be there when it goes up into the sky. It's very important."

"Are you going to bring more of your friends to Earth?" Soren asked, deciding it was as good a time as any to bring it up.

"What do you mean?" Leumas asked.

"Other aliens. Like you. Are they going to come to visit the council?"

"You...ah...know about these things?"

"Yes," Soren said emphatically as he watched Leumas closely to see his reaction.

"How long? How long have you known?" Leumas tentatively asked.

"Oh...for a long time."

"Well, then...why didn't you say anything?"

"Because you were all trying to keep it a secret, so I'd thought you didn't want me to know."

"How do you know about it then?"

Soren watched as Leumas appeared torn between surprise and curiosity.

"I can sense them, some of their thoughts."

"Their thoughts...are you sure it is their thoughts? Think hard, Soren, this is very, very important."

"Well pretty sure. It's like they would talk verbally and would say one thing but in their thoughts they meant something else?"

"I see. I couldn't have summed it up any better than that," agreed Leumas.

"It's kind of cool. I'd really like to meet some of them, to see what they look like."

"Well, I think we better talk to your mom about this first. Then we…"

His words were interrupted by the announcement that there was a visitor at the door.

***

Copolla's head throbbed unmercifully as he pressed the entry notification button to the quarters of Sarah Carlson. His stomach had settled somewhat with the exception of an occasional rumble that sent acidic tasting bile up into his throat. He quickly learned that as long as he was calm, he could minimize the effects of the upset stomach. He pressed the entry notification button again, this time depressing it with more force.

*Calm down...*he reminded himself, realizing his disposition was extremely volatile, and that he had to be cautious not to act in any manner that would cause suspicion. Seconds passed as he continued to wait. *What the hell is taking so long?*

As his impatience for someone to answer grew, he raised his hand in preparation to pound on the door, then lowered it, reminding himself that the human would never act that way. He snickered at the thought, being careful not to shake his head too much, because any movement brought pain.

Finally, the door slid open. He immediately recognized Leumas standing before him. He had to pull all of his resources together to not reach out and grab the vain bastard, and choke him until he was a very thorough blue in color. Bile violently surged into his throat and he swallowed the bitter tasting fluid. He forced a thin smile, bordering on a sneer, to his lips.

"Edward, good to see you," Leumas said.

The loudness of his voice caused a new sensation of pain to shoot through Copolla's head and he felt himself wince.

"Are you all right?" Leumas asked.

"Yes. I'm just not feeling well...terrible headache," Copolla said as he touched his temple. It was easy to play this part because his head actually did feel on the verge of exploding.

"You look a little pale, too," Leumas added.

So would you if you just finished throwing up your guts, Copolla thought as he waved his hand in dismissal.

"Maybe you should have a doctor check you out."

"I did. It's just a touch of flu or something. Really, I'm fine, but thanks for asking. How are you doing, Leumas?"

"Confused, but then what's new," Leumas said with a broad smile.

"Happens to the best of us." Copolla scrutinized the smile on Leumas' face. It reminded him of the same sickening expression Leumas wore the day he told him that he had information that would remove him from the council. He pictured his hands reaching out and grabbing Leumas by the throat. Grabbing it and squeezing until the eyes popped out of his head.

"Come on in," Leumas said, stepping out of the door entrance.

Copolla followed him into the room, looking to see who else was there. He expected to find the female, but didn't see her or the boy. *Where are they? I must see the boy...now! NO! Can't be too anxious. Samuel wouldn't do that.*

"Where's Sarah, and the boy?" he asked.

"Sarah's resting. She had a rough night."

"Oh? Something wrong?"

"It's Soren," Leumas said as they arrived at the chairs in the living room. He offered Copolla one chair as he took the other.

"What about him? Nothing serious, I hope."

"There have been some interesting developments, but I imagine you want to talk with Sarah about the test launch tomorrow. I'll let her know..."

"That can wait," Copolla interjected. "I'm concerned about the boy. Tell me about Soren. He's okay, isn't he?"

"He's resting," Leumas said, as he stood and began to pace around the living room. "It's really strange how lately he's dropped one surprise after another on us."

"There have been a lot of surprises lately," Copolla said, reminding himself of his own appearance in the body of the human. "Yes. Many surprises...some good and some not so good. You think you reach the end of something and then there you are--smack dab in the middle of something else. Keeps us on our toes though, doesn't it?"

"What do you mean?"

"Oh nothing, it's just my meandering. So what'sgoing on with Soren?" Copolla cursed himself for letting his mouth run away. He had to remember he was Edward Samuel, not Copolla. Samuel was practical and not a philosopher.

"Are you ready for this? First he lets us know that he has telepathic ability to communicate."

"Really," Copolla said, his interest piqued. *So the boy does have the power. Excellent. Excellent...*

"Yes. And he can get through even Sarah's mental block."

"Is that powerful?" Copolla asked, knowing full well that it was. He had to play the role all the way if he was going to get everything from Leumas.

"Extremely," Leumas said emphasizing the word. "I've only known three who could do that: Greg, Sarah and our dearly departed Copolla."

"Humph," Copolla uttered. He felt his face contorting with anger and knew Leumas had probably seen it, too. He had to say...or act like he felt the same anger and revulsion. "Yeah, that bastard."

Leumas nodded in agreement and went on. "But that's only the beginning. He also has the ability to go into a mind and reshape what that being perceives as real. He can show them any memory they might have, or probably create a new one."

"That's amazing," Copolla said as he delved into his private thoughts. *A perfect genetic alteration, and undoubtedly one of a kind.* The power of such a capability would be mind-boggling. He felt a smile appear on his lips and allowed a low bit of laughter to escape. His mind raced with the possibilities. If all he had to do was change or alter the perception of what one saw, there would be no need for armies or expensive war machines. One simple thought would do the work of thousands.

"Amazing doesn't begin to describe the ramifications of such power if it could be harnessed safely. But unfortunately it is not without a significant cost."

"What do you mean?" Copolla sensed there was another part to this story. Leumas never gave full answers without someone having to drag all the information out of him. It was a trait Copolla had despised for years and looked forward to be rid of forever...that was, after he tortured Leumas for as long as he could.

"The power drains his body dangerously low of vital fluids, mainly electrolytes," Leumas explained. "He can only maintain the perception or memories for a few minutes or less before he slips into severe dehydration and collapses."

"That could pose a problem to using the power effectively."

"Using the power? You can't even be considering risking the child's life in order to gain an advantage," Leumas said as he stared intently at Edward.

Copolla struggled to make his expression look compassionate and hurt from the accusation Leumas had just asserted. He even managed to force some moisture into his eyes. "You don't think I am more concerned...about...this power thing then I am about Soren, do you?"

"No, of course not," Leumas said as he put his hand on Edward's shoulder. "I didn't mean that...it's just been quite a strain lately."

Copolla slowly allowed his hurt look to change back to his normal expression. He had to struggle to keep from laughing at his own actions. But his internal humor faded quickly the longer he looked at Leumas' smug face. His stomach surged.

"I understand," Copolla said, touching Leumas' hand that was on his shoulder. He wanted to rip it off and break every bone in it, to start with, but instead shook it warmly. "You probably need some rest."

"I will, later. I promised Sarah I'd keep an eye on Soren while she rested."

"Is he still asleep?"

"No. At least he wasn't a few minutes ago. That was when he dropped his next surprise."

"And what was that?" Copolla asked, curious at what other surprises the boy was capable of.

"He knows a great deal about the council. He even knows that I'm an alien." Leumas shook his head in puzzlement.

"How did he find that out?"

"He claims that he just sensed it. He says he's known for a while but hasn't said anything because he knew we had been trying to keep it a secret from him."

"Quite perceptive, isn't he?"

"Oh yes. But that just opens this issue up even more. If he can perceive what is going on around him even when separated by physical objects, imagine what he could do if he was standing next to you? That makes him…"

"Very formidable," Copolla added, but then quickly clarified, "if he were to fall under the wrong influence."

"Most definitely," Leumas agreed. "Sarah and I have decided to keep this to ourselves for now. We're going to run some medical tests on him to ensure that what goes wrong doesn't have any lasting effects, and maybe isolate what is causing it."

"Makes sense. The child's safety is paramount. You wouldn't want this kind of thing getting out. It might cause hysteria."

"Or worse yet, someone might want to kidnap him in an attempt to isolate and use that type of neural power. I'm ordering the security tightened even above what I already have in place."

"No need to get overly paranoid, Leumas," Copolla said, thinking ahead to how he was going to get the child out of the compound. "You don't want to alarm the boy or give the impression you are hiding something that has suddenly become more valuable. That gives it away and defeats what you wanted to achieve."

"I understand, but I think it's needed. Don't ask me how or why I think that, I just do."

"Well, you know best in these matters," Copolla said trying not to sound condescending. "If you need anything from me, just ask."

"Thanks. I have to…ah…" Leumas yawned. "Sorry."

"That's quite understandable. You're exhausted, I can tell just by looking at you. Why don't you get some rest? I have a few hours to kill before Sarah and I have to leave. I can watch Soren. And if the chair is comfortable, maybe I'll even catch a few Zs myself."

"Well…"

"Go ahead. Get some sleep." *You idiot. How blunt do I have to be? Get the hell out of here.*

"Okay. Thanks, Edward. I'll be back in about two hours."

"Fine." Copolla smiled. That should be plenty of time to take a look at the boy.

"Sarah is in her bedroom if you need to wake her."

"Fine." Copolla waved a hand at Leumas. "Now go."

As he heard the door swoosh shut behind Leumas, Copolla sighed. "Finally! I thought he'd never leave."

He made his way down the hallway, knowing the layout of the quarters from the mind of the human. He stopped outside Sarah's bedroom and pushed the partially closed door open enough so that he could peer in. He saw Sarah lying under a blanket and he could see the slow but regular breathing of a deep sleep. He leaned back and closed the door, satisfied that she wouldn't be waking up anytime soon.

He made his way back down the hallway to Soren's room. When he peered in, the boy's eyes met his, and he watched a grin emerge onto the boy's face.

"Uncle Edward!"

"Hey, kiddo," Copolla said, stepping farther into the room until he was alongside the bed. "Feel like some company?" He ruffled the boy's hair, remembering that this was something the human Edward did when he visited.

"Sure. Where's Uncle Leumas?" Soren asked as he pushed what he thought was Uncle Edward's hand away.

"I sent him to get some rest. He was starting to act...you know, kind of stupid, or should I say, more so than usual." Copolla chuckled at his own words. Soren laughed along with him also.

"That was just a little joke, a private joke between us real humans to get us warmed up. Uncle Edward wants to play a game, okay?"

"Sure!" Soren agreed. "What kind of game?"

"I'll explain it to you as we go along."

CHAPTER
TWENTY THREE

"If I could have changed anything, I would have destroyed the Earth a long time ago."

Copolla

"It'll be fun," Copolla said as he smiled at Soren. "You trust Uncle Edward, don't you?"

Copolla didn't want to waste much time talking with the child, but he had to make sure about some of the facts and perhaps he might learn something that the inept Leumas had missed. He also had to lay the groundwork for future action he was already thinking about. Leumas tightening security wasn't going to help matters very much, but there was nothing he could do about that without raising suspicion.

"Sure," Soren answered without any doubt in his voice.

"And there's a prize if all your answers are truthful," Copolla added. "And it's a very nice prize, too."

"What kind of prize?" Soren asked.

"We'll talk about that later," Copolla said. "That's part of the game, not knowing what the prize is. It's a secret. Secrets are always better, did you know that?"

"No. My mom and Leumas say secrets are not always good. Bad people hide behind secrets because they are too cowardly to come out into the open."

"Well. That certainly is a mouthful." Copolla sighed. Soren's response was just what he would have imagined the female human and Leumas telling the child. He would grow up to be weak, not understanding the importance of secrets and how you can use them against your enemies. Such stupidity!

"Well, there are certain special kinds of secrets that are okay," Copolla said. "Your mom and Leumas probably just forgot to mention those kinds. The kind I'm thinking of will be between you and me. That's an okay secret because we're good friends, right?"

"Well, I guess so," Soren answered.

"And with this kind of secret, your mom and Leumas will also get a prize if you can keep our secret. Can you?"

"Sure," Soren agreed. "They'd like that kind of secret. Let's start the game of questions. Are they like riddles?"

"Sort of." Copolla launched into a series of meaningless questions and answers with the child, warming him up so to speak.

"Now," Copolla finally paused. "Tell me, how long you have had this power?"

Soren's smile and exuberance quickly faded from his face. "I'm not supposed to talk about it."

"I know. But that's with strangers. I'm not a stranger. Leumas told me it was okay for you and me to talk about it."

Soren appeared to think about it for a few seconds and then said, "I guess you're right."

"Good," Copolla said reassuringly. "Now remember it's important that you answer quickly so as not to lose points in the game. Got that?"

"Got it!" Soren exclaimed, clearly anxious to start.

"So, how long have you had this power?" Copolla asked again.

"It just started."

"Good answer. You're earning points like crazy! Next question: Did you use it on your mother and Leumas at the same time?"

"Yes!" Soren said loudly.

"Was it hard?"

"I don't understand the question."

"Oh, sorry. Was it hard for you to control both of their thoughts at the same time?"

"No."

"Good answer. Lots of points there! Do you think you could do it on more then two people?"

"Maybe, but I might need some help."

"Help from whom?" Copolla asked.

"From...I don't know," Soren answered. He sounded frustrated that he couldn't give a better answer.

"Why did you say it then?" Copolla asked.

"It just popped into my mind when you asked it. I don't know what it means. How am I on points?"

"You're almost there," Copolla said, indicating by holding up his hand and using two fingers to indicate a tiny space in between them. "Maybe you want help from Leumas or your mom?"

"No, it's not them. It's from someone I don't know."

"How can that be? How can you want help from someone you don't even know?"

"I don't know!" Soren stated again, this time his face contorting with obvious frustration.

"How about your father?" Copolla guessed. "Maybe it has something to do with him?"

"No. Not that. That's different. I'm sure of that."

Copolla sat in silence for a few seconds. He didn't think the boy knew anything else and he saw no point in pushing him too far...not yet anyway. Once he got him away from here, he could open up his head and go exploring. The consequences wouldn't matter then.

The distant beeping of an alarm clock from another room interrupted his musings. The human woman, he thought, she'll be in soon to check on him.

"I didn't win the prize?" Soren asked.

"Of course you did," Copolla said as he watched the boy's face immediately brighten.

"Y--e--a--h! I won the prize!"

"But I don't have it with me," Copolla said slowly, as if wanting to draw the boy's disappointment out further. He wanted to laugh at the way he had the child dangling like a puppet. "I promise to bring it very, very soon. Maybe even on my next visit."

"I have to wait?"

"Yes, I'm afraid so. But that means the prize grows even bigger!"

"It does?"

"Oh yes, in fact, I think the surprise for Leumas and your mom is growing bigger, too. I can't wait to see their faces when I give it to them."

"H--o--o--r--a--y!" Soren screamed loudly.

Copolla's involuntary reaction was to raise his hand to swat at the boy for yelling and possibly attracting his mother's attention. Catching himself, he quickly moved his hand toward his mouth and held his finger up to his lips and made a quiet sound.

"You have to be quiet. If your mom or Leumas hears about any of our little talk, all prizes are cancelled. Especially yours!" he said as he pointed his finger at the boy. "Do you understand? I want your promise."

"Yeah, sure." Soren made the cross his heart motion with his hand.

"Good then..."

"Soren? Are you all right?" Sarah's voice called.

"Fine, Mom," Soren called back and smiled at Uncle Edward. "Everything's fine."

***

Sarah finished dressing for her trip to the launch site in Florida, then stepped into her son's bedroom. She was expecting to see Leumas, but instead saw Edward.

"Oh--hello, Edward."

Although it puzzled her, wondering what happened to Leumas, she immediately smiled at the sight of the President. Edward had been like a father to her over the past six years. He was a caring man that always looked out for everyone else, never himself. And he had...

Damn, she thought as the sight of Edward triggered the earlier memory provided by her son. Her wedding day. Edward was the one who had married her and Greg. She looked away from him as she felt herself beginning to tremble. She forced the memory away, afraid the tears would come again.

"Hi, Mom," Soren called.

"Hi, honey," she said to Soren, then turned to face Edward. "Edward? I didn't know you were here. Where's Leumas?" she asked as she walked up to the side of the bed and smiled at Soren.

"We were just playing a little game, Mom," Soren said.

"I know, honey, but you need to rest now. Okay?"

"But I have..."

"Soren," Sarah said more firmly.

"Okay. Night, Mom. Night, Uncle Edward," he said as he turned on his side and closed his eyes. Sarah turned her attention toward Edward.

"I sent him away to catch an hour or two of sleep," Copolla said. "He looked terrible. I had some time so I figured I'd help. It's the least I can do."

"That's sweet of you," she said as she walked up to him and moved to kiss him on the cheek. "Thank you."

As she was about to kiss him, he suddenly jerked away.

"Edward? What's wrong?" He seemed uneasy about something, not his usual easy going personage.

"Oh, it's... I haven't been feeling well lately, probably some kind of bug or something. I don't want you to get it. Can't have us both not feeling well with such a big event coming up."

"Of course not," she said, hearing the tiredness in her voice.

"Are you up for this?" Edward asked. "You're not looking too well yourself."

"I'll be fine. It's just been a very trying couple of days."

"So I've heard. Leumas has explained the developments."

"Regardless, I can't miss what I've been preaching about for the past six years, can I? I imagine the whole world will be watching the launch, considering all the economical, social, and political ramifications of such an important event."

"You can be sure of that," Edward agreed. "Are we sure everything will go as planned?"

"Absolutely," Sarah answered confidently. "The ship was built in strict accordance to the council specifications. It's a proven model, been in service for many years."

"Well, I guess then we have nothing to worry about, do we?" Edward asked.

Sarah looked at him, perplexed. There had been something in his tone of voice that struck her oddly. She wondered if he'd ever sounded like that before. Or was it just her present state of mind that made it sound that way? She wasn't sure...she wasn't sure of anything anymore.

"Sarah, is something wrong?" he asked.

"Nothing," she said shrugging off the feeling. "Is it time to go?"

"Yes...it's time to get this show on the road. We'll shuttle back on the helicopter and board Air Force One."

"I'll call Leumas and tell him we're leaving."

"Tell him I said...goodbye also, will you?" Edward said and then smiled.

***

Sarah and Edward mingled with the guests in the reception area that NASA provided for them to watch the launch at the Kennedy Space Center. In the distance they had a clear view of the launch pad where the unmanned spacecraft, simply called *Constellation*, waited to leave the Earth on its maiden voyage.

The ship's shiny surface shimmered in the sunlight. Its material as well as its shape was a completely new design. Many people, mainly the older rather than the younger, commented on its resemblance to the shape of the crude model ships used in the old Flash Gordon movies. Its body was cigar-shaped with fins on its sides and at its end. Some even called it a smaller version of the old dirigible or blimps.

The launch site was typically used for launches of the space shuttle; however, the entire space shuttle project had been placed on hold with the miraculous advancements made in the past few years, which if successful today, would completely revolutionize space flight for the planet. Unlike its predecessor the space shuttle, the *Constellation* required no booster rockets filled with tons of rocket propellant to get it into orbit. Instead it would slowly climb to orbit using only a fraction of the amount of fuel that the shuttle and its booster rockets currently required to break the Earth's gravitational hold. Once in orbit, it switched to its new hyper-drive motor and was free to go anywhere it chose to without worrying about replenishment for years and years. Representatives from virtually every nation were present to see the launch of not only a spacecraft, but what they hoped would be a new leap in economic development around the globe. But initiatives like this did not come at a small expense. Billions of dollars had been invested by almost every country on the research and development of the spacecraft. The more you spent on anything, the higher the public interest was and with that, the greater risk for fallout if something should go wrong.

Sarah quickly became immersed in the proceedings, and for the moment, put her concerns about Soren to the back of her mind. Although she was not a scientist or engineer, she had been in charge of an even tougher part of the space program--selling it to the world. And sell it she had. Her approach had not been the macho image previously used to try to promote the space exploration program. Instead she symbolized it in the average person way, showing how the benefits gained from space travel boosted the standard of living of everyone around the globe. There were tons upon tons of minerals in space, minerals highly desired by corporations. Construction methods and manufacturing in space alone would resolve unemployment in every country and actually produce a shortage of labor.

If there were any doubters, and of course there were some, after the completion of the hyper-drive engine that would enable travel within and outside of their own solar system, the remaining countries signed on. This created the biggest coalition of countries ever seen in the history of mankind. Today's test would be one of the last steps to accomplish that.

The technological part of the program had been the easiest. All the design and specifications came from proven technology--the council. The ideas or concepts had been slowly introduced into the minds of human scientists by influencing their thoughts, to nudge them in the right direction. After that was accomplished, the council stood back and watched the concepts come to life. The human scientists claimed all the discoveries, and the ball kept rolling in the movement to explore the solar system and move out into space.

As Sarah mingled with the guests, she smiled and greeted them. Many of them she had become close friends with her over the past six years. They exchanged ideas and strategies on how best to boost public awareness and confidence in the space program and the movement toward outer space. There had been some extremely shaky moments, Sarah recalled, but they had weathered through them all to reach this point. She couldn't help but feel a twinge of pride in what she had accomplished, but that was not without a bit of regret also as she thought about Greg.

The whole idea had been his--getting the people of Earth moving out toward space. Although he hadn't exactly had a plan at the time, one did present itself through Leumas' suggestion to relocate the council to Earth and begin the slow release of technology. *Greg...I wish you were here to see this with me...*

"T minus one minute," the voice sounded from the speaker. There was a flurry of activity as the various representatives from governments took their seats.

Sarah rejoined Edward at their assigned seats. "This is going to be wonderful," she said. "In a few moments, we shall see our dreams and destiny fulfilled."

"Yes, it certainly is," he agreed, without looking at her. "Another insignificant race shall join the cosmos in their quest for the answers."

"T minus thirty seconds," boomed from the speaker.

"Edward, are you okay?" She wondered why he was talking like this lately, little phrases here and there that seemed out of character for him.

"Fine, never better. Why?" he asked as he looked at her.

"You just sound a little off today."

"It's nothing. Just getting caught up in the excitement." He turned back to watch the launch.

Sarah was about to say something else when the voice from the speakers began the final countdown.

"Ten--nine--eight--seven--six--five--we have initial engine start. Four--three--two--one."

Sarah watched as the ship began to lift off the pad. Applause from the crowd and cheers of well-wishes ensued. The ship quickly accelerated as it moved into its planned orbital trajectory.

"Constellation has lifted off and is on..."

A brilliant burst of light lit up the sky. Everyone turned in that direction. A few seconds later, the rumble of an explosion rocked the building. Sarah felt her stomach tighten in horror at the thought of what had just happened. *No...it can't. It's not possible...*

Edward turned toward her. "I don't think that was supposed to happen," he said.

"I don't understand. Everything was checked and rechecked."

Many of the country representatives began to crowd around her asking for an explanation.

"This is mission control," the voice sounded over the confusion of people talking. "We have confirmation that the explosion was the spacecraft *Constellation*."

Sarah, still shocked, said nothing. "It's time to go," Edward said to her. They rose from their seats, Edward's hand grasping Sarah's elbow to make her move. "We will look into this immediately," Edward said to the crowd as they moved toward the door. "We will get you a preliminary report as soon as it's available."

The President's Secret Service contingent reacted quickly, and safely ushered them through the door.

"What could have happened?" Sarah asked as she paced the floor with her arms akimbo.

"I don't know. But if everything was checked and rechecked, the only other remaining possibility was that it was sabotaged from within."

Sarah stopped and looked at him. "That's not possible. First, security has been extraordinarily tight. Second, there were no communicated threats."

"All I know is we have a lot of pissed-off countries that have a lot of questions they want answers to and we don't have any."

"I'll get in touch with Leumas. I'm sure the council was monitoring the launch. Maybe they noticed or detected something that went wrong," Sarah said.

"Tell him to hurry. We're not going to be able to hold off the international pressure for long on this one."

"I'll coordinate from here. Where will you be?"

"I'm heading back to Washington. I have some other matters that need looking into. Keep me informed of your progress."

"I knew Copolla only used me for my brains.
But then, I was using him as well. It's what life forms do."
Ambassador Alpha

"Well done, Alpha," Copolla said, as he talked on his personal communicator from his secure office at the White House. "It's only been five hours since the explosion and they are in mass chaos trying to figure out what happened. I couldn"t have done it better myself."

"Thank you," Alpha's voice sounded through the tiny speaker.

"They are still combing through the wreckage as we speak searching for clues as to what went wrong." Copolla paused as if waiting for Alpha to say something. When nothing came, he asked, "They will find something, won't they?"

"Of course," Alpha said quickly. "The transponder used for the detonation was enclosed in a blast-proof container. They will have their evidence as you wish."

"Excellent," Copolla said as he grinned. "Has the council shown any interest?"

"A meeting is scheduled for tomorrow."

"You'll have to tell me how it goes."

"I shall give you a report after it--"

"The boy," Copolla interjected, as he remembered his conversation from earlier. "I want young Soren to be watched closely."

"He is secluded from--"

"I don't care! Find someone who can get on the inside. Any information is better than no information."

"I understand, but why the boy?" Alpha asked. "Did you see something that--"

"Never mind my reasons!" Copolla shouted. "Have you forgotten the rules of our association?"

"No...ah...of course not," Alpha stammered.

"Good then. Now, I have things to do. Is there anything else?"

"No...er...yes."

"Which is it?"

"Yes. The young female child. She has had some episodes lately, something to do with her physically."

"The nature of the episodes?"

"She has had seizures of some type and loses consciousness for a short period of time."

"How many of these has she had?"

"At least two documented occurrences, both within the past two days."

"And she recovers fully after each event?"

"Yes, but she has no recollection of the passing of time. She claims to just go to sleep."

"Interesting."

"Do you want me to have her examined? Perhaps a brain culture would reveal the source of the seizure."

"No. I don't want her touched yet. Are there recordings of the events?"

"Yes."

"Good. Send them to me. I want to see this firsthand." Copolla placed his elbows on the large desk and placed his hand together in steeple-like fashion which he brought to rest under his nose.

"As you wish. Is there anything else?" Alpha asked.

"No. I'll be in touch soon. It's time to set things into motion for the next phase."

Copolla terminated the communication. Within seconds, the information from Alpha was received on his computer via a secure link. He wasn't exactly sure why he felt this anxiousness to look into these occurrences. The female human child was just extra icing on the cake. Or was she? If there was…

A knock at the door interrupted his thought.

"Come in," he called.

Army General Bradstorm, the chairman of the Joint Chiefs of Staff, entered the office. The four highly polished stars on his shoulders glistened in the light.

"Mr. President," he said, coming to a halt in front of the desk, standing at attention. "Reporting as requested."

"Thank you, General," Copolla said as he observed the features of the human: the square chin, the hardened face. It was exactly what he wanted.

Copolla had planned on using influence to get what he needed, but he decided to forgo it on the General. Influencing tended to deaden the brain somewhat on these humans. He needed a man who could use his brains to achieve the desired outcome he wanted. By the looks of the man, this should be fairly easy. Besides, after the general did what needed to be done, chances were he would have an unfortunate accident anyway, when the time was right.

"Please have a seat," Copolla said, indicating a chair.

"Thank you," the general said as he sat.

"General, I know you are used to orders flowing down from the Secretary of Defense, but I have something I need for you to do."

"Sir?"

Copolla knew that he was going against the grain here by not using the normal chain of command. The next few sentences would be crucial to his success.

"What I am about to ask you to do must be kept secret for the time being. No one is to know about this conversation."

"Sir, I don't understand."

"The item deals with national security, General, and only on a need-to-know basis. I have my reasons for wanting to keep this low key. If you feel you can't work under those guidelines, then we are finished here and I'll find someone else who can do this. Take a moment to decide."

The general looked indecisively at Copolla for a few seconds as he appeared to think about what he was going to do. As he decided, his indecisive look faded and the earlier determination returned. "You can count on me, sir."

"Good then. Now, if a scenario comes up and you have no choice but to use a name in authority, use the Vice President, not mine. Any further communication will be with him, not me. That is a critical point to this unusual situation. I must not be implicated in any way in order for this mission to be a success...even after its conclusion. Is that clearly understood?"

"Yes, sir!"

"Good. Now here's what I want you to do. For this mission, I want you to select a group of individuals you can trust and who follow orders unquestionably. I also have a very specific list of equipment you are going to need. Some of which is cutting edge and never used before."

"An overseas mission?" the general asked.

"Oh, no," Copolla said and couldn't help but laugh. "No, not overseas. We have a greater threat right here at home. This mission is in the United States. West Virginia, in fact."

***

Leumas sat at the center of the council hall waiting to begin the discussion on the mishap of the interstellar spacecraft test. Earlier, Sarah had called, telling him she couldn't leave the space center just yet, so he would have to conduct the session without her. The NASA investigation was continuing but still hadn't revealed any cause for the disaster and the pressure was mounting by the hour for a statement about what had happened. Also, Edward had returned to Washington in preparation of holding a press conference.

Leumas had seen the disaster as it happened, watching it from Sarah's quarters on the television, and immediately dispatched an investigation team to look into it. What could have gone wrong, he didn't have a clue. Unfortunately, the more he thought about it, the more he feared what Sarah had told him about Edward's comment: possible sabotage. He hoped it wouldn't become more then just that, a possibility.

"This meeting of the United Council for Developing Worlds shall come to order," the roll taker announced as it returned to its seat. Members of entirely different shapes and sizes scrambled, crawled or leaped to their seats. The hall grew eerily quiet.

Leumas began, "We shall withhold any routine business for this meeting and immediately move into the investigation of the failure of the interstellar spacecraft. Is the investigation committee ready?"

A member from Arcturia 734, called Sdrien, which looked like a cross between some form of ape and a canine species, rose immediately from his seat. Leumas had chosen Sdrien because his species was admired for their doggedness in researching problems until an indisputable cause was found.

"I am ready," Sdrien said, his voice sounding coarse and deep.

"Please proceed," Leumas said.

"I have analyzed the telemetry of the spacecraft, and found no operational flaw. All systems were functioning appropriately and in accordance with required parameters."

"Then why did it explode?" a member asked.

"I assumed that if the spacecraft was operating as it should, there must have been an outside factor involved, something that was not part of the spacecraft but affected its operation. I reviewed all telemetry going to and coming from the spacecraft, and found an anomaly. Please direct your attention to the viewer."

Leumas turned toward his display and watched as the image of a narrow bandwidth appeared.

"This is the telemetry pattern going to the spacecraft. It provides the input to various systems onboard the craft. I will now enlarge it to isolate each command path."

The band grew segmented and tenfold in size. "I will now remove all communication signals coming from their flight control."

The image began to get thinner as the segmented sections disappeared from the screen. After a few seconds, only one line remained. Leumas felt his stomach began to churn with impending trouble.

"This is the anomaly. This signal being sent to the spacecraft did not originate from their flight control, yet is hidden within the standard command sequence signal. It is also on a frequency not used by any known humans in either a commercial or military practice."

"Who does use this frequency?" Leumas asked.

"I cannot pinpoint a specific user; however, I can say that this range of frequencies is generally used by this council."

There was a low murmur from council members.

"For what purpose?"

"Generally, for the sending of coded or encrypted messages."

"So it cannot be traced?" Leumas asked, but he already knew the answer. He had himself used the frequency for just that purpose.

"No, it cannot."

"Can you determine what the purpose of this signal was?" Leumas questioned, although to him it appeared obvious. He just didn't want to believe any of this was happening.

"Unknown. Not enough data."

"If we speculate," Leumas said, "that *we* weren't required to send a signal to the spacecraft, then whoever did more than likely had something to do with the disaster. Do you agree?"

"It is a possibility, but it cannot be substantiated," Sdrien said. "I do not wish to speculate without further confirmed data."

"Would there be any details from the wreckage that could shed some light in the investigation?"

"Possibly, if we…"

"A moment please," Leumas said as he saw a flashing image on his screen. It was the alarm indicating an urgent communication from the security officer. He pressed the receive button. "Yes, lieutenant," he said softly.

"Co-leader Leumas, there has been a breach in the security perimeter of the compound area."

"Use the usual decoy devices in position," Leumas said, but he quickly realized that they would have done that without calling him.

"They have no effect."

"Define the breach," Leumas asked.

"Low flying helicopters, military version."

"Military? They of all people should know of the restricted air space. Did you try communicating with them?"

"They refuse to answer."

"Projected destination?"

"On current course, they will arrive over the landing field in thirty seconds."

"Well, they won't see anything with the cloaking device that covers the landing area," Leumas said. "It should…"

"Telemetry reports indicate they have just activated a cloaking device negate field."

"That's impossible…they don't have one of those devices…only we…do…"

A claxon alarm sounded in the council chambers. Council members turned to their screens on their desks to see the cause of the alarm. Leumas knew they were now receiving the same information he was from the automated alert system.

The security officer continued. "They are hovering over the landing field. Sensors indicate they are gathering data."

"Bring in one of our security ships from orbit to prevent them from leaving the area. Put the security force on high alert. Stun weapons only. If they get out of the helicopters, I want to know the minute a foot touches the ground."

"Yes, Leumas," the lieutenant answered coolly.

Leumas returned his attention to the council members. "Your attention, please," he said. "There is no cause for alarm. We appear to have a human aircraft that has inadvertently stumbled upon our facility. I am going to get in contact with the appropriate people and see what has happened. We will reconvene later to finish our investigation."

Leumas quickly departed before anyone could ask any questions. He headed for the communications center to get in touch with President Edward Samuel.

**

Sarah watched as the debris from the spacecraft was brought into the large empty hangar at the NASA facility designated as the collection point for the investigation. Her preliminary meetings with flight control officials and engineers revealed no cause for the sudden explosion of the craft. All indications were that everything was going as it should, in accordance with every test they had conducted in the months preceding the launch.

"I want an engineer over here," a voice cried from an area where a new load of remnants had been deposited. Sarah moved in that direction as did a handful of NASA people. As she came closer she caught pieces of the discussion.

"I have no idea," one engineer said.

"Let me see it," another voice called out. Then a few seconds later the same voice spoke again, "No, never seen it before."

"Excuse me, Miss McClendon," a voice behind her said. Sarah recognized the voice as John Hagen, the senior engineer on the spacecraft project. "Let's see what the boys have found," he said to her as he moved through the crowd toward the center.

Sarah followed him as closely as she could to get through the mass of people. As he reached the center, one of the men handed him the device that had caused the stir. It was a heavily charred black box about the size of a cigarette pack but about twice as thick. On the ends of the box-like item were what appeared to be places a wire connection could be made. A vanilla colored ticket dangled from one of those areas; the number 75 written on it indicated the location where it had been found.

The look of puzzlement on the chief engineer's face indicated he didn't know what he was holding. Sarah knew that if anyone could identify any piece of this spacecraft it would be John; he had been instrumental in all aspects of design from the beginning of the program and had been key to keeping everything on schedule.

"Are we sure it came from the wreckage?" he asked.

"Yes, sir," a man said as he flipped through paper on his clipboard. "Number 75. It was found in part of the nose cone and became detached during transit."

"Strange. It doesn't look familiar."

As John turned it over and over in his hands, looking for any type of clue that might reveal what the small box was, one end slid open.

"What's this?" John said as he tilted the open end down. A smaller device slid out and landed in his plastic-gloved hands. The smaller box appeared to be unscathed from any charring whatsoever.

"Will you look at this?" he said as he studied the contents of the box. "I've never seen any kind of circuitry like this before."

"What do you mean?" another engineer asked.

"I mean I don't recognize this design." John looked at the young engineer who had asked the question. A fog of silence settled upon the crowd, quickly followed by murmurs of what the lead designer, the man who had signed off on each piece of the craft had said.

Sarah could only watch and listen as other engineers gathered around John as he showed them what he was referring to. His preliminary assessment was unsettling. What would technology unknown to these engineers be doing on the spacecraft? Where did it come from? Who put it there? Her mind quickly came to the choice that it had to be from the council. No one else had the technology. But only ideas and concepts were provided so that the engineers would come up with the design themselves. There would never be a direct transfer of any actual working components.

"Let's get this down to X-ray and see what we've got," John said.

"I'm going with you." Sarah quickly fell into pace alongside him.

Other engineers followed along. Sarah stopped and turned toward the growing trail of people.

"Perhaps it would be best if the rest of you continued working on the other debris," she told them. "Don't you agree, John?" She tugged forcefully at his elbow.

Sarah's Presidential position carried the obvious clout and although she rarely used it, she felt it extremely important to limit the possible discovery of alien technology for whatever reason it was here.

John looked at her inquisitively at first, but then turned toward the other engineers and said, "Yes, everyone keep looking through the debris."

The crowd looked dismayed, but gradually accepted the direction. Sarah and John continued on their way. As they walked, Sarah wiped at the perspiration that had accumulated on her forehead and couldn't help the feeling that something was not right and that this was only the beginning.

CHAPTER
TWENTY FIVE

*"If only I had known earlier, maybe all of this could have
worked out differently, and he would still be alive today."*
Vice President John Bishop

Vice President John Bishop walked into the reception area of the oval office. The standing joke that circulated about the vice president was that he was a neat freak. His appearance always reflected an uncanny attention to detail; most figured it was a leftover trait from his military service. His suit was neatly pressed, not a wrinkle to be seen, and hung perfectly on his five-foot-six inch frame. His weight was a little over the desired amount for his build, but he carried it well. He wore his hair neatly combed back and his eyes had an energetic exuberance that always fascinated people.

"Morning, Gladys. How are you today?"

"Good morning, Mr. Vice President. I'm very well, thank you." She turned her head to look around the office and then said, "He's a little fussy this morning. He's been calling me every five minutes to find you."

"These are trying times at the moment. I think everyone is a little on edge."

"I know, but I've never seen him so...upset. You better go right in. I don't think you want to keep him waiting."

"Thanks."

Bishop entered the inner sanctum of the oval office.

"John," Copolla said. "Thanks for coming."

"Mr. President."

"Have a seat, John, We have something very pressing we need to talk about."

After John Bishop had been seated, Copolla sat opposite him in another chair, staring at him intently. He wasn't sure if his consciousness still possessed its ability to apply influence, but he was going to find out in the next few minutes. Unlike the general, he needed Bishop to perform a crucial part of his plan in an exact manner that necessitated the use of influencing his thoughts.

"John, there are some unusual events coming into play that I need for you to be ready for."

"Yes. What..."

"Listen!" Copolla said firmly.

Bishop's face reflected a surprised expression at the outburst.

"Listen," he repeated. "Things have been happening for a while now, strange things defying explanation. I wasn't sure until recently, but the unfortunate accident of the interstellar spacecraft...I'm sure it was sabotaged."

"What? How could that be? Security was extremely tight."

"Someone...or should I say something, got through."

"I don't understand."

"You will," Copolla said and then pushed his thoughts to Bishop.

::*The spacecraft was sabotaged by a group of aliens that do not want us to attain space flight capability. They have been on Earth for years controlling our actions.*::

Copolla stopped and waited to see the effect it had on the man. The Vice President just continued to stare at him, his face blank and emotionless.

"John?" Copolla finally said. "Did you hear me?"

"Ah...yes. Is this true? I just can't believe this. But how did this all happen? How do you know about this? What are we..."

::*Silence! Just listen and I will explain the rest.*::

Bishop's body shuddered violently as if he had just received a jolt of electricity.

::*You have uncovered a plot at the highest level of our government. You have recently learned that I, President Edward Samuel, have been part of this alien conspiracy from the beginning, since I was elected President. I allowed these aliens to take control of an area in West Virginia. I thought it was for the betterment of mankind, but you discovered what I was doing and knew it was wrong. I am misleading the country and the world. The aliens mean us nothing but harm and they must be expelled from Earth. Evidence is being uncovered at NASA at this moment that you will use to prove the sabotage was done. You will take control of that material and use it to prove your point when the time comes. Also, you have already ordered a clandestine reconnaissance flight to check out the target area in West Virginia. Do you understand?*::

"Yes, I understand," John said, his voice flat and emotionless.

::*You will announce this at the time I tell you. Then you will threaten to launch a military strike unless these aliens leave Earth. Until that moment comes, I will make all the announcements. Is that understood?*::

"Yes."

::*Yes, what?*::

"Yes, Mr. President."

"Good, very good, John," Copolla said as he closed off his thoughts and returned to normal conversation. He couldn't keep from smiling.

"Now don't you have some business at NASA you better take care of immediately?"

"Er...yes. I do," he said slowly, as if he had just remembered something.

::Oh and one more thing.:: Copolla shot back into his thoughts. :: Don't forget to bring back the lead engineer to speak about the unusual discovery. But not the woman Sarah Carlson. She has other business to attend to. You will tell her that she has "sensitive business" to take care of. Say no more than that, she'll know what it means.::

**

Sarah sat with John Hagen, the chief engineer from NASA, at a small table outside the engineering X-ray facility. They sipped coffee as they waited to hear the results of the mysterious item found in the wreckage.

Sarah was grateful that John had sent the rest of his staff off to continue searching the debris for anything else that might be of interest. Damage control was her main mission at the moment. She didn't know exactly what she was going to do until she found out what they discovered about the mysterious item. She wanted to call Leumas and brief him about this latest issue, but she didn't want John straying off and perhaps bringing someone else in to look at the data when he received the X-rays, so she stayed with him the entire time.

"It's just so odd," John was saying as he absently sipped his coffee. "I mean it's nothing like I have ever seen before."

Sarah knew if the item was of council technology, all hell was going to hit the fan if it was announced that alien technology was involved. "John, I understand your concern, but I think if there is something odd about this device, we should keep the results amongst senior staff for now."

"What do you mean? Why would..."

"Here you go, John," a technician said, interrupting their conversation. He carried the sheets of X-rays and the small box to where they sat, handed them to John and then walked away. John looked at Sarah for a few seconds as if he wanted to ask her something further about what she had been saying, but quickly returned his attention to the materials. He laid the X-rays upon the light table and clicked the switch that activated the bulb underneath the glass top.

Sarah watched as his eyes scanned the images. He swapped films without saying a word and continued his meticulous study of the images. After a few minutes of unbroken silence, he switched the light off. He sat back and took a large gulp of his coffee and then looked at Sarah dead on.

"What's going on here?" he asked.

"What do you mean?" Sarah asked.

"I have a feeling you knew that this technology is well beyond anything we have ever done. Sure, I recognize some of the components, there are similar types in this advanced technology of the spacecraft, but there are other things here that I don't have a clue about. I might hazard a guess as to what its purpose may have been, but that's not the real issue at the moment, is it?"

"Look...John, like I was saying earlier, the President doesn't want anything right now that would further harm the space program. It's bad enough we have this tragedy already. You know how fast public opinion can be swayed when something like this happens. We've seen it many times in the past with other tragedies that caused years of lost time. No need to muddy the waters any further, at least not publicly. We'll leave this component in your hands to study and see what you come up with."

"That's not exactly an answer," he said.

"I know, but it's the best I can do for now. If you don't trust me, then I'm sure President Samuel will be more than happy to discuss any issues you might have."

"Well," he began and hesitated. He stared at Sarah for a few seconds, then at the small box he held in his hand. "I suppose," he continued slowly. "I suppose if he can shed a little insight on this, then I can wait that long before saying anything."

"Thank you." Sarah felt a sigh of relief escape her lips, but his words still left a big question in her mind. "John, you said you might be able to guess at what its purpose was?"

"Yes, but this is just a guess. The layout of circuitry might indicate it was a transmitter or receiver of some type. But what bothers me is the outer box, the one that it was contained in."

"Yes?"

"The only function it has that I can tell is it performs as some form of shield to the enclosed device. It's made of some material I've never seen before and it's incredibly strong."

"Shield from what?"

"That's what I don't get. If this device was part of the problem with what happened, it doesn't make sense that whoever placed it there would want it to be found. It would have been disintegrated in the blast. No evidence of any tampering."

"It's as if they wanted it to be found," Sarah said.

"Exactly," John agreed. "It's as if whoever…"

"Excuse me," a loud voice sounded from the corridor, interrupting John.

Both John and Sarah turned in that direction. A group of military policeman were moving quickly toward them.

"Stay right where you are, please," the one in the lead said.

"Is there a problem, Lieutenant?" John asked.

As the lieutenant arrived at their table, he eyed the small box and X-rays that were lying upon it. "Is that from the wreckage of the space craft?"

"Yes," John replied. "What…"

"All debris is to be secured until further notice," the lieutenant said as he motioned for one of his men to collect the box.

"By whose direction?" Sarah asked.

"Vice President Bishop," he answered.

Sarah was surprised at this turn of events, but she thought perhaps Edward had directed this action to stall any further discovery of what she was becoming more sure was an alien sabotage.

"I was just going to take it back to the hangar," John said.

"We'll take it back," the lieutenant said.

"But I was going back there anyway, I could…"

"You're coming with us," the lieutenant said.

"Where?"

"Just come with us, sir."

"I'll find out what's going on, John," Sarah said as she rose from the table. "I'll call President Samuel and get this cleared up." She turned to the lieutenant. "Where are you taking him?"

"The same place you're going," the lieutenant said as he motioned to his men. Two men now stood next to Sarah and John.

"What's happening here?" Sarah asked. "I am…"

"I know exactly who you are. I have my orders."

"Never ask what else can go wrong because usually it does."
Leumas

Leumas keyed in the coded channel that would link him to President Edward Samuel. As he waited for the call to go through, he watched the picture on the monitor of the helicopter that hovered over the UCDW landing field. What the hell was going on? From probable sabotage to having the site of the council revealed. He touched a control on his desk and the image zoomed in on the occupants of the helicopter. By their actions, they were obviously photographing the craft on the landing field. But how they broke through the security barrier remained a mystery. Not even council ships without the proper equipment could do that.

"Yes, Leumas," Edward Samuel's voice answered. "How nice to hear from you."

"Edward, we've got a problem here. There's a military helicopter hovering over the landing field, taking pictures."

"What?" Edward said, sounding surprised. "How did they get in there?"

"Somehow they got through the restricted airspace and the coded barrier."

"Who the hell authorized this? I'm going to have some general's butt over this one! Probably some weekend warriors doing some training and veered off course and think they entered the twilight zone or something."

"I hope so. You know what could happen if any of this was leaked."

"I know...I know. I don't know why they are there," Edward said, "but I'll get them out of there in a few minutes. Damn military brats. I don't know what they think they are doing. I'll make sure they get debriefed and understand that what they saw is classified."

"Understood, Edward. I'm going to have our security ship send a neutronic pulse to destroy the images they recorded."

"Good. I'd better take care of this immediately. What's happening around here lately? Is there anything else that's going to go wrong?" Edward asked.

"Let's hope not," Leumas offered and terminated the conversation. He opened up a channel to the duty watch officer.

"Lieutenant, have the security ship fire a neutron pulse at the craft to destroy their film recording equipment. I repeat, fire a neutron pulse only. Understood?"

"Yes, Leumas," the lieutenant responded. "Neutron pulse only."

Leumas sat and watched as the helicopter continued to hover, waiting to see it called off by Edward. While he waited, he couldn't help but think about what Edward said about what else could go wrong. He had to admit, everything was certainly not going the way it was supposed to lately...the issues with Soren, the interstellar spacecraft disaster, and now--

His screen lit up as the helicopter exploded in a flare of bright light.

"What the hell?" He watched as the flaming fireball diminished, leaving only a tangled wreck of twisted metal that fell to the ground. He pounded the communication switch with his fist for the duty watch officer channel.

"Lieutenant, what the hell happened?" Leumas demanded.

"I don't know, sir! I'm checking..."

"I told you to just have them send a neutron pulse!"

"Yes, sir, that's what I told them!"

"So what happened?"

"One minute, I'm getting conflicting reports on the communication the ship received."

"What? What do you mean, conflicting reports?"

"I'm analyzing the data link." There was silence for a few seconds.

"Lieutenant?" Leumas said impatiently.

"The message was tampered with. It appears that someone coded a message over my carrier telling them to destroy the human ship."

"Trace it!" Leumas demanded.

"I'm trying," the lieutenant said.

Seconds ticked by until finally there was a response from the lieutenant. " I can't bring it down to an exact location because it's coded and encrypted."

"How did someone break into our coded and encrypted message?" Leumas asked and felt the chilling reminder of the council meeting only minutes before.

"I don't know."

"Well you better find out. Immediately change all the codes."

"Yes, sir!"

Leumas sat back in the chair and let out a scream to vent his anger. He knew he had to call Edward and tell him what happened, but his mind was racing with the fact that somebody was playing them--or him-

-for an idiot right now, and they were winning. The more he thought about it, the angrier he got. The helicopter had used a field negator to breach the compound. The only place a negator could have come from was a council world. The mysterious communication signals also were from someone in the council. Logically thinking, who would gain from the destruction of the interstellar spacecraft and possible exposure of the UCDW to the humans? Only one group came to mind, the movement back to Zire faction.

He was going to talk with Ambassador Alpha after he told Edward the bad news.

***

Copolla listened as the secure communication device beeped, notifying him of an incoming call. He knew it would be Leumas calling to inform him of the unfortunate destruction of the helicopter. He snickered and tried to avoid going into hysterics, but he couldn't help it. He loved leading Leumas around like a dog on a leash. He began to laugh loudly and uncontrollably. "Poor Leumas. Poor old Leumas! Everything just seems to be going wrong..."

Alpha had done well, he thought. Alpha was a genius at times; Copolla couldn't deny that. If only the ambassador had the guts to do something with his ideas...but then he would be dangerous and he would outlive his usefulness. Oh well, things had a way of catching up to people. All in good time...all in good time.

The communication device continued to beep. Copolla cleared his throat and picked it up.

"Yes, Leumas," he said trying to sound nonchalant. "I called the duty officer and told them to get that helicopter out of there. Don't tell me it's still there?"

"No, Edward, it's not here."

"So what's the problem then?"

"The helicopter has been destroyed."

"What?" Coppola said, trying to avoid another comical outburst. He thought redundancy and shock would be the appropriate response to display at this time. "What do you mean destroyed? There was a crew on there...young Americans."

"Someone got into our secure communications and sent the order to destroy the helicopter instead of just firing the neutronic pulse like I wanted. I'm sorry."

"You're sorry? Wait a minute! You're supposed to be the technologically advanced aliens. I thought you had safeguards to prevent this kind of stuff? How could something like this happen?"

"I don't know," Leumas said. "We're looking into it right now and..."

"Well I think you'd better go find out, Leumas. Don't you? This is going to take some serious damage control on my end. You've really put me on the spot."

"I know, Edward, I know. I'm sorry. I will find out what happened, I promise you. The loss of life of the people on board the craft is inexcusable. Those responsible will be punished."

"I certainly hope so."

"Edward, I know it may sound unkindly of me in lieu of the loss of lives, but I have to make sure about one issue."

"What?"

"For some reason which we have not ascertained yet, the craft was able to penetrate the null field barrier, and you know that shouldn't have happened. We're looking into that also. I'm worried that there may have been communications from the craft. Did you check to see if there was any data transmission that may have contained images or conversations of the crew about what they saw here?" Leumas asked.

"There was none. Apparently your communication safeguards were still in place," Copolla answered.

"Good. We wouldn't want another incident like we had with that reporter, Ray Schume. He almost did us in."

"Yes. He almost did," Coppola said, remembering how he had fed the human reporter information about the council. It had almost worked. He remembered how he'd had them all scampering around trying to put out the fires he created. It had been such fun...until his son had screwed everything up.

"Well, if you're sure everything is secure on your end, I'll get to work trying to get things straight here."

"Yes...that sounds like a good idea, Leumas. You do that." Copolla terminated the communication before Leumas could say anything else.

He turned his gaze toward the computer and clicked the mouse several times until he reached what he wanted. He sat back and watched the video feed the helicopter had sent. It clearly showed the landing field at the UCDW compound, which contained at least two dozen alien spacecraft. He watched as the camera zoomed in on a number of craft, showing the detail of them, clearly depicting a technology that was evidently not human. The images continued for several seconds and then there was a surge of bright light and the screen went blank. "Perfect," Copolla said. He composed a note to the chairman of the Joint Chiefs of Staff, General Bradstorm, telling him to ensure the Vice President received a copy of the video. As he finished typing and was about to send it, Copolla had a change of mind and added another line to the note, telling the general to come and see him about another matter. Although he hadn't wanted to use influence on the general at first, now it really didn't matter anymore because he had fulfilled his purpose. Now all he could become was a problem, and Copolla wasn't going to have any of that.

It was time for an accident...no, that would be too boring. A suicide sounded more dramatic. Copolla was sure there was an open window or something the general could fall out of. And of course a note indicating some form of complicity in this whole affair should also do nicely.

***

Sarah and John Hagen were escorted by the military police to a room at the NASA headquarters building. They were ushered inside and left alone. Sarah couldn't help but feel leery when she heard the door being locked from the outside.

"What's going on?" John asked.

"I don't know, but I'm going to find out," She took out her cellular phone and dialed Edward's number. Just about as she was going to press the send button, the sound of the door being unlocked caught her attention. She decided to wait until she saw who was entering.

Vice President John Bishop walked into the room and smiled at her. Some of her unease quickly passed. Although John had not known of the council on Earth, he had always been supportive of their efforts in the space program. Leumas, Edward and Sarah had agreed that after Edward finished his last term, and if John showed interest in running for President, he might prove to be an advantageous predecessor for Edward.

She breathed a sigh of relief and greeted him. "Mr. Vice President," she said, not using his first name in the presence of John Hagen. "What's going on? Why have we been detained?"

"I apologize, Ms. McClendon, but there have been some unusual developments that required Mr. Hagan not to speak with anyone about what he has uncovered. I apologize for the gruffness of the military police but there wasn't any time to spare given the seriousness of the discovery."

"Unusual developments?" she asked.

"Yes, President Samuel has informed me that the unique item that was discovered can severely damage our efforts. For reasons of national security, he has placed me in charge of the situation so that it wouldn't go public."

"How did you hear about it so soon? It was only hours ago."

"Word travels fast when there's a mystery. The rest you'll hear about later at a briefing. President Samuel asked me to relay to you that you have some sensitive business to attend to, so I won't delay you anymore."

She recognized the coded response, "sensitive business." Edward would use this term when there was a need for her to return to the UCDW. "Yes. Thank you. What about Mr. Hagen?" she asked.

"President Samuel would like to speak with him. I am personally going to escort him to the White House."

Well that would hopefully resolve this problem, she thought. That was what John had asked for; to talk with the President about what he'd discovered, and Edward would no doubt secure his secrecy. Hopefully that would all work out and keep the item that had been discovered out of the press until they could find out what was going on.

"Well, I think that about covers things for the moment," she said to Bishop and then turned toward John, who was still looking confused. "I think you'll get that conversation after all. I hope that will resolve any concerns you might have."

"Me, too," he said and smiled. "This is all a little overwhelming for an engineer." They shook hands and Sarah left the room.

Walking down the hall, she came to a ladies' rest room and stepped inside. She checked to ensure the stalls were empty, then removed her cellular phone and dialed the number that would transfer her to Leumas at the UCDW compound. She waited impatiently as the signal was routed and encrypted. Finally Leumas' voice came on.

"Sarah, where are you?" he asked.

"Still at NASA. What's happening?"

"We had an incident with a military helicopter that dropped by to have a look at our place. It's a long story but the short of it is that someone has infiltrated our command control systems. Instead of a neutron pulse to erase their film, our security ship in orbit fired a laser blast that destroyed the helicopter and all aboard."

"What? Oh, my God."

"Plus there are indications that the spacecraft accident was not an accident but a deliberate act. All evidence points back here, to someone at the council."

"I was beginning to suspect that," she said. "The device found...or should I say the device that was meant to be found, clearly indicates an advanced technology."

"Any chance of us getting a look at that device?"

"Maybe later. Right now it's on the way to Washington with Vice President Bishop and the lead NASA engineer who discovered it. I assume Edward will quell the engineer's concerns and bury the device so the public doesn't get wind of it."

"Right. He's doing the same for the incident with the helicopter. I don't know what we'd do without him."

"I know. I know," Sarah agreed. "He's wonderful."

CHAPTER
TWENTY SEVEN

"I had no idea what I had become involved with. Now...I wish I still didn't."

John Hagen: NASA

When the door closed, Vice President John Bishop turned his attention toward John Hagen. "Well, Mr. Hagen, I think we need to talk about some of these things that have been happening. You may not realize it, but our national security has been breached."

"Breached? I don't understand."

"This device you've found. It's clearly not from this planet, is it?"

"How did you know that?"

"I've suspected many things over the years but only recently are they becoming clearer and I see what has been going on. I didn't want to speak with Ms. McClendon here because I suspect she may be involved with some of this."

"Sarah? But she's been key to all our efforts. You can't mean that she's done things to hinder what we are trying to accomplish?"

"Not everyone is as they appear. Didn't she try to convince you to keep silent about what you found?"

"She did seem anxious about downplaying the discovery," John offered. "But it doesn't make sense."

"You'll be surprised how deep this goes, Mr. Hagen. Very surprised. The important thing is that we have proof that we can bring to the American people and the rest of the world. And you will be right there on the stage with me."

"What about the President? I thought we were going to talk with him. Isn't this something he should bring to the people?" John asked.

"He won't."

"Why not?"

"Because he's at the center of the conspiracy, Mr. Hagen. He's been a major player in this from the beginning. In fact, it has been Ms. McClendon and President Samuel all along."

"All along in what?"

"They have been working for an alien race, keeping an eye on what we were doing. Now that we are getting too powerful, they blew up our spacecraft. They don't want us to get any more advanced. They want to hold us back, to keep us from making our way out into space so we can see what a mockery their so-called council justice system is.

Well...we have a little surprise for them now. We know about them and we know where they are."

***

"That should just about do it," Copolla said aloud in the empty oval office as he replaced the telephone in its holder. "Everything is in motion. Just one more step to accomplish."

A knock sounded from one of the doors that only his Secret Service agents knew of, reminding Copolla that he had summoned one.

"Come in," Copolla said in an almost jovial tone, then remembered that jovial would not fit the motif of the upcoming conversation and quickly added, "please."

The door opened and agent Tee Morris entered the room. A tall and broad shouldered man, he radiated the picture of health and strength. He was the only council member planted within the Secret Service to maintain close contact should the President ever need assistance of a special nature. The idea had been Leumas', Copolla knew from the memories of the human; quite a smart move considering Leumas' usual ineptness.

"Yes, Mr. President," he said as he closed the door.

"We've got one hell of a problem. The worse thing that could have happened has occurred." Copolla contorted his face as if under great emotional stress. "We're all going to be exposed in a matter of hours, if not less. They have learned everything and there isn't a damn thing I can do about it."

"What's happened?" Agent Morris asked.

"Vice President Bishop has found out about the council location. They have video secured from a helicopter that somehow penetrated the council area. They also have all the data on me and my affiliation with the council."

"How did they…"

"I don't know. If I knew about the leak, do you think we would be in this predicament right now?" Copolla asked as he mixed anger and fear together.

The effect was wonderful, he thought, as he watched the confusion on the face of the council idiot as he searched his thoughts for the required procedure in the case of such an event.

"Of course not," Agent Morris said as his face regained some of its composure.

"And now I just heard they have evidence that indicates complicity of the council in the destruction of the interstellar spacecraft. Put two and two together and we're what they equal." He grabbed a large briefcase and began throwing articles into it even though he had no idea what they were. He was just doing it for effect to show his fear and hurriedness.

"Do you wish to initiate evacuation procedures?"

"Yes, immediately. As soon as they hold their press conference, it'll all be over for me. No one will understand what we were doing and hysteria will begin. It'll be the greatest witch hunt in the history of this office, and the country for that matter. There will not be any opportunity to try and resolve this from here. We have to get to the council where maybe I can make someone understand through reason. But until that time, they'll impeach me and who knows where it will go from there. The same for Ms. McClendon."

"Where is Ms. McClendon?"

"Fortunately, I was able to warn her and she's already on her way to the council. I need to get there and confer with Leumas and her on our next move to see if we can find our way out of this mess."

"Understood," the agent said. He removed a cellular phone from his inside suit jacket and pressed a key. "Code Oscar. I repeat: Code Oscar. Immediate departure." He replaced the phone in his jacket. "I have initiated the procedure for the Secret Service. Code Oscar indicates immediate danger and that you are to be secretly evacuated from the White House. We'll take the private helicopter I have at the commercial airfield and land directly at the secondary landing zone at the council headquarters."

"Good, then what are we waiting for? Let's go."

As Copolla followed Agent Morris out the door, he smiled.

***

"Yes, I understand," Christine repeated to the voice on the telephone. When she had answered the phone, she had immediately recognized the voice that belonged to the man she knew as Alpha. "How long will she be gone?" she asked. "I need to know what to pack for her and what...hello? Hello?"

The voice at the other end of the phone was gone. She slammed the receiver back into the wall-mounted receptacle.

"Asshole. How the hell do they expect me to get the child ready to go somewhere and not give me an idea of how long she's going to be gone. And have her ready to leave in ten minutes. Who the hell do they think they are?"

She stomped around the kitchen for a few moments, stewing over the phone call and the abruptness of its ending. As usual it took her a few moments to realize that she was being angry for no good reason when the epiphany of the situation struck her. *I'll be able to take some time off and party. What the hell am I being angry about? Get the kid packed up, then hit the street.*

She walked quickly, with renewed vigor in her step, taking the stairs two at a time as she headed for Cindy's room. The child was sitting on her bed reading a book. *How smug she is*, she thought, as the child hadn't even looked up from her book when she entered.

"Get some things packed," she said. "You're going on a little trip."

"Where?" the girl asked, still not looking up from her book.

"That's not important," Christine answered coolly. "Just throw some clothes in a bag."

"How long will I be gone?"

"I don't know. And stop with all the questions. Just get packed. Someone is coming by to pick you up in a few minutes."

"Who?"

"Didn't I just say to stop with all the questions?" Christine answered, feeling her earlier good mood quickly dissipating. She hated the way this small child could make her feel so stupid at times. She wondered if she did it on purpose just to piss her off. "Get moving--now!"

Cindy finally looked up at her. "Okay, okay," she answered as she closed the book and got up from her bed. She knelt on the floor and pulled a small bag out from underneath the bed, then opened a dresser drawer and began placing things into the bag.

"How am I..." Cindy began to ask when the doorbell sounded.

"That's probably your ride. Let's go," Christine said as she grasped Cindy's hand and virtually yanked her away from the dresser.

"I haven't finished packing," Cindy protested.

"Don't worry about it," Christine muttered as she moved with the child toward the door and out of the room. "I'm sure they'll give you everything you need."

The doorbell rang again. "I'm coming, I'm coming. Keep your pants on!" she shouted as they made their way down the stairs.

Christine opened the front door. On the doorstep stood a small man, even smaller than her five feet. He was bald, with elfish looking ears, but his face reflected a sternness that seemed not to fit the rest of his appearance.

"Is she ready?" the man asked with a surprisingly deep voice.

"Right here." She pulled on Cindy's arm and brought her around to the front of her.

The man looked at the child for several seconds before speaking. "Hello," he said finally, his face losing the stern look and becoming cheerful and friendly.

"Hello," Cindy said. "Where are we going?"

"A trip. A fun trip. You do like fun things, don't you?"

"Sure."

"Okay, see that car over there?" he asked, as he pointed to a white car parked in front of the small house.

"Yes."

"Good. Now go to it and get in. I'll be there in a moment."

Christine didn't know what it was, but she somehow "felt" his words in her mind. She started to move in his direction, feeling something drawing her as his words reverberated in her mind.

"Not you," he said to Christine as he raised his hand. "Just her." He indicated Cindy by pointing his other hand.

Suddenly the feeling or sense of urgency that had settled upon Christine left her with the same speed as it had arrived. Cindy, without further comment, walked out of the doorway and headed to the car. The man watched as she got into the vehicle and closed the door.

He turned his attention back to Christine. "I have something for you." He reached into his jacket. "Mr. Alpha has sent you a bonus for your fine work. A little something extra to help you enjoy your time off."

"That's awfully nice of him," Christine said. "It's been a while since he sent any kind of bonus."

"I'm sure this will not disappoint you in the future...because you won't have one. Future, that is."

"What are you talking about? Hey..." Her words trailed off as she saw what he removed from his jacket. It appeared to be some kind of gun, but it looked odd, almost like a child's toy. It reminded her of what they called a derringer, the kind of gun that the western gamblers used to pull out from their sleeves or boot. He pointed it at her chest.

"What is this? Some sort of a joke?" Fear made her voice tremble.

"A joke...of course not. This is for you," he said as he handed her the weapon. "Mr. Alpha felt very strongly that you should have this fine piece of equipment. After all, you never know when something like this might come in handy."

Christine took it from him, feeling the coolness of the small gun-like weapon. "What am I supposed to do with this?"

"Do? Oh yes. Sorry, I forgot."

Christine felt something jam into her thoughts, obliterating everything else except for the one thought that repeated itself over and over again.

::After I leave, wait one minute and then press the gun to your forehead and pull the trigger. Is that clear?::

"Yes," she agreed, feeling nothing but the imperativeness of the single thought that resonated in her mind.

"Good. Now you have a nice night...whatever is left of it for you, anyway."

"Yes..." she answered as that same thought repeated over and over again in her head.

::After I leave, wait one minute and then press the gun to your forehead and pull the trigger. Is that clear?::

"A gift is sometimes not what it appears to be—believe me, I know."
Cindy Carlson

Cindy watched as the small elfish looking man left the house and came out to the car where she waited. She knew she should be cautious, but any opportunity to be away from Aunt Christine was something to be cherished and taken advantage of. She would have to be careful how she acted, remembering that she was physically a child in everyone else's eye, not wanting to raise any suspicion from the mysterious visitor.

When he got in, instead of starting the car up right away, he sat and looked out into the darkening street as evening settled upon the city, his hands gripping the steering wheel as if he were driving down some imaginary road . Then, without taking his eyes off the outside world he was observing so intently, his hand moved under his jacket as if searching for something, then returned it to the steering wheel of the car.

Cindy watched the man curiously, wondering why he was looking so intently at the surroundings of her neighborhood. There were homes, one after the other, lined up on the street. Nothing that she thought warranted such attention. The expression on his face, the slight slanting of his lips to indicate fascination and almost wonderment, added to her bewilderment. It appeared to her that he was taking some form of pleasure from his observations.

Although she had no idea who this person was, she thought she could sense that he wasn't here to harm her, like the doctor did when he came to visit. Plus the doctor never took her anywhere, and time away from Aunt Christine could only be an improvement of sorts given the rarity that the opportunity ever presented itself. But she also felt or knew that he was not a nice man by nature. She knew that in his own way he could be just as bad as the doctor was. Still, something told her that for the time being he wouldn't harm her because he'd been told not to.

"You're not from around here, are you?" she asked.

He turned toward her and smiled. "No. I'm from somewhere very far from here. This is my...first time in this area."

"I thought so," Cindy said as she nodded in agreement. "I can tell these things."

"Well, aren't you the perceptive one," he said smiling again.

The smile attracted her attention for some reason. Not so much the smile itself, but the "feeling" from it. It had a calming effect on her. Her thoughts grew sluggish, like the way your lip felt after you got a shot at the dentist's office. You knew it was there but it felt mushy and you couldn't tell if it was moving or not.

"Where are we going?" Cindy asked.

"Somewhere where you'll see things you never knew existed. A very secret place, or at least it was. I understand all that is changing as we speak. Anyway, then you're going to go on another trip to a new... place and see even more wonderful and exciting things and meet new people. Sound like fun?"

"I don't know, you're not being very specific," Cindy said. "Where is this place and why didn't Aunt Christine come with us?" *Slow down*, she told herself. *Don't rush him.*

"All in good time child, all in good time," he answered. "As far as your Aunt Christine is concerned, she has a previous engagement she can't miss. A very soon engagement if I..." A beeping sound interrupted his talking. He looked away from Cindy, his attention drawn back to the house.

Cindy turned in the direction where the strange man was looking. She saw a bright light that lit up all the windows of her house. She squinted and held her hand up to her eyes, shading them from the brightness. It looked as if every light switch had immediately come on and then slowly faded out.

She turned back to the man and watched as he continued to stare at the house. His hand moved under his coat and silenced the device that had continued beeping while she had watched the intense light appear and then quickly dissipate.

"What was that?" she asked. "Is Aunt Christine okay?"

"Of course! Better than ever," he said, sounding happy. "She must have opened her gift that I gave her. Well, let's be on our way," he said as he started the car.

"What gift?" Cindy asked, her interest piqued. If there was anything that could distract her from any form of rational thinking, it was the words "gift" or "present." The concept had always been something unique to Cindy and instantly made her forget everything else. She had rarely ever received one, and now to hear that Aunt Christine had gotten one from this mysterious visitor was more then she could imagine, and all her conscious efforts were now centered upon this event.

"Just a token from Mr. Alpha," he said and then paused, staring at her. "Oh, that's right, I almost forgot. Mr. Alpha also mentioned that you really like gifts. Can you open the glove box?" he asked as he pointed in that direction. "I forgot to give you your surprise."

"Surprise?"

"Yes. Go ahead. Open the glove box."

Cindy opened the glove box and saw a small box covered in pink wrapping paper.

"This?" she asked. A sense of caution rose in her mind. *Gifts from a stranger…not good! But what could it do to harm me? If he wanted to do that, why bring me out to the car? It's okay.*

"Yes. Come on now and open it. I love surprises, don't you?"

"Sure." She removed the box and held it in her hands. A surge of warmth shot through her. The box seemed alive. *Silly! How can a box be alive?*

"Go ahead. Open it!" he implored her.

"Okay, okay!" she said, but still hesitated at tearing at the paper. She felt as if her entire body was suddenly wrapped up in the box. The gift wrapping was the prettiest she had ever seen. The best Christine ever did was wrap up her birthday gift in aluminum foil. This…this work of art, she thought, seemed a shame to tear apart.

"What's wrong?" he asked.

"It's just so pretty." She caressed the ribbon that formed the bow in the center.

"Wait until you see what's inside."

Her thoughts screamed to her, *"OPEN IT!"* She couldn't resist it any longer. She carefully pried the edges of the tape so that she could unfold the paper without ripping it too much. Eventually she made her way to the small box and opened it up. Inside the box, wrapped in soft silky feeling paper, was a little teddy bear. It was the cutest thing she had ever seen.

"Do you like it?" he asked.

"It's so pretty."

"Well, take it out and hold it in the palm of your hand. It may be a small bear, but it's a special bear made to sit in your palm."

She removed the bear, placed it in her right palm, and held it upright with her left hand.

"It's so adorable and…ouch!" she cried. The sudden jab in her palm caused her to drop the bear. It fell silently to the floorboard of the car as she grasped her right hand with her left and examined her palm. In the center was a red spot where something had poked her. She felt a wave of drowsiness come over her and the world around her begin to go gray and fuzzy.

The shock of betrayal forced her to one last realization. "Drugged... why?" she murmured.

"Lesson number one," he said. "Knowing the weakness of a potential enemy is extremely important. By using that weakness to lull them into carelessness, it makes them do things they might have reservations about. Lesson Number two: Things that are pretty and look harmless are not always what they appear. You're lucky, though. This time you will wake up in a couple of hours. Your Aunt Christine won't ever wake up. In fact they'll have a hard time finding all the pieces."

Cindy slid back in the seat and closed her eyes.

***

Reporters assembled in the White House press room awaiting the preliminary press conference by the President of the United States on the interstellar spacecraft explosion. It was already twenty minutes past the announced starting time and apparent restlessness settled over the assembled journalists as they formed groups and speculated about the delay. Finally the door opened and several officials came through. Murmurs ran through the crowd of reporters as they saw that the President was not among them. Instead Vice President John Bishop stepped up to the podium.

"Ladies and Gentleman," he began. "Let me start by saying that this is by far the most difficult day of my life and for this country. What I am about to tell you is all verified information. Let me begin by saying that what happened in the sky off the coast of Florida a short time ago was just the tip of the iceberg."

Several reporters sat up in their chairs as they listened, obviously intrigued by the opening comments of the Vice President.

"I regret to inform you that the interstellar spacecraft was sabotaged. A bomb was planted onboard and detonated shortly after takeoff, destroying the vehicle."

Murmurs rumbled through the reporters.

"Was it terrorists?" A voice called out.

"Has anyone claimed responsibility?"

Others chimed in asking more questions while others stood from their seats and began waving their hands to be recognized. Cellular telephones appeared magically in their hands as calls were made to their parent offices.

"Please," the Vice President said, raising his hands in a halting gesture. "There will be no questions until I have finished."

He waited for a few moments as they settled back down and became quiet.

"We arrived at this conclusion based upon a detonation device found in the wreckage and examined by the Chief engineer from NASA, Mr. John Hagen." Vice President Bishop indicated to one of the men who were seated on the stage.

The Vice President continued, "We have learned that a terrible shroud of darkness and deceit has been placed over the American people. A man that we all put our trust in has led us astray. This man has made a pact with a group of individuals that only had one thing in mind, to keep the people of Earth from expanding outward into space. This act of sabotage was their way of proving that they can stop us."

A deathly silence settled over the room as the reporters hung on every word the Vice President spoke, waiting for him to name this incredible and dastardly traitor.

"Along with this discovery, other certain incredible and frightening evidence has recently come to light that takes this betrayal even further. Without saying anything more, I want to show you this evidence we have brought here today to lay before the American people. If you would please direct your attention to the screen, we will show you something unimaginable, and let me remind you that we will not answer questions until the conclusion of the briefing. I will let General Bradstorm explain what you are going to see. General."

General Bradstorm stepped up to the podium as images flickered and then came into focus on the screen. Vast mountainous and woodland areas were displayed.

"This footage is from the surveillance camera from an Army National Guard helicopter," the general said. "Shot only hours ago while it was conducting a training exercise. The area we are seeing is in a rural section of West Virginia, an area that includes several thousand acres of national forest."

Images of a compound containing several buildings appeared. "This is the secure military compound. Once a military remote communications site, it was modified six years ago and is now used by the American government for private meetings and secure gatherings of national interest. It also served as a primary retreat for senior White House officials, but chiefly for the President of the United States."

Images of more woodland areas appeared as the helicopter continued on. "What we discovered lies approximately sixty miles away." The images on the screen changed and now showed the distinct shapes of about a dozen spacecraft parked in an open area of a meadow. As if interpreting the initial thoughts by the audience of the reporters, the General added, "Yes, they are what they appear to be, Ladies and Gentlemen. They are alien spacecraft."

"But General…" one of the reporters began in a sarcastic tone. He was quickly cut off.

"These images have been analyzed by our best scientists. There is no doubt about this whatsoever," the Vice President added.

"Also," the general continued, "we conducted some seismic studies of the area from our geological satellites to see what might have attracted that many alien spacecraft to one area. What we have been able to determine is that some form of underground environment has been secured in the mountains in this area. Our assessment can only conclude that we have been invaded and occupied by an alien race, maybe more than one, judging by the different configurations of spacecraft seen. As to why these spacecraft have not been detected in the past, I can only assume that they have some kind of anti-radar device that blocks them from being detected, which may have recently failed and the error was undetected."

The images on the screen suddenly flared with a bright white light and then went blank. "The helicopter was destroyed by what we must assume was another alien ship in orbit. There were no survivors. We are pretty confident that the aliens believe they destroyed the craft before it could transmit any of the pictures back to us. We are continually monitoring the area for any movement of these forces and we have placed our military forces on alert and have targeted the area with short range missiles." The general returned to his seat as the Vice President returned to the podium.

"One must find it hard to imagine how all of this could have happened without anyone seeing any signs. But with the thrilling excitement of the space program and the promises of a bright future through that end, our attention was conveniently diverted. I believe this was done purposely to keep us from seeing what these aliens are up to. Even though technologically superior to us, even an alien race would have to infiltrate the workings of our defense and similar organizations to keep up the appearance that everything was normal. Therefore it is an obvious assumption that they were assisted in some way…from the top office of the country and his chief assistant for the space program. I am sad to say that President Edward Samuel and Sarah McClendon have been in alliance with these aliens since the day he took office."

Several members of the press stood in disbelief.

"Perhaps it would be best if you asked your questions at this point," the Vice President said.

"Where is the President? Why isn't he here to comment on these accusations?"

"The President is missing. From what we can tell, he left with a Secret Service agent about two hours ago."

"Is there evidence that incriminates him?"

"Yes. We have found his file of communiqués with the alien organization, as well as Ms. McClendon's. All will be released at a later date as soon as we finish our own investigation."

"If the President is missing, what happens to the chain of command?"

"I am acting President in his absence."

"Will be there a military strike on the alien compound?"

"We don't know yet. We are still examining the area and conferring with our allies. This is obviously something that has global implications; if aliens are here in the United States, they are probably elsewhere on the planet as well."

"Vice President Bishop, you remember the accusations reporter Ray Schume made six years ago? He disappeared after that. Do you think there is any connection?"

"I can only speculate at this point, but I think we can all form our own conclusion on that issue, knowing what we know now."

***

Sarah arrived back at the council headquarters and decided before going to see Leumas that she could spare a few minutes to stop and check on Soren. As she entered her quarters she found him sitting on the sofa, staring at the television screen.

"Soren," she called. "Mom's home."

Soren didn't move from where he sat. He continued to stare directly in front of him, not noticing her presence. Sarah took a few anxious steps closer.

"Soren? Soren, can you hear me?" She touched his shoulder. As her fingers made contact, she heard a snap and immediately received a painful jolt that shot through her fingers and straight up to her shoulder. Her knees began to buckle, but she recovered quickly, grabbing onto the end of the sofa to keep from falling. *Christ!* she thought. *What was that? That was not just static electricity.*

Soren broke his gaze from directly in front of him and looked at Sarah for the first time.

"Hi, Mom."

The nonchalant tone in his voice scared Sarah. "Soren, are you alright?"

"Sure," he answered. "I was just...thinking."

Sarah cautiously sat down on the sofa, fearing another large discharge like the one that had almost taken her down previously. She was careful not to get too close to him for the moment.

"What have you been thinking about?" she asked.

"Dad," he said.

Dad. No other word could affect Sarah like that one as she felt a surge of emotion wash through her. She knew that as Soren got older he would ask more questions about his father, but that didn't make it any easier on her. Explaining to Soren what Greg was like forced her to remember, and that was still a painful event.

"What about him, Soren?" she asked, trying to keep her voice calm and even.

"Just thinking of how wonderful it would be to have him here. It would make us both very happy, wouldn't it?"

"Yes. Yes, it would. Very happy," Sarah agreed and reached out for him. There was no shock this time as she felt her son's warmth against her skin. She hugged him tightly and kissed his head.

"Everything is going to be okay, Mom. I know it."

The waves of emotion pummeled into her mind and she imagined Greg was here sitting on the sofa next to her and she was hugging him instead of Soren. ::*Sarah,*:: she heard him say in her mind. ::*I love you.*::

All her senses felt his presence. She could smell him, she could feel the way his skin was soft and sweet...but knew that it couldn't be real-- Greg was not here! She pulled back from Soren...or was it Greg...no, it was Soren. It had to be! Greg wasn't here he was...dead. *No, not again!* She screamed in her thoughts. She couldn't go through this again!

"Soren, what did you do!" she cried.

"Nothing, Mom. What's wrong?"

"You pushed those images into my mind again, didn't you?" she asked. Her voice sounded harsher than she wanted.

"No. I didn't do anything. I was just hugging you."

::*Are you sure, Soren?*:: she sent telepathically.

::*Yes, Mommy, I didn't do it.*::

"Then what..."

Alarms sounded in their quarters followed by a computer voice. "The compound is now in a defensive posture. All security personnel report to their assigned position."

CHAPTER
TWENTY NINE

"Chaos is my most useful tool wherever I go and whatever circumstance I face."

Copolla

As Copolla stepped from the shuttle in the human form of President Edward Samuel, he heard the alarms and the computer automated voice announcing that the compound was in a security alert status. He couldn't help but smile at what he had caused.

Perfect, he thought. *It's already begun. That will make the next step even easier.*

From the shadows he saw the familiar shape of Alpha step out.

"Mr. President." He made a motion with his tentacled hand to his lips that indicated their speech might be monitored. He walked up to Copolla and placed a small device about the size of a thumbnail onto his clothing. Copolla immediately recognized it as a communication blocking device that would prevent his voice from being heard.

"It is safe to speak now," Alpha said.

"Always the cautious one, eh, Alpha?" Copolla said as he smirked and uttered a laugh.

"I do not wish to take any risks," Alpha answered dryly. "If something were to go wrong, my future would be in question, even my life."

"Smart. Very smart," Copolla said and thought, *Always looking out for number one. Highly commendable. I would do the same thing.* "But have no fear, it appears everything is going as planned," Copolla said as he motioned with his arm in the air to the commotion of the alarm and voice warning being announced.

"Yes. I anticipate that there will be no reconciliation in the near future with the Earth people and the controlled evacuation announcement will be coming soon."

"You're so right there," Copolla agreed. "The hornet's nest has been stirred sufficiently enough for that. I imagine the government is in an uproar at this very moment trying to figure how all of this could have happened. Isn't it wonderful?"

"It should provide sufficient distraction and aid the process."

"What of the girl?" Copolla asked.

"She is sedated and on board my ambassadorial ship."

"Good. Good. I don't think it will take very long to escalate to the point where I can convince the council that it is time to go. Be prepared to leave on very short notice. Is everything arranged?"

"Yes."

"Well then, I better get to work and meet with Leumas so I can convince him that I need to be on the first ship out of here...with the young master, Soren. After all, the welfare of the child comes first, doesn't it? We wouldn't want anything to happen to him, now would we?"

Alpha's face betrayed no sign of appreciation of the humor as Copolla laughed heartily.

When Copolla saw this, he slowed his laughter, wiped the spittle that had appeared at the corner of his mouth, and eyed Alpha cautiously.

"You know, Alpha, I really wish you would display some kind of emotion at times. It makes me nervous, makes me think that maybe you don't trust me."

Alpha showed no emotion as he responded, "Very amusing."

***

"Soren, you stay here. I'm going to find out what is going on," Sarah said, raising her voice over the automated alarm.

"Okay, Mommy. But I didn't do anything wrong. Honest," the boy said emphatically.

"I believe you...but something is happening and I'm worried for you. It may be affecting what it is I'm feeling or sensing. We'll talk about it later, okay?" She kissed him on the forehead and hugged him. "I really have to go and help Uncle Leumas."

"Okay. Mommy?"

"Yes, Soren?"

"Everything will be okay."

"I hope so, honey. I hope so."

Sarah stepped out into the corridor. As soon as the door closed behind her she let her emotions wash out of her. She leaned against the wall for support as the tears came. With clenched fists she pounded against the wall, not knowing what else to do.

Why is this happening? Is there no end to this madness? My own thoughts have been more than enough to punish me all these years, now my own son adds to it. Oh God, please...why is this happening?

The computer voice repeated, "The compound is now in a defensive posture. All security personnel report to their assigned position."

Sarah focused her thoughts on the computer voice. She wiped away the tears that lingered and took in a deep breath and slowly exhaled. *Get moving, Sarah! Stop your whining and get your ass moving! You have responsibilities. Leumas will need your help.*

She straightened up and got moving. By the time the door to the command center opened, she had cleared her mind and was ready to work.

"Leumas, what the hell is going on?" she asked as she entered the main control room of the council.

"You haven't been watching the news or been in touch with your office lately, have you?" Leumas said as he pointed to one of the monitors that had the news channel on.

"No, why?" she asked, not looking in the direction he indicated. "I've been busy trying to avert a catastrophe at NASA."

"Well, aside from that, all hell is breaking lose. The compound has been exposed to your military and it has just been made public. Forces are moving in and surrounding the area. Watch this," he said as he keyed a monitor. A grim-looking news reporter for CNN came into view.

"This day has seen two shocking announcements from Vice President Bishop. First, that an alien presence has been detected in West Virginia. Second, that President Edward Samuel and his assistant Sarah McClendon are and have been involved with the alien conspiracy since they entered office. Vice President Bishop has indicated that their main goal has been to deceive and distract the people of Earth, while the aliens plotted a takeover of the planet. Military forces are preparing to..."

"Oh, my God," Sarah said as she placed her hand up to her lips. "What about Edward? Have you spoken..."

"He will be arriving shortly. He was able to escape with the council Secret Service agent we assigned to him."

"How can this be, Leumas?" Sarah asked as she felt her entire world collapse around her. All the years of work now vanished before her. All of hers and Greg's dreams of peacefully moving the Earth out into space slowly faded from existence.

"I don't know. But it's all out in the open now and I don't see any way to talk our way out this time."

"What are we going to do?" Her voice sounded small and unsure.

"I'd thought we wait for Edward to get here and see if he can do anything. The military forces don't pose any significant danger to us for the moment. More importantly, we know there is someone on the inside of the council who has caused all of this to happen."

"Why? For what end?" Sarah asked.

"It appears to simply expose us to the people of this planet. If Edward can't convince them that we are not here to take over, and they decide that they don't want us here, council law says we have to leave the planet."

"That's it? Game over? We uproot the entire organization?"

"Yes. It's that simple. And isn't it amazing that this is exactly what some of the council members wanted? To return to Zire."

Sarah, shocked by the sudden news, felt her mind ready to explode. What were they to do? "But Earth...is my home...and...Greg's home. We just can't leave like we were some criminals..."

Leumas walked over to Sarah and grasped her hands. "It doesn't look good for you or Edward. The news says they have already sworn in Vice President Bishop as President, they're calling Edward and you spies and charging you with espionage all in a matter of hours."

"But John Bishop, he's a good man. I can't believe he would do any of this."

"Somehow he's been convinced. It's done. No sense in dwelling on it. Sarah, I know this all comes as a shock, but I need for you to be strong. We have the council to think about. There are decisions that will need to be made."

Sarah's face changed from the look of shock and awe to one of understanding, of purpose.

"You're right," she agreed and tried to sound as positive as she could. "The greater good is at stake. Even if it means we lose Earth as a potential member of the UCDW. But I still want to talk with John Bishop when Edward gets here. There may still be some chance."

"I agree," Leumas said, smiling. "We'll figure out something...we always do. But preparations still have..."

"Leumas," a voice spoke from his terminal. "This is Dora."

"Yes, Dora. What is it? I'm kind of busy at the moment."

"Yes, Leumas, I know. I have been monitoring events. Are you handling the stress..."

"Dora, was there something you wanted?" Leumas asked.

"Yes, of course there is. I have detected a disturbance matching your search parameters."

"What is she talking about?" Sarah asked.

"I have Dora keep an eye out for anything out of the ordinary that might mean something other than what it appears to be."

Sarah nodded. She knew that Leumas kept a constant watch for any activity that might indicate any plots against them or the council.

"What kind of disturbance?" Leumas asked Dora.

"An electromagnetic disturbance that has all of the characteristics of the previous one reported with the exception of location."

"Where did it occur?"

"Its location was in quadrant one, directly above this compound. There is a probability of over ninety percent that they are almost identical in comparison to each other. There is a…"

An alarm sounded from Leumas' console. He turned and stared at it with a puzzled expression on his face.

"What's wrong now?" Sarah asked.

"The room sensors have detected an intruder in the…ah…room…"

"What room? What's wrong, Leumas?"

"It's the room where Greg's body is in stasis."

"Like we don't have enough going on right now to worry about," Sarah said angrily. "I'll take care of this. Have someone from security meet me there."

"But Edward should be here any minute. Why don't you let security handle this?" Leumas offered. "Please, Sarah?"

"No! This won't take long. I may not be able to do anything about what is happening in my own country and even on my own planet. But when it comes to this, no one will mess with the only man I ever truly loved in my life. This won't take long, I promise you."

Part Three

RETURN

OF THE MIND

CHAPTER ONE

"Time, as they say, is just a drop in the bucket. However, it is the ripples caused by that drop that causes things to change."

Greg Carlson

He was home. He didn't know how he made that decision but he knew it as sure as he knew anything. H-O-M-E...

Greg opened his eyes, immediately sensing that what he was seeing was through his eyes, his own physical eyes and not through his thoughts confirming that he was no longer in the purely energy state of his mind. It was cold, quite cold where he was. He lay on his back, looking through a glass enclosure of some sort staring upward at the ceiling. Searching his thoughts, he assumed the enclosure was a stasis container as he had requested when he left for that final battle with Copolla. It seemed like it was only yesterday.

He tried to raise his arms. It took quite a bit of effort as his stiff limbs were slow to respond to his request, and felt the coolness of the glass on his hands. He pushed upward until he heard and felt the vibration of the motorized mechanisms kick in. There was a loud hiss as the seal of the container broke and he immediately felt the rush of warmer air entering the chamber.

Greg patiently waited for the cover of the chamber to rise, hoping the inrushing warmer air would ease the stiffness of his movements before he tried to get out. When the top had opened to its fullest extent, he knew he should probably wait until his body warmed, but he couldn't. He was home. He pulled himself upright to a sitting position, feeling the stiffness of his entire body as it tried to resist. He removed the wires that were attached to his chest for monitoring his vital signs.

He was able to look around the room from his sitting position. He saw that lights were coming on, probably from sensing his warming body temperature. He could make out the shadows of the walls and the sole seating bench that occupied the otherwise empty surroundings.

Slowly, he climbed out of the stasis chamber, his body warming up but still not used to moving freely. He had to remember that his body had lain in the chamber for six years without any movement other than what had been supplied by electrical impulses sent into it to keep nerves active and prevent atrophy. When his feet touched the ground, his knees buckled. He held onto the chamber for support. He was not ready yet to go anywhere, even though he wanted to find Sarah and Soren as soon as he could. A few minutes of sitting on the bench as he continued to warm would be best.

Using the side of the chamber for support, he inched his way slowly to the bench. He sat down abruptly, causing his body to scream out of every muscle and joint, protesting the sudden landing. He grimaced as his body reverberated in an echoing sensation of jolts of searing pain. The sound of a door opening drew his attention from the pain.

"Who's in here!" a woman's voice screamed. "This area is off limits! Security will be here any second. You better come out right now."

Greg's body tingled with the immediate recognition of Sarah's voice. Looking in the direction of her voice, he could only make out her outline as a dark figure, silhouetted by the bright light that came from the corridor.

"S..a...r.....a.....h," Greg croaked but his voice had no volume. And then he realized what he needed to do. ::Sarah::, he said in his thoughts.

::What? Who's there? Who...?::

::Sarah, it's me!::

::Greg? Is that you?::

::Yes, my love, it's me. Come and help me. I'm still quite cold from the stasis. Can't move too well or speak::.

::You're really here? I'm not dreaming this?::

::Yes, I'm here, sitting on the bench. Come.::

"Greg?" her voice called, piercing the silence. She sounded pessimistic, Greg thought as he reminded himself it had been six long years for her.

He watched as she moved into the now-brightening room where he could see her. To him there had been no lapse of time. He saw her as if he had left her only hours ago when he departed to meet Copolla and his attack fleet. But he had to remember it was not the same for her. She'd had long years with only the company of loneliness and the despair of his death. He knew this was going to be difficult for her and he had to be careful.

As she continued to come closer, she suddenly stopped. Greg could see her eyes, wide open as if in shock or disbelief, as they looked at him cautiously. She turned her head toward the stasis chamber and back at him as if to confirm that the body that now sat on the bench was the one that had actually come from the chamber. He saw the fear in her eyes, the fear, he thought, of having had her hopes vanquished many times before, and the feeling that it would happen again.

"What? How? How do I know I'm not hallucinating this?" she said, her voice quivering. "Maybe it's all in my head. Maybe it's not real. Another dream...Soren? Soren? Are you causing this? Don't... please..."

::*Soren is not causing this*,:: Greg said softy in his thoughts.

"I can't...I don't..."

::*Sarah--Mrs. Carlson*.:: Greg sent his thoughts. ::*I told you I'd be back. Didn't I? After all, we didn't have a honeymoon*.:: He mustered every ounce of energy in his body and raised an outstretched hand toward her. ::*Come, my love, take my hand*.::

Sarah cautiously took the last few steps toward him, her eyes fixated on his outstretched hand. When she was close enough, she stopped, slowly raised her hand and reached for his. He saw her hand trembling as the distance between them closed. As their fingertips touched, Greg felt the euphoric surge of energy caused by their telepathic mind link, and reaffirmed by their physical contact, making him feel whole. When her slender fingers reached his palm, he enveloped them in his own and squeezed them tightly. The warmth surged through him, helping to ease any of the remaining pain he suffered.

"Oh, Greg...it really is you! It's you. My God..." Sarah said as she moved the remaining step closer to him, her hands now reaching for his face.

"Sarah," Greg said his voice low and soft, but now discernible. "Yes, it's me. I'm back."

"You're here! Truly here!" Tears ran down her face as she kneeled down to where he sat and engulfed him in her arms. "Here! With me... here!"

"Yes, Sarah, I'm here...I'm home," he said and suddenly felt a sudden twinge of guilt remembering that the caretaker had told him he would not be staying indefinitely, and that would tear her up again. But for the moment, he relished her physical and mental company, feeling his body recovering quickly from the effects of the stasis.

"I've missed you so much," she cried.

Greg gently eased her away so he could look at her. Tears streaked down her face as she smiled at him. He kissed her gently on the lips several times. They both smiled and laughed in between the tears that flowed down both their faces and pooled on their skin, joining together. They hugged for several minutes, words not needed at this point as they bathed in the aura of happiness and love.

"Soren?" Greg whispered into her ear as they remained embracing. "Is he all right?"

"He's...fine," she said.

Greg thought he heard some reserve in her voice.

"I'll take you to him in a little bit," she added. "Can you stand?"

"Yes, I think so." He rose slowly from the bench, feeling only a little disoriented and weak.

"Where have you been?" she asked, as she slid her hand around his waist to support him.

"A place that...well, it's hard to explain. For now, let's just call it a place for lost minds. It's a very long story but the one thing you have to understand is that time didn't have any meaning there. To me...it's as if I was just here with you yesterday."

Sarah looked at Greg, the shock evident upon her face. "But...it's... six years..."

"I know. I know. I'll tell you all about later, okay? I'm home now and everything's going to be fine," he said as he touched her cheek gently with his fingers.

"Okay," she agreed. "But I want to know everything from the time..." Her voice drifted off as her eyes grew large with the shock of something she had forgotten.

"What's wrong?" Greg asked.

"Oh, Greg, you couldn't have come back at a worse time. I know that sounds horrible to say, but everything is collapsing around us."

"What's happening?"

"The council's been exposed! Edward and I are now considered conspirators with the alien race that's trying to take over the planet. Everything we've done, everything we've accomplished...all gone."

"How did it happen?"

"Betrayed...by someone inside the council."

"Inside the council?"

"Yes, it had to be because they knew how to manipulate their way through our systems. It almost seems as if some of Copolla's cronies may still be around. It has all the attributes of something he would do. But at least we're sure he's dead."

Greg stopped walking and stood looking at Sarah. The mention of Copolla's name attacked the wonderful feelings of seeing Sarah and being home. It also reminded him of what he had been sent back to accomplish.

"What's wrong?" she asked.

"Just the mention of that creature's name," he answered, as he forced a smile back on his face. In that moment, Greg decided that the explanation of his return and the hunt for Copolla could wait for a little while. It didn't seem as if things could get much worse at the moment anyway. "I know I have to get with Leumas, but I want to see Soren first, just for a few minutes."

"Come on, I'll take you there. We can have Leumas join us in our quarters."

Greg squeezed her tightly around the waist and they continued walking.

"It's so great to have you back, Greg," she said. "Promise me you'll never leave me again."

"I'll do my best," Greg answered, but he kept his eyes straight ahead as the doors to the passageway opened and they stepped out into the brightly lit corridor.

***

Soren sat quietly on the sofa in the living room, facing the entrance to the quarters. He had changed his clothes and now wore a pair of slacks and shirt rather then the jeans and sweatshirt he had on earlier. His hair was neatly combed and his face was flushed with color as if he had been physically exerting himself earlier.

His gaze was drawn to his small hands that he held in his lap. He smiled when he looked at them, as if they were something new. He watched as the aura of light that surrounded them danced in intensity and changed color. To him, it looked as if they were on fire, but it didn't hurt. The flames of numerous colors moved as he lifted a finger or gently raised his hands a few inched above his lap. As he moved them more and more, he saw a trail of rainbow of color that followed them like the wake of a fish in shallow water. He laughed as he moved them through the air causing a barrage of color and patterns. He tried to draw images with them as he moved in awkward motions to create birds and animal patterns. The colors blurred together and totally encompassed his vision, leaving a curtain of color before him.

"Yeah...it's so pretty," he said as he stopped moving his hands and watched the colors slowly dissipate into the air around him.

The sound of the door opening drew his attention and the colors immediately vanished. The two figures he had been expecting entered the room.

***

Holding Sarah's hand, Greg stepped into his quarters. Again he reminded himself that although he looked upon them as if he had just left them hours ago, it had been six years in actual time. But as his gaze settled on the familiar surroundings, he saw Sarah had not changed a thing, and the familiarity of the area immediately offered a sense of calm and belonging.

"Soren?" Sarah called, driving Greg's attention to the area where she was looking.

"Here, Mom." Soren stood from where he had been sitting.

Greg tracked the voice as it led to the small child standing in the living room watching them. His heart thumped heavily in his chest as he looked upon the small child, their child, his son. A first impression seized Greg that he was somehow older than he looked, older than his six years, but quickly dismissed it because what did he know about how a six-year-old child would look. This thought quickly dissipated from his mind as it was replaced with another, a single word that Greg knew, but did not understand what it meant right at this moment and why it had resurfaced suddenly. *Balance.*

"Soren," Sarah said cautiously. "Do you know…"

"Daddy!" Soren screamed and ran toward Greg.

Greg knelt and raised his arms to meet Soren as he lunged into his embrace. He scooped up the child and hugged him tightly. He tried to stand but his knees resisted the added weight.

"Easy, Soren, Daddy's still a little weak," Sarah said, her voice still sounding as if tears lurked in it somewhere.

"It's okay, Sarah," Greg said as he remained on his knees hugging Soren. He drew the boy closer and kissed the top of his head. He was surprised at the strength Soren had in his embrace and felt the warmth of the child flow into him. There could be no understanding of a child until you held your own in your arms, feeling the life within it, and knowing that you were responsible for its existence.

"I knew you would come back," Soren said as he gently backed away from the embrace.

"You did," Greg said. "How did you know?"

"I just did," Soren said in a childish voice that exuded a confidence and a certainty that there could be no other explanation.

"Well, I guess you were right," Greg agreed and smiled at the child. He glanced toward Sarah and noted that her expression had become somewhat guarded. "Sarah? What's wrong?"

"It's something we can talk about later," she said.

Greg heard the caution in her voice and the feeling from her that now was not the time to discuss the subject.

"Does Uncle Leumas know you're back?" Soren asked.

"Not yet? I was…"

"I'll tell him!" Soren exclaimed. "Let's surprise him! Okay?"

"Sure," Greg said. "Why don't we…"

"I've already called to him. He's on the way!"

"But how? You've been here!"

::*Like this!*::

Greg received Soren's words in his thoughts and winced at the strength of them. "Easy, Soren. I guess we do have to talk about some things." Greg glanced toward Sarah again.

::*Like father, like son,*:: she replied simply to Greg's mind.

"You have to hide!" Soren said. "Come to my room."

"Okay, but let me have a minute with Mom."

"Hurry!"

"I will, go ahead and I'll meet you."

Soren ran off toward his room.

"He's telepathic. What else?" Greg asked.

"It all just started. But what really has me concerned is that he also has the ability to take thoughts and place them in the mind of others. It's as if he can replace the reality of a person with whatever thoughts he chooses."

"Not just the suggestion?"

"No. He makes you see and feel everything as if you were there reliving that moment. Believe me, I know. He's done it to me."

"Incredible."

"Dangerous, too. The process drains him physically to the point he shuts down. It's scared me to death. I've had the doctor look at him, but I didn't tell him anything about what he can do. I figured if that word got out, he'd be in even more danger. But the doctor was very concerned that whatever caused his body to become so weak could harm him drastically if not treated. I've told Soren that I don't want him to do it anymore. I don't know what else to do. It's so frightening and I'm worried, Greg. He's a child and he thinks it's a game...he could..."

Greg saw the glimmering of tears in her eyes.

"Dad!" Soren yelled from his bedroom. "Come on!"

"Coming," Greg called, and then turned back to Sarah. He reached for her hand and squeezed it tightly. She moved closer. Greg kissed her, this time much slower, enjoying the sensuous feel of her lips against his. When they parted, he said, "We'll figure this out later. I promise. Love you."

"I love you, too."

Greg released her hand and went off to join Soren in the bedroom.

*"Perhaps I never should have tempted fate by trying to alter the Leader's
vision of the future. I feel a sense of foreboding that it will only lead to my
destruction in the end."*

Ambassador Alpha

Cindy slowly awoke. Her eyes struggled to focus on the blurred
images she saw directly above her. Slowly they came into focus and
she realized she was staring up at a low ceiling. She didn't recognize it
and that realization, of not being in her room at home, reminded her
of the strange man in the car, the gift, and then total darkness.

She went to move her hands to rub her eyes and discovered that they
were restrained. She tried to move her legs and felt the same result. Yet
she saw no ropes or belts that were strapped over her. Unable to move,
she felt a cold wave of fear and helplessness descend over her.

The normal reaction for a six-year-old child would have been to cry
and scream out. Instead, because her mind was analytically developed
like someone much older, it forced her to apply reason to what was
happening.

The two basic questions appeared in her mind: *Why am I here and
where am I?* Obviously the "why she was here" question could not be
answered directly without outside data. There was a reason of course,
because everything had a reason. She had been removed from her
home without Aunt Christine. Either Aunt Christine said it was okay
for her to go, or someone made Aunt Christine let her go. But Cindy
remembered the bright light she had seen in her house, the gift given
to her Aunt and compared that to the so-called present she had been
given. If Aunt Christine's gift had done something to her as the gift
she had received, then her Aunt was also in trouble. If that were true,
she had been kidnapped and Aunt Christine's services were no longer
required. Cindy began to doubt if she would be going back to the house
ever again.

All of these thoughts didn't explain why she was here, but it painted
her a picture in her head of those that had removed her. They didn't
care what they did or who they hurt. This thinking did not bring her
closer to the answer of the question of why she was here, but it made her
wonder why her captives risked so much. Why was she so important?

The sound of the door opening drew her attention from her thoughts.
In stepped the elfish looking man that had removed her from the house.
He stared suspiciously at her and spoke. "You're awake?"

"Yes...where am I...what do you want?" she asked, forcing her voice to sound scared. She forced tears to her eyes. "Why can't I move?"

"You're strapped down. They're magic straps, invisible. If you promise to behave I may let you up. As to where you are and why you are here, that's not for me to answer."

"I want to go home!"

"Can't help you there. Besides, we're going to go on a trip as I promised you earlier."

"Where?" Cindy asked, trying to get information, but keeping her voice as childish as possible.

"Can't help you there either, but I can guarantee you it is somewhere very special. In fact, it's so special only one hum...or person has ever gone there."

Human. Cindy's precise analytical mind picked up on the way he had tried to not say it. *Human.* To not use the word would indicate that others involved were...were what? Not human? If so, then what would they be? Aliens? And if they were aliens involved, how did she fit in all of this?

Listen to what you're saying, she said to herself. *Aliens from space! Little green men...well, not exactly little and green, but this one did look somewhat odd. And what was it that he gave Aunt Christine?*

These thoughts were wild and unbelievable, but something gnawed at her consciousness. Hadn't her life been somewhat odd and unusual? All her life with Aunt Christine, she had always wondered about the form of treatment she had received. She had been watched as if someone wanted to see what she did and how she did it, like a lab animal. Was she human? Were her captives alien? Or was it vice versa? She didn't know. All she understood was that she was not a six-year-old child, at least not in any mental capacity. She was special is some sort of way, that much she was sure of.

"Are you daydreaming?" the elfish man asked.

Cindy pushed her thoughts aside and looked up at him. Deciding to risk being bold, she took a direct approach. "Why did you say 'human'?"

He stared at her for a few seconds. The earlier look of suspicion returned to his elfish face and then broadened into a grin. "You picked up on that. Very perceptive. They said you might be smarter then you acted."

"Who said? What are you talking about? I'm just a little child..."

"Too late. If you want information, you'll have to get it somewhere else. I just follow orders."

"Why can't you tell me where I am and why I'm here?"

"All in good time."

"So you're just a doer? No individual thinking allowed?" she asked and quickly wished she hadn't. One of the concepts she still hadn't grasped was talking over the head of an adult. It was usually not accepted very well and the consequences usually weren't good.

The man's grin faded slightly at the edges as he said, "Just for that, you can stay where you are for a while longer."

He turned and left the room, closing the door obviously harder than was required.

Cindy exhaled deeply. "Smart move," she muttered. She knew she tried to push too hard too fast. Patience and her love of presents were her two biggest weaknesses and if she didn't learn how to control them, she was going to get into trouble.

"Get into trouble?" she said and giggled sarcastically. "I'm already in trouble."

***

Greg stood in the doorway of Soren's room. His eyes scanned the posters that hung on the walls. Most were of science fiction, spaceships and alien worlds. The words "like father, like son" immediately flashed through his thoughts. He felt regret for having missed the first six years of his son's life and wondered if he would even have the chance to see more than a glimpse before he was summoned back. Where was the... *balance?*

"Come on, Dad," Soren called. "He can see you from there."

"Okay," Greg said and stepped farther into his son's room. He sat on the bed and called Soren over. Soren bounced onto the bed next to him. Greg placed his arm around him.

"Soren, I know there are things we need to talk about. But when Uncle Leumas gets here, he and I, and probably Mom are going to have to leave. There are some things happening that need to taken care of very soon. Do you understand?"

"Sure, but afterwards we can play right?"

"Of course. I would like to spend a lot of time with you. After all, we haven't spent any time together since you were born. I've been away."

"Sort of, but I have you up here," Soren said, pointing to his head.

"What do you mean?" Greg asked.

"Some I borrowed from Mom's thoughts of you," he said cautiously. "From the times before. Mom really likes you."

"Yes. I know. I like her, too." Greg smiled sheepishly. "Mom has told you not to do that anymore, right?"

"Uh-huh." He nodded. "Uncle Leumas, too. He said I have to learn how to control my thoughts so I don't hurt myself or anyone else."

"That's right. What about…"

"Wasn't the dark place scary?" Soren asked enthusiastically.

"Dark place?" Greg asked. "What do you mean?"

"The dark place. Where you were all this time?"

"What do you know about it?" Greg asked, curious about Soren's interpretation of where he had been. Greg barely understood it himself until the caretaker had explained it.

"It must have been scary until people were there."

"People? How did you know…" Greg's word were cut off by the sound of the door opening in the living room and Soren's shout.

"Uncle Leumas is here! Come on!" Soren shouted and grabbed Greg by the hand. He led him over to the door but not out into the passageway.

"Soren -- wait!" Greg said firmly, getting his son's attention. "What do you know about where I've been?"

Soren hesitated before answering. "Just that it was somewhere else. Far away in a place where there weren't people…real people."

"How did you get this idea? Did someone tell you?"

"No. I just had dreams about it. I saw some things. That's how I knew you would be coming back."

Greg wondered how on Earth Soren could have known or sensed any of this. Could there be some form of neurological connection between them? Was there some way Soren received some kind of feedback from his own mind? Or was there a psychological aspect at work here?

"What else?" Greg probed deeper.

Soren's gaze dipped below Greg's and he spoke softly. "There's someone else. It was dark. Very dark. Someone evil. They were there, too. A very bad person. Sacred me." Soren's voice trembled, near tears. "He wants me, too."

Greg reached out and hugged Soren. "Don't worry. They won't get you. I'll protect you."

"Promise?" Soren asked, looking up into Greg's eyes.

"Promise," Greg said and kissed him on the head.

"Can we surprise Uncle Leumas now?"

"Okay."

***

Leumas stepped into Sarah's quarters as soon as the door opened. He saw Sarah standing in the living room, and his attention was immediately drawn to the expression on her face. Her cheeks were flushed with color, and she looked as if she had just had some kind of emotional outburst.

"Sarah, what's wrong? Soren told me to get here quick! I hadn't heard from you since you left to investigate the intruder alarm in the stasis chamber. What's…"

"Everything's okay, Leumas. I'll explain in a second. How is the situation?"

Leumas exhaled deeply. "It's quiet for the moment. Edward just arrived on the shuttle and I told him to meet us here. The council wants to hold an emergency meeting." He brought his attention back to her. "Are you all right? You looked flustered. Sarah, what's going on?"

"I'm fine. Really fine," Sarah said. She then turned toward Soren's bedroom. "Soren?" she called. "Uncle Leumas is here."

Leumas turned in the direction of Soren's room.

"Surprise!" Soren screamed as he appeared in the passageway.

"What surprise?" Leumas asked as he watched the boy emerge into the living room. As Soren moved from his room, Leumas saw that his left hand was extended behind him as if pulling something along. "What's going on? Come on, Soren, this is not the time for games."

"Is there ever a good time for games?" a voice called from behind Soren.

Leumas' mind immediately recognized that voice. He felt an instantaneous shiver run through his body and his breath vanished from his throat as if he had just been punched in the stomach.

Greg appeared behind the boy. "Hello, old friend."

For a few seconds, Leumas could not utter a sound or move. Finally, he gasped in a weak voice. "Greg? Greg! It's you? You're here?"

"It certainly appears that way," Greg replied as he walked up to Leumas and extended his hand. "It's good to see you again."

Greg's hand hung in the air that separated the two of them. Leumas scrambled within his mind the possibilities of what was happening. An imposter? Some form of shape shifter? He had to be sure! ::*Dora,*:: Leumas sent in his thoughts. ::*Examine the male subject before me and identify.*::

::*Working, one moment.*::

As he waited, Leumas examined the man that stood in front of him. He wanted to believe so much that this was really Greg. But his mind forced him to recall that not more than a few days ago, he had looked upon Greg's body lying in the stasis chamber without any consciousness within it.

"Don't you believe it's me?" Greg asked.

"Let's say I'm a little skeptical," Leumas replied.

"Well, what would it hurt to shake my hand? Please," Greg said as he held out his hand with emphasis.

"I suppose it wouldn't," Leumas said as he slowly reached out and took the offered hand. He felt the warmth that it contained. That warmth was suddenly accompanied by a onslaught of thought that flooded his mind.

::I still owe you for the two rings I borrowed for the wedding. Had to come back and get straight with you on that...and to say thanks for catching onto the walking time bomb of the reporter Schume. He would have killed us all if you hadn't caught onto him.::

Leumas' face broke into an expression of happiness as any remaining doubt that he harbored quickly vanished. The thoughts of guilt over Greg's death that had plagued him earlier dissipated into nothingness as he glimpsed his good friend. "No one else knew that you borrowed the rings from me that day...except for Sarah."

Leumas turned toward Sarah and saw that she was smiling and nodding at him. He saw her eyes were filled with tears but her smile conveyed they were not from fear, but from happiness. He turned back toward Greg. "It's really you! You're back! You're really back!" He drew Greg into his embrace and hugged his best friend.

"It's good to see you, too," Greg said.

::Confirmed identity.::" Dora said.

::Thanks Dora, but I knew it before you did.::

"But how? When? Where?" Leumas stuttered, as he and Greg separated. His heart pounded in his chest. "I have to admit..." Leumas looked toward Sarah cautiously. "I wasn't sure if you were ever coming back. It all seemed so unreal, the whole thing."

"Unreal. What I experienced felt the same way. I guess the hardest part is that time had no meaning for me. For you, six years have passed, but for me, it's like it was...yesterday."

Sarah came alongside Greg and grasped his right hand. Soren took his other hand.

"But you're here now. You're home," Sarah said as she placed her head on his shoulder.

"My daddy's home!" Soren shouted.

"Yes, he is," Leumas agreed as he playfully swiped at Soren's face. He marveled at the sight of the three people he loved the most, finally together, the way it should have been all these years.

He never wanted to forget this moment, the culmination of true happiness. He doubted that he could ever truly explain the feelings he possessed at the moment if he was ever asked to describe it. Leumas sent a thought to Dora.

::*Dora, please record the image of Greg, Sarah and Soren.*::

::*Image recorded.*::

::*Thank you, Dora.*::

"Getting back to your question," Greg said. "It's a long story and I promise I'll explain later. But first I think we need to look at what's going on."

"The short view is that it's a mess. The word catastrophic barely defines it. Somehow the entire operation has been exposed in a matter of days. The humans know everything, our location, our influence on the space program, Edward and Sarah's involvement. Everything."

"How?"

"All we have are suspicions right now. Definitely someone working from the inside, but at this point we don't have much information," Leumas said, then quickly added, "Now that you're back, we might be able to do something."

The sound of the arrival notification at the door drew their attention. Sarah made her way to the door and pressed the open button. Edward Samuel stood in the doorway.

"It felt good to be home again, yet the impending thought that it would all end kept nagging at my subconscious. I knew I should tell them but I couldn't."

Greg Carlson

"Hello, Sarah," Copolla said in Edward's voice. "Glad to see you made it safely back. I understand that Leumas is here and..." his voice drifted off as he looked past Sarah and saw Leumas standing in the living room with another person. He couldn't see exactly who it was from his line of view, so he leaned slightly to the right. His eyes narrowed in on the image of Greg.

What? My son is alive? But he was dead! How can he be standing here?

"Edward, come on in," Sarah said as he felt the grip of her hand on his arm. "We don't want this getting out just yet."

Copolla stepped into the room, his eyes still locked on Greg. Mixed feelings of rage and surprise flowed through him. His son, his own son who had tried...no, not tried, *had* caused his death and ruined his plans. Anger quickly squeezed out his initial surprise. He wanted to grab his son by the neck and choke him for ruining his plans.

"Edward." Greg stepped forward. "It's good to see you."

Copolla fought to control his emotions, but his body shook with uncontrolled rage. Slowly, he schooled his face into a look of surprise and watched as his son offered his hand.

"Edward, are you all right?" Greg asked.

"Greg? How...when..." he said, forcing a stammer into his voice. "My...my...God...you're back...truly back?"

"Yes. I'm back. For a moment there you looked like you'd seen a ghost."

"Well...yes, I thought I actually was seeing a ghost. My God, it's good to see you," he said as he grasped Greg's hand and shook it. "When did you...ah...get back?"

"Just a little while ago."

"How did you...well, I mean...how did you get back from wherever it was you were?"

"A long story, which I promise I will tell everyone later. But I think we have more immediate concerns right at this moment."

"Yes. Yes, we do," Copolla agreed. *Let's get down to business and replace all this human emotional bullshit, shall we? You're always looking at the big* picture, aren't you...my son? Well you better take a long look because you won't have it for long!

"I'm glad to see you were able to get out in time," Greg said.

"The situation is continuing to deteriorate quickly, I imagine. I was lucky to get out. If it wasn't for our planted agent in the Secret Service, I may not have gotten out and would be under arrest."

"Hi, Uncle Edward!" Soren shouted. "Are you really going to jail?"

Copolla turned toward Soren. "Well, hello there, Soren. Don't worry, I don't think I'm going to jail just yet."

"You better not, we have our game to finish playing, remember?"

"Of course I do," Copolla said and winked at Soren. "I remember. You make sure you don't forget."

"Soren," Sarah said, "we need some time to talk. Can you go and play in your room for a while?"

"Okay, Mom."

"I'll see you later, Soren," Greg called.

"Okay, Dad," he said and then ran up to Greg. Greg knelt down and hugged him. "Love you."

"Love you, too. Off you go now," Greg said.

When Soren had left the room, Sarah spoke first. "Do you have any idea how they found out, Edward? It just all happened so fast."

"No. I'm not sure. But whoever is involved got to the VP, John Bishop, and also the chairman of the JCS. That's why the military came in for a look. Once I saw what was happening, I knew I couldn't explain my way out of it so I came here."

"The important thing right now," Greg said, "is to figure out how much time we have before things get really ugly. Any ideas, Edward?"

Copolla thought about his own timetable before answering. "Well, there are certain protocols that have to be followed before any action can be taken. It all depends what the reaction is. If they perceive a significant threat, they may attempt a strike."

"Worse case scenario, Edward, how soon?" Leumas asked.

"I'd say twenty-four to thirty-six hours."

"You said strike. What kind of strike?" Sarah asked.

"Possibly nuclear," Copolla answered, trying to sound grave. "You have to remember that this compound is in a secluded area which means less risk to the number of people."

"We can't have that," Greg insisted. "There has to be some peaceful way of talking our way out of this."

"I agree with you whole-heartedly," Copolla said, "but who is going to talk to them? They won't trust Sarah or me. They see you and they will remember the incident with Schume a few years ago. I think we need to sit this one out, maybe even permanently unless we can regain their trust. Let Leumas start a dialogue with them and see where that goes."

"He's right about us not being able to be involved," Sarah interjected. "The best thing for us is to be out of sight."

"Also," Copolla began, thinking that now was the appropriate time to insert his plan. "As far as the rest of us, I would recommend an immediate evacuation of critical council members and their families. I don't want to sound like I'm giving up my own planet, but I'm a realist and I only want what's best for my world. And if that means disappearing forever, I can deal with that. But I feel like I'm part of the UCDW, and the council has many other planets to be concerned with besides Earth. We need to get established somewhere else so we can begin planning our next move. A mass and peaceful exodus might give the people of Earth a degree of confidence that might cool things a little."

Silence settled amongst the group as everyone digested what Copolla had said. He waited impatiently for them to acknowledge that his plan was the only viable one. *Idiots,* he thought to himself. *It takes them so long to see the obvious.*

"I think it's time to announce to the council I'm back," Greg said. "They obviously know what's happening and if I can link the two together, my return and the departure from Earth, they might see it in a positive light. Leumas, you start the evacuation plan and then see what you can do about opening a dialogue with Vice President Bishop."

Copolla smiled as he watched Greg and the others.

What a shame it is that I will have to kill my own son. Greg is the only logical thinker amongst this band of misfits. But he's too set in his dreams of galactic peace nonsense to salvage anymore. I gave him a chance before and all he did was try to kill me...his own father. What kind of respect is that for a father who gave him the greatest gift of power that could have been used to dominate the other races? Instead he chooses to be passive. Such a fool! But there's still hope--there is Soren; young enough to be molded and shaped into the weapon that will reduce the galaxy into utter submission. And that's just the way I want it.

"I never wanted the religious overtone to dominate over the organization. In the end, religion and politics never mix successfully. However at the time, I couldn't stop what they wanted."

Greg Carlson

The hall of the council was filled with chaotic sounds as members communicated in their different tongues with each other. Leumas could tell from the tone and pitch of their voices that they were worried.

"Best to get this done as soon as possible," he said to Sarah as they stood in the corridor that led to their seats.

"You're right. But where is Greg?" she said as she looked down the empty corridor. "He said he would meet us here."

"He said he had something to do. But we can't wait. They're impatient as it is."

"Let's go then."

The two walked into the hall and were met with an immediate cessation of sounds. Deathly quiet enshrouded them. They quickly made their way to the speaker's podium. Leumas stepped forward.

"Members of the Council, as you all know by now, our situation has been compromised here on Earth. Our connections with the local Earth government have been severed and we are now perceived as a threat to this world."

The chamber was engulfed again with the sound of voices. Leumas waited for it to settle down again before continuing, but during that interval he heard the calls he feared the most.

"Return to Zire!"

"Call in the defense force!"

"Neutralize the Earth's defenses!"

"Place the planet under martial law!"

"Return to Zire!"

"Please...please. Allow me to finish before we open the floor to questions," Leumas said, his anger rising at the mention of returning to Zire. He truly suspected some of the members involved with the movement to return to Zire were involved in all of this somehow and may have cost them years of work on Earth and caused irrevocable damage to the process.

"How all of this happened is still being investigated, but given the light of the circumstances we were discussing in this chamber only hours ago, it appears evident that it was someone amongst us who initiated our discovery. There have been those of you..."

"Leumas!" a voice called out.

All eyes looked in the direction of the voice that dared to interrupt. A lone figure stood in the aisle of the last row of seats, cloaked in a hooded robe.

"You stand ready to accuse. But is this the appropriate time?" the mysterious visitor didn't pause at the end of his question but continued. "I shall answer my own question and say not."

"Who are you and why do you interrupt?" the master at arms, stationed at the head of the hall, questioned sternly.

"I am obviously a member of this council, otherwise I would not have been allowed in this great hall we built eight years ago when many feared the remaining threat of Copolla's hold. That should suffice for credentials for the moment. I have come here today to be heard. Does Leumas refuse me?"

Leumas looked at Sarah to see if she knew whom this person was. She shrugged. He returned his gaze to the speaker.

"I refuse no one the opportunity to be heard in the hall of the council, but please be brief as time is of a critical nature."

"Thank you," the hooded figure said, still not moving from where he stood. "I have only a few things to say to my fellow council members. Do not forget what we have done here. Do not forget what we overcame and swore to abide to, whether here on Earth or wherever the council chooses it should be. In our haste, let us not be foolish, but wise with what we have learned through our struggles and successes. What we have learned does not change over time. Only we change and within that change, sometimes we forget. Do not forget. I ask this as a fellow council member and as a friend to all of you."

"You speak wisely," Leumas said softly. "And you speak the truth. But I do not recognize you or your garb."

"Who I am is not as important as the organization for which I am proud to be part of."

Sounds of approval and applause resounded in the hall. The mysterious visitor now took purposeful steps and walked down the aisle toward the main speaker's area. As he did, he carefully slid the hood up and over his head, exposing his face for all to see. Greg stopped and slowly turned in a circle for all the members to see him. The applause came to an immediate halt and the eerie silence returned.

"I have returned as promised," he said.

***

Greg was sure the council members who immediately recognized him were undoubtedly scanning his body and checking his DNA template to ensure that he was the real thing. A few seconds later, when apparently satisfied that he truly was who he said, he heard the statements that he knew would come.

"He has returned!"

"The prophecy has come true!"

"It is as he said it would be!"

"Most Holy!"

"A true leader!"

Greg raised his arms and waved them slowly in a motion to quiet the hall. When it was quiet again, he began carefully, knowing that these first words would be the most impressionable.

"I have not come back because of prophecy or religious fervor. I have come back because the time has called me back. We find ourselves amidst a great crisis again, but it is not something new to us. We shall overcome this as we have many others in the past, as we will have to do in the future, and we shall do it rationally and without hidden agendas."

Greg made his way up to the main speaker's area. As he met Leumas, he shook his hand and winked. He then turned to Sarah and hugged her.

::Nice entrance, huh?:: he sent in his thoughts to Sarah.

::Only you could pull something like this off. Nice touch.::

::Thanks. Love you too.::

He returned his attention to the council. "If our time here has come to an end for whatever reason, we shall follow the procedures established and not go down a path blinded by fear or mistrust. As you all know, it was the very misconceptions brought about by not understanding what was happening that caused the great war that almost ended all life in this galaxy and led to the creation of this organization so many years ago."

He turned to Leumas and placed his hand on his shoulder. "As my good friend and I know so well, we stood in the great hall on Zire eight years ago in front of the council. Sarah and I refused membership. Do you remember what the outcome was then?" he asked Leumas.

Leumas immediately recited his response. "If a planet refuses membership, they shall be left alone to develop in their own way. As long as they harm no other planet of the council, they shall be left in peace."

"That's correct," Greg agreed and then returned his gaze to the rest of the council. "Earth has now refused membership, and we shall now leave them to their own peace. The council shall return to Zire and close down this facility with the hope that sometime in the future, there may be a call to reopen it again. We shall leave under the same premise by which we arrived, one of unity and peace."

"What of the trouble in our midst," a voice called out.

"We shall resolve that when we return to Zire," Greg said calmly. Then in a more serious tone he spoke slowly, "I would caution those of you who are involved, to look within yourself and bring an end to this foolishness, for it serves no purpose here among such a noble group of life forms."

Leumas and Sarah joined Greg. They each joined hands with one another and then raised them above their heads in show of unity. Thunderous applause rang through the hall of the council for several minutes. Greg and Sarah left together while Leumas remained. When the hall quieted Leumas spoke. "Let us all prepare for departure. Launch sequences shall be coordinated through central control. Please be ready to depart within twenty-four hours. Destination: Zire."

***

Copolla sat in the back of the council hall as the members filed out. He studied the looks on their faces as he acknowledged their greetings to the Earth president.

Such a pitiful lot. How easily they are swayed by a mere rhetoritician. Just a few words and they think things will be exactly as they were before. Aren't they going to be surprised when I add a little more turmoil to their lives.

"Mr. President," Alpha said as he approached Copolla. Several other members continued to pass by on their way out. "Please accept my apologies for the turmoil your world is under."

"Thank you, Ambassador Alpha. These are certainly trying times we find ourselves in. We are fortunate that the great and omnipotent leader of the council has returned to guide us through these troubling times. We would be lost without him."

The last few remaining members passed the two figures on their way out of the hall. They were now totally alone.

"Did you hear him speak," Alpha said in a low but euphoric voice. "With mere words, he took turmoil and chaos and made it serene. There was something in his words that had a calming effect, don't you think?"

"Yes, he really laid it on thick, didn't he," Copolla said with a sneer. He didn't like what he heard in Alpha's voice. "The boy can speak, there's not any doubt about that. And he probably coated those words with a little bit of "influence" as well. Recognize a charlatan when you hear one, Alpha."

"It's an unfortunate occurrence, his return," Alpha said nervously. "This may alter our plans to…"

"There will be no altering of anything," Copolla snarled. He gripped the armrests of the chair he sat in and squeezed them with all the force his human body could muster. The fact that he did not cause any physical damage to them only angered him further.

"But how can we compete with a return from death? He has returned as he promised. The prophecy has come true!"

"Silence, you fool!" Copolla screamed. He grabbed a handful of Alpha's council robes and balled it around his hands, squeezing the fabric so that it tightened around Alpha's neck. He pulled Alpha down toward where he sat, to within a few inches of his face. "Have you forgotten that I, too, have returned from death? But don't hold your breath waiting for me to make any pretty speeches like him. I don't have to. They will fear me more than before because they think I will seek revenge…and I will. I will kill as many as it takes to complete my destiny. *As many as it takes!* I'm going to harness the power available in Soren and use it to make him and the rest of the council crawl on their bellies to ask for my mercy!"

Copolla rose from his seat and released his grip on Alpha's robes. He used his hands to straighten the area where he had balled the robes together. A small smile appeared on his lips.

"Do you want to be one of those crawling to me for mercy, Alpha?" he asked as he poked Alpha firmly in his chest with his hand.

Alpha involuntarily moved backward from the force of Copolla's push.

"Or do you want to be part of the power and great things I am going to do?" Copolla continued. "But I caution you, Alpha, if you're not with me, you're against me. My enemy." Copolla returned to his seat. "Please, take a few seconds and decide your fate. I'll wait right here."

Alpha shook noticeably for a few seconds. He moved his lips but no sound came out.

"I'm sorry, Alpha, I didn't hear you? Did you say something?"

Finally Alpha managed to stammer out the words. "I…want…I want to…be with… you, honorable Copolla."

"Good. Now that that is settled, get your ass in gear and stop your worrying. Get the ship ready to go. It won't be long now. I just have one or two more things to do."

Alpha turned and began to move away.

"Oh, and, Alpha," Copolla called.

Alpha turned back to face him.

"If you change your mind again, I'll kill you in the most horrific way imaginable. And you know I have quite a vivid imagination, don't you?"

Alpha did not respond.

"The same goes for any of our merry band. Make sure you spread the word that there will be no more chances."

***

Greg, Sarah, and Leumas met in the control center of the council after the meeting.

"Well, what do you think?" Greg asked the group. "Will they go along?"

"I think so," Leumas answered. "I think you were right about them associating your appearance as a positive event with the return to Zire. We have some maneuvering space for a while anyway."

"We'll need it. I'm still concerned about any early response that Earth might..." Greg paused as he looked around the room. "Where's Edward?"

"I saw him in the council hall earlier." Leumas glanced towards the door before continuing. "And I...well...has anyone noticed anything different about him?"

"What do you mean?" Sarah gave Leumas a puzzled look.

"I don't know. It seems like he's a little off somehow. Something barely noticeable but I can't put my finger on it."

"He's obviously under a lot of stress," Sarah added. "When the test of the ship failed, he had enormous pressure on him by other countries and he was a little short tempered with me. But given the situation, I can understand that. Now he's been isolated from his own home world and that's bound to cause some feelings of inadequacy and extreme emotional embarrassment."

"Edward's resilient." Greg poured himself a cup of coffee and then added. "I'm sure he'll bounce back."

"You're right." Leumas nodded. "I guess that kind of abrupt change to anyone's life would cause them to be a little off. It was probably nothing anyway. Speaking of abrupt changes, how is Soren taking your return?"

"Pretty well, so far. But I'm only gauging that on the short period I was with him. As soon as I get the chance, I want to talk some more to him about these powers he has. He was alluding to something earlier, but I didn't get the chance to really look into it."

"There'll be plenty of time after we get settled on Zire," Leumas offered.

Greg thought that he might not have that much time. He felt guilty having not told Sarah and Leumas that he was only here until he did what he had to do, find Copolla and send him back. He knew he would have to say something soon about the arrangement of the caretaker and the maintaining of the balance.

"Greg?" Sarah called.

"Ah...yes."

"What was that? You seemed lost in your thoughts."

"Oh nothing. I was just thinking..."

"I'm here," Edward's voice called as he walked into the room. "Sorry for the delay, I was waylaid by some of the council members after the meeting. By the way, well done, Greg. I thought the way in which you entered and the words you used were perfect."

"Thanks, Edward. Let's hope it works."

"So what's next?" Sarah asked as they sat down in the chairs that circled a small table.

"The problem has grown," Leumas said. "The rest of the world is now up to date on what has been going on. There's even talk about joint action against us."

"That does complicate things." Greg sighed. "Too many nervous countries can be a potential for disaster."

"Any suggestions?" Leumas asked.

"I think we should send a message to the White House and the rest of the world telling them that we're leaving, peacefully. Spell the whole thing out to them from the beginning, don't hide a thing," Greg said earnestly. "But it must be sent before we start leaving. We don't want them to think we are launching a major attack or anything and have all hell break loose."

"I have people working on the evacuation sequence," Leumas said. "I'll make sure that no one leaves before we are ready."

"I'd like to offer a suggestion." Edward's voice sliced through the momentary silence. "If I may...I know I'm not much of a help anymore as President, but..."

Sarah reached across the table and touched Edward's hand. "Your advice will always be welcome here, Edward."

"Of course,' Greg added.

"Thank you. I've been thinking about what role I can play when we get back to Zire, and I thought that you may still need a representative from Earth and seeing as how I am available, I thought I'd take the job."

"Superb idea, Edward," Sarah said. Greg and Leumas also agreed.

"There's something else," Edward added. "I mentioned this earlier and I still believe it is even more crucial now. In regards to the evacuation, what I was going to suggest is that we must move the figures of authority safely away from any potential trouble. That means all of you," he said pointing at Greg, Sarah and Leumas. "Call me the pessimist, but I don't feel totally comfortable that whoever is at the cause of all our troubles will just take a break during such a vulnerable period. If I were in their shoes, I would use it to cause more trouble. When you want to derail the train, you remove the vital parts such as the engine, then the rest of the cars have no one to follow."

"He may have a point," Leumas said. "We still don't have any clue yet as to who was involved in our discovery. It wouldn't hurt to be cautious."

"Agreed then," Greg said.

"One more thing," Edward added abruptly before anyone could say anything else. "That goes for Soren also. And as I don't really have much to do at the moment, I'd be honored to take him with me and ensure his safety."

"Well...why don't you talk to him about it?" Sarah turned toward Greg. "Okay with you?"

"Sure." Greg nodded.

"If he agrees, then fine," Sarah said. "I just don't want to worry him about all of this along with everything else that has been happening with him. See what he says when you ask him?"

"Of course, of course. Yes, I'll do that," Edward agreed and smiled warmly.

"Okay then." Greg rose from his chair and began to pace. "If the security issue is settled, let's figure out what we are going to say to this world."

"In the hours and days after Edward's disappearance I was faced with the toughest decisions of my life."

Vice President John Bishop

The members of the former and now absent President Edward Samuel's staff rose as Vice President John Bishop entered the briefing room.

"Please, ladies and gentlemen, take your seats."

Everyone sat as they watched the Vice President enter the room. He immediately made his way to the chair that he occupied under normal circumstances, the one to the left of the President's chair. Then, stopping abruptly when he realized the Secretary of State was sitting there, the de-facto Vice President, he caught himself and took the head seat.

"Old habits," he said. "Well, this has turned out to be one hell of a day, hasn't it?"

Nervous bits of laughter and exaggerated facial expressions greeted his question.

"Let me begin by saying that no one is as surprised as I am about what has happened. In fact, I almost still can't believe it. I find myself almost not believing the words and thoughts I am saying and thinking. However, there are certain facts of this situation that cannot be ignored and that is the purpose of this meeting. I have asked the Joint Chiefs of Staff to brief us on what they feel our options are militarily. However, I have not given up in trying to seek some other solution. There is a lot that we do not understand and the rest of the world is waiting to see what we decide to do. With that said, I will turn it over to General...."

Bishop paused as he saw that the general sitting at the table was not General Bradstorm but General Corprosal, the assistant chief.

"I'm sorry," he said, looking at the general. "Where is General Bradstorm?"

"General Bradstorm is dead, Mr. President. Apparent suicide."

The other members looked questioningly at one another around the table. Bishop saw the look on their faces and understood their feelings because he was having the same immediate reaction: that the general had probably been involved in the conspiracy.

But, that didn't make sense, Bishop thought. *Why would the general that uncovered the alien base kill himself?* Something was not right, but there were pressing issues that needed more attention at the moment. They needed information and a plan of what the hell they were going to do.

"That is...unfortunate," Bishop said slowly, breaking the silence. "Did he give any reason?"

"No, sir."

"Well, ah...are you ready to brief us?"

"Yes, sir."

"Please proceed."

General Corprosal began. "During the past few hours we have tried to get as much information as we can about the aliens. As you all already know, they have been inhabiting an isolated area of West Virginia. After examining satellite imagery of the past few years, we have determined that they have been there for approximately six to eight years."

"General, why has this not been noticed before on this imagery?" one of the senior staff asked.

"Simply because the changes in the area were so subtle and negligible, they were not detected by our satellites. When we reexamined the imagery, we programmed the computers to search for any abnormalities regardless of how small."

"So why have we suddenly discovered them now?" someone asked.

The General hesitated before answering. He glanced in the direction of President Bishop and received a nod to continue.

"That is an excellent question, but unfortunately one that I do not have all the answers to. What transpired was this: for some reason a routine flight was diverted to this area of West Virginia. However the flight apparently contained some specialized equipment that allowed them to penetrate a...I'll call it a cloak of some sort, to penetrate a cloak and see the alien craft that were there. Why the flight was there and what the equipment was, I have no idea and no one can tell me anything. All of the crew was killed. All agencies, including the FBI and CIA, have flat out denied any involvement."

"This part still remains a mystery," President Bishop added. "At some point we need to come back to it. There are many questions we need to know the answers to in order to fully understand what has happened. But let's move on for now. Please continue, General."

"From what we can determine from the weapon that destroyed the helicopter, it was fired from hundreds of miles away, from something in Earth's orbit, and is comprised of a type of energy we have not encountered before...nor would we have any way to defend against it. We have imagery of the alien craft, but honestly we don't have any way to evaluate them. Given this and the technology for what they apparently have done here in complete secrecy for many years, I feel that we are looking at an alien race of immense technological capabilities, well beyond anything that we are capable of, including any conventional weapons."

"Thank you, General," President Bishop said. "Any thoughts?"

"I have a few things," Paul Jordan, head of the Secret Service said. "Not answers, but more questions."

"Go ahead, Paul," Bishop said.

"It's obvious that they infiltrated our government at some of the highest levels, including my own organization, but I don't see why? If this alien race is so technologically advanced, why did they need some of our people? Why not just take over with a show of force? This leads me to some possibilities: either they aren't strong enough to take us over, or they want to do it secretly for some reason, or they don't want to take us over at all and there is another reason for them being here. The General has pretty much eliminated the first one of not having the strength. So secretly they want to preserve our infrastructure for whatever reason, maybe for future occupation or some other purpose in mind. Is it just me or is there something that just doesn't make sense here?"

"Those are interesting questions, Paul," Bishop said. "Why sabotage our efforts when they could have easily destroyed them? Unless there is something beneath all of this. But until we get more information, we'll be going in circles." Bishop returned his gaze to the general. "General, what are our nuclear capabilities and what do you think the effect would be?"

"We can bring to bear just about any of our arsenal on this area, but if we can't deliver it on station, the effects could be catastrophic to the United States and even the world."

"What do you mean?"

"If the aliens have orbital capability, which apparently they do by what we have seen with the destruction of the helicopter, they could shoot down anything we launched. That would cause a detonation in the atmosphere and release wind blown radiation, which could travel anywhere."

"Can't we get something in there another way?" a voice questioned.

"We're probing that area as we speak, nothing big, just some special ops teams trying to get a feel for other defenses. If we could get in that way, we could detonate a nuclear weapon remotely. It would eliminate all the surface elements, but I can't say for sure about the underground areas. We don't know exactly how deep they are."

"What about the rest of the world?" a member asked. "Are we in contact with anyone else?"

"Everyone has placed what capability they have on high alert," the general responded.

"And that means what?" someone asked.

"It means that they have more than likely keyed in the coordinates for the area and locked them into their firing systems in the event something goes wrong."

"I don't like this," someone else said. "Too many fingers on the trigger."

"I think we've got some time," Bishop asserted, "but not much. I've spoken with the major governments and told them what we know so far, which obviously isn't very much. With Edward Samuel gone and with the common knowledge that he was involved, that has them skittish."

"General, this nuclear strike...what about the surrounding areas?"

"The size weapon we use will determine the radius of the blast. But there will undoubtedly be civilian casualties and long time effects on the area. I would recommend we begin an evacuation immediately of everything within a hundred miles of the area, just as a precaution."

Silence enshrouded the room. President Bishop slowly looked at each person sitting at the table. Their eyes were all upon him as they waited for him to say something.

"Begin the evacuation of the area. General, I want only the preparations to be made for a nuclear weapon drop on the site. I want it to be made perfectly clear that only I will make the decision when and if the time comes. Is that understood?"

"Yes, Mr. President," the general answered. "Understood."

"If there are any other ideas or options anyone might have, now is the time." Bishop said.

"Have we tried communicating with them?" another member asked.

"Not yet. We've been waiting to see if they would try first. It's an option, but up to this point we…"

A door to the room opened and a harried-looking aide entered. "Excuse me, Mr. President, but we have an incoming message from the alien group. They wish to speak with you."

"Well, I guess it's time to exercise that option we just spoke of," Bishop said.

***

Soren sat in his room looking at a book that had pictures of the planets in them. He knew he would not find one for Zire, because it wasn't in their solar system. It was in the solar system of Alpha Centauri, approximately four-point-three light years away. He had been able to piece together what was going on from things he heard and sensed from everyone around him. They would soon be on their way to this other planet, leaving Earth, maybe for good.

For whatever reason, he was picking up new things; glimpses of thoughts or feelings from the people around him. He could sense an urgency that was not there before. This was how he was able to put together the need for their movement to this other planet.

There was also someone or something else that he didn't know. Something strange... It was very confusing. He felt as if he should know it or them, but didn't. However, this other person or thing was leaking into him not glimpses, but a feeling of some sort, an energy that ran through him. He no longer became weak from the strain of his mind, but he thought that perhaps that was because his dad was home now, and not in that faraway place.

He was glad his dad was home. It made him feel proud that everyone was happy to have him back. But now Soren was faced with another decision that was difficult to make. The decision whether or not to tell his father about everything he'd done and everything he knew about. He wasn't sure if his dad would be angry about it or not. But that could wait until later...there was still time.

Soren shrugged as he closed the book and placed it on his bed. A moment later he heard the door opening and the voice of Uncle Edward.

***

Edward Samuel walked down the passageway that led to Sarah and Soren's quarters. Two guards, which Leumas had ordered placed outside of the quarters, acknowledged his presence and allowed him to enter. He couldn't help but laugh to himself at the simplicity of his task the appearance of the human life form afforded him.

"Soren?" he called when the doors closed behind him.

"Hi, Uncle Edward," the boy called as he came from his room and entered the living room area.

"Are you ready?" Copolla shot out.

"Ready for what?" Soren asked.

"Today is the day! Have you forgotten?"

"My prize? Is it about my prize? Is it? Is it?"

"Yes, my boy, it certainly is about your prize!"

"Where is it?" Soren asked as his eyes darted over Edward and around the room.

"Ha-ha. Did you think I would bring it here? Silly boy."

"Well, where is it?"

Copolla looked around the room as if he didn't want to be overheard, giving the appearance to Soren that it was secret. Then he bent over and whispered to the boy, "I had to hide it on board one of the ships. I didn't want everyone to get jealous."

"Let's go get it then!"

"Well we can't just yet because of all this stuff that's going on," Copolla said. "You've heard we are all going to go on a trip away from here, right?"

"Of course, the evacuation," Soren stated simply. "We're returning to Zire."

"Yes, of course, the evacuation. You're such a smart boy, aren't you? Anyway, if you come with me, I can give it to you then, otherwise you are going to have to wait for a pretty long time until we get where…"

"Okay! I'll go with you, Uncle Edward."

"Well, you're going have to ask your mom and dad if it's okay. But remember you can't tell them about the prize. That's still a secret."

"Got it!" Soren said enthusiastically.

"Just tell them something like…well…maybe Mom and Dad want to be alone for a while. Give them some privacy. Do you know about privacy?"

"Of course I know about privacy," Soren said and thought for a minute, then proudly stated, "Removed from public view."

"That's right. My, my, my, you are a smart boy." Copolla smiled. "And smart boys always get the best prizes."

"Yay!" Soren shouted.

"Okay, I've got to do something now, but you get ready to go soon. Your mom and dad will be back here and then you tell them about going with me. Got it?"

"Got it!" Soren imitated a salute with his tiny hand.

Copolla returned the salute in a mock-serious gesture. "You know, you would make a good soldier."

"In what army?" Soren asked.

"That remains to be seen, my boy. Just remember when the choice presents itself, you want the more powerful one."

"Greg's return brought a reassurance back to the council that Sarah and I could never provide for them. I do not feel slighted knowing this, only humbled."

Leumas

"Mr. President," Leumas said as the image of John Bishop appeared on the screen of one of the monitors in the control center. "My name is Leumas."

"Well...ah...Mr. Leumas, I assume you are in a position to speak for whoever it is you represent?"

"That is correct."

"And you are an alien race from another planet?"

"That is also correct, sir," Leumas said, trying to keep his voice warm and friendly. "However, I would offer that 'races' would be a better explanation because there are many different ones involved. And please, just call me Leumas."

"As you wish," the President responded coolly. "You say many races? I am surprised that you appear quite human in shape?"

"Yes, I do. My world, as well as some others, do have similar humanoid characteristics, with some subtle differences," he said as he held up his hand and spread his fingers apart revealing the webbing in between them. "For the moment, we felt it was best that my appearance would suit our initial discussion."

"How do we know this isn't some kind of hoax?"

"I think we're beyond that, don't you, Mr. President? Obviously we are here and you have seen some things already that have convinced you that we are who we say we are."

"Yes, I suppose so." Bishop paused for a moment and then spoke. "You said 'we.'" Is there more than one in charge?"

"Yes, but that is not important right now. We have more pressing issues to discuss before the situation escalates. We know that you have some units probing the perimeter of the compound as we speak. They will not be harmed, but there are some safeguards in place that will prevent them from getting too close...for their own safety."

"I understand," Bishop replied warily.

"Mr. President, I want to begin by saying that whatever you currently believe or have been told, we pose no threat to your country or the rest of the planet. We will take no offensive action whatsoever. Our only wish is peace for everyone."

"Mr. Leumas… excuse me, Leumas, under the circumstances, I find that difficult to believe given the methods and means by which you have established position here and your act toward the helicopter that you destroyed."

"Sir, as to the helicopter, I offer my sympathies of the loss of human life. It was not our intent to harm them. What happened was indeed a grave and unfortunate accident, one of which I am not at liberty to discuss at the moment because we have not completed our investigation of the incident. As to the need for secrecy of our presence, it is or was for the best interest of the planet. May I explain?"

"Go ahead."

"I am a representative of an organization called the United Council for Developing Worlds, which is comprised of many other planets. Our main goal is to help civilizations develop their technology in an orderly fashion and to become part of the organization. This equalization process allows for planets to preserve their resources, avoid unnecessary social burdens and peacefully coexist in the galaxy."

"Why Earth?" Bishop asked with no further clarification to his question.

"That is a long and complex story. But for whatever reason we have entered into this affiliation, we have been secretly assisting your scientists with technology that you have seen come to fruition the past few years. We do not just hand over the technology, but allow your own people to realize a critical piece of information and then let them develop it. As to why we have physically relocated here, for right now, to keep things simple, I'd say mutual interest of all."

"If all this is true, then why the secrecy? Why not just announce your intentions?"

"For the very reason we are speaking right now: the obvious mistrust or concern of an alien invasion. You have to admit your literature and media is plagued by the concept of an alien invasion and the enslavement of the planet."

"Mistrust?" the President blurted. "You invaded our government! Doesn't that sound like an 'invasion' to you?"

"Not invaded. We gave Edward Samuel a choice. He agreed that the advancements and gains would outweigh the risk of the secrecy of our presence. Our whole arrangement is based upon trust."

Leumas saw the expression of disbelief on the President's face, and he could tell the man was going to rebuke what he had just said about trust. "Before you say anything, Mr. President, I would like to mention one more thing about this organization. We are very careful about what and how we do things. What has recently happened, the mishap with the interstellar spacecraft and the revealing of our presence, has all been the work of a clandestine group within the organization whose aim appears to be the exposure of us."

"Politics?" Bishop said in a puzzled and surprised voice.

"Yes. Basically that's what we are taking about. Although there is nothing that can be done to undo this, if you decide that our presence is not welcome, all you have to do is tell us to leave and we will. We will not go against your will."

"That's it? Just say, 'Leave,' and you will all disappear?"

"That's correct. We will leave peacefully and not return until asked."

"Really?" Bishop said somewhat sarcastically. "You'll have to forgive my pessimism, but how do I know we can trust you?"

"You don't," Leumas said plainly. "Call it a...leap of faith if you will. But if you ask us to go, we will leave Earth during the next twenty-four to forty-eight hours and you will not hear from us again. Until we receive your decision, we will not make any sudden movements and we would like to believe that you will not either. We do have the planet under constant surveillance."

"This will be a difficult event without any assurance that you and your organization can be trusted."

"I understand that, Mr. President. If there is any way I can facilitate the decision process, I shall be more than willing to help. We seek a peaceful resolution regardless of what you decide. These initial hours are crucial and we hope that reason and rationale will override any other methods that might lead to a less desirable outcome."

President Bishop remained silent for several seconds. "Where is Edward Samuel?" he finally asked.

"He is with us, as is Ms. McClendon. It appeared that their safety was in jeopardy."

"He has caused this office much disgrace by his actions, and...also my friendship."

"Sir, Mr. President," Leumas began sincerely. "I would ask that you not judge either of them too quickly or harshly. Both of them always had the best interests of the country and planet first before anything else. I, too, have worked very closely with them and consider both of them very dear friends."

President Bishop stared intently at Leumas. "It's all so hard to believe."

"Yes, I imagine it is," Leumas agreed. "I truly wish we could have met under better terms. You have much to think about. I will leave this channel of communication open. We shall await your decision."

***

"So how did it go?" Greg asked as Leumas entered his quarters. Sarah and Edward sat on the sofa in the living room with him.

"I think, considering the circumstances, that it went pretty well. Of course there was the obvious skepticism, as you can well imagine, having gone through the same things yourselves. But overall, I think it was positive."

"Do you think there is any possibility that they might ask us to stay?" Greg asked.

"Highly unlikely," Leumas quickly answered.

"Not likely at all," Edward added firmly. "Remember, we're not talking about just one country, we're international at this point. The whole world will be watching the United States. Even if there was the wildest thought about some kind of alliance, all hell would break loose."

"Well, the ball is in their laps," Leumas said.

"Court," Edward said firmly. "Not laps! If you're going to quote American sayings, then get them right!"

"Yes...court, that's what I meant," Leumas said, staring at Edward in surprise at the outburst over the little slip with words. Greg and Sarah also eyed Edward because of the remark.

"Sorry," Edward said. "Please go on."

"Now we wait," Leumas continued. "The best thing we can do is nothing, just watch and make no sudden movements as a sign of good faith."

"What of the evacuation process?" Sarah asked.

"I'm going to suggest that we be ready to go, but wait until we hear something. I wouldn't want them to think that we said one thing and do another. Tensions are very high across the planet."

"That's probably a good idea," Greg agreed. "We have surveillance of the entire planet in place so we can stop any action they might try. Correct?"

"That's right," Leumas said. "We can easily neutralize any attack. If they..."

"I disagree," Edward said, abruptly interrupting Leumas. "The current situation places all of us in unnecessary harm. I think the evacuation should start immediately. This is ludicrous! They *aren't* going to change their minds."

"Edward?" Greg questioned. "We're not in any immediate danger."

"This planet is like a wounded animal. We don't know how they are going to react and that makes them extremely dangerous. *You* most of all should realize that."

Greg looked intently at Edward. He considered Edward's words, remembering his and Sarah's first encounter with Leumas. "I know what you mean, I remember my initial reaction. It was quite scary."

"And I know John Bishop and the pressure that's on him," Edward continued. "He has no choice but to place the nuclear arsenal on alert and be prepared to use them, not to mention prepare the rest of the world to do the same. It's not just the United States we need to be thinking about. It's the rest of them. If they were to make a consolidated strike, could we stop them all?"

"Edward, you're talking about a global attack," Sarah argued. "I doubt that…"

"I know what I'm talking about!" Edward shouted. "And the longer we wait, the better the chance that something will happen!"

The outburst caught all of them off guard. Greg looked at Edward, perplexed as to why he was reacting so emotionally.

"Edward," Sarah exclaimed. "I've seen you under a lot of pressure before and you never reacted like this. There's something else, isn't there? Something you're not telling us."

Edward just stared at them, his eyes wide and his face tinged with red, looking as if he were ready to explode.

***

Copolla silently stared at them through Edward's eyes, his gaze darting from one to the other. He wished he could grab each one and strangle them until their eyes exploded. *You, idiots. You all deserve to die! You want to believe that everyone is rational. Such fools!* He stood and paced the room while they watched him suspiciously. *Stop it!* he chastised himself. *All this is going to do is raise their suspicions. Appeal to their emotions, their true weakness, and do it now!*

"I'm sorry," he said, his voice shaky. "Please forgive me." He urged moisture into his eyes. "I never want to interfere with what you think is best. After losing what I achieved, and seeing the hopes of my planet destroyed, I just can't help feeling strongly about this."

He wiped at his eyes with his fingers. "But my emotional reaction is just what you can expect from the people of this planet." *Good…good. Yes, that's the angle to use.* "I…I don't want anything to happen to you, any of you. You're like family to me."

"Edward, we understand," Sarah said as she came alongside him and placed her arm around his shoulder.

"It's okay," Greg said. "With what you've been through, it's understandable that you are concerned. We all are."

"I know how you feel, Edward." Leumas patted him on the back. "When Copolla destroyed the council, I felt as if I had lost everything I had worked for, as well as many good friends. I felt as if my world had been torn away from me. I guess that's why I can't let go of the paranoia that I feel about him or his cronies."

You fool! Copolla thought. *The incredible thing is that for once you're actually correct! Hey, everybody! Leumas has the right idea – it's a miracle! This is going to be so much fun! I'm going to love killing you myself this time, Leumas.*

"Thank you all. I just want you to understand that these are irrational times and we still have a saboteur amongst us. Until we get someplace safe, we are at risk. All of us. And if something should happen to any of you, I just couldn't forgive myself because it was I who made the ultimate decision to introduce this planet to the UCDW. You are all here because of me."

"All right, Edward." Greg agreed. "What do you think we should do?"

"Start the evacuation immediately, just a few ships to move you, Sarah and Soren to safety. Leumas can stay here in case he has to talk with Bishop."

"Leumas?" Greg asked.

"I'll have to tell Bishop something so they don't get nervous about our movement," Leumas said.

"Perhaps I should talk with him," Copolla said.

"But I thought we agreed you shouldn't have any contact with him?" Sarah asked.

"That's what I thought, but maybe I was wrong," Copolla offered. "Maybe the familiar face will help. Bishop and I were friends after all. I think if I appeal to him under that friendship, he would understand that a few ships leaving would pose no danger."

"I don't know," Greg said, shaking his head. "I'm afraid it might make them nervous."

"Please, Greg," Copolla murmured. "Let me try."

Greg looked at Sarah and Leumas, and then returned his gaze toward Edward. "Okay, Edward, you talk with him and see what you can do."

"At first I regretted being stuck with the human body, but as things progressed, the sense of irony was just too delightful to ignore."
Copolla

"Hello, John," Copolla said, as the image of John Bishop appeared on the screen. He noted the look of both surprise and contempt that appeared on the President's face.

"Edward, this is a surprise. I didn't think we would be hearing from you again."

"Well, here I am."

"You've created one hell of a mess, Edward. How could you…"

"Yes, I imagine I have created a mess, John. But let's not get into that right now. The alien leader, Leumas, was kind enough to allow me a few moments to talk with you and to offer whatever reassurance I can that their interest is one of peace, and again to reiterate that they will abide by whatever you decide."

"I appreciate you taking this opportunity, but of course you can understand that you have a slight credibility issue at the moment."

"Agreed. I know there is nothing I can do to salvage that at the moment, but what is more important is the global outlook, what we referred to as the Verizon concept, remember? That is what I am worried about: all those countries and many with some form of nuclear potential. I'm worried someone might take matters into their own hands."

A brief moment of recognition flashed across the President's face. Copolla hoped it wasn't enough to raise the suspicion of others who might be watching at this moment and realize that he had just initiated a coded response.

Copolla had searched the memory of Edward Samuel, and discovered the coded methodology that the president would use if he were under duress or held against his will in a terrorist scenario. *Verizon concept* was the initial start of the message with the understanding that the word "three" would start the coded section. The message would be divided into thirds, with only the first statement being the one that was meant to be adhered to. The remaining two thirds would mean the opposite from the spoken word and should be acted upon accordingly.

"The Verizon concept is kind of convoluted at the moment," Bishop added, "but I understand your concern."

Copolla saw the brief recognition in Bishop's face. *Perfect*, he thought.

"John, I know emotions are high and I don't want any accidents to happen that everyone will regret. There have obviously been enough mistakes here already, we don't need any more."

"No. We certainly don't need any more." Bishop agreed.

"Good. That's why I am contacting you on their behalf. There are *three* issues I need to communicate with you. I want to be clear on each one, so forgive my simplification and redundancy."

"I'm ready."

"First, a ship will be departing from this area. I want to ensure you that this is purely a routine event. When the ship departs, do not attempt any offensive action against it. It will leave the Earth and not harm anything."

This will be my ship, Copolla thought. *Do not touch it.*

"I understand," Bishop said.

Good, now here comes the best part. I hope this idiot will understand that it all means the opposite.

"Second, another ship will depart shortly after that. As with the first, it will leave this planet. Do not attempt any hostile action, and none will be taken toward you. Disregard the media, which has been running rampant with the stories of an attack being launched on Washington, DC."

This ship will not leave Earth. Attack this ship because it will have orders to attack Washington.

"Thank you for that reassurance," Bishop said.

"Third, another ship will leave after that; follow the same principles as I mentioned previously. Also, I want to emphasize as strongly as possible that any attempts to attack this area will be foolhardy. The defensives are impenetrable."

Attack this ship as well. Then attack the compound because they will be vulnerable for attack.

"Did you get all of that, John?"

"Yes, Edward, I understand. But as I mentioned earlier, how do we know that they...you can be trusted?"

Copolla knew that this was going to be the toughest part, how to get them to believe that he was an unwilling participant in this after he had gone through all the effort to convince them otherwise. The story had to be a sincere one, something that would appeal to the human. Copolla first thought about reciting one of his poems, but this almost made him laugh and he decided against it. He had searched the memories of the man whose body he possessed and thought there might be a way, if he could do it right.

But first, he had to make this channel secure so no one but John would hear it. If Greg, Sarah or Leumas did, it might ruin the whole thing. He glanced at the console and saw the button he was looking for. He casually moved his elbow and nudged the switch to the up position, making the communication secure. When they asked him later, he would tell them he had accidentally hit it with his elbow.

"John, I've switched to a secure mode," Copolla said while distinctly changing his voice to reflect urgency. "I don't know how long I will have it before they discover what I've done. Believe me, I know exactly what you mean. If I were in your position, I would think the same thing. I know it looks as if I was a willing participant to all of this, but I wasn't. I never was."

"Edward, we have all the evidence. It's plain to see."

"I know, I know. But they had my family John...my kids. You remember when my wife died of cancer."

"Yes."

"They killed her. It wasn't the cancer. They wanted to make an example of what they would do if I didn't follow their orders explicitly. I had no choice."

"But the years, Edward. You had years to reveal this in some way."

"I couldn't. They were watching me and my kids. You have to believe I tried," he implored. Copolla knew the longer he tried to convince him, the more the chance of an error would creep into the conversation. He thought he had raised enough doubt in Bishop to pull this off.

Bishop's face reflected confusion as he tried to make sense of all this. "But Edward, your children—where are—"

"John, they're coming. I have to sign off. Please believe me! God Bless the United States of America. I hope that some day you will all understand and forgive me for what I have done. Good bye."

Copolla switched off the transmit button and sat back in the chair. Within a few seconds, he found himself laughing uncontrollably. Tears came to his human eyes and rolled down his cheeks.

Seconds later he heard the door opening to the communications center. He regained his composure but left the tears. Leumas, Sarah and Greg entered.

"Edward." Leumas asked. "What happened? I was watching the communication and then it blacked out."

"I must have accidentally hit something with my elbow. I...I was just so emotionally wrapped up, I guess, I didn't watch what I was doing. I'm sorry...I didn't mean to screw it up."

"I understand," Leumas said and placed his hand on Edward's shoulder.

Copolla wiped at the tears. "You'll have to excuse me," he murmured.

"Perfectly normal in this case," Leumas said.

"That was a very noble thing you did, Edward," Sarah said as she came up alongside Edward. She grasped his hand with her own and squeezed it gently. Greg joined them and added his hand to hers.

Copolla hid his smile with his hand and turned his head away from them. "Thanks for understanding," he said. "All of you."

"Edward, what is the Verizon concept you mentioned?" Sarah asked. "I haven't heard the term before."

Copolla looked at Sarah as he felt anger rising. *How dare you question what I have done!*

Easy, he cautioned himself. *Just explain it and they will move on.* "It's for the inner cabinet circle. It's the term we use to describe the nuclear capabilities of other countries. I used it because I wanted to show John that I was still thinking in terms of the organization, and second to emphasize what I think the serious issues are. They can control what they do, but it's the other countries I'm more worried about."

"Good move," Sarah said. "Building on familiarity and purpose. That should help."

Like I need your approval…you dumb human!

"What do you think? Does he believe you?" Greg asked.

"I can usually read John pretty well, and I think I may have gotten through to him. But I would suggest that we have the first ship depart within the next two hours, just as we indicated. The longer we wait the more skeptical he may become. I would like to take the first ship with Soren if I may. I think I would feel better knowing that he was out of harm's way."

Greg looked at Sarah, who nodded. "All right," Greg agreed.

"Then, the next two ships at two hour intervals," Copolla suggested.

"I'll make the arrangements," Leumas offered.

***

The image of a teary-eyed Edward Samuel faded from the view screen. Silence enshrouded the office of John Bishop, which also included the Secretary of State, Norman Grates, the Chairman of the JCS, General Corprosal and the Secretary of Defense, Hal Burton.

John Bishop felt extremely tired as he exhaled a large breath and leaned back in his chair and stared at the ceiling trying to make sense of this mess.

"Mr. President, you don't believe him, do you?" Secretary of State Norman Grates asked.

"I don't know anymore," he said softly. "Edward Samuel used the appropriate code and procedures. If he is telling the truth, this could be a key moment in determining the future of the planet. But who do we believe? The man we think was a conspirator with the aliens, or the aliens themselves? If we wait too long to decide, many people might die. Or they might leave as they said they would and this nightmare would be over."

"Mr. President, I think the aliens are doing a characteristic maneuver," Burton said. "The first ship is just a test, a scout ship to see if it will be attacked before sending the more important ones. But this also proves that there may be a weakness in their defenses if they are concerned enough to send a scout ship. Isn't that correct, General?"

The chairman of the JCS nodded. "I have to agree with your astute assessment, Mr. Secretary. If I were in their position, I would do the same thing."

"But what if Edward is telling us what the aliens want him to tell us?" Grates asked strongly. "It could be a trap."

"But that doesn't make sense," Bishop said. "The only reason they would set a trap would be unless they aren't as powerful as they say they are. Let's face it, if they were superior in all respects, they would just do what they want, right, General?"

"Yes, sir."

"So that leaves two possibilities: either they aren't as powerful as they say they are, which I find hard to believe after seeing the way they destroyed the helicopter, or the aliens are telling the truth and Edward is lying. Which one do you think it is?"

John Bishop waited, but no one said a word. He scanned the faces of each man sitting at the table. One by one they looked away. But he saw the look in their eyes and knew what it meant; no one wanted to make the wrong decision. A decision that could get a lot of people killed.

"I guess nobody here is a gambling man," Bishop finally said with discouragement in his voice. "I can't say I blame any of you. Thank you all," he said, dismissing the group.

They left the room, leaving him in silence, something that seemed strange after the constant meetings and discussions over the past twenty-four hours. John Bishop stood and walked around the large conference table. He stuffed his hands in his pocket, an old habit that he could never seem to break and one that the reporters constantly picked up and criticized him for. He laughed at the thought. *Yeah…in times like these, they would probably say I made the wrong decision because I had my hands in my pockets.*

"To trust or not to trust, that is the question," he said aloud and found himself laughing at his cliché. Could Edward be trusted? Maybe, maybe not. You would think you would know someone after all these years of working together and being friends.

Come on, John, he said to himself. *Analyze the choices and go with your instincts. Either way, you're screwed. If you let the ship go, you'll be accused of being weak. If you attack, and you've underestimated their capabilities, the planet suffers the consequences. COMPROMISE THEN! You need more time. Maybe the staff will come up with something! So...let the first ship go. If Edward is correct, and it leaves without any problem, then fine, that adds credibility to Edward's statement. When it comes time for the second ship...then...I don't know.*

"The plan made perfect sense. Copolla hid his presence in such a maniacal way that he could not be detected...until it was too late."

Sarah Carlson

Greg and Sarah walked along the passageway with Soren between them, each of them holding one of his hands.

"Are you sure you want to go with Uncle Edward?" Sarah asked.

"Sure, he's a lot of fun," Soren replied eagerly.

"We'll only be a couple of hours behind you," Greg added. "We'll meet at..." Greg wondered what he should say. If he told Soren another planet, he might not be able to handle that right now.

"Zire," Soren added. "I know that's where we are going."

"How?" Greg asked. He looked at Sarah, who looked dumfounded as to how Soren had known.

"I know most of the things that Mom, Uncle Leumas and Uncle Edward didn't want me to. I thought that if they wanted to keep a secret, then it was better if I didn't tell them I knew about it."

"Like what?" Sarah asked as she stopped and placed her hands on her hips.

"This place, the council, the other aliens and the meetings, all of it," Soren said matter-of-factly.

"How did you know?" Greg asked.

"I just did. Sometimes when I slept I had dreams about it, I could see things going on. And then other times I could hear things; the way Mom and Leumas would talk sometimes, especially when they thought I was asleep."

"Young man, you were eavesdropping on me?" Sarah said.

"Well...kind of. Don't be mad at me, Mom. Please."

"I'm not mad, Soren. I just wish you had told me about this earlier so I could have helped you understand it."

"I think he already does," Greg said. "Don't you?"

"I think so," Soren said confidently. "Most of it anyway."

"Well, that makes one thing easier," Greg said, thinking that he and Sarah wouldn't have to explain that much to him now. "But we still have some other things to talk about yet, don't we?"

"Yes." Soren agreed.

Sarah looked at Greg questioningly.

"He has some interesting thoughts about where I was," Greg told her. "Some interesting and accurate thoughts."

"Soren, how did…" Sarah began, but stopped. They had reached the area where Soren and Edward would get into the shuttle to reach the ship they were traveling on. Leumas and Edward were standing on the platform waiting.

"We'll get into this later," Greg said as he reached for Sarah's hand and squeezed it reassuringly. "Promise," he added.

"Hey, Soren," Edward called. "Ready to take a trip?"

"Sure," Soren agreed eagerly. "We're off to the planet Zire!"

Leumas looked at Sarah and Greg, an expression of surprise on his face that Soren knew where they were going.

"Yes, he knows," Greg said. "But we didn't tell him a thing. He just figured it out on his own, so there isn't any point in hiding anything from him from this point on."

"Really," Leumas said. "But how?"

"We'll talk about that later." Greg turned to Soren. "Come and give me a hug, big guy." Soren ran up to Greg and hugged him. "You be good and we'll see you soon."

"Okay, Dad. Love you."

"Love you, too."

"Everything set, Leumas?" Sarah asked.

"Yes, shouldn't be any trouble. I've notified John Bishop of the launch, and he has informed everyone else globally. We also have redundant coverage just in case, both in orbit and here."

"Soren…" Sarah kneeled down to his level. "You behave for Uncle Edward, okay?"

"Sure, Mom." Soren hugged her.

"I love you."

"Love you, too, Mom. And don't worry, everything will be okay. I promise," Soren said.

***

Greg heard the words Soren said, but it was not so much *what* he said as *how* he said them. Sarah also must have heard something because she looked at the boy with a perplexed expression for a few seconds and then turned toward Greg.

::*I know, I heard it too,*:: Greg said in his thoughts to Sarah. ::*Something in his voice. It's as if he knows something that he's not telling us. We'll get to the bottom of it when we get to Zire.*::

"We'll be fine," Edward added as he gripped Soren's hand in his own. "Don't worry about anything. I'll take care of Soren as if he were my own son."

"Thanks, Edward." Greg briefly shook hands with his friend.

Sarah hugged Edward and kissed him on the cheek. "Thanks."

"My pleasure." Edward turned toward Greg. "We're really like family, aren't we? All for one and one for all."

"Right," Greg agreed. The remark struck him as odd in that he couldn't picture Edward saying something like that. It was too cliché. He dismissed the thought quickly, though, and reminded himself that Edward was not President anymore, and he was entitled to let his guard down now.

"Let's go, sport," Edward said to Soren. "Climb on in the shuttle."

When they were both situated in the shuttle, Soren waved one last time.

Greg, Sarah, and Leumas returned the wave. Edward raised his hand and said, "See you on the other side."

The shuttle sped off to the launch area and the waiting ship. Greg, Sarah, and Leumas walked to the control center to monitor the launch.

"Leumas," Greg said as they walked along the passageway, "have you had a chance to look into who might be involved from the council in all of this mess?"

"I've had some of my resources looking into it, but we're not getting much. The only thing that tends to resurface is this little group that wanted to move the council back to Zire."

"Well, the outcome has certainly suited them. But would they be capable of the sabotage and the leak of information?"

"Possibly. But I don't know for sure. I've been meaning to get with the one that they consider their leader, Ambassador Alpha, and see what he knows. But events have overcome me. As soon as we're done here, there won't be much until the next launch in two hours, so I'll try and get with him then."

"Good. We need to resolve the internal issue quickly so we can get settled on Zire and back to business."

"Back to business?" Sarah questioned. "When we get back to Zire, the only business I want to see is you and Soren getting to know each other."

"Of course," Greg added. "I will. As soon as things settle down, I promise." Although he wondered how much time there really would be. He had to find Copolla and didn't even know where to begin looking. For all he knew, the caretaker might have been wrong and Copolla was not on Earth, but on Zire where he might have laid a trap for them.

"Leumas, have you set security protocols in effect on Zire?"

"No, why?" he asked.

"I don't know, call it a hunch. But I think we need to be careful. I mean, what if we're wrong? What if this is all a plan to get us off Earth and right into a trap on Zire?"

"Why do that?" Sarah asked. "Have you seen this in some vision, Greg?"

"No. I'm just thinking out loud, that's all. After all, Copolla destroyed the council and sent the galactic leadership into turmoil on Zire before. If someone felt that it could be symbolic again from the same standpoint, wouldn't the council be left open to attack again?"

"I see your point," Leumas agreed. "I'll have security perform a deeper check and establish the protocols. It doesn't hurt to be safe."

"Thanks. I don't want you to think I'm paranoid, but..." Greg's words were interrupted by a yawn. "Oh, I'm sorry."

"You're tired and need some rest," Sarah said. "Your body is not used to all this activity. Remember it sat in stasis for six years."

"I sometimes forget that," he said and smiled.

"That's why you have me around, mister." Sarah wrapped her arms around his waist. "I'm going to make sure you take care of yourself. I lost you once, and I'm not going to lose you again."

Greg found himself drifting into her deep blue eyes. No other woman could ever mesmerize him the way Sarah did.

"Ahem," Leumas said. "We're ready to launch here."

"Oh, sorry, Leumas," Greg said.

"Quite all right, you two. I always thought you made a cute couple. After all, if it wasn't for me, you probably never would have met. So you really have me to thank..."

"Don't start that again, Leumas," Sarah chided playfully. "But we promise, we won't ever forget that." She stepped up behind him where he sat and placed her arms around his shoulders and gave him a brief hug.

"Okay, they're off," Leumas said as the image on the screen showed the craft lifting off the ground and quickly accelerating out of view.

"Any movement from Earth forces?" Greg asked.

"Nothing. Sensors indicate they are tracking it, but other than that, all is quiet."

"So it appears Edward got through to John Bishop."

"For the moment anyway," Sarah added.

"That's it," Leumas said. "They are out of range of any potential weapon, and safe and sound. Now I've got some things to do." He rose from the chair. "Why don't you two get some rest. Who's going next, by the way?"

"Sarah," Greg answered. "She's going on the next flight. I'll take the last one."

***

"Well, we're on our way," Copolla said to Soren, who sat in the seat next to him. "You know what that means?"

"My prize?" Soren asked.

"Yes, my boy, your prize. Your long-awaited prize."

"Where is it?"

"It's in one of the cabins. Come on, I'll take you."

They both rose from their seats and walked to the rear of the small craft. There were two doors at the end of the short passageway.

"In there," Copolla said, indicating the door on the right.

Soren tried the doorknob but found it locked.

"Oh, sorry." Copolla pressed his thumb to the scanning faceplate. A click could be heard as the door unlocked. "Go ahead, it's all yours, just as I promised."

Soren turned the handle and opened the door. He stepped into the small cabin, his eyes scanning for an indication of some kind of present.

"I don't see it."

"It's up there, on the sleeping bunk," Copolla said. "Go ahead and climb up."

Soren climbed the ladder-like steps and peered into the space.

"There's someone…"

The sound of the door closing and the lock being engaged drew his attention from the sleeping bunk. He jumped down and tried the door. It was locked. He banged on the door with his hand.

"Uncle Edward, the door is locked," he called loudly.

"Yes, it is," Copolla said from the other side. "It's locked to keep you in there for the time being. Hope you enjoy your surprise."

Soren heard footsteps walking away. He moved from the door and returned to the ladder. He went up the few steps and peered into the sleeping space.

"Who are you?" he asked.

***

Greg gently kissed Sarah as she lay asleep next to him in their bed. He allowed his hand to gently trace along her smooth skin, reveling in the warmth and softness his fingers felt. She briefly stirred and he stopped, not wanting to wake her. He pulled the sheet up to her shoulder and she settled back into undisturbed sleep.

Greg couldn't sleep. He felt restless and uneasy with the thought that all of this would end and he would be returned to that nothingness that the caretaker managed. He tried to relax and he allowed his mind to wander. He pictured Sarah sitting on a barstool in a bar from the early fifties setting, eight years ago, scared out of her wits. Yet even then, he had thought she was beautiful as he remembered sneaking glances at her when she thought she couldn't see. He felt a smile form on his lips as he remembered. How things had changed from that day on. He wished they could be that way again.

After watching the successful and uneventful launch of the ship, they had returned to their quarters to prepare for their own departure. However, finally alone, they were engulfed with each other and the feelings they had not yet been able to share since Greg's arrival.

Without any words spoken, realizing that time, as usual, was a precious commodity that always eluded them; they went to their own bedroom and made love. Their clothing marked their path, hastily discarded on the way. Their passion was strong and uncontrollable, as if it was their first time making love. Their telepathic connection enhanced their feelings; not only were they able to share the physical sensations of lovemaking, but they shared their thoughts and feelings, which bathed them in an aura that was like nothing they had ever experienced.

However, lying here now, Greg couldn't shake the dreaded feeling that it might be the last time they would be together like this. The caretaker's words kept coming back to him...*balance*. It reminded Greg what he had been sent back to do: to find Copolla and somehow send him back to the caretaker and end his own physical existence. Yet, from the moment he had arrived, the chaos of the current situation had kept him busy and had not yet begun to track down Copolla. But as the events unfolded, he had begun to realize they had all the markings of something that Copolla had orchestrated.

Still there was something else that he couldn't put his finger on. He couldn't go to Leumas or Sarah for help, not yet anyway, with everything else that was going on.

The thought that he was missing something continued to plague him. Copolla. There had been no messages from him, no blatant threats against the Earth or the council, and those were things Copolla would characteristically do. He loved to torture with his taunting and promised annihilation. Why the different strategy this time? Why had Copolla changed his usual methods? If anyone was a creature of habit, Copolla was without a doubt...so why the change?

Sarah stirred in her sleep and she snuggled closer to Greg. Her arm wrapped around his naked waist. He smiled at her touch and the momentary distraction it provided from the questioning of Copolla and his motives.

The change? What had been different this time? he thought.

The obvious answer came to him. What had changed was that Copolla was not in his own body. It had been destroyed and he had been forced to take another physical shape. But whose? It couldn't have been just anybody, because with all that was happening, it would have to be a position of authority of some kind in order for him to be able to do the damage so quickly and thoroughly. One of the council members maybe? Maybe, but most of the damage had been done at the Earth governmental level, especially the Presidential level, with Edward's and Sarah's involvement revealed, the space program interference and the discovery of the compound by the military. But the actual sabotage had been done at the council level. Could there be two people involved, one in the council and one outside of it? Maybe...but how would he find out?

He got out of bed and quietly went into the living room. He stopped to look out of the large window that normally provided him a wonderfully sharp view of the blue ridge mountains of West Virginia. But instead of the clear visage, dark, foreboding clouds of a thunderstorm obscured the mountains. A bolt of lightning flashed, clearly showing its origination and path, quickly followed by another. Greg stood and watched as the lightning lit up the sky with its beauty and wrath. Many more bolts flashed across the sky, yet Greg remained fixed in his position. Then, as if in synchronization with his own thoughts, a flashing bolt triggered a thought, a possibility.

The entry notification of the door sounded. Greg got up and pressed the button. As the door opened, it revealed Leumas in the passageway.

"Leumas, perfect timing," Greg said. "Come on in."

"Well, I'm glad my timing was good somewhere. I can't find Alpha to ask some of those questions we had. It's as if he's vanished into thin air."

"Before we go into that, I have something to ask you. I don't want to lose this train of thought. It's probably nothing, but..."

"What?"

"When I returned," Greg began, thinking about the lightning bolt he had seen. "Was there any outward sign, some event or energy discharge? Anything at all you would consider abnormal?"

"Energy discharge," Leumas repeated. "Like an electromagnetic burst?"

"Well, yes, I suppose that might be a possibility to consider."

Leumas pondered the thought for a few seconds. Greg saw his expression of puzzlement turn to one of recognition.

"What?" Greg asked, seeing the look.

"It's...well...odd that you ask. You may recall that I've had Dora monitoring for any unusual events that might be the beginning of something against the council from any leftover Copolla fragment?"

"Yes, I remember, go on," Greg said impatiently.

"I recently had her change her program parameters slightly, and she found an anomaly. It occurred a few days ago, then another very similar electromagnetic burst occurred when you returned."

This was too close to be coincidental, Greg thought. Two life forms came back, two electromagnetic disturbances.

"Where?" Greg asked.

"I forget the exact location off hand, but I remember when it happened because I called Edward to ask if he had detected anything unusual. Air Force One was in the area of the disturbance."

"How close?"

"Very close if I remember. About the exact area."

"In the exact area of the disturbance?" Greg asked to confirm.

"Yes, why? Greg, what does..."

"And the two disturbances were the same?" Greg asked, ignoring Leumas' question.

"Virtually identical."

"Was anyone else on the plane?"

"Just the flight crew, I believe. Edward was returning from some meeting overseas."

"Was there any reports of anyone acting strange after the incident? Any reports about anything that seemed out of the ordinary?"

"I don't know, but if there had been something odd, I think Edward would have mentioned it."

Edward would have mentioned it, Greg thought. Edward would have mentioned it unless it had happened to him. If Copolla had taken his form, then all that had happened made perfect sense. "No...it can't be. How could we have missed it?"

"Missed what? Come on, Greg, what are you talking about?"

"I'll explain in a bit. But first I want you to check on Edward and Soren's ship. Find out where they are!"

"But…"

"Just do it, Leumas, please."

"Okay. Okay," Leumas said as he walked to the computer station in the room. He pushed a button and then spoke. "Control, patch me the current trajectory of the ship that launched one hour ago." Greg stood beside him as he waited for the image to be displayed.

"There is no live trajectory to project. Tracking sensors have been disabled on the craft," a computer voice responded.

Greg's stomach sank with fear that his suspicions might be correct.

"What? Why was I not notified that this had happened?" Leumas asked. "I am supposed to be notified when anything out of the ordinary occurs."

"There was no abnormality. The ambassadorial override code was used as justification of the action. Normal operating procedure."

"Wait a minute. Uh-uh. There weren't any ambassadors on that ship."

"That is incorrect," the computer politely stated.

"Well then, whose authorization was used?"

"Ambassador Alpha."

"Well that explains why I couldn't find Alpha," Leumas said.

"I think it's worse than that," Greg added. "Computer, project trajectory based on last readout."

"Unable to project. Tracking sensor was taken off line as soon as craft left solar system."

"So Edward, Alpha, and Soren could be anywhere?" Greg mused aloud. "Why would they do that unless they were trying to avoid being tracked to wherever it is they are going."

"There are two additional life forms on board at departure," the computer said.

"Identify," Leumas stated.

"One was the pilot, Argusa. The other is unknown."

Greg paced the room. He wondered if he had waited too long in addressing this issue about Copolla, thereby helping him kidnap his own son.

"Unknown? How can that be?" Leumas asked.

"No scan on file," the computer responded promptly.

"But that's impossible. Everyone here is required to be scanned when they enter the compound area."

"Apparently we have another mystery," Greg added resentfully. "But I think I've found part of the problem…and he has my son."

"Who has your son? Alpha?" Leumas asked.

"Alpha's part of it, but it's Edward that's the real problem."

"Edward? How the hell can he be the problem?"

"Simple. It's not Edward, not mentally anyway."

"What the…"

"Greg, what are you saying?" Sarah's voice called as she entered into the living area. Greg and Leumas turned in her direction. "What's going on? I heard you say that Soren is missing?"

"I'm going to try to contact the ship," Leumas said as he approached the computer terminal.

Greg reached out for Sarah's hand and gently pulled her away from where Leumas was, to obtain some privacy. "Sarah, I haven't told you everything…how I got back and what happened to me where I was. There just wasn't any time with everything going on."

"What is it, Greg? But…what about Soren? He's with Edward… Is he in danger from Edward?"

"From Edward, no, but it's not Edward anymore."

"There's no answer," Leumas said.

"I didn't think there would be, not yet anyway. But you can bet there will be a message soon."

"What the hell is going on?" Sarah asked.

"This place where I went…" Greg paused, trying to choose his words carefully. "It's like a …a hotel or something where the energy of one's mind goes. They…and don't ask me about them because I don't understand who or what they are…they maintain some kind of balance there, good energy and bad energy or good people and bad people. I went there when I became detached from my body. My arrival caused some kind of imbalance and some bad energy was released. It returned along the same path as I traveled, which brought him to Air Force One, Edward's plane, where he assumed control of Edward's body."

"Who or what was it?" Sarah asked.

"It was Copolla," he said and watched as the fear and disbelief appeared on Sarah's and Leumas' faces.

CHAPTER NINE

*"Never let anything get in the way of your appetite for revenge.
It tastes sweet whether hot or cold."*

Copolla

"Alpha," Copolla said as he entered the flight cabin but stopped as he immediately smelled something familiar...singed flesh, the smell of death by a laser blast. A quick look revealed a body of a short elfish-looking alien lying upon the floor. He had been shot at point blank range with a laser pistol. Copolla knew that Alpha hadn't the guts to do it; he must have had someone sneak on board and kill the pilot before he got here. "How are we doing? Better than this poor unfortunate soul, I hope," he said, indicating the dead body. He gave it a swift kick and it slid into the corner.

"Er...fine," Alpha said hesitantly. "I don't believe they have figured out what has happened yet. There have been no attempts at communication or interception."

"Why should they?" Copolla said sarcastically. "They have left their good friend Edward Samuel, the former President of the United States, in charge of their son. What could possibly go wrong?" He laughed broadly, his chest heaving in great breaths and spittle flying from his lips. When his fit of laughter subsided, he continued. "I never thought things would have gone so well in this puny human form." He placed his hands on his chest. "But it actually made everything so easy! I have stolen what they value the most and all it took was you and I."

"I also disabled the tracking sensor as soon as we cleared Earth orbit. The Ambassadorial override should hide any immediate concern."

"Very good, Alpha, you've done well. You seemed to have overcome your earlier reservations," Copolla said smugly while remembering their conversation in the council hall. Alpha didn't reply, so Copolla continued. "Have you sent the messages?"

"Yes. Everything will be prepared as you requested."

"What about monitoring the next craft departure from Earth? Will we be able to see what happens?"

"Yes. I have left a connection to the observation cameras."

"Good. Good. It will be interesting to see what the humans do when the next two craft depart. I honestly can't guess. Humans are so damn unpredictable. But I have to admit, I think I can have much more fun if my three best friends: Greg, Sarah and Leumas, survive -- so I can torture them later. I mean...stranger things have happened. They might decide they choose to live and join with me, seeing as how they can't get rid of me."

"What about the boy?" Alpha asked.

"He's locked up."

"Is he harmed?"

"Harmed? Well, of course not. Really, Alpha. We're talking about my grandson here. Besides, he came along willingly to claim his prize. And, I might add, I have kept my word. He's becoming acquainted with his sister."

"Do you think it wise to put them together?"

"Why not? You've had the girl under observation for years and you said there is nothing there as far as powers. Isn't that correct?"

"Yes, Copolla, that is correct. But she was never introduced to her twin brother."

"It's not a problem. If she had the power, she would have shown evidence of it by now whether she knew her brother or not. You're not touting this fanatical religious or legend thing about the son again, are you?" Copolla said with obvious disdain.

"No. I just want to make sure that everything goes as planned."

"You're like an old woman at times, Alpha, you know that? You worry about everything. Look, we know the boy has power, and he's very smart. It won't take him long to figure this out now. What I want is for him to become fond of his sister so that we can use her to leverage the power out of him if he doesn't want to use it the way we choose."

"And if it doesn't work?"

"Well, if it doesn't work, the boy will have to be killed. If I can't have him, to use the power the way I choose, then nobody shall," Copolla said and smiled. He looked around the cabin and then returned his gaze to Alpha. "Now, what do we have to eat?"

***

Soren went up the few steps of the ladder and peered into the sleeping space.

"Who are you?" he asked as he looked upon the dark-haired girl in the bunk. Her hands were bound together and tied to a metal bar. He knew he had never seen this girl before, yet there was something vaguely familiar about her.

"How about untying me?" she said.

Soren looked at her warily.

"Neither of us wants to be here," she added. "Do you know where we're going?"

"I thought we were going to Zire, but I don't know now."

"Zire?"

"Zire is a planet in the Alpha Centauri system about…"

"Four-point-three light years away. I know. I read about it," she interjected.

"That's correct," Soren agreed, somewhat surprised at her response. She didn't look to be older then he was, yet she seemed to know a lot. "I'm Soren."

"I'm Cindy."

Soren reached up and untied her hands. "There you go."

"Thanks," she said as she stretched her arms. "That's much better."

Soren climbed down the ladder, followed by the girl.

As she stood next to him, Soren saw that she was about the same height as he was. "How old are you?"

"Six."

"Me, too."

"How did you get here?" she asked.

"I came with my Uncle Edward. But something's wrong with him. He's acting very strange. I've never seen him do these kinds of things before, like acting mean or playing a bad trick on me."

"Do you know the other one?" she asked. "The other man?"

"I didn't see anyone else. Why are you here? Do you know about the aliens and the council?"

She smiled.

"What's so funny?" Soren asked. He thought maybe she hadn't understood him or maybe she thought he was playing a joke on her. Then he realized what he'd said probably did sound strange.

"Nothing. It just completes the puzzle."

"What puzzle?"

"I have suspected many things," she said in a low voice. "Earlier, when the man, or whoever it was, came to get me, he said some things and I started thinking. I always thought something strange was going on. My Aunt Christine was like a keeper. And the others would come and check me every so often as if they were waiting for something to happen. Maybe I was a test or something. So…do you know if I'm human or alien?"

"I don't know? You look human to me."

"Are you human?"

"Sort of."

"What does that mean?"

"I think I'm half and half," Soren said, recalling bits and pieces of the memories he had extracted from his mother. "But I'm not sure."

"Maybe I am, too, and that's why we're here."

"I don't know," Soren answered. "All I know is the reason why we were leaving in the first place was because the council has to leave Earth."

"Why? And how do you know so much about it?"

"Because it was a secret and somehow they found out. Something to do with the rules they have. I hear my mom and dad talking about it. They're kind of the leaders of the council along with Uncle Leumas. He's an alien, and he has this skin between his hands."

"This is so interesting," she exclaimed. "You're lucky to have parents that are involved with this kind of stuff. I love reading about space and alien worlds! I've read everything I could get my hands on. Tell me more!"

"You can't blab any of this. It's supposed to be a secret."

"Well, it isn't anymore," she shot back. "Besides, do you really think I would blab to anyone? I'm not like that...you know...like a little child."

"No, I guess not," Soren agreed. He was beginning to enjoy talking with her. She was the first person his own age that he felt comfortable with.

"But then again," she continued, "I wouldn't be here if I hadn't fallen for that trick with the present he gave me."

"Me, too," Soren said. "I fell for the prize trick. So I guess we both gave into our weaknesses."

They both laughed with an established familiarity between them.

"What about your family?" Soren asked.

"All I know of is Aunt Christine. I called her 'Aunt' but I don't think she was really my aunt. She was just doing a job, pretending. I never knew my parents. Aunt Christine said they were killed in some car accident or something right after I was born."

"Sorry," Soren said.

"Where are your parents now?" she asked.

"They were supposed to be coming along, but now, I'm not sure."

"So, these are really bad aliens then?"

"I guess," Soren agreed. "They must have planned to kidnap us from the start."

"I wonder why me?"

"What do you mean?" Soren asked.

"Well, if your parents are the leaders of this council, these bad aliens must be planning to use you in some way to make them do something, or you are valuable in some other way. That would make sense, too. But that doesn't explain why I'm here. Maybe it's just a coincidence."

"Or you have something that they want," Soren suggested.

"Like what?"

"Maybe it's just you?"

"What do you mean?"

"You know," Soren began hesitantly, "we're not like other kids. I can hear it in the way you talk, just like I do. We know things, things the grownups know."

"Yeah," she agreed. "I'm tired of having to pretend all the time that I'm a regular six-year-old kid."

"Me, too, but we still like being treated that way sometimes. I mean, we get presents and prizes sometimes. You know, we're a lot alike."

"Yeah, I guess we are," Cindy said and smiled. "But I think you're different in some way than I am."

"How so?" he asked.

"I don't know. It's just...a feeling I have."

***

"No! It can't be," Leumas said. "Not Copolla! He's dead -- dead!"

"Believe me, I couldn't understand or fathom this either. But all I got from this caretaker was that some sort of balance had to be maintained," Greg said. He felt his earlier frustration now compounded with the anger and fear of the people closest to him.

"After all this! Everything we've been through! We just can't get a break," Sarah said as she walked over to Greg. He saw the tears streaming down her face, but he also saw the anger in her eyes as well. "And this bastard has our son?" she said.

"Yes," Greg answered as he reached out for Sarah and drew her into his arms. He felt her body tense and relax as if unsure of what it wanted to do. He couldn't help feeling guilty about waiting to divulge this information.

"I still can't believe it was Edward," she said as her voice echoed into his shoulder. "Of all people, the odds of Copolla ending up in someone so close to us."

"Can you imagine what he must have been thinking when he was here, among us?" Leumas asked. "He was laughing the whole time as he maneuvered us into this predicament. The nerve of that...that creature!" He slammed his fist on the table.

"It was all a distraction," Greg said. "He wanted us preoccupied so that he could come up with a reason to leave and take Soren with him."

"Well, it worked," Leumas agreed. "Right down to the smallest detail. But why Soren?"

"That's the easy part," Greg said. "You've both seen the powers he possesses. And you probably mentioned that to Edward. I think Copolla will try to get Soren to use those powers, or he will copy Soren's genetic makeup and he'll create his own little army. He won't need many and you know how patient he can be. Or he'll use Soren against us, or me, by threatening us with Soren's life if we don't do his bidding."

"What are we going to do?" Sarah asked as she pulled back from Greg.

"We've got to figure out where he will go," Greg said. "If we know that, then maybe I can send my mind to Soren and help him to escape."

"I'll have our ships begin looking along their last known trajectory," Leumas said as he began inputting information.

"I don't think they'll find anything," Greg said. "He's too smart for that. But in case they get lucky, have them just locate and follow, not intercept. If Copolla knows what's happening, there's no telling what he might do."

Sarah began to pace, her steps unsteady. She stopped and placed her hands on the back of a chair for support. "This is like a horrible nightmare that just won't end. Promise me, Greg, that this time we're going to make sure this ends one way or another. I can't take this anymore."

"I promise, Sarah." In his thoughts he said to himself, *no matter what the costs.*

"And whoever else is responsible is going to pay dearly," she continued. "Including the mysterious passenger in the ship."

"That's gnawing at me," Greg said. "For some reason, I feel it's important. Who could it be, or why was it so important that we not know who it is?"

"Someone that was not scanned at any of the entrance portals," Leumas said as he continued to type. "Why was it so important that they were smuggled inside? Would we have recognized them?"

"But a pre-flight scan is required, isn't there?" Sarah asked.

"Yes, but the computer can't match it to anything unless they were officially scanned and titled at the port of entry."

"But the DNA pattern of the initial scan would still be on file, wouldn't it?"

"Yes, but if we don't know who it is, it would be like looking for a needle in a haystack," Greg said.

"This person is probably a conspirator of Copolla," Leumas said. "I'll have the computer run a comparison to all DNA on file for council members in the database, including those linked to Copolla's henchmen. Maybe they were here once before and their genetic blueprint is still on file from a past visit."

"As soon as you're done there, we need to try to make a list of where Copolla might go," Greg said. "Where would he still have any influence left?"

"Greg, can't you search by projecting your mind?" Sarah asked. Greg heard the pleading in her voice for some hope for their son.

"Yes, but if I don't know where to go, I could be searching for a long time and when we do find out where they are, I might not have any strength left to do anything." He grasped her hand and squeezed it. "We'll get him back, I promise. Even if I have to turn myself over to Copolla in exchange for Soren."

"No!" Sarah pleaded. "I won't lose either one of you!"

"Shh..." He placed his finger on her lips. "Let's take this one step at a time."

"Oh, Greg," she murmured. "Why can't we just have normal lives for once?"

"It wasn't meant to be that way, I guess. Our destiny is somewhere else."

"Is that you speaking or is that some vision where you've seen it?"

"I don't know," he answered. "It's hard to tell anymore what is a vision and what isn't. I always wonder about the two children. I thought..."

"Greg! Sarah!" Leumas shouted. "You better come here and see this."

"What is it?" Greg asked as they walked over to where Leumas was peering into the screen.

"The computer found a...ah...match."

"Who is it?" Sarah asked.

"That's a good question, seeing as the closest DNA matches to our mystery passenger are you and Greg."

"That's Soren," Sarah stated.

"No, it's not," Leumas said. "I've isolated the strands." He pointed to the screen. "This is Alpha, this is Argusa, a pilot with known ties to Copolla, this is Edward and this is Soren. Now, this one here..." He tapped the screen with his finger. "...is the mysterious one and it's not Soren, but the DNA says it's a very close relation, female, and about the same age as Soren."

"What?" Sarah asked. "A close relation? What are you talking about?"

A close relation...another child? Greg thought. *The vision! There were supposed to be two children, a boy and a girl. Two would maintain a -- balance. That's what the caretaker meant. Balance...balance...balance... that's it!*

Leumas spoke, "I'm talking about..."

"Twins," Greg said, finishing the sentence for Leumas. "There were two children, not one."

Sarah stared at Greg. He saw the shock and awe on her face as she tried to comprehend what she was being told. Even he felt sickened by the dastardly things that had been done to them, but he also knew now was not the time to get wrapped up in a wave of emotion. That wouldn't help save their children.

"But how?" Sarah croaked. "The doctor -- Doctor Caruso -- would have told me if there were two children..."

"Not if somebody had gotten to him," Leumas said. "Made him lie to you about the second child."

"Leumas, do a quick check on the whereabouts of the doctor," Greg said. He then grasped Sarah and gently nudged her over to the side of the room.

"Greg, how can this be? Why does this keep happening?"

"I don't know, Sarah. I just don't know. But it's done and we have to focus on how we are going to get them back. I need you to be strong and to think this through. I know it will be incredibly difficult wondering about our daughter, what's she like and where has she been these past years. I know because I have the same thoughts and questions. But right now, we need to be together on this so we can figure out something."

"Did you know?" she asked.

"No, not as first, but now that I think about it, it has something to do with what the caretaker hinted at. For some reason he didn't come out and say that there were two children, but in a roundabout way he hinted at it."

"I should have listened to Leumas and used the council doctor," Sarah said. Greg heard the chastising tone in her voice. "He said it might be risky. But I had to be stubborn and insist on using Doctor Caruso. I never thought..."

"Don't condemn what you did," Greg offered. "It wasn't your fault. There was no way you could have known what was going to happen."

"But how did they know? How did they know I was going to have twins?"

"Someone probably used a medical scanner on you. It would have revealed to them that you were carrying two children before any human doctor would have noticed it."

"But why would they take the child?"

"Probably because they wanted to see if she developed any unique powers that they could use or control. Or maybe just to make it appear that my vision was invalid."

"Copolla, that bastard," Sarah muttered.

"No, not then. Remember, he was gone. It must have been one of his supporters. Like a sleeper cell that remained hidden."

"Or someone in the movement to return to Zire," Leumas interjected. "If the vision had no credibility, then they could use that to discredit Greg. Sounds like Ambassador Alpha."

"Perhaps they are one and the same," Greg offered.

"What about the doctor?" Sarah asked Leumas. "Have you found anything?"

"Both he and his family disappeared shortly after your delivery," Leumas said. "No trace whatsoever as to what happened to them. It's as if they vanished off the face of the planet."

"Not vanished. Probably killed so that there wouldn't be any trail to follow. That pretty much solidifies the theory of someone on the council being in on it," Greg added.

"What do we do now?" Sarah asked.

"We have the second launch window coming up real soon. Do we still want to launch? I don't know if we can trust the little armistice that Edward...I mean Copolla negotiated, do you?"

"We might as well," Greg said. "Even if they do attack, it shouldn't be a problem, should it?"

"Not for us, but for the planet it might be, if they use nuclear weapons."

"Well, I guess we have to make sure they don't then."

"How will we do that?"

"A little influence might help," Greg said.

"But we can't get close enough now."

"You can't, but I can. I think it's time I paid a visit to President John Bishop, or at least his thoughts anyway."

"I tried to keep things from the bastard, but he was too powerful. Little by little he gained access to all of my thoughts. I never felt so defiled in my life."

President Edward Samuel

"So what is your decision, Mr. President?"

John Bishop scanned the eyes of the cabinet members who sat around the table. Having been officially sworn in as President a few hours ago, he now felt the full brunt of the nation upon his shoulders. He thought it ironic how his first major decision, the one he would be remembered for, might also be his last.

The Secretary of Defense, who had proposed the question, nervously tapped his fingers on the table.

"How much time do I have?" Bishop asked.

"Approximately fifteen minutes, Mr. President."

"And you all concur that we should go ahead and follow Edward Samuel's suggestion that we launch a strike?"

"Sir, we would suggest it either way. We don't have a choice."

"But if we wait to see what their intentions are, we might avert all of this," Bishop asserted.

"Sir, if these aliens have the ability to do what they have done, we don't think they can be trusted. And if we let them get off the ground, we might lose the initiative. Our only option is to nuke the entire area."

"But why tell us what they are going to do? Why not just do it?" Bishop argued.

"The only explanation is that they are taunting us."

"What about evacuation?"

"Not enough time and it would cause mass panic and chaos."

"And if they are as powerful as they appear, what about a plan against a retaliation strike?"

"If they are that strong, then there is nothing we can do."

Bishop stood from the table. "I'll be back in a few minutes with my decision." He didn't wait for any response as he left.

He closed the door to his office, noting the time so he could clock off his fifteen minutes. He sat behind the desk and looked out the window. His options weren't many. If agreed to the strike and the aliens were destroyed, the toll of the residual radiation would be disastrous. If the aliens weren't destroyed, their retaliation would be the same result.

What the hell am I going to do?

***

"I'll be right back," Greg said as he squeezed Sarah's hand. He was lying on the couch in their living quarters. Leumas continued to monitor from the terminal in the quarters for any signs of the ship Copolla had taken with the children.

"You sure you're up for this?" she asked as she moved the hair from his forehead with her fingers.

"I have to be. We can't have all our work on Earth be destroyed by a nuclear strike. I wouldn't want to think that it happened because of what we started."

"I know," she agreed. "Let's just hope that John Bishop is susceptible to the idea."

"Oh, he will be, one way or the other. Keep you fingers crossed. Love you."

"Love you, too."

Greg closed his eyes and cleared all thoughts from his mind. He remembered his teaching from the alien visitor, Vague, who had trained him in the process of projecting his mind from the body's physical confines to one of energy that could travel great distances. He carefully formed in his mind the image of his link back to his body, his lifeline, and then formed the image of the White House. Slowly, he felt his consciousness blend into the structure.

Sarah had given him the basic layout of the building and indicated where the President would probably be. Greg's consciousness moved through the concrete and other materials searching for him. Luckily he found him exactly where Sarah had predicted. He was alone, which would make the process even easier.

John Bishop sat at his desk, his hands propping up his head as if he were unable to keep it raised on its own ability. His hands covered his face, giving him the appearance he didn't want to see anything. Greg surmised that he was looking at a man faced with a decision he didn't want to make.

A voice came over his intercom. "Mr. President, they're waiting for you."

John Bishop removed his hands from his face and sat up. Greg saw the exhaustion in his eyes and the indecisiveness in his face as his facial features grimaced as if in pain.

"Thank you, Carol. Tell them I'll be right there."

Greg formed the words in his thoughts and pushed them.

::*There will be no attack.*::

"What?" John Bishop said as he stood and looked cautiously about the room. "Is there someone here?" After a few seconds, a cynical smile formed on the edges of Bishop's mouth. "If you go crazy now, John, that won't help matters."

Greg pushed his thought harder. ::*You will not order a strike. Everything will work out peacefully.*::

John Bishop stumbled back a step and fell into his chair. He raised his hands to his temples and massaged them with his palms.

Too hard, Greg thought. He needed to find just the right amount. He lowered his consciousness as close to Bishop's mind as he dared and pushed again, this time with less force and hopefully more accuracy. ::*You will not order a strike. Everything will work out peacefully.*::

Greg knew he had attained the proper level when Bishop's haggard and worried looking face appeared to smooth out a little and become slightly relaxed as if the answer to everything that troubled to him had become perfectly clear.

::*Do you understand? There will be no attack. Edward Samuel cannot be trusted. Everything will work out peacefully. It is best to wait and allow the aliens a chance to honor your decision and leave on their own accord. Call it…a leap of faith.*::

"Yes," Bishop replied.

Greg decided that John Bishop deserved to know the truth about everything that had transpired during the presidency of Edward Samuel. Perhaps someday he could use it to prove the usefulness and the purpose of what had actually happened during the council's time on Earth. In his thoughts, Greg formed a synopsis of the images and voices he'd experienced on his trip back from wherever it was he had been. He imagined encapsulating them into a single package and placed them into the mind of Bishop with the instruction to be released slowly over a few days.

"Mr. President, they are waiting for you," the voice of the secretary called over the intercom.

"I'm on my way," Bishop said.

::*Remember, insist that they wait forty-eight hours, to allow the aliens time to leave. Do you understand?*::

"Yes."

::*Good. Now get--*::

Greg felt the presence of something else in Bishop's mind. He wasn't sure how to define it; it was as if he had bumped up against something in the dark. A shadow of something, but it was wearing off or disintegrating. It was a remnant of something that had been here earlier. Influence? There was some sort of a residual in Bishop's mind, a leftover of neural energy. Someone had been in here and it didn't take long for Greg to realize it had been Copolla.

This residual appeared as a fibrous strand to Greg's consciousness similar to the one he maintained to his own physical body, although this one was much finer. It reminded him of a strand of hair. Could it be used, he wondered, like a piece of evidence to track down the killer, like DNA analysis? Could he use this as a way to track Copolla? He wasn't sure. But how would he get the strand back in order to use it? If he returned to his own body right now, he wouldn't be able to follow it from there, he would have to follow it from where he was, here, and right now. But could he maintain his own lifeline while following this one?

"Mr. President," the intercom sounded.

They're waiting for him. He needs to get in there and tell them, Greg thought. *The problem here is solved for the moment.*

"I'm coming, Carol," Bishop said. "Be right there."

Greg began his exodus from Bishop's mind. He knew he had no other choice but to follow the strand of energy and only hope it led him to Copolla and the children. He focused on the strand of energy and allowed his consciousness to flow into it. Everything went dark as he was sucked into a tremendous vacuum--hurtling him somewhere. He only hoped it was the right place and not some trick that Copolla had laid for him.

***

John Bishop entered the meeting room and sat at the head of the table. For the first time in the past few hours he felt confident of what he was about to do.

"Gentlemen, after great and painful consideration, I have decided. There will be no attack at this time."

"Mr. President," the Secretary of Defense began. "Do you realize what is at stake here? If we lose the element of surprise, we might not get another chance."

"Of course I do. My conscience will not allow a pre-emptive strike without exhausting all efforts to a peaceful resolution. Nor can I trust the word of Edward Samuel. We don't know if he's telling the truth, code or no code. Hell, at this point we don't know who is telling us the truth and who isn't. But I do believe that if these aliens were going to destroy us, they would have done it already. Therefore, we will give them forty-eight hours to depart the planet. At the end of that time, if they haven't left, we will launch an attack. Is that understood?"

Nods of affirmation came from the other members around the table as Bishop looked at each one of them.

"Gentlemen, I know that I am asking a lot of you. Call this a *leap of faith*, if you will. I can't explain it to you, but I have never believed more strongly in anything than what I am telling you right now. I'm asking you to trust me and to pray with me that everything will work out peacefully."

He scanned the faces of the people sitting around the table. He saw hope and he saw fear in their expressions. At this point, he knew there wasn't anything else he could tell them that would calm their fears. Now all they could do was wait.

"Well then, I believe I need to talk with this Leumas character."

***

"Yes, Mr. Bishop," Leumas said.

"I'll be blunt, Mr. Leumas, er...Leumas, forty-eight hours is the length of the patience of the people of this country. We will make no threatening action toward your departure as long as you live up to that expectation."

"That's fair enough," Leumas agreed.

"However if you do not leave in that time..."

"I understand perfectly. Is there anything else, Mr. Bishop?"

"Just one thing," Bishop began, but then hesitated. "I don't understand and there are many questions still unanswered, but if you're so technologically advanced as it appears you are..."

"Yes."

"Then how did we discover your presence?"

"Mr. Bishop, there are some things that are constant throughout the galaxy, regardless of the level of technology. Politics and those seeking their own personal gain at no thought of the cost. We are both presently a victim of both counts."

"I see, well...I think I do."

"Our presence would never have been detected by your people. It was revealed by someone within our group who wants us to leave Earth and return to the original location of the organization I represent, and by another life form of much more devious concerns who was working inside your own system."

"I see what you mean now. Politics."

"Yes. But don't get me wrong, there are always those who wish for nothing but good for their people, their world and the other worlds in the galaxy. I'm referring to Greg Carlson and Sarah McClendon. One you are familiar with and the other you may not be."

"I know Ms. McClendon. We interacted frequently. I always had the utmost faith and confidence in her abilities. I also remember Mr. Carlson. He was involved in that reporter's accusation, Ray Schume, I believe his name was. That was a few years ago. What a side show that became."

"That's correct. It was an interesting period, but we weathered it and everything got back on track. And Edward Samuel, I know you probably have formulated your own thoughts about him, but I would temper it by saying this: the Edward Samuel you last saw was in the shape of him, but it was not really him."

"I don't understand."

"Perhaps that is better, in this particular instance. Just remember him for the good things he did accomplish."

"You know that's not how it works. One 'aw-shit' wipes out all those 'atta-boys.'"

"How well I do know it," Leumas said remembering his own time of being in the same situation when he first began the indoctrination process of Greg and Sarah. "Well, Mr. Bishop, there are things I need to attend to."

"Same here."

"If anything comes up, you'll be sure to let us know?"

"Yes. But there...well, there is one last question I'd like to ask."

"Yes?"

"Will you come back?"

Leumas smiled. "Only if you ask us to."

"How will we..."

"You've been given the tools to reach out. Now it's up to you. Trust me, you'll know when the time comes. Goodbye, Mr. Bishop."

Leumas disengaged the view screen and the image of John Bishop faded out. He keyed up the compound global communications channel and made the announcement to begin the return to the planet Zire. Then he spoke with security to ensure that the departing ships would still be protected, just in case they needed it.

He keyed in the code to contact Sarah, who remained in their quarters with Greg.

"Sarah, I just finished speaking with Bishop. Everything appears to have worked. How is Greg?"

"He's still unconscious."

Leumas heard the concern in her voice. "He must have finished with Bishop a while ago. I wonder why he hasn't returned?"

"I don't know."

"Can you tell if anything is wrong? Can you sense anything from him?"

"No."

"Maybe he's found something else?" Leumas suggested.

"I...don't know," Sarah answered. "But if he has gone somewhere else, he must maintain the link or he won't get back."

Leumas heard the break in communication as Sarah terminated the conversation. There was nothing to do now but wait, and he hated that part most of all.

CHAPTER ELEVEN

"I knew she was like me in a certain way from the first time I met my sister."

Soren Carlson

"I think it's time I talked to our little friends," Copolla said to Alpha as he wiped his mouth with his sleeve. They were seated in the dining area of the craft, which was just off of the main control area. "How much longer until we reach Acuba?" he asked.

"A few hours," Alpha replied. "But don't you think the council will look there for you?"

"Not at first. They will probably assume that I would not go to the last place I was: too obvious. By the time they discover that I have gone there, it will be too late. Then we will go to the least expected place they would think to look for us: Zire, right underneath the council's nose."

"An intriguing plan: risky but intriguing."

"One must have the backbone to take risks. That seems to be a trait that is missing these days," Copolla said, his facial features contorting into a disgusted look.

"I'm curious about the child. How will you proceed?"

"Simple. If I can't convince the boy to do what I want, I will threaten the girl's life. I don't believe in wasting time."

"How exactly will you use the child's power?"

"Alpha," Copolla said, sarcasm clearly evident in his voice. "Here I thought you were the smart one. I was sure that by now you would have figured it out."

"Please forgive my ignorance."

Copolla eyed him warily. He wondered if Alpha was mocking him. "It's obvious that the child has power that exceeds the sum of his parents. Not only can influence be used, but the ability to go into someone's mind and dissect it into tiny pieces. Just imagine it; there are so many ways that he can be used. For instance, all he has to do is go into the mind of someone and pick out the one thing that terrifies them and he can make it so it continually plays in their thoughts. How's that for controlling their actions?"

"Control by fear. Very effective."

"That's only the beginning. Imagine a group of them going from planet to planet. We won't need a large armada of fighting machines.

We can do this by just having them going into the minds and capturing their loyalty."

"Ah, very clandestine and subversive. Very good."

"Yes. It won't attract much attention either. That's the real beauty of it."

"Where shall you begin?"

"With the council members first; we'll isolate them one by one. I'll use their fear to put me back in leadership."

"But you don't need the council. Why bother with it?"

"It's just a point I want to make. Leumas ousted me and then my son turned against me. I want the rest of the council to pay for what they did."

"I see," Alpha replied, his voice sounding cautious.

"Don't worry, Alpha. I'll be sure to leave enough of it for you to control and use however you see fit."

"Your generosity is magnanimous."

Copolla gazed at Alpha. "Alpha, do I sense a streak of sarcasm in your voice lately?"

"No, of course not. I am honored to be part of your plans."

"Good. Otherwise maybe we need to have a little talk again."

"No, Copolla. There is no need for that. I shall comply and follow with whatever you decide to do."

"Well, that's good to hear." Copolla rose from his seat. "You stay here and monitor council ship movements. I'm going to formally introduce our two friends to one another."

***

"Why do you think I'm different from you?" Soren asked Cindy.

"I have a way of getting a feeling or sense about things sometimes. With you, I can sense that there are things you can do with your mind, but I can't. But somehow, I feel like I'm a part of it. I don't know — it's hard to explain a feeling."

"I can do things," Soren said. "But they hurt me in a way, make me very tired and weak."

"I've had that happen to me, too. Aunt Christine would get really mad when that happened."

"What were you doing?"

"I don't know. I never really remember."

The sound of the door being unlocked turned their attention from each other.

"Well," Copolla began as he entered the compartment and locked the door behind him. "Are we getting acquainted?"

"What's going on, Uncle Edward, or whoever you are?" Soren asked.

"Very good, my little friend, very good. Your analysis is correct. I am not your Uncle Edward although I do share his physical form. You've heard the expression that beggars can't be choosy."

"What is…"

"You can call me Copolla, after all, that is my real name. Now, aren't you curious why you two have been brought together?"

"I've heard of you," Soren said. "You're supposed to be dead."

"Yes, well sometimes things don't always work out the way you want them to. Now get back to my question."

"You're going to use us some way to get at the council and my mom and dad, aren't you?"

"Correct again. You're so smart. Can you tell me why she is here?" Copolla said, pointing at Cindy.

"I don't know," Soren said, ensuring he kept a puzzled look on his face.

"Can't you see the physical similarities in yourselves? You both look very much alike because you are brother and sister."

Both Soren and Cindy looked at one another before returning their gaze to Copolla.

"But you have differences," Copolla continued. "You, Soren, have significant powers, where she has nothing to offer. Do you know what that means?"

"No," Soren answered.

"That means that she is expendable. If I decide she is not worth keeping around anymore, I'll snap my fingers and she'll be gone."

"You are an evil and disgusting person," Cindy said.

"Silence!" Copolla roared. "Or the first thing I will do to you is cut out your tongue."

Cindy backed up a few paces from where she was standing.

Copolla returned his attention to Soren. "Now, I am going to have you use your powers to perform certain alterations in the thoughts of others."

"I can't," Soren said. "I promised I wouldn't because it hurts me. They said if I did it again, I might die."

"We'll just have to work around that little problem, now won't we? Your so-called parents just didn't want you to realize the power you have. You can't believe half the things they tell you. Now, I want to have a little private demonstration of the abilities."

"I can't..."

"Use those words again and she dies right now! Then after I kill her, I will dissect your puny little brain and take what I want! Is that understood?" Copolla's face burned with hatred. "I don't hear you," he said as he removed a weapon from his belt and pointed it at Cindy's head.

"Yes. Yes, I understand," Soren answered.

"Good. That's much better. Now, there is an alien in the craft. I want you to go into his mind and find out the thing that he fears the most. Do you understand?"

"Yes."

"Good then, do it now."

***

I hope this works, Greg thought as his neural essence raced through space, following the strand of energy he had detected in John Bishop. He had passed through the Earth's solar system and was now heading toward the star system of Alpha Centauri. He kept part of his mind focused on maintaining his tie to his own physical body back on Earth. He knew the penalty all too well of losing that attachment--a mental oblivion.

The outline of a ship appeared directly ahead of him, he urged himself forward faster. In seconds he was able to recognize it as a council craft, and the one he was searching for because the energy strand disappeared into it. He slowed his speed and focused his thoughts on becoming part of the ship. He remembered having to do this exact same thing when he rescued Leumas and Sarah from Acuba when Copolla had them kidnapped. The memory of that experience reminded him of what had caused his mind to lose contact with his physical body back on Earth: learning that Copolla was his biological father.

He felt his consciousness merge into the ship. Once stabilized, he traveled through it, searching for the central control area by following the cable runs. After a few seconds he found what he was looking for. He was in the main control area and could see everything around him, including the alien who sat at the controls, and the dead body of another alien that was pushed into a corner.

Feelings of disgust attacked Greg's consciousness at the sight of the body. He fought to control his emotions; he couldn't afford to be distracted at this point. He had to remain focused on his tie to his own body back on Earth if he was going to survive. Whoever it was, they were beyond any hope, so Greg cast aside the image and turned his attention back to the one that was behind the controls of the craft.

He assumed this alien was the ambassador called Alpha. *First things first*, he thought. He didn't really have a plan of action already formulated, so the logical thing to do before confronting Copolla was to get the craft's tracking beacon turned on. Any other direct attempt at changing course would evoke suspicion from Copolla, who Greg knew was impervious to influence. If the locator beacon were turned back on, this would allow Leumas to locate the vessel and send help. But he needed to get Alpha not to see it. The only answer was to make him believe that it was supposed to be turned on in the first place.

Greg formulated the thought in his mind and gently pushed. ::*You have forgotten to turn the tracking beacon back on, per Copolla's orders. Do it immediately and he will not discover your error.*::

Greg watched as Alpha's face went blank and he reached for the switch and flipped it to the on position.

Satisfied he was easily able to influence Alpha, Greg pushed the next thought. ::*Slow the craft to interplanetary speed. Copolla said he wasn't in any hurry.* ::

Alpha easily completed this task as well. *Perfect*, Greg thought. With the locator on and the ship slowed to a crawl, Leumas would get someone here and hopefully assist in whatever it was he was going to do.

Satisfied, Greg began to back out of Alpha's sphere of neural energy. Suddenly he felt an influx of energy and sensed the presence of another form entering Alpha's mind.

***

Soren lay back on the bed and prepared to project himself into the alien's subconscious as directed by Uncle Edward, or Copolla, as he had told him.

Cindy came over to the bunk and sat down next to him.

"You be careful," she said. "I haven't had a chance to pick on you yet. It's kind of neat knowing I have a brother."

"I will," he said and smiled. "We'll be okay, I promise. Can you stay next to me?"

"Sure. I won't move. I promise."

"This is just so touching," Copolla said mockingly. "Get on with it, I don't have all day!"

Soren closed his eyes and focused his thoughts toward the alien, Alpha. He entered into the darkness of his mind and opened himself up to sense where the thoughts of fear were located. As he waited to decide what direction to pursue, he felt something, a shadow of energy passing by him. He felt a sense of familiarity of having sensed this energy before.

::*Soren? Is that you?*::

::*Dad? What are you doing here?*::

::*That's a long story. Didn't we tell you not to use this power? It weakens you too much and it's very dangerous.*::

::*I didn't have a choice. Copolla said he would kill Cindy.*::

::*Cindy? Cindy...is that her name?*::

::*You didn't know either?*::

::*We just learned of her existence a short while ago. Is she okay?*::

::*She's fine as long as I do what he wants.*::

::*What does he want?*::

::*He wants me to prove my power by finding what scares this alien the most so he can use it to control him. A test.*::

::*I see. I can't say I'm surprised. Look, you get in and out real quick. I'm going to drop in on Copolla and see what I can do to stop him.*::

::*Okay.*::

::*You be careful, Soren.*::

::*I will.*::

::*Love you, son.*::

::*Love--*:: Soren's thought ended abruptly.

::*Soren, what's wrong?*:: Greg called.

Suddenly Soren found himself growing very weak. The images around him began to diminish into nothingness.

::*Dad! I can't maintain...*::

::*Soren? Soren!*::

***

Cindy saw Soren's body suddenly jerk spasmodically. When she looked closer, she also noticed he was covered with sweat.

"What's happening?" Copolla asked.

"I don't know," she answered.

Soren's hands were now shaking continuously, adding to the symptoms of having some kind of seizure.

What am I supposed to do, Cindy thought, feeling helpless.

::*Cindy, can you hear me?*::

"What?"

"I didn't say anything," Copolla said. "Are you crazy as well as useless?" He laughed.

::It's okay, Cindy. I'm communicating to you in your thoughts. I'm your father. I know you may not be able to communicate the same way with me, and that's okay. We can work around that for now. Soren is in trouble and I need for you to try and help him. I want you to take his hand, hold it and talk to him.::

Cindy grasped one of his hands in hers and squeezed it gently.

::Good, now talk to him.::

"How long is this going to take," Copolla barked.

"I don't know."

"I'll be back in a minute. I have to check on something. Ensure that he is done by the time I get back."

Cindy watched as Copolla got up and left, locking the door behind him.

"Soren, where are you?" she said as she grasped his other hand in hers, now holding both. She tried not to be alarmed by the cold and clammy feel of them. "Are you all right?"

Soren's body stopped shaking and now lay still. "Soren?"

::I'm here,:: he answered in her thoughts. ::I'm okay. Whatever you're doing, don't stop. I feel fine now.::

Cindy noticed that he had stopped sweating and the cold clammy feeling she had from his hands had been replaced with warmth, feeling normal.

"I'm just holding your hands," she said and shrugged.

::Soren, Cindy, this is Dad. Are you sure you feel okay now, Soren?::

::I feel perfectly fine now. I feel stronger somehow.::

"I'm feeling like a middleman in this conversation," Cindy interjected. "You are both talking through me."

::Is it causing you any discomfort?::

"No, but it feels really weird having these voices buzzing through me," she said and giggled.

::You're acting as some form of conduit or anchor,:: Greg said. ::Cindy, are you sure you feel okay?::

"Fine, never better."

::You must be connected somehow to Soren, boosting his strength and maintaining some sort of…::

::Balance,:: Soren said completing the sentence.

::Yes. Interesting choice of word, but correct. Perhaps because you're twins, there was some form of separation of abilities that only work as they're supposed to when you are together, physically touching. We know that if Soren uses his power without being in touch with you, Cindy, it affects him in a bad way. I guess your presence acts as a safeguard of some sort. Neither of you can do it without the other. It ensures a balance.::

"But why can't I communicate with my thoughts like you can?"

::I don't know. Maybe all your power is in the form of being the stable influence for Soren so that he can do what he is meant to do.::

"Speaking of 'meant to do,' Mr. Not-so-nice-guy will be back soon and will probably want some results. Whatever we are going to do, we need to do soon," Cindy offered. "I hate to see him get mad."

::I think we'll give him exactly what he wants. Soren, I have an idea.::

"Life with Greg was wonderful even with the moments of not knowing whether he would leave and never come back. I never could get used to it."

Sarah Carlson

"Greg, where are you?" Sarah said as she sat on the edge of the bed holding his hand. "Don't you go and leave me again...please. I couldn't go through that again."

She felt the tears coming and this time did not even consider holding them back. She let them flow freely from her eyes and down her cheeks.

::Greg,:: she thought. ::Come back. Please...::

She tried to focus her thoughts and send them, hoping that they would reach him wherever he was, as she had done when he'd gotten separated from his body before. But this time she couldn't clear her mind of the images of the children, a boy and a girl, somewhere in the hands of a treacherous madman. A girl she hadn't ever seen before. She wondered if she looked like her or Greg.

"Sarah," Leumas' voice over the communication circuit causing her to jump. She caught her breath and answered.

"Yes, Leumas."

"We've got him," Leumas exclaimed. "The location beacon just came online. I've ordered ships to intercept. Are you ready to go?"

"But...Greg?"

"Don't you get it? It has to be him that caused the beacon to come on. Alpha or Copolla certainly wouldn't have done it. It's Greg all right! He's alive and well and causing hate and discontent for them--God, how I love that guy!"

"Thank God is right," Sarah said and breathed deeply. "How long until we intercept them?"

"About an hour," answered Leumas.

"I hope that's soon enough."

***

Copolla unlocked the door and stepped back into the room. Both Soren and Cindy were sitting up on the bed.

"Well?" he asked.

"It's done," Soren answered. "I have what you wanted."

"Excellent. Now tell me."

"I can't exactly tell you, I have to show you."

"Show me?"

"Yes. I have to place the image in your mind for you to see it."

"Trickery, boy?" Copolla eyed Soren warily. "I'll warn you right now that anything you do will come back tenfold on you and your sister. I'm impervious to all attempts at influencing."

"There's no trickery. You asked me for something and I know what it is. I will place the image in your mind so you can see what it is that Alpha fears the most."

"Go ahead then, but remember, if there is any trickery..." He pulled his gun from his belt and pointed it at Cindy. "...she'll be the first to know."

Soren lay back down on the bunk. Cindy remained next to him holding his hand. He closed his eyes.

::Copolla, dear father,:: the thought rang in Copolla's mind, surprising him. He had been expecting the young boy's voice, but instead immediately recognized Greg's voice. ::I want you to release the children.::

::You! What are you doing here! How dare you interfere! You can't harm me::

::I know I can't, but how can I stand by and let you harm my children?::

::They will not be harmed as long as the boy performs what I want him to do.::

::Is this what it has come to? You would use children to obtain what you want?::

::Whatever it takes, my son. You had your chance. I offered it all to you but you decided you wanted to be a do-gooder for the insignificant planet and galaxy. And look what it has gotten you... treason amongst your own kind. Your life is falling apart everywhere you look. Chaos and the powerful have always ruled and always shall.::

::I know these are bad times. But I can't let it get any worse. I will do whatever it takes to get my children back. Just name the price.::

::My price? I'll tell you what my price is...::

***

Soren entered into Copolla's mind. He could hear the echoes of the conversation of his father and Copolla. That was the diversion his father had said he would do while Soren searched for Copolla's essence inside of Edward's body.

As he scanned the hallways of his mind, he saw that Copolla's habitation of his Uncle Edward's mind appeared as large black splotches, all intertwined and connected to each other, covering the doors where Edward's memories and thoughts were contained, keeping them trapped and allowing Copolla to have free reign.

Soren formed an image of a steel door in his mind and it appeared in the wall next to him. The door was made of thick metal and contained nuts and bolts the size of his hand. Next Soren opened the door and lined the walls of a similar design, allowing it the shape and structure of a fortification, designed to keep things in, not out.

Next he grasped one of the black splotches and began to pull it off of the door it covered. It was not willing to come away easily. He pulled harder and it came away with a violent snap. Soren dragged it over to the room he created and tied it to the far wall. His hands had become covered with the black film and he felt its slimy essence.

He didn't know how many of these infectious things were here, but they stretched as far as he could see. At this rate it would take a very long time to clean out his uncle's mind and rid him of Copolla's presence. He hoped his father knew what he was doing.

He focused his energy and pushed the thought into the room he had designed, allowing the energy to become absorbed into the walls and ceiling so that it emulated the thought of safety and isolation from the rest of the mind. Next he began arbitrarily picking adjoining areas that were covered and ripping and tearing at them, knowing that these were bits and pieces of Copolla's mind.

***

::My price is you! You can make your child do what I want. If you have him do my bidding, I won't harm the other child or your wife.::

::I can't allow that.::

::But you just said you would do anything?::

::I know, but I didn't really mean it. I just needed the time.::

:: Time? You fool! Then we have nothing more to discuss.::

::Oh but we do,:: Greg added. ::You might not be able to understand it, but I am willing to give up my own life to save my children.::

::What are you talking about?::

::I came prepared to bring you back to where you belong. I have been given the ability by the caretaker to mutate my own energy into a cancerous type virus. This virus shall consume everything in the brain that you inhabit.

I will die in the process but you shall be gone also. A price that I feel is worth the sacrifice of my own life.::

::You wouldn't dare.::

::Father, you should know me by now. I don't make idle threats. It's already begun, can't you feel it?::

Copolla frantically tried to focus his thoughts by trying to remember things and found that there were gaps where there weren't any before.

::You forget, I am holding a weapon on your daughter.::

::There is only one way to save yourself. I know what it is. If you want that way out, you best put the weapon down.::

::You bastard!:: Copolla screamed.

::Yes. Yes I am. The more time you wait, the more of yourself you lose. Personally I don't think it's a bad thing, but perhaps you might think differently about that.::

Copolla felt his hand release the gun and it clamored against the hard steel deck.

::There!::

::Good. Now listen very closely. There is a room, only one place that can hide your subconscious from the virus. I suggest you find it very quickly, there isn't much time left by the way..::

::I will be back! Somehow--someway you know I will be.::

::Yes, I do know. But in between now and then, there will be peace and happiness for a while and that's better than nothing, so I guess we'll have to settle for that.::

::You fool!::

::Like father, like son.::

***

Soren watched as the movement of the elements of Copolla's mind began to progress slowly on their own into the room he had created. Then suddenly, as if detecting some form of urgency, they quickly picked up speed and he could hear the onslaught of more and more of the infectious elements of Copolla's mind as they were sucked into the room. He thought he could almost hear the ranting of Copolla as they swooshed by. As the last strand entered, he slammed the door shut and double bolted the door.

He thought to his father: *::He's in there, Dad. He fell for the story-- hook, line, and sinker. How were you so sure he would believe you?::*

::*Because he knows I am sincere and never bluff or lie, only this time I did. Also self-preservation is one of Copolla's landmark traits. He will do anything to survive if he thinks there will be a chance to escape.*::

::*What about Uncle Edward?*::

::*I don't know, we'll have to see. Now you get out of Edward's mind and stay with your sister. Help is on the way. I'll place the thought of sleep into Alpha's mind so he won't cause any trouble. Then I will return to my own body. Okay?*::

::*Okay.*::

::*Oh--and one more thing, Soren, when I get there, we need to talk about some things, young man. Or should I call you Caretaker?*::

::*Not exactly.*:: Soren answered meekly.

***

Edward Samuel awoke to find himself lying on the floor in a strange room. *Where am I?* He thought as he slowly sat up. His body felt sore and he had a terrible headache.

"Hi, Uncle Edward?" he heard.

Turning to his right, he saw Soren and a young girl that he didn't recognize.

"Soren, where are we?"

"We're on a spacecraft. I don't know exactly where we are but don't worry, help is on the way."

"How did we get here?"

"It's a long story. Don't you remember anything?"

"Well, I don't know. I remember sitting in my office at Camp David and then I was...arguing with someone."

"That was probably Copolla."

"Copolla!" Edward said, alarmed at hearing the name. "He's dead!"

"Not exactly. He was able to come back to Earth and take over your body. He's locked up in a safe place in your mind."

"In my mind?"

"Uh-huh. My dad and I were able to trick him."

"Your dad? He's back?"

"Uh-huh."

"Boy, I did miss a lot. Who's this?" he asked, pointing to the mysterious girl.

"This is Cindy, my sister."

"Your sister?"

"Uh-huh. Say hello to Uncle Edward, Cindy."

"Hello, Uncle Edward," she said.

"Wait a minute," Edward began. He was totally overwhelmed by all these things he was hearing. It made his head pound harder. "You mean to tell me you have discovered you have a sister, your dad is back, and Copolla was using me--or my body--to do what he wanted?"

"Correct!"

"And he's still here?" he asked as he pointed to his head.

"Correct again. All locked up."

The ship momentarily jarred from the docking of another craft.

"That should be Mom, Dad, and Leumas," Soren stated.

"Good. Maybe they can explain what the devil is going on. I'd like to know who's running the United States if I've been away? I'm sure with all the confusion, I need to get back."

"We're not going back, we're heading to the planet Zire. All of the council is coming, too."

"Leaving Earth? Everyone?"

"Yes."

"Is it because of something I...or Copolla did?"

"Yes, I think so."

"My God, what have I done? What has that bastard done?"

"No matter how many times I woke to seeing Sarah's face staring at me with that frightful and pained look, I always promised myself that it was the last time."

Greg Carlson

Greg opened his eyes and smiled as he saw Sarah standing over him.

"Hi there," he said.

Sarah reached down and hugged him. He could feel her body move as she sobbed into his shoulder.

Greg wrapped his arms around her and pressed her close, relishing the feel of the warmth of her.

"It's good to be back," he said. For the first time since returning, he felt at peace knowing that he now understood everything. "Everything will be fine now."

Sarah, without releasing him, spoke. "Greg. No more of this. The risks, the not knowing if you will come back...I can't take it anymore."

"It's done. Or at least I think it is. We've reached a balance of some sort. I'll explain it later."

"The children? They're safe?" she asked.

"Yes. They're fine."

Greg scanned his surroundings.

"We're on Leumas' ship?"

"Yes. When the beacon came on, Leumas assumed it was you that did it. We left Earth immediately and brought your body with us."

"How soon until we arrive at the ship?"

"Should be anytime now," she answered.

"Good."

"Greg, did you see her?"

"Yes. She's as beautiful as you. And smart as a whip. She and Soren, well, they make one hell of a team."

"Like you and I?"

"Better."

"Then the vision you had? It's true? The children shall lead the council?"

"Yes. All will be as it should be."

***

Greg, Sarah and Leumas stepped onboard the ship, quickly making their way to the cabin where everyone was.

Greg opened the door and stepped into the compartment. Edward, Soren, and Cindy were sitting on the floor in a close-knit group. It reminded him of being on a camping trip; he almost expected to hear them singing campfire songs together.

"Well, don't you look like the cozy bunch?" Greg said, but couldn't help his eyes from focusing on Cindy. She looked just like Sarah...the same dark hair and facial features. "Hello, Cindy, I'm your father, in person this time, not in your mind."

He watched as she rose quickly and stepped over to where he stood. Greg knelt down and opened his arms. She dashed into them without any reservation. Greg hugged her tightly.

"I'm so sorry, Cindy. If only we had known," Greg said.

"I know, Dad, I know," she said.

"Cindy?" Sarah said from behind Greg.

Greg released the girl and gently maneuvered her toward Sarah. "Cindy, this is your mother."

Cindy, again not showing any hesitation or reservation, ran into Sarah's arms.

"Oh, baby!" Sarah exclaimed as her voice broke into sobs of relief and excitement.

Greg turned his attention to Soren and Edward.

"Are you all right?"

"Fine, Dad," Soren quickly answered. "But I think Uncle Edward is a little confused."

"A little confused is the understatement of the year," Edward answered. "But it is sheer delight to see you whole again, Greg. Welcome home."

Edward stood and embraced Greg.

"Thanks. It's good to be back, Edward."

"Now will someone please tell me what the devil has been going on?" Edward asked.

"Let's get off this ship," Leumas interjected as he stepped forward. "There's an uncomfortable stench. We'll be more comfortable on my vessel. But first I want to meet this young lady who's been avoiding me." He turned to where Cindy and Sarah still embraced.

"Cindy, this is your Uncle Leumas," Sarah offered as she turned the girl in his direction.

"Hello, Uncle Leumas," she said.

"Hello to you, too, young lady. May I say that you have inherited your mother's fine features fortunately and not your father's."

Greg gave Leumas a sarcastic look. "Leumas..."

"Thank you," Cindy responded.

"Well, now that we are all introduced, let's get off this tub."

***

"I'm sorry, Edward," Sarah said.

Her apology, although heartfelt as it was, could do nothing to stem the anger and humiliation that Edward was feeling. When Sarah completed explaining everything that had happened, Edward felt Greg place his hand on his shoulder.

"What a mess Copolla made," Edward muttered. "Destroyed everything. The council's work, my presidency, my family... everything."

"It's not a total disaster," Greg said. "Earth has the spacecraft design to do with as they please. Wasn't that one of our goals?"

"True. But look at the cloud of alien conspiracy and mistrust Copolla left behind. How would you react?"

"It'll take a while for them to get over it," Sarah agreed.

"And I'm left with that bastard in my head?"

"Until we figure someway to get him out of there," Greg responded.

"And he can't get out again?" Edward asked, his words pointed and searching for reassurance.

"I don't think so," Greg answered.

"I don't like the sound of that," Edward said. "We can't take any chance of this madman ever getting loose again and destroying the hopes and ambitions of people."

"We'll figure out something."

Edward didn't like the uncertainty of the situation and the potential risks involved. He looked at Greg and Sarah, good friends who had put all they had on the line the past few years to save the council and Earth. He could ask nothing more of them now. It was his turn.

He replaced his saddened outlook with one of a more conciliatory acceptance. "You're right, we'll get through this somehow. We always do."

"You need to rest now, Edward," Sarah said. "You've been through a lot the past few days."

"And you have a new member of the family to get acquainted with," he said. "She's a beautiful young lady."

"Thank you," Sarah said and gently kissed him on the cheek. "Get some rest."

"I will. You two get out of here."

Greg and Sarah left the room.

Edward went over to the liquor cabinet, thankfully provided by Leumas, and found what he wanted...a bottle of Scotch. He filled his tumbler with ice and then poured in a small amount of Scotch. He looked at the glass and then added some more. He took his drink and sat near the view port window.

Thoughts surged into his mind, images that he didn't remember but the people in them were recognizable. There was John Bishop, General Bradstorm, and other members from his staff. *These must be images from when Copolla used my body*, he thought. He wanted to know more of what had happened and what Copolla had done. He reached out for these images in his mind, pleading to see more of them.

The glass of Scotch fell from his hand and shattered on the floor.

"I know you're there..." he said. "I can feel the filth."

::*I will get out.*:: The voice in his mind rose from the depths.

::*Not if I have anything to say about it.*::

::*You won't be able to stop me. I am too powerful!*::

::*Don't bet on it.*::

Terribly powerful laughter erupted in his mind. Edward clasped his head with both hands.

"No! No!" he cried.

::*You can't stop me! Nobody can stop me!*::

***

Greg made his way back to their quarters after being alone for a while in the observation deck of the ship. He wanted a few moments to think and sort things out before he talked with Soren.

When he entered, Sarah was sitting with Cindy and Soren, showing them pictures from a family album.

"This was my mom, that would be your grandmother, and..." Sarah looked up. "Greg, where have you been? We were looking for you."

"I was just wandering for a few moments, thinking about some things."

"We were going to see Leumas. I think Cindy has a crush on him."

Cindy blushed. "Mom! Yuk!"

"Oh, sorry," Sarah said as she hugged Cindy. "That was supposed to be a secret, huh?"

"Why don't you two go ahead. I want to talk with Soren for a little bit."

"Ah...okay," she said.

Greg saw the inquisitive look. ::*It's okay. We just have a few things we need to talk about. I'll fill you in later.*::

"I guess we can go and do the girl thing, right, Cindy?"

"Sure."

Sarah rose and grasped Cindy's hand. "We'll be back."

"See you later," Greg said as he opened the door for them. When they had left, he turned his attention to Soren. "Ready for a little talk?"

"Sure, Dad."

Greg moved to the couch and sat next to Soren. The questions and partial realizations that had been hounding him were now ready to be released.

"You've had the power for quite some time, haven't you?"

"What do you mean?" Soren asked, sounding puzzled.

"Tell me the truth, Soren, there isn't any need to hide anything any more."

"Yes. How did you know?"

"No one else knew about the caretaker, yet you mentioned him when we were talking about my experience. It was you who created the caretaker, wasn't it?"

"Yes."

"Why and how?"

"It started by just dreaming about you. Mom showed me movies of you and her so when I went to sleep, it was on my mind. Somehow my thoughts became linked to yours and I saw that you were in some kind of oblivion, nothing but unfocused energy. By creating the caretaker, I was able to force your consciousness back together by giving you purpose."

"Yes, you did," Greg agreed. As he thought back, he couldn't remember anything before he started conversing with the caretaker. "But the way I found my way back, the memories..."

"You did that. No one else could, you just needed a little push to get you to consider the possibility."

"I see. But what about having to return there when I was done? Why did you make that statement if it wasn't really true?"

"That was just to reiterate the balance issue. If you kept thinking about it, I thought it would lead you to Cindy."

"And it did, but if you knew about Cindy, why didn't you just tell someone?"

"I didn't know who it was. I sensed something but I wasn't sure where or who it came from. All I knew was that this missing link would complete what was lacking and everything would be resolved. I don't have an exact link to her like I do to you and Mom and if I said anything, Mom and Leumas would have freaked out."

"Probably, but you still should have told them," Greg said forcefully. Then in a more gentle manner he added, "No more secrets, okay?"

"Okay, Dad."

"As far as the link to Cindy, I think that's part of the safety mechanism or something. I hate to say the term, but you two balance each other appropriately. She doesn't have the mental powers you possess, but she provides the stabilization features that you need."

"I can't use my powers without her?"

"It's extremely dangerous. You could damage your body and your mind if you do. Do you understand?"

"Yes."

"Together you can do wonderful things, but you must agree to them. There can be no onesidedness. You and Cindy are to be...I hate to coin another term, but 'the caretakers' of this power. Do you understand?"

"Yes."

"Good. Now, explain to me about bringing Copolla back? Were you involved in that?"

"I didn't do anything as far as Copolla was concerned. I was told he was coming back."

"Told? By whom?"

"He came to me in a dream. The man said he knew and liked you and that you had worked with him before. He said his name was Vague."

"Vague?" Greg said as the image of the alien who had taken the shape of the old historian, Robise, appeared in his mind. It was through Vague's assistance that he had learned the ability to allow his mind to travel and thereby defeat Copolla.

"Yes," Soren answered. "I checked the archives and your personal logs and found his name and that what he did was in fact to help you. So I trusted him when he told me and I told you. He was a good person, right?"

"Yes. Yes he was. And he told you Copolla was coming back?"

"Yes. And then one day this showed up," Soren said as he handed a data crystal to Greg. "He asked me to give it to you when you returned."

Greg eyed the crystal. "Did he say how Copolla got back?"

"He said that some of the others of his organization found out what he did and that he was in trouble for interfering and altering the timeline, something about only being able to do so much. As punishment, for his actions, Copolla was returned with the understanding that whatever happened afterwards on its own, would stand. Do you understand all of this?"

"I understand...or I think I do. This other organization is from the future and they mean well, but they also believe in not doing too much damage to the timeline, even if it betters the future."

"Why?"

"Because one little change, even if it helps a lot of people, alters the fabric of time itself. For instance, they could change one little thing, say they prevent an accident that saves someone's life, and although it's a good intention, it could cause a hundred people to not be born. It's like a domino effect. The fact that they gave me the power to defeat Copolla six years ago must have affected the timeline in a worse way than they had imagined."

"I think I understand it now," Soren said.

"But it still doesn't explain what we are going to do with Copolla."

"Maybe there is something about that on the crystal?"

"Might as well take a look at it." Greg rose from the sofa and went over to the terminal. He dropped the crystal in and pressed "Play." The image of the alien he had come to know as Vague appeared before him. He looked just as he remembered him, his skin old and wrinkled from age, the long white lab coat, the wisps of white hair that appeared to dance about his head and that friendly and benevolent face.

"Hello, Greg. If you are seeing this that is good because you have returned. I'm sorry we won't have a chance to meet in person. Soren has probably explained to you what has happened and why we seem to be at another impasse with history. Hopefully this time we will end Copolla's reign of cruelty once and for all. But the cost will be high, it always is and for that...I am truly sorry. Good bye, my friend."

"What the..." Greg began but was cut off by an emergency warning siren.

"De-pressurization warning," the computer voice shrilled.

CHAPTER FOURTEEN

"Death, whether alien or human, is never easy to comprehend."
Leumas

Edward dashed out the door of his compartment.
::Where are you going to go? Hmmm?:: Copolla chanted.
"Wherever I can to be rid of you."
::That's impossible. I am inside your mind. Soon it will be mine again. They think a child can hold me behind a door. The door is made of steel. Steel can bend if enough force is placed upon it. Little by little, it bends and more of me slips out.::
As Edward turned the corner, he saw Sarah and Cindy walking towards him.
"Edward?" she called.
"Sarah, go! Get away!"
"What's wrong?"
::Take her and the child. Kill them! Kill them! We don't need any of them to control the universe!::
"No!" Edward screamed as he willed the thought away. But he felt the strength inside his mind growing.
Sarah stepped closer. "Edward, what's wrong? Is it..."
Edward fought to resist, but the anger and rage inside of him proved too strong. He grabbed Sarah and Cindy.
"Edward, you're hurting us!" Sarah screamed. "Stop!"
Edward's eyes were drawn to the life pod placard on the wall. Gripping Sarah and Cindy with one arm, he pressed the button that opened the door. The door slid open revealing a small compartment that would hold at the most two people. His eyes located the panel labeled "door override." He opened it, reached in, and ripped out the wiring and circuitry. A computer voice from within the pod exclaimed: "Warning. Door override disabled. Do not use this life pod. Improper door closure will result in improper atmospheric seal."
::Yes, jettison them into space. Yes...Yes...Yes!::
Edward, poised to push Sarah and Cindy into the faulty pod, hesitated as he felt the tears that had released from his eyes make their way down his cheeks. He felt his grip loosen and then he relaxed his arm altogether.
::What are you doing? Finish it! I command you!::
"Sarah, there isn't much time. Go! Please hurry!"
"Edward, we can help you if..."

::*You will do my bidding!*::

"Sarah...go!"

::*Stop! You will kill them!*::

"Run!" Edward yelled as he felt his arms rising to reach out and grab them again. "Get through the door! Hurry!"

::*Stop them!*::

"No! You're the one that needs to be stopped once and for all!"

Edward stepped into the pod, fighting to maintain what little control he could. He was waiting to hear the passageway door shut and lock. Seconds ticked by and then he heard the *whoosh* sound of the door closing.

::*You can't kill yourself!*:: Copolla chided. ::*You humans value life too much to waste it.*::

::*Not when it comes to a choice such as this,*:: Edward shot back. ::*You make it very easy.*::

Copolla laughed heartily.

"Let's see you laugh this one off!" Edward screamed as he reached for the manual explosive detaching lever and pulled it.

***

Greg almost fell over Sarah and Cindy as he turned the corner. They were sitting on the floor next to the pressurized door. Sarah was crying as she hugged Cindy

"Sarah, are you two all right, I heard..."

"It's Edward," she said and pointed behind her. "He's acting as if Copolla is back in control. I think he has defeated the door mechanism and he's going to depressurize the pod. You can't..."

There was an explosive sound as the pod detached.

"Damn!" Greg screamed. He pressed the wall communication device. "Control, is Leumas there on the bridge?"

"What the hell is going on?" Leumas' voice responded. "Who launched the pod? The door is open and..."

In the background, Greg heard the computer's voice from main control responding to Leumas' question. "Life pod occupant is Edward Samuel. There are no life signs."

"No, it can't be...how...why?" Leumas's voice stuttered in what Greg surmised was disbelief.

"Yes, it's Edward," Greg said. "Sarah says Copolla was trying to take him over again and Edward wouldn't allow it."

There was silence for several seconds.

"Is that bastard finally gone?" Leumas asked.

"Gone for good," Greg answered. "And so is a very good friend."

The cost will be very high. Greg remembered Vague saying.

"Greg," Sarah spoke, her voice crackling. "Let's take Edward home."

"Yes, of course," he answered, as he gently grasped her hand.

"He was a nice man, wasn't he?" Cindy asked.

"Yes, honey, a very nice man," Sarah replied. "He did a lot to help his people."

"Leumas, can you have someone retrieve Edward's body? We're going to take him home to Earth before we go to Zire. I can give you a hand…"

"I'll do it myself," Leumas answered. " I…want to do it myself. Please."

Greg heard the pleading in Leumas' voice. "Yes, I understand. And one other thing," Greg continued. "Get me a direct line to President John Bishop."

CHAPTER FIFTEEN

"No matter where I go in this universe of ours, I will call no other planet home except for where I was born, on the planet Earth."

Greg Carlson

Greg and Sarah, Soren and Cindy, and Leumas stood in silence next to the freshly covered grave in the Arlington National Cemetery in Virginia. Their eyes were fixed upon the lettering of the tombstone, which read: Edward Samuel, 1952-2008, beloved husband and father, caretaker of the United States of America and of the planet Earth.

"Greg," Sarah said, breaking the trance-like silence. "Perhaps a few words before we go?"

"Yes, I was waiting," he said as he looked around as if he were expecting someone. "But maybe we should go ahead."

"Edward. Friend..." Greg began, then paused.

The sound of vehicles approaching caused him to stop. Everyone turned in that direction to see three Suburbans come to a stop nearby. Men quickly jumped out of the first and third vehicle and were easily identifiable as Secret Service agents by their calculated movements in searching the area. Seconds later, President John Bishop exited the middle vehicle and walked towards them.

"John," Sarah said as she met the President. "Thanks for coming. I know it couldn't have been easy to make the decision to risk coming here."

"Sarah, I...well, Edward was an old friend. I've done a lot of thinking. And thanks to the thoughts that Greg left with me and after you explained the entire incident and then what happened out there in space, I thought it only proper to pay my respects. I only wish that the rest of the world and his family could know the truth."

"I know, and someday they will. Come and meet the rest," she said as she guided him along. "I believe you and Leumas have met."

"Yes, we've spoken before. Mr., er...I mean Leumas, a pleasure to meet you in person."

"Mr. Bishop," Leumas said as he shook Bishop's hand. "Thank you for having the courage to come today and believe in the future."

Bishop nodded and smiled.

Sarah moved him toward Greg.

"This is Greg Carlson, my husband."

"Greg," Bishop said, offering his hand. "Thanks again for the information you gave me. I have to admit it was a little overwhelming when it released in my thoughts, but I'm glad you did. There is a lot to think about."

"Yes, there is, Mr. Bishop."

Sarah moved him along. "And these are our children, Soren and Cindy."

Bishop kneeled down to the children's level. "How are you. A pleasure to make your acquaintance."

"Hi," they said in unison.

Bishop rose and returned to stand on the opposite side of Greg, Sarah and Leumas.

Greg started, "Edward was a friend to us all. He was a man of vision for his country and the world. He willingly made the ultimate sacrifice, his own life, to ensure that the evil would not be loosed among us. We lay him to rest today with the hope that his sacrifice will not be in vain, and that his vision will live on in the sprit of others, whether human or alien. I know I will never forget him. May you rest in peace, good friend."

Greg produced a red rose from his pocket and placed it on the grave.

Sarah stepped up next. "Edward was like a father to me," she began. "We worked together in our dream of moving out into space. He made more accomplishments than had ever been thought possible in such a short time. It is through his legacy that the people of Earth will indeed move out into space and explore the galaxy and meet the other races that await them. When they do come, Edward, they shall be reminded of what you have done here. I promise you. God bless."

Sarah placed a red rose on the grave and then joined Greg and the children.

Leumas came forward next. "I helped Edward Samuel to be elected President of the United States. He had everything he needed to be the President already, I just evened the playing field and he did the rest. In the years I knew him, he was my friend and one of the most compassionate humans I have ever met. May he find peace in the comfort of the knowledge of his accomplishments and know that he leaves behind many friends who would have gladly changed places with him. Rest well, my human friend."

Leumas placed his rose on the grave and stood next to Greg and Sarah.

"Edward," John Bishop said. "My friend and colleague who had the confidence in me to be his Vice President. I thought of you as I would a brother, yet here today I cannot help but feel like Judas, in that I betrayed your trust and confidence as I take over your position. I wish

I could tell you that I will clear your name so you could be remembered as the great person you were, but it will take time. All I can assure you is that I will continue on with what you began and hope that I can follow through on the legacy you started. Rest in peace, good friend."

John Bishop placed his rose on the grave and joined the rest of the group.

"Well, I have to be going," Bishop said. "Things haven't quite settled down yet and there are all kinds of discussions about how we will protect ourselves from another alien invasion."

"Everything has been removed from Earth," Greg said. "The chambers are closed down and sealed. When we leave, there will be nothing left of our visit."

"I wish..." Bishop said. "I wish it could have been different."

"It was a risk from the beginning," Greg said. "We all knew and understood that. Perhaps as the people of Earth reach out to space and meet other races and beings, they will understand what we did."

"That won't be for a long time," Bishop said softly.

"Oh, you never know," Greg offered. "With the advancements in technology you have in your possession, you'll be out there before you know it."

Bishop nodded and smiled. "I hope you're right, Greg. Good-bye."

The President walked off and returned to the vehicle, followed by his Secret Service entourage. They sped off quickly, leaving the small group to themselves.

"Well, time to go," Leumas said. "We have the council waiting for us on Zire."

"Starting over, another new beginning?" Sarah asked.

"In a way," Greg said. "But as long as it is a beginning and not the end, I guess we can live with that."

"The children, what of their beginning?" Sarah said. "Will they have to live a life in fear because of their powers?"

"For the time being, they will be children, nothing more," Greg answered. "No one needs to know of their powers beyond us. Together, no one can harm them. But hopefully they will never have to use the power again."

"There will be a religious fervor," Leumas warned. "Your return and the acknowledgement of the second child as was in your vision. There will be some that say that it is the legacy, the destiny that you have foreseen."

"And let them believe it," Greg asserted. "Because it is true. It is as I have seen it and if that vision holds the fabric of the galaxy together, well then...so be it."

"And after?" Sarah asked.

"I don't know. I've not seen anything beyond that point. Maybe there is a limit to my power, or maybe I was shown what to see by our time altering friends. I don't know anymore. I guess from here, we'll have to play it by ear." He shrugged. He was amused at his own lackadaisical approach to the situation and laughed for the first time since he had returned. It felt wonderful.

Leumas and Sarah joined him. When their laughter subsided, the group of friends and family closed in upon itself. They, in turn, hugged one another.

"Leumas, would you take the kids back to the ship? We'll be there in a minute."

"Sure, Greg. Come on, you two. Last one back to the ship is a rotten scrinkbug!"

Soren and Cindy looked at one another in confusion, acknowledging that neither one of them had any clue of what a scrinkbug was, but they smiled and took off running for the ship.

"Well, are you ready to go to Zire?" Greg asked Sarah.

"Home?"

"No. Earth will always be our home. And we will be back. After all, that was part of the vision, remember? We shall pass control of the council to our children, on Earth. Earth will once again become the center of the universe."

"But…" Sarah began.

"No buts right now," Greg said as he pulled her close to him. "We have a long time before we have to worry about all of that. There is something very important we haven't done and it must be taken care of immediately."

Sarah's face grew sullen. "There's something else? Another commitment?"

"Yes, and a very important one. We have responsibilities, you know?"

"I know." She sighed. "What is it?"

"We haven't had that honeymoon yet."

Sarah smiled and hugged Greg. They turned and walked arm in arm to the awaiting ship.

"Tell me, Mr. Carlson, can you afford to buy a girl a drink?"

"Why, Mrs. Carlson, I believe I can. In fact, I know of this old speakeasy right out of the forties. I've had dreams about it. Reminds me of the first time we met…do you remember?"

"Yes…I most certainly do. That's where I met the man of my dreams. In fact, he's one of a kind."

TONY RUGGIERO

Tony Ruggiero has been publishing fiction since 1998. His science fiction, fantasy, and horror stories and novels have appeared in both print and electronic mediums. His other published novels include:

Operation Immortal Servitude. The US military has developed a new weapon to its arsenal—*vampires*. Tony brings his Navy experience to this dark fantasy series: The Team of Darkness declassified files. Coming soon are Book II: *Operation Save the Innocent*, Book III: *Operation Face the Fear* and Book IV: *Operation Endgame*.

Alien Deception. Thought you knew how the political system worked? Remember, nothing is as it appears...nothing. Your whole life you think you understand who and what you are and then one day you learn that it is all a lie. So what do you do? You have lunch with the leading candidate for President of the United States...you and your alien friends.

Tony is also a contributing author to *The Fantasy Writers' Companion* from Dragon Moon Press. Other collaborative work includes *The Writers for Relief Anthology* and *No Longer Dreams Anthology* and *Breach the Hull*. He also released in podcast and print format a collection of his short stories called *Aliens and Satanic Creatures Wanted: Humans Need Not Apply*.

Tony retired from the United States Navy in 2001 after twenty-three years of service. He currently resides in Portsmouth, Virginia. While continuing to write, Tony teaches at Old Dominion University, Saint Leo University, and Tidewater Community College in Norfolk, VA.

Please visit his webpage at www.tonyruggiero.com.

www.ingramcontent.com/pod-product-compliance
Lightning Source LLC
Chambersburg PA
CBHW072318020726
47501CB00002B/556

* 9 7 8 1 8 9 6 9 4 4 5 7 9 *